JESUSITA

For Stephanie
Enjoy
Ronald L. Ruiz

JESUSITA

RONALD L. RUIZ

First Edition   ISBN 13: 978-1-937484-33-0

AMIKA PRESS   53 W Jackson BLVD 660 Chicago IL 60604   847 920 8084
info@amikapress.com   Available for purchase on amikapress.com

Edited by Jay Amberg and Ann Wambach. Cover art by Hugo Anaya. Cover photography by Billy Alexander. Author photography by Amanda Wilson. Designed and typeset by Sarah Koz. Body in Espinosa Nova, designed by Cristóbal Henestrosa in 2010. Titles in ITC Golden Cockerel, designed by Eric Gill in 1930, digitized by Richard Dawson, David Farey & Phill Grimshaw in 1996. Thanks to Nathan Matteson.

MY THANKS TO
    Jay Amberg, who made this book possible
    Amanda, for her never-ending support and work
    And Ren McClellan, for his insight and encouragement

AUTHOR'S NOTE

BY 1975, California had the eleventh largest economy among nations of the world. Its biggest industry, agriculture, had been built on the backs of legal and illegal immigrants.

The 1848 Treaty of Guadalupe Hidalgo granted United States citizenship to many thousands of Mexicans living in the American Southwest. Between 1850 and 1910, tens of thousands more Mexicans immigrated to the United States to work, particularly as miners, railroad builders, and field hands. The Immigration Act of 1917, which set strict quotas for most immigrant groups, waived requirements for Mexicans, in part because agricultural growers wanted the availability of inexpensive labor. In the late 1920s, California growers also imported 31,000 Filipino men in an attempt to further reduce labor costs. The Filipinos were prohibited from buying land or marrying Caucasian woman.

During the Great Depression of the 1930s, thousands upon thousands of legal and illegal Mexicans were deported or pressured to leave the U.S. under the so-called Mexican Repatriation Movement. With the entry of the United States into World War II, however, the situation again changed dramatically. An extreme labor shortage occurred throughout the nation, especially in its agricultural fields. Consequently, the Mexican Farm Labor Program, often referred to as the Bracero Program, was instituted in 1942. Under the Bracero Program, an estimated 4.6 million Mexican nationals crossed the U.S. border as farmworkers. In some places, camps were established where workers were fed, clothed, and housed. In other places, laborers lived on the ranches and farms where they worked.

In the 1940s and 1950s, many farmworkers quit the Bracero Program after finding better jobs and living conditions in cities and towns. They were then considered illegal immigrants. Some of these workers found it easy and convenient to bring their families to the U.S., immediately providing better living conditions for them as well. *Jesusita* begins in October, 1945.

✝ I

JESUSITA AND her four children are working and living on a ranch fourteen miles south of Fresno. The ranch is no different than the one they left four days before. There is nothing one can see anywhere except rows and rows of vines and the sky and an iron white sun above them. Twisted brown stalks rise four feet from the ground sending leafy vines with clusters of grapes in every direction. The grapes bow the vines so that they hang down around the stalks creating hut-like spaces. The rows are separated by six-foot paths on white, chalky, sandy soil that becomes blistering hot as the day progresses. Big wooden trays covered with waxed brown paper have been placed every few feet apart. On them the harvested grapes will be laid to dry. There is some shade under the vines near the stalks but the workers must be careful when working or resting there because spiders and wasps aplenty have nested there. Jesusita, Sergio, and Yolanda are picking grapes while Paulina is tending to Concepcion by dragging her around the ranch in a lug box, trying to keep her out of the sun, as her mother instructed, by moving her from under one row of vines to another as the sun shifts. Now Paulina has been stung by a wasp and is writhing and crying on the burning sand. Jesusita looks in every direction for help but there is no one in sight. She sends Sergio and Yolanda back to where they were picking before the contratista finds the five of them huddled together, not working, and fires them. He had been reluctant to hire them, to let them on the truck yesterday morning, but she had assured him, begged him, that she and the two older ones were experienced, fast pickers and that Paulina would take good care of the young one and keep her out of everyone's way. They desperately need the work. Work is becoming scarce. The season will end in one or two more weeks, and just three days ago she gave Agripina Aguirre a big part of her summer's savings as a deposit and first and last months' rent on a garage in Fresno where they will live through the winter.

She tries to quiet Paulina, but the more she tries, the louder Paulina cries and the more she thrashes. She has dragged Paulina out of the blistering sun and under the shade of vines and has stationed herself so that she can see the contratista coming. Paulina is a sight to behold. Her clothes and hands are chalky white and her face is a dirty brown, streaked everywhere with grape juice. Her hair is matted with sweat and dirt and juice. When she keeps rubbing her right temple, Jesusita remembers hearing that a bee sting could be fatal if it pierced the brain. She tries rubbing the girl's forehead and temple but that only makes her squirm more.

Then Concepcion begins to cry. Jesusita had forgotten the youngster who is in a lug box in the middle of the row in the blazing sun, the drag rope lying useless in the sand. Concepcion is struggling to take her clothes off. "Tengo calor, Mama. Tengo calor." Every morning, the workers begin picking as soon as there is daylight. They start the day wearing three or four upper garments so that as the morning grows hot, sweat soaks the first and second layers and they become a coolant, an air conditioner, as the afternoon heat becomes fierce. "No, no! No te quites tu suéter!" She goes to the box to put Concepcion's sweater back on, but then remembers that last night as they slept huddled together under the shelter of grape trays, the child had moaned that she was cold. The nights are getting cold and last night Concepcion's undergarments were still sweat-wet, chilling her. Maybe it would be better to let Concepcion take off her sweater, let it dry off. She hears another family of pickers two rows over and becomes aware of Paulina again.

She hurries back to Paulina. This is no time to be worrying about Concepcion being cold tonight. Paulina is still moaning, rubbing her temple, and turning her head in the sand. Maybe that other family can help. Jesusita stands and looks over the vines for the other family. But even as she does, she knows that she can't ask them for help. All summer long, and this job has not been an exception, she has held herself and her family aloof from the others. She is not one of them and will never be one of them. Nor will her children be. Rogelio's death has brought her closer to them but this is as close as they will ever get to her and hers. Not for a moment will she be beholden to any of them or ever let them think that she and her children are like them.

She hears the contratista approach the other family, and she turns and runs, stumbling in the hot sand and leaving Paulina, hoping he won't find her. She reaches Sergio and Yolanda who have stopped working and have turned and are staring at the writhing, crying Paulina in the sand. "Hurry, he's coming! We have to work fast! Don't leave a single bunch of grapes on the vine and be careful how you set them on the trays!" A few minutes later he's there. He is a thin, wrinkled old man whose khaki fedora distinguishes him from his workers. "You and your kids do good work, señora. And you work fast. But the girl who looks after your little one has been stung by a bee. It's not serious. But you should go, take a few minutes, and comfort her. She's lying back there in the next row."

IT HAD been a long summer. When Rogelio was killed in a truck accident in March, Jesusita did not know what she would do. Sergio was fifteen, Yolanda thirteen, Paulina eleven, and Concepcion three. Two years before in the dead of the night, the family had crossed the border at Mexicali and made their way to Fresno where Rogelio had found steady work the year before. Because of Rogelio's steady job, they did not have to follow the crops in California as migrant workers six or seven months out of the year, unlike many families in the barrio. Thus the older three children had had the benefit of two full years in American schools. The three spoke English and read and wrote it in varying degrees. Jesusita's options were limited—return to Mexico's abject poverty or follow the crops like other barrio families hoping for a better life.

In late April, she joined the caravans of families headed for Coachella Valley and the spring fruits and vegetables. Then back to the Central Valley and melons, peaches, plums, figs, and apricots. Next, over to the Coast for lettuce, tomatoes, peppers, and strawberries, returning to the Central Valley for the grape harvest and the final six weeks of the season.

The living conditions were grim. They ate under makeshift shelters of fruit boxes or fruit trays or under trees or even vines. Water had to be hauled in using whatever containers were available, sometimes far from the ranch house or from an irrigation ditch. Handcrafted pits were their stoves to cook whatever nonperishable foods they were able to carry with them or to warm what canned goods they could buy from rural stores. Their toilets were always but a few feet from their shelters wherever there was the least chance they could be seen by others. Their human waste was covered over by dirt as best they could. Leaves were used to clean themselves. They slept on the ground either over or under the few blankets they carried.

From the beginning Jesusita decided to winter in Fresno. She had lived there for two years and knew the resources that would be available to her there and the schools that her children could be enrolled in five or six months each year.

AT THE end of the season Jesusita and her children make their way to Agripina Aguirre's house on the outskirts of Fresno. In her big backyard stands a twelve-by-twenty-five-foot garage. Its sides and roof are made of sheets of rusting, corrugated tin nailed to an assortment of wood framing. The floor is dirt. It has a small, wood-burning stove, but there is no water, no electricity, no window. It has but a single door. After more than six months of makeshift shelters at ranch after ranch, the garage seems like a bit of heaven to Jesusita. An outhouse is at the far corner of the lot. That too is a huge improvement over the holes they had to dig, usually by hand, to bury their waste at the ranches. With the door shut, the garage is dark but during the day there are enough holes and slits in the corrugated tin to be able to see. For night she will have to buy a kerosene lamp. Water can be had at a hand pump near the house.

Once they have brought their few belongings and moved in, Jesusita sets about to make the garage more homelike. She, Sergio, and Yolanda scour the alleys behind downtown stores for discarded cardboard boxes and behind grocery stores for wood crates. Box by box, crate by crate, they carry and drag them, trip by trip, to Agripina's garage. There they break down the cardboard boxes and lay them over the garage dirt to make a smooth, clean floor. The crates will be their tables and chairs. She pays pennies to grocers for their discarded flour and burlap sacks. These they take to the Salvation Army and stuff them with clothes and rags from a salvage bin; these are their mattresses. But the nights have turned cold and the first night on the new mattresses is especially cold. Lying there in her clothes, kept awake by the cold, it occurs to Jesusita that they could fill more sacks and use them as quilts. The next day they return to the grocers and then to the Salvation Army.

Except for occasional dunkings in ditches and creeks, the family hasn't bathed in months. Jesusita buys the biggest tin tub she can find. At the end of the first week, heating water on the woodstove, the family bathes in shifts with those not bathing sitting at the far end of the garage with their backs to the bathers.

Aside from the weekly bathing, the woodstove is lit only once a day for as long as it takes to cook dinner. As the nights grow colder, Concepcion huddles closer and closer to the stove after dinner. One especially cold night, Concepcion is able to rest her hands against the stove's iron sides less than an hour after dinner. "Lumbre, Mama. Lumbre, más lumbre!" Concepcion shouts.

"Cállese!" answers Jesusita, as she sits on her mattress mending by the kerosene light. The little one continues, "Lumbre, Mama. Lumbre, más lumbre!"

"Cállese!" Jesusita repeats several times. Concepcion doesn't shut up. Jesusita explodes, throwing her mending aside and springing to her feet. In three or four quick steps, she yanks the little one from the stove, screaming, "There is no money! We have no money!" The little one begins to cry. Jesusita becomes outraged, swatting her hard wherever her hand finds her. "We have no money!" she keeps screaming. The child howls as she is dragged across the cardboard floor and thrown onto the girls' mattress and then has a quilt hurled over her, muffling her howling.

There is an uneasy silence among the other three who are sitting around the kerosene lamp with open texts they have just received, struggling to make some sense of the chapters they have missed. They pretend not to see or hear. Their eyes are glued to their books. When Mama gets like this, they never know what to do. She is constantly telling Sergio that at fifteen, he is the man of the house. But when she gets like this, he feels like a frightened, helpless little boy. There's nothing to do except pretend that it isn't happening and hope that her fury won't be turned on him. Yolanda defends Mama whenever she and Sergio talk. She reminds him time and time again that Mama had never been like this before Papa died. But for Mama, where would the four of them be? Mama has worked incredibly hard for them, and it is only right that she should expect much of them too. As a result, whenever Yolanda falls in the path of Mama's wrath, she feels doubly wronged. Paulina is deathly afraid of Mama when she gets like this. She, more than any of the others, seems to raise Mama's ire, no matter what she does.

Two nights after Concepcion was yanked from the stove, Paulina, shivering, says to no one in particular, "Oh, it's so cold in here."

Jesusita leaps up off the cardboard and, before Paulina knows what is happening, slaps her across the face, knocking her down and taunting her with, "Cold! You say you're cold! Cold are you!" shaking the girl hard. "You're cold, are you? Are you cold?" determined to get an answer out of her. The crying child is too terrified to answer.

"Are you cold? Look at me! Answer me! Tell me you're cold! I said look at me!"

The girl can't look at her. It is not the screaming or the shaking but the eyes that are terrorizing her: huge, rage-filled, hate-filled eyes that threaten worse things. The others see those eyes. There is no pretending now. They all know those eyes. "It's like she wants to kill you, tear you to pieces," Sergio has said. "She's crazy when she gets like that."

Jesusita doesn't stop, and Yolanda finally pleads, "Mama, don..." Only to have Mama turn on her with that look, silencing her. Turning back to Paulina, "You're cold, are you! I'm going to show you what cold is! You're going outside!"

"Mama, it's cold and dark out there," Yolanda pleads. Once again a look quiets her.

Jesusita opens the garage door, pushes Paulina outside, and slams the door shut. She stays at the door, tense, straining to hear the girl, guarding against the girl becoming so loud that Agripina or some other neighbor might hear her. Paulina's crying; her pleas are growing louder. "Mama, please let me in. I'm freezing. I'm scared. Please, Mama, open the door."

Jesusita flings the door open and hisses, "If you don't shut up and stop your crying, you're going to get a beating you'll never forget!" The girl believes her, and the pleas become stifled sobbings. Thirty-five minutes later, Jesusita opens the door. "Get in here and get to bed!"

She orders everyone to bed. She turns off the lamp and lies down on her mattress fully clothed. She can't sleep. She's tense, and every few seconds her body jerks. As much as she tries, she can't stop the jerking. She can't think. She can only feel, and after a while the feeling is clear: she is struggling against the sense that she has done something wrong. But she has done nothing wrong. She wishes she could cry. But she vowed to stop crying months ago at one of the ranches. She had cried so much alone at night that one night she felt that she couldn't cry anymore. It was more than being tear-drained; it was the conviction that tears were useless, that tears weakened her and made matters worse. Life is what it is, she tells herself constantly. In order for her and her children to survive, she has to be strong. Her children have to be strong or they will never survive. They have to learn now that life is hard; they have to learn now to be brave and withstand the brutal hardships of life. She has done nothing wrong. They have no money. They are down to their last pennies. For more than a week they have eaten boiled beans or boiled lentils. She has rationed the tortillas to one a day for each. And now the lentils are gone and they have enough beans for maybe three days. The firewood costs money and it is almost gone. She has done nothing wrong.

Early the next morning, she puts the beans to soak. The longer they soak, the less firewood they will need. She counts the last five tortillas. Tomorrow there will be beans, just beans. And the day after? She's not sure, she doesn't know. She has been down to the Power building so many times looking for work that Mr. Jim has taken to locking the back door so that she can't go in and ask him again. The last time he yelled at her, "How many times do I have to tell you? There's no work! I have my crew! Just because you cleaned here last year for a few weeks doesn't mean that you have a job here every year!" She has tried other office buildings, even waiting outside in the dark hoping that someone won't come to work and they will need her. No one has needed her.

She has taken to sending Sergio out after school to every house in the neighborhood and beyond asking if they need yard work. After a week of "no's," she doesn't believe him and begins following him, hiding behind trees and bushes and fences to watch as he knocks on each door. His luck is no better than hers.

Darkness now comes just after five and brings with it a cold that slices through the corrugated tin as if it wasn't there, at times making the inside of the garage seem colder than outside. This night is one of those nights. Concepcion has laid down on the girls' mattress, covering herself with her quilt. Yolanda and Paulina are sitting on the mattress too, quilt-covered, doing their homework. Sergio, with jacket and cap on and hands in his pockets, alternately sits and rises and paces back and forth, sits and rises, waiting for the appointed hour when he can light the fire. Jesusita sits next to the kerosene lamp mending. She knows they are cold, but no one has dared mention the cold. She has foregone her quilt to show them, even though she too is cold. Her thumb and forefinger pressed against a needle are numb. But she has ordered that the fire can only be lit at 6:30, making best use of the firewood to cook and heat. Tonight is the coldest night yet, and for a moment she thinks of starting the fire early, but only for a moment, because in two or three days they will be out of firewood. She continues sewing, apparently self-absorbed, as if she is completely unaware of the cold. Until every part of her body feels caked in cold, so cold that she can no longer guide the needle. She stops sewing. She sits, waiting. At 6:23 she can wait no longer. "Sergio, start the fire."

There is excitement in the garage. The little one yelps. Yolanda and Paulina rush to help Sergio with the fire, rumpling up paper and handing him kindling. The paper glows yellow-orange. The kindling lights. Then Sergio crosses three half-logs on the kindling. But instead of flames, there is smoke. Sergio blows into the stove. More smoke, lots of smoke. The girls peer into the stove's door. Thick smoke. They blow. Smoke begins pouring out of the stove. Sergio closes the stove door. He waits a few minutes. He tries again. He has to be careful with the kindling: there's not much left. More smoke. He closes the stove door and kneels with his head down. Everyone, even Jesusita, is watching. He tries a third time. Same result. He pulls out one of the blackened half-logs. He examines it and says, "Mama, it's green. It won't burn."

When Jesusita sees the smoke the third time, she knows. Sergio need not have spoken. Everyone turns and looks at her. She doesn't see them. Her look cautions them. They dare not speak. But it is not what they think. She is thinking of Agripina, the fat woman who lives in the front house, her landlady. She will have to crawl to her now, beg from her. There is no other way.

SHE REMEMBERS the first time they met. She will always remember that day. She is standing on the front porch. Agripina comes to the front door. She raises her fat face and looks down on her, not saying a word. Her stance and her look say it for her: *What do you want?* Jesusita has worn her only dress and has scrubbed her face, her hands, and arms in a drinking fountain and pulled her greasy hair back in a tight bun. But there is no hiding what she looks like now. A month ago while standing alongside the contratista's truck, she happened to see her face in its side mirror. It shocked and scared her. It was the face of an old woman, creased, darkened, grim, tight—not unlike the faces of old, peasant, Indian women whom she had always looked down on. Later that same day as she approached a grocery store window, she slowed and looked at her image, hoping to refute what she had seen earlier. Dressed in the pants and shirts that she wore every day in the fields and with her hair pulled back, she looked like a small, stooped old man. There was a time when she might have cried over this but now she cries only over survival. Still, for a few moments, she remembers the looks men used to give her and all the little things they used to do for her before Rogelio and in the first years with Rogelio. Those looks have been long gone, just as mirrors and windows will be. Agripina sees what she is now. She sees the ragged dress and the needy, penniless face. *What do you want?* her look says.

Jesusita speaks first, before the fat woman can close the door. The sound of her words almost fails her. "I hear that you have a garage for rent?"

Agripina studies her from on high. *She has money? Perhaps she's not a beggar?* "Rent it to who?"

"To me."

"To you? Just you?"

"No, to me and my kids."

"How many are you?"

"We're five."

"You and four kids?"

"Yes."

"No man?"

"No man."

"You're sure?"

"I'm sure."

Agripina studies her some more. *She's trash and that dress is probably the only one she owns. And the kids can't be any better off.* But the garage has been vacant for almost a year now and she could use the money. To guard against those kids, she can make everything except the garage, the yard around it, the outhouse, and the water pump off-limits. *They have to be a very sorry-looking bunch. What will the neighbors think?* But if she keeps them back there, who will be the wiser? *But does she have money?* "The garage is big, clean, and in good condition and I get thirty dollars a month for it."

"I can pay that."

"I ask for the first and last months' rent in advance."

"I can pay that."

"And a thirty-dollar deposit. Which means that you pay me ninety dollars before you move in."

"What's a deposit?"

"That's if you break or destroy anything while you're in it, I get to keep the thirty dollars to fix it."

"What's there to break or destroy?"

"Plenty. It's in good, clean condition now and I want it that way when you leave."

Now it is Jesusita who pauses, who looks down and away, thinking. Ninety dollars will take a big part of her summer savings. But the season will be ending soon and the weather is changing. The nights are getting colder. They will need shelter soon. She looks back up at the fat woman, wide-eyed and noncommittal, saying nothing.

"Do you have the money?"

"Yes."

"Let's see it."

She pulls out a wad of mostly one dollar bills from her dress pocket.

"Are there ninety dollars there?"

She nods, not knowing if she should nod.

"You're sure?"

She nods again.

"Alright, I'll show you the garage. Wait here while I get the key."

She watches as the fat woman moves her girth away from the door through the front room. She takes tiny, shuffling steps. Her huge calves seem joined or pasted together. She wonders how a woman that big can pee without wetting herself. The floor protests as she moves. Her only free motion is the swinging of her short, club-like arms. In Mexico, she would have served as the lowest of maids in many a house. In some houses she would not even have been allowed to cross the back door threshold. Then it occurs to her that *she* has not been allowed to cross the fat woman's back door threshold.

Three and a half weeks later, they move in. They come in single file along the walkway on the side of the front house. Sergio first, the two older girls, the younger girl, and Jesusita. She knows the fat woman is watching. She can *feel* her watching. They carry an assortment of flour sacks and paper bags. Once they are in the garage, they do not come out. Jesusita orders everyone to sit down in the darkness of the windowless garage and be quiet. It's almost as if they're hiding. She's hoping that the fat woman hasn't seen them, but she knows she has. Fifteen minutes later, there's a knock on the door. A shaft of apprehension strikes. She should have known. She whispers to the older ones to move the sacks and bags to the back of the garage, away from the door. She opens it. Agripina is all but in the garage.

"Oh, I see you're here."

"Yes."

"When's the furniture coming?"

"Tomorrow," she says before she can stop herself.

"I hope so. There's nothing in there except the woodstove."

"I know."

"Where are the children?"

"They're in here."

"You'd better get some lamps. It's dark in there."

"I know."

The next day Jesusita, Sergio, and Yolanda carry and drag the scavenged cardboard boxes and wood crates to a temporary site in an alley a block from the garage. Their plan is to move them into the garage after nightfall, avoiding Agripina's watchful eyes. Just after dark as they enter the backyard with the boxes and crates, Agripina is standing in the screened-in back porch with the light on. "What do you have there?"

"Boxes."

"Boxes? Boxes of what?"

"Empty boxes."

"Empty boxes for what?"

"For the floor."

"What floor?"

"Our floor."

"Your floor?"

"The garage floor."

"Where's your furniture? You said it was coming today."

"They stole it."

"Who stole it?"

"I don't know. Some people."

"Where was it?"

"With some friends."

"Some friends?"

"You don't know them. They don't live here."

"Where do they live?"

She's said enough. She doesn't want to answer but somehow feels compelled to answer. "In Kingsburg."

"Did you call the police?"

"No."

"Why not?"

"Because they had already called them."

"Who called them?"

"The people in Kingsburg."

"Where are the other kids?"

"In there," she looks toward the garage.

"You left them alone?"

"Yes," Jesusita nods, beaten.

"I saw no smoke. It must be cold in there. Do you have lamps yet?"

"No."

"It has to be cold and dark in there."

"I know."

"Have they eaten yet?"

"No, but they will."

She lets them pass, carefully examining every box with those watchful eyes. Inside the garage it is just as Agripina has said, cold and dark. "Mama, tengo hambre," the little one whines. "Shhhh!" Jesusita threatens. "We'll eat as soon as we're finished."

There are more boxes in the alley. If they leave them there, they might not be there or might be damaged in the morning. But she can't go out there now. She can't take another grilling by Agripina. She'll wait, if need be, until Agripina goes to bed.

"Mama, tenemos hambre."

"Shut up!" she snaps. "Shut up! Sit down and be quiet!" Fifteen, twenty, thirty minutes pass. She can't tell. The only clock they have ticks on in the dark, unseen.

"Mama, tenemos hambre."

Her urge is to hit Concepcion, but she can't tell where she is in the dark. She gropes her way to the door and cracks it open. The back porch light is off. "Sergio, Yolanda, vengan. Quietos."

The three make their way to the front house. When they are a few feet from it, the back porch light flashes on. "Where are you going now?" She is standing in the back porch looking down on them through the porch's screen.

"To get more boxes," Jesusita answers.

"More boxes?"

"Yes."

"You need more boxes?"

"Yes."

"Where are the little ones?"

"In the garage."

"Have they eaten?"

"Yes."

"What did they drink? I didn't hear the pump, and I didn't see you bring in anything to drink?"

"They weren't thirsty."

"This had better be your last trip. I can't have you going back and forth in my yard all night long."

"It will be tonight."

From the alley they drag and carry every box they can, of necessity leaving some behind. When they return, Agripina is still standing in the lighted porch above the only way into the backyard, casting a shadow over the entryway, but not enough to darken anything. "Why so many boxes?"

"To cover the dirt floor."

"You're going to use those wood boxes to cover the dirt floor?"

"No, we will use those for tables and chairs."

"Tables and chairs?"

"Yes, until they find our furniture."

"Until who finds your furniture?"

"The police."

"What police?"

"The police in Kingsburg."

"How do they know how to contact you? Where you live?"

"I gave them the address."

"What address?"

"This address."

"What is it?"

She pauses. She doesn't know. The pause grows longer. She feels cornered, panicked, trapped. "Please let us go," she pleads. "We have to eat."

"I thought you said you had eaten?"

"Only the younger ones."

"Then why were they crying that they were hungry when you were gone?"

She feels herself crumbling. "We have to go."

"I have to warn you that the Welfare Department takes kids away from their parents when they're neglected, when they haven't been fed."

She turns. There is nothing more she can say.

Agripina is there in the morning when they bring more boxes. "How many more times are you going to be dragging those boxes in here? They make a horrible noise."

"Yolanda, pick up your boxes."

"I can't, Mama, they're too big."

"I said, how many more times are you going to be dragging those boxes in here?"

"Not many." But Jesusita doesn't stop. She doesn't look up or around at the fat woman. The garage is in sight. She quickens her pace and one of the boxes drops. She tries to lift it as she moves. It falls flatter. Now it is the loudest of the dragging boxes. She doesn't care. She moves faster. In the garage, she sits on the ground rubbing her face in her hands, thinking that she has made a mistake but reminding herself that there were few places. And now with the season over, there are none.

She clears the garage, sends the little one outside with Paulina. Then the three cut and lay the cardboard. Finished, the floor looks much better. She feels better. She is about to bring Paulina and Concepcion back in, when she sees Agripina standing in the doorway. Agripina steps inside uninvited. She looks around at the floor without commenting. Then she says, "If your little one continues to make the noise she's making out there now, you're going to have to keep her inside. Neither I nor the neighbors need to put up with that."

For the first time Jesusita hears Concepcion crying in the backyard. She has become so accustomed to hearing Concepcion crying that she doesn't know what to say. Fear grips her. There is no way she can keep Concepcion in the garage all the time. She sighs, her shoulders sag. She has had enough.

Agripina plods on. "I see you don't have a lamp yet."

Jesusita looks away and shakes her head.

"And you have no firewood. You can't raise these kids, especially the little one, in the cold and the dark. You're not even cooking. How are they eating? How are you feeding them?"

She stands mute. Ever since Rogelio died she has lived in shame. When will it end?

"You know, if someone, if any one of my neighbors found out about this and reported you to the Welfare Department, I've already told you what they would do."

She says nothing. She looks down. At some point Agripina will tire and leave.

"I guess you've been sleeping on the dirt. And now the cardboard. I don't see any mattresses. No blankets. Woman, it's cold at night. And you mean to tell me that you're going to sit and eat off those boxes? Until your furniture comes? You know what? I don't think you've ever owned a stick of furniture in your life. Have you...? I know you haven't. I don't like this. I don't like the conditions that these kids are living under. If you don't change your ways soon, I just might have to call the Welfare Department myself."

She makes no response, not even a flinch.

Agripina stares down on her. The children watch. After a while, Agripina turns and walks away in disgust.

That afternoon Jesusita buys a used kerosene lamp in China-town and five dollars of firewood from a neighbor. What she has left from her summer savings will feed them maybe for two weeks or until she can find work. Before she goes shopping, she leaves Sergio in charge with strict orders. He is to keep the garage door open about a foot, just enough to let in light and the warmth of the day so that when Agripina comes snooping, the garage won't be dark and cold. Everyone, especially the little one, is to stay inside until she returns. If Concepcion starts to cry, for whatever reason, he is to cover her mouth tightly until she stops. If a stranger or strangers come, he is to tell them his mother is out buying food, lamps, wood, mattresses, and blankets.

She doesn't leave until she is convinced, by repeatedly peeking out the garage door, that Agripina is neither hiding in the back porch nor looking out the kitchen window. Then she walks softly, quickly, some sixty feet to the side of the house. Once there she hugs the house wall and ducks under the windows that look out onto the walkway. Reaching the front porch, she hurries out the gate onto the street.

When she returns, Agripina is sitting in the back porch. "You know, Jesusita, there is no need for you to tiptoe, to go sneaking in an out of the backyard. Unless, of course, you have something to hide. Are you stealing something from me? Is there something about your past that you haven't told me? What is it, Jesusita? Why must you sneak in and out of here?"

She pauses just long enough to hear the first accusations before she continues on to the garage as quickly as she can, without a word.

Inside the garage, there is great excitement. "Show us how it works, Mama!"

"Turn it on, Mama! Turn it on!"

"Is it ours?"

"Can we keep it?"

"Can we keep it lit 'til we fall asleep?"

She lights the lamp.

"Oohhh!"

"Wow!"

But she doesn't answer. She's lost in thought. *We have to go. We can't stay here. But go where? She has our money.*

When the woodman comes there is more excitement. "Now we can have a fire!"

"Now we can cook!"

"Now we'll be warm!"

The woodman stacks the wood and leaves.

"Let's make a fire, Mama!"

"Let's see how it works!"

✠ 18

She shakes her head no. They can't start a fire. The stove will get dirty and Agripina will want to keep some of the deposit.

She sends Yolanda outside with the little one. Sergio and Paulina follow. Alone she thinks, *We can't stay here. I have to get our money back. I have to.* Outside she can see the kids starting to play. *But where will we go?* They need shelter. *What will we do? I don't know, but that woman is driving me crazy. I can't take any more of it. We have to go.*

Outside she starts toward the back porch door. Agripina is not in the porch nor at the kitchen window. But when she reaches the cement landing and before she can knock, the kitchen door opens, a light goes on, and Agripina steps into the back porch. "What is it? What do you want?" Whatever, if any, reservations she might have had about leaving are, at that moment, swept away.

"I want my money back! We're leaving!"

"Leaving? You've only been here two nights."

But then Agripina sees those bulging, rage-filled, hate-filled eyes that had so terrorized Jesusita's children and are about to explode now and are telling her to let the woman do whatever she wants.

"You've only been...," she starts to repeat, and the eyes widen. She stops, frightened. There is no talking to this woman. She doesn't know what to do or say.

"I want my money back! I want my money back!"

"Please don't look at me like that."

"I'll look at you any way I damn please! Give me my money back!"

"I can't give you your money back."

"You can and you will!" She yanks at the porch door but the latch holds.

"I held the garage for you for weeks. I could have rented it ten times for more than I rented it to you. Now everybody's settled for the winter and I will lose everything."

"I want my money back!"

"Stop looking at me like that. You're threatening me. I'll call the police!"

"Call them!"

19 ✠

"If I call them, they'll take you away. You're illegal. And your kids will end up in the shelter."

"You make me lose my kids and you'll wish you were never born!"

Agripina whimpers and steps back from the door, away from that twisted face and those evil eyes.

"I want my money back!"

Shaking her head, Agripina starts to cry.

Jesusita yanks at the door again, but the latch holds. "I want my money back!"

Sobbing, Agripina says, "I don't have your money. I spent it a long time ago. I was behind in my house payments. Your money's gone. I don't have any money to give you."

"Liar!" Again she yanks at the door. Again the latch holds. She kicks the door. She steps back. She rubs her mouth with the top of her fist, thinking. Then her body slumps.

"Come in and search if you want. I don't have your money."

Jesusita screams, "You stay out of our lives! You stop watching us, watching everything we do! Understand?"

Agripina nods, a handkerchief covering most of her face.

"Stop complaining about everything we do! Criticizing everything we do! Understand?"

Agripina continues nodding.

"Stay away from the garage and stay away from my kids! Understand?"

Yes, yes, Agripina nods, beaten, repentant.

"And stop watching us! I mean it, if you know what's good for you! Stop watching us! Do you hear?" She turns and leaves and, seeing her startled kids watching, yells at them, "Get in there! Get in that damn garage!"

In the days and weeks that follow, Jesusita knows that Agripina is still watching. She can *feel* her watching. At times she has even stopped at the back porch on her way in or out of the backyard and has raised herself up to the porch screen and looked down into every corner of the porch hoping to find Agripina stooped somewhere there waiting for her next peek. But Agripina has not been there. Jesusita peeks or turns quickly to the kitchen window that looks out on the backyard and the garage. But Agripina has not been there. She's become convinced that Agripina must be watching by cracking open, ever so slightly, the bathroom door that leads out onto the porch. It has to be the bathroom door. Because she *knows* Agripina's watching. She has to be watching. Every time she leaves in the late afternoon to go downtown to look for work, Agripina comes out on the front porch and greets her, smiling uncomfortably, mumbling a few words about nothing, never looking at her but always managing to ask if she's found work yet. "No," says Jesusita, steely-eyed, looking directly at the nervous woman. "Oh, well, that doesn't matter. It's not important. I'm sure you will soon enough." She smiles weakly, nodding, avoiding those eyes.

But it does matter. Jesusita knows that it matters as much to that greedy woman as it does to herself—that the fat woman has to be worried about the winter's rent. So she adds, "Nobody wants to hire me. It'll probably be like this all winter."

Now Jesusita must see Agripina again. She wraps her shawl around her and steps out into the night air. The yard is dark, and she thinks that Agripina can't possibly be watching now. But when she knocks, Agripina is quick to answer. She couldn't have been far away. She had to have seen her coming.

"Yes, my dear?" A high, too-pleasant voice.

She has not turned on the back-porch light. They are standing in the dark, inches apart, separated by the wire screen. "Agripina, I need five dollars." It is not so much a statement as a demand.

"You need five dollars?" Her words carry a taste of incredulity. But the tone is soft, still sweet.

She wishes the porch light were on. She'd like to see Agripina's face.

"Why do you need five dollars, my dear?" The voice is even sweeter, girlish.

Now she thinks that Agripina might be enjoying this. If that screen wasn't there, she would slap that fat face, choke that cow neck. "I need five dollars." Still firm, still a demand.

"But you're not telling me why you need it, my dear."

She's enjoying it. She wants her to beg. She won't...but the kids are cold and hungry. She's cold and hungry. "We have no wood for the stove. We have no money to buy wood. We can't cook. It's cold. After tomorrow we will have no food."

"Well, we haven't gotten to tomorrow yet, have we?" Still sweetly. "We're still on today, aren't we? Right now, today, all you need is some wood for the stove. Isn't that true?" There's nothing sweet about Agripina's voice now. It's the voice of their first days in the garage. Still evil.

"I need five dollars."

"You don't need five dollars now, my dear. What you need now is firewood. You've said that yourself."

"Please, Agripina, please." She's begging now. But it doesn't matter. They're cold and hungry.

"No, I won't give you five dollars. I won't even loan you five dollars when you don't need it." Her voice is strong, bold now.

"Please, Agripina, please."

"I said no, and no is no!" It is her first voice. "There is some firewood in the basement. You can take what you need and only what you need for tonight. I will deduct that from the rent you've paid. That's all I want to say. That's all I want to hear. It's cold out here." The kitchen door opens and closes and she is gone.

Later that night, as Jesusita and Sergio gather firewood by lamplight in Agripina's basement, it seems to her that she and her children have always and will always live in shame. But Mr. Jim comes looking for her the next morning and offers her work cleaning office buildings. He advances her a week's pay. Three weeks later she rents two rooms in the home of another cleaning woman. She tries several times to recoup her deposit and the balance of her rent money, but Agripina will not answer her door.

✝ II

"I'LL GIVE you a nickel if you touch it," the man whispers.

Angie hears him but doesn't think he is talking to her. She is curled up on her side in her seat with her thumb in her mouth looking up at the black-and-white cartoon on the huge screen.

He pokes her and leans closer as he whispers, "I'll give you a nickel if you touch it."

She turns, sits up. "Touch what?" she says quietly. It is dark in the theater, and she can't see what he wants her to touch.

"Give me your hand and I'll show you."

"Gimme the nickel first."

He puts the coin in her hand and says, "Now give me your hand."

She switches the coin to her right hand and gives him her left hand. He takes her hand and puts it on something warm and hard. "Just keep it there for a little while."

She does for a little while and then brings her hand back and curls up again on her side and finishes watching the cartoon.

When a cowboy movie begins, he pokes her again. "I'll give you a dime if you rub it for a while."

"A dime?"

"Yeah, a dime. But you have to rub it until I tell you to stop."

"Gimme the dime."

He gives the six-year-old the dime, and she gives him her hand.

He takes her hand and places it on the warm, hard thing and says, "Put your fingers around it." She does and he says, "Now rub it up and down until I tell you to stop." He guides her hand at the wrist while Angie goes back to watching the good guy on his horse chasing two bad guys on their horses. She hears the man making noises like something is hurting him, and then he whispers, "Stop! Stop!" releasing her wrist. She pulls back her arm without ever losing track of the chase on the screen.

After a while he leans closer again and whispers, "Do you come to the movies often?"

"Only on Saturday when my mom has men company."

ANGIE HERRERA and her brother, Saul, and their mother Madelena live in a two-room apartment on a nameless alley in Fresno's Chinatown, half a block from the Ryan Theater. All Angie needs to do to get to the Ryan is to walk to the end of their alley, turn left on Tulare Street, go past one store, and she is there. Earlier that Saturday as her mom gave Saul the dime that will get them into the Ryan, she said, "I have a man friend coming to visit me, and I want you kids to stay and watch the movies two times. I don't want you back before 6:30. Understand?"

"Yes, Mama."

Once in the theater, Saul, as always, seats Angie in the front third row and then goes off with his friends who have the run of the Ryan.

As it turns out, Mama has the same male company for five successive Saturdays, which means that Angie gets to go the Ryan five Saturdays in a row. Each Saturday the man comes and sits next to her as soon as Saul leaves. And each Saturday when she leaves the Ryan, she has fifteen more cents than she had when she entered, more money than she has ever had in her life. She goes to Louie Kee Market almost every day and buys candy—more candy than she has ever had in her life.

Her problem is where to hide her money and her candy in their tiny, two-room apartment. If either Mama or Saul finds the money or the candy, they will want to know where the money came from. She can never tell that because she knows that there is something wrong with touching the man's thing, something she shouldn't be doing. She has seen some of Mama's men friends with their things big and long and hard like the man's thing, and each time her Mama has gotten mad, has scolded her for looking, and each time the men have hurried to cover themselves so that she can't see. If looking at that thing is bad, what must touching it be? But there doesn't have to be anything wrong with it if only she knows, if nobody else knows. And she has never had so much candy in all of her life.

After the fourth Saturday, there is no doubt that she can never tell anybody what she has been doing with the man. As she and Saul leave the Ryan on that Saturday and start down their alley, they see that some of Saul's friends and some older guys have circled Polly Wang, who is crying. Polly Wang is a third grader who lives in the alley too. All the Mexican boys are always laughing at Polly and calling him "puto." Angie doesn't know what "puto" means but she knows it can't be very nice. As they near the group she hears Georgie Ramirez, the oldest and biggest boy, saying, "You're lying, Polly, you're lying. Bobby saw you and the man." Polly is shaking his head and crying. "All we want to know is how much money he gave you. You better tell us or I'm gonna kick your ass."

The boy standing next to Georgie says, "You're lying, Polly. I saw you and that man down there by those bushes. He had his big fat dick in your ass and you were letting him."

"If you don't tell us how much he gave you, I'm not only going to kick your ass, but, after that, I'm gonna tell your mom and dad about how you're going around in the Ryan touching and sucking on men's dicks and getting fucked by them in the ass."

Shaking his head, Polly slobbers, "You can't tell them. They don't talk English or Mexican."

"Yeah, but I can get one of them Louie Kee girls to tell them in Chinese.... You always got a lot of money, and it's about time that you start sharing some of it with us. So how much did that man give you?"

"He only gave me fifty cents, and I already spent all of it."

"You're a lying sack of shit!" Georgie grabs Polly and punches him hard in the face. Angie screams and runs crying to their apartment.

On the sixth Saturday Mama has no male visitor. Still Angie asks if she can go to the movies.

"Movies? You want to go to the movies? Where am I supposed to get money for your movies? You think we're rich or something?"

"You had money last Saturday, Mama."

"That was then. This is now. I don't even have enough money for the rent. The landlord has given me until this payday to pay it. Otherwise we'll be out in the alley. No, you can't go to the movies."

Angie goes to the Ryan anyway, walking back and forth in front of it until she tires and sits down on the sidewalk next to it. Soon she is pacing in front of it again—until Saul sees her. "What are you doing here, Angie? You heard Mama. She's got no money. So there's no movies. What do you think—they're gonna let you in free? Only Mr. Ryan gets in free."

It is months before Mama has another Saturday afternoon visitor. When Angie returns to the Ryan, she is careful to sit in the same seat in the third row. But the man doesn't come, not only on that Saturday but on the following Saturday. Over the next two-plus years, the times that Angie goes to the Ryan are few, and the man is never there. Soon he is forgotten.

When she is nine, he is there again. He leans over and whispers, "Hi, remember me?"

"I think so." She's not sure.

"Remember what we used to do down there in the third row?"

"I remember."

"I've been in here lots of times looking for you, but you've never been here."

"I didn't have the money to come."

"It's only five cents."

"I know. But my mom doesn't have money."

"Do you still want to do what we used to do?"

"How much will you give me?"

"You're older now. So I'll give you fifteen cents to touch and rub me, and if you let me touch you, I'll give you thirty cents."

"Touch me where?"

"Down there where you pee.... And if you let me do that I'll give you five cents more so that you can come to the show every Saturday. That's thirty-five cents. I bet you've never had thirty-five cents. Have you?"

"No."

"So you want to let me touch you while you touch me?"

"Ok."

For the next three months Angie goes to the Saturday afternoon movies every week. She goes alone. No one at home is the wiser. Neither Saul nor his friends ever have enough money to go to the movies. And on Saturday mornings, once Saul dresses and has a bowl of cereal he is gone, not to be seen again in the little apartment at least until six. If Mama is there on Saturday mornings, it won't be long until she too is gone, because she has finally found a boyfriend who can welcome her at his house. The money Angie is earning every Saturday is wonderful. And she has found a hiding place for it and her candy under the apartment eaves behind an abandoned bird's nest. It doesn't take much to put a box on a kitchen chair and hide or retrieve it. But one day Louie Kee himself announces before a store full of customers, "Little girl, where you getting all this money from? Do your Mama and Papa know how much money you have?" Angie scoops up her candy and soda and hurries out of the store. Though it means walking blocks and blocks out of her way, Angie solves this problem as well. She takes her business elsewhere, buying her candy, ice cream, and sodas at five different stores in and out of Chinatown. It is years before she steps into the Louie Kee Market again.

Then, a week before her tenth birthday, just as unexpectedly as he returned, the man does not come. Still, so certain is Angie that he will be there the following week, that she takes a good portion of her savings and buys herself a birthday present. She pays a street woman ten cents to go into a thrift store with her and help her buy a blouse that she has seen in the window. She wears her new blouse every day, instead of the frayed, stained blouse she has worn for two-and-a-half months, hiding it in her lunch bag until she gets to and later when she leaves the school. She wears it until Saul notices it at school. "Where'd you get that from?" Later that day, she tosses it into a garbage can on her way home from school. The man doesn't come to the Ryan that Saturday or the following Saturday. Doggedly, she goes to the movies every Saturday until her savings are gone.

Then she is twelve and her body is changing, enough so that her mother warns her several times, "You better not go getting pregnant on me. Because I'm telling you right now, I'm not taking care of any more kids. I've done my taking care of kids, and you're not going to be bringing another one into this house."

"How am I gonna get pregnant if I don't even have a boyfriend?"

"You will. You will. And I'm telling you right now, boys, men don't stay with one female. They'll tell you they love you and love you 'til they find something they think is better. And if you get pregnant, you won't see them no more. They got what they wanted and they sure don't want to be around any baby. So I'm warning you, I'm not taking care of another baby."

"I don't even have girlfriends."

"I'm not talking about girls. I'm talking about boys."

In fact Angie has no boyfriend, and there is none in sight. Not the way she looks and dresses. As for girls, the only girls close to her age that live in the alley are Chinese. They go to Confucius school every day after school and all day Saturday and never associate with anyone not Chinese. As for school, she is too ashamed of where and how they live in the alley to ever invite any of those girls over. And her clothes are the shabbiest in the class.

She passes the Ryan on her way into and out of the alley but no longer thinks of the man. Then one Sunday afternoon, out of sheer boredom, Angie decides to go to the Frank H. Ball Playground. As she leaves the alley, a man standing on the sidewalk near the curb on one side of the Ryan motions to her. She stops and looks at the man quizzically, longer than she would normally look at any stranger, any man. *Could this be him?* she thinks. It's been so long and because of the darkness, she never really knew what the man looked like. This man is short and dark, very dark. Darker than most Mexicans. Somehow more like a Chinaman, with kind of slanty eyes, but way too dark for a Chinaman, yet more like a Chinaman. The man motions to her again. She goes up to him.

"You want to go to the movies?"

He's speaking English but with a funny accent, not the accent of a Mexican or a Chinaman. Did the man have an accent? She doesn't think so. But she can't remember. It's been so long. "I don't have any money."

"I give you money."

She can't remember.

"I give you money. You sit with me. Oᴋ?"

He has a quarter pinched between his thumb and forefinger. "Oᴋ."

He gives her the quarter. "Sit in number three row and wait for me. Oᴋ?"

She is fingering and looking at the quarter. A ticket is now seven cents. He didn't give her seven cents. He gave her a quarter. There could be a lot more. "Oᴋ."

"You go first. I come a little bit later. Sit where two people can sit, but remember row three. Wait for me."

It has to be him. Otherwise how would he remember row three? "Oᴋ."

Once he is seated, he turns in the darkness and whispers, "Can I touch you?"

"How much will you give me?"

"I already give you twenty-five cents."

"That was to get in the show."

"Show only cost seven cents. I pay you with the change."

"No. That's for the show next time."

"Next time?"

"Yeah. I can meet you here again."

"How much you want for me to touch you now?"

"Fifteen cents. But if I touch you, it's more."

"How much more?"

"Fifteen cents more."

He sits back. But only for a moment. "Ok, I touch you," putting his hand on her thigh.

She grabs his hand and holds it firm. "No, gimme the money first."

He sighs and sits back again, this time reaching into his pocket with his free hand for the coins. His other hand is still on her thigh, held tightly by Angie. He is anxious. He fingers two coins in the darkness, hoping they are the right ones, wanting his hand free as soon as possible. "Here," he whispers.

"Ok." She takes the coins and frees his hand.

Seconds later, breathing heavily, he whispers hard, "Touch me."

"Give me the money first."

Again he reaches into his pocket with his free hand and pulls out all the coins his fingers can find. "Here."

"How much is this?"

"I don't know. I don't care. Take it all. Just touch me. Grab it."

His name is Santiago, and he tells her that he can only meet her on Sunday afternoons because he works six days a week. They meet for two months of Sundays. After the first Sunday it is always the same. She meets him on the sidewalk a few steps from the alley on one side of the Ryan and says she needs a quarter to get in. He protests that he gave her a quarter the last time, and she says that she is sorry but that she has already spent the change and needs another quarter to get in. He says that it only costs seven cents to get in, and she says she knows but that she needs a quarter to get in. Grudgingly he gives her another quarter. But once inside, he is well organized. He has a dime and a nickel in his front left pocket and a dime and a nickel in his back left pocket, and he is sure to sit on her left side. It usually takes no more than a minute for him to tighten and groan and push her hand away, rest for another minute, and then whisper, "I'll see you next Sunday," and leave. She always stays and watches the rest of the movies. Mom and Saul are never home, and it is better than sitting in that empty, dirty, little apartment by herself.

After their second meeting, Angie hears people on the street referring to men that look like him as Filipinos.

"Mama, what are Filipinos?" she asks when she gets home.

"Why do you ask?"

"Because I see a lot of them walking around Chinatown on Sundays all dressed-up."

"They're from the Philippines, some little islands in the ocean far from here. They brought them over here to work in the fields. The ranchers like them because they work hard and long hours for cheap. They like them better than the Mexicans because they don't bring their families with them, and the ranchers don't have to be bothered with kids running around in the fields or men and women fighting. They weren't allowed to bring any women or children with them. So they live alone, usually a bunch of them in one house. They're not dangerous or anything like that but be careful of them—because they don't have any women and it's against the law for them to have white women. And a man without a woman will be looking for one anywhere he can find one. Mexican women don't like them because they're funny looking and their talk sounds like Chinese and they stink. But they won't bother you because you're too young. But if any of them do, just tell me and I'll take care of them."

THERE ARE seven of them. They live together in a small, white house on the western rim of Chinatown. They are short, dark, small-boned men, soft-looking because of the paunch they develop on their little frames. They wear their Sunday slacks high up on the beginnings of their stomachs. They are quiet, respectful men who slip in and out of Chinatown stores practically unnoticed. They carry Spanish names and surnames, perhaps the only vestige of Spain's early conquest of their home islands. They do not speak Spanish but rather a sharp, clipped language that Angie will never understand. They work as many days and hours as they can in the fields; aside from the work, there is nothing for them in America. Except during the harvests, Sunday is a day of rest on the ranches. After Sunday morning breakfast and weekly chores, they don their one set of dress clothes. And with slicked-back, black hair and shiny, pointed shoes, they start down the slight incline into Chinatown to walk through streets and sit in stores and shops, until most of the afternoon has passed, and they can start back to their house and begin preparing Sunday dinner.

Then one Sunday as Santiago is about to leave the Ryan, he pauses and whispers to Angie, "Next Sunday after we finish here, I want you to come up to my house. It's near the playground. I have friends there that live with me. I have told them about you, and they would like to meet you. They're nice and will treat you nice, and I think you can make a lot of money there. But remember, I found you first. You are mine first."

✝ III

YOUNG OSVALDO Montes remembers being driven through the streets of Mexico City on his way to school, lessons, and other places. Those are his earliest memories. He will always remember them. What he sees on those drives is so different than what he sees at home. The people are very poor, and everywhere they are trying to sell things that even he knows are worthless. They are dirty and badly dressed. It is the children that fascinate and haunt him. Their noses are always running with snot. He can see the sores that the snot causes above their lips. Their hair grows in many different directions and lengths. They have scabs on their faces and arms. Many are barefoot even on the coldest days of December and January. Their feet are filthy, covered with layers of dirt and dust and splotches of many things. If they wear shoes, they are the shabbiest of huaraches that are coming apart. Their pants are either enormous or too small. He knows that they know that they are not to approach him, not get too close to him, even in the car. Raoul, one of the family chauffeurs, has only to wag his index finger at them a few times without even looking at them when the car has slowed or come to a stop, to have them shrink away like street dogs.

"What do they want, Raoul?"

"They want money, sir."

"Why don't you give them some?"

"Because I have no money to give them, sir."

"Not even a few centavos?"

"If I did give to just one, the car would immediately be covered with all of them, like maggots, sir."

"Why are they so poor?"

"Because they were born that way, sir."

"Why wasn't I born that way?"

"Because you were lucky, sir."

"But they're just like me, aren't they? I mean they have arms, legs, eyes, feet, mouths. Sometimes I see them laugh and run and talk just like me. "

"It's not the same, sir."

"They're people too, aren't they?"

"There's a difference, sir."

"What's the difference?"

"I don't know how to explain it, sir. But there is a difference, a big difference."

On other days he sees them running and ducking in and out of vendor stands, chasing each other, laughing, giggling and shouting at one and all, using sticks as toys and rolled up rags as balls. And he thinks that they have to be more fortunate than he who can never play as recklessly and as randomly as they, but instead must play by appointment with a select, cautious few under the watchful eyes of one of his nannies or guards behind the high walls of his home.

As he grows older what he sees continues to upset him. Four-and five-year-olds with their little boxes of Chiclets, "Two for five centavos, señor"—already trying to sell their tiny packets of gum to people who don't have a centavo to spare. Children standing behind people eating at taco stands asking, without much luck, for a few centavos to buy a taco of their own or asking for a bite of a taco or scavenging pieces of tacos left behind. Beggars' children standing next to their sidewalk-seated parents, staring off into the distance as multitudes pass without so much as a look. The number of disfigured and/or handicapped children seems to grow. How can he have so much, and they so little?

One day, when he is old enough to drive, he says that he has an errand to run and insists that he will drive one of the family's seven vehicles there alone. The chauffeurs are aghast. They tell him that his father would never permit that. He answers that either they let him do as he wishes or he will have them fired. He leaves the estate alone. They follow: three in two cars. He drives to the poorest section of the city, parks at a huge mercado, and enters and sits himself at one of the open-air food stands. He orders a plate of nopales and rice and beans. The other customers and vendors watch in disbelief and little by little move away from him. He eats alone and asks for more tortillas. The three chauffeurs, armed with pistols, watch from a distance, certain that all hell is about to break loose. When he finishes eating he leaves a large tip—causing a great commotion. The chauffeurs follow him out of the mercado and on the road at a safe distance. Later, they debate whether they should tell Don Osvaldo. If they tell Don Osvaldo, young Osvaldo might have them fired. If they don't tell Don Osvaldo and he finds out, then for sure they will be fired. That night they tell Don Osvaldo.

"Have you lost your mind? Have you gone crazy? Do you have any idea of the seriousness of what you've done?" His father is almost shouting. This is his manner when he is belittling people, and he is always belittling people. His money gives him that right. He is pacing, waving his arms. His brow is knotted, his eyes are angry. "Do you have any idea what could have happened to you if they had known whose son you are? Do you? Do you?" Most people are afraid of him. He keeps them that way, either because it gives him more power or because he just enjoys it. "Answer me! Answer me!"

Osvaldo doesn't answer. He's not afraid of him. At seventeen, he understands all too well that it is his father who is dependent on him and not the other way around. His father needs him. He has five sisters and no brothers. How many times has his father said to him, "Someday this will be all yours. You will pick up where I have left off. Don't you understand that you could have very easily been kidnapped?"

His father's voice softens. It is caring. He is beginning to think that he might be the only person in the world that his father loves. Everyone else, including his mother and his sisters, is afraid of him. And he keeps them that way. "Who wants to kidnap me?"

"Osvaldo, don't act stupid. Don't you understand how much you could be worth to those animals? A ransom of millions of pesos. Don't misunderstand me. It's not the money. For you, I would pay whatever they asked, even if it left me penniless. You know that. What I worry about is what they could do to you, even if the ransom has been paid. They could maim you, mutilate you, kill you, even after they got the money. It happens all the time."

"Nobody bothered me in that mercado. Nobody was going to kidnap me there. I ordered and ate a taco just like everybody else and then left."

"What I don't understand, Osvaldo, is why you want to associate with those people? What can they give you? They have nothing. They are dumb, illiterate. They know nothing. They can talk about nothing. They are filthy. They stink. Most of them don't have soap. They wouldn't know what to do with it if they saw it. The woman who served you—she was the cook, wasn't she? And she took your money, didn't she? You handed her your money and she continued cooking and serving you, didn't she? That can be dangerous, you know."

Don Osvaldo is still wearing one of the gray suits he always wears to the office. *How many gray suits does he have? How many gray suits does he need?* His father says they are all different. He's even brought some out to show him how different they are. But they all look the same to him. When the tailor comes to their house to measure him for another gray suit, they laugh at the poor fools who buy ready-made suits from the big department stores thinking that no one will know. Not once does the tailor ask his father why he needs another gray suit. If he ever does, his father will probably answer it's to go along with one of the dozen pair of black shoes that he always brags come from Paris. His father will never understand. "I suppose," he answers.

"You suppose! Do you have any idea how many times she had handled money before you came? All those coins and bills carry germs, Osvaldo, dangerous germs. Many of the people who eat there are dangerously ill or have been in contact with someone who is dangerously ill. They give her their money with all its germs and she goes on cooking and handling your food. Do you have any idea how long her food has been out in the open air, exposed to every kind of fly and insect? Why would you want to eat their food, Osvaldo, why?"

"They're people, Papa, people just like you and me."

"No, they are not, Osvaldo! They are nothing like you and me. They have nothing to offer this world, our world, nothing to justify their existence other than their despicable need to continue to propagate more and more children into that hideous world of theirs."

"If they have nothing, then why don't you give them some of your money? You're always telling me that you're one of the richest men in Mexico. Give them some of your money. It won't hurt you and it might help them have better lives."

"Osvaldo, you are young yet. You have a lot to learn. In time you will learn that you don't help people just by *giving* them things. In fact you hurt them, you weaken them. You take away their self-reliance, their self-respect, their independence. No one ever gave me anything and look where I am. I did it by hard work and perseverance. If those people you're talking about just went out and got a decent job and worked hard at it and persevered, you would immediately see how much better their situation would be and how much more they would respect themselves. This idea of spreading the wealth without the recipients working for it will only lead to disaster.... Do you have anything to say for yourself?"

"Not really, except I think those people in the mercado and on the streets are people, and we should help them."

"Please, don't get me started again. Until further notice, you will be driven to and from school and everywhere else by one of the chauffeurs."

"I thought the Mercedes was mine."

"It is. But one of the chauffeurs will be driving you in it until you can show me that you've regained your common sense."

Two weeks later, Raoul was stunned to see young Osvaldo come out of the house dressed in shabby, soiled clothes and get into the car. "Are you going to school like that, señor Osvaldo?"

"Yes. Let's go."

"Is this for some sort of school function?"

"Yes. Let's go. I don't want to be late."

When he dresses like that again the following day, Raoul mentions it to Don Osvaldo.

"What? What did he do when he got to school?"

"Both days he went into the school dressed like that and both days at 3:00 he came out of the school dressed like that."

Don Osvaldo calls the school and speaks to the principal who tells him that young Osvaldo has been causing quite a stir coming to school dressed the way he has been lately. He has attended classes, but on both days he has left the campus at the noon hour and on the last occasion had returned late for class.

"The next time he dresses like that, I want you to go back to the school that same morning and be there before the noon hour. Park far enough away so that he can't see you. When he comes out, follow him. I want a full report."

Raoul knows where the boy is going. But Don Osvaldo will never believe him and will only become furious with him if he tells him—and will want him followed anyway. So he says nothing.

The boy waits a week before he dons his shabby clothes again. When he gets into the car, Raoul says nothing. Later that morning as he drives back from school, he is tempted to go directly to the mercado. But if his hunch is wrong, there will be hell to pay with Don Osvaldo. The boy leaves the campus at the noon hour. He hails a taxi. After four blocks, Raoul is certain he is going to the mercado. Rather than follow the cab, he takes a shorter route and enters the mercado before the boy does. He stands off to the side and waits. The boy enters and goes to another open-air stand and takes a seat at the counter. From behind, he looks like any of the other customers. Raoul thinks that two of the customers take note of the latest arrival longer than usual, but no one moves away from him. The boy tries to engage the customer on his right and then the one on his left in conversation, but neither will talk to him.

Don Osvaldo is outraged. He screams at Raoul. "Why didn't you go up and yank that little son of a bitch away from the counter in front of all his low-life friends! Then no one would want the little bastard back again!"

"Boss, I thought that would only make things worse. Then they might have guessed who he really is and taken him hostage."

"I don't give a good goddamn what you thought! Your job isn't just to stand there and watch! Your job is to put an end to this shit! Don't you understand?"

"Yes, boss."

"Don't 'yes' me! Not after you didn't do a goddamn thing!"

The screaming continues until Don Osvaldo thinks of his rising blood pressure. Then he stops and glares at the bowed Raoul for a full minute before he yells again, "Get out of my sight, you worthless piece of shit!"

Later that day, Don Osvaldo leaves word that he is to be notified immediately the next time young Osvaldo leaves the house dressed shabbily. He does not have long to wait. The next morning the boy climbs into the vehicle wearing clothes he has bought from a cripple who had laid out his wares on the sidewalk near the mercado: a pair of wrinkled, soiled brown pants; a shrunken, faded flannel shirt; and canvas shoes worn-out at the toes. Raoul tells him that he's forgotten something and goes back into the house and calls Don Osvaldo at his office. "He's at it again, boss."

Don Osvaldo is waiting when Raoul returns from taking the boy to school. "This has got to stop and since I can't rely on you, I'll stop it myself. Get Felipe and Juan in here. The four of us will go in two cars. I want everyone armed. Whatever presents itself, we must be ready."

They park a block away from the school. Don Osvaldo and

Raoul are in the front car; Juan and Felipe are behind them in the second car. "One never knows what can happen to the first car, but they'll never be expecting a second car." The boy emerges just after twelve and gets into a taxi.

"I think I know where he's going, boss."

"Where?"

"To the mercado. If we take a shortcut instead of following the taxi, we can..."

"I don't give a damn what you think. All your thinking has gotten me nowhere. Correction. It's gotten me here. Just follow that taxi and shut up."

The taxi leaves young Osvaldo off at the entrance. Instead of going into the mercado, the boy weaves in and out of the crowd of people on the sidewalk, some of whom are standing and eating at taco stands. The boy nods and greets two older, unkempt men. Tears well in Don Osvaldo's eyes. *Is this what my son has come to?* The boy stops at one of the filthiest stands and smiles warmly at the worn woman at the stand who is cooking, serving, taking and changing money, and tossing refuse off the stand down somewhere near her feet. Street dogs vie for it. Don Osvaldo fights back tears. *What's wrong with the boy? What's gotten into him? He never smiles at me like that.*

"What do you want us to do, boss?"

"What do you think I want you to do? Get him the hell out of there. You and Juan go get him. Have Felipe follow you at a distance. If there are any problems, tell Felipe not to be afraid to use his gun."

"Do you want to come with us?"

"Are you crazy?" He's shouting now. "Have you *ever* seen me associate with that garbage? Have you *ever* seen me get near those pigs out there? Just because my son has gone crazy doesn't mean that I don't know who I am—doesn't mean that I've lost all my self-respect! You make another insinuation like that and you had better start looking for another job!"

The two men creep up behind the boy and, as he is biting into a

✠ 40

taco, drag him away from the stand out toward the street and the waiting car. The boy struggles and screams. The crowd is startled. A few start to follow the boy and men. Felipe fires his gun into the air. "Get back! This is none of your business! Get back!" They need no further warning.

In the car, Don Osvaldo's shouting begins anew. "Have you lost your mind? Don't you know whose son you are? Have you no respect for your family? Shame on you for having dragged us down into the armpit of the world!" The shouting goes on halfway across the city. When they reach the estate, Don Osvaldo says, "From now on until further notice, Felipe will accompany you whenever you leave these premises. He will sit in the classroom with you at school. He will go with you to any and all social functions and be with your every move. The only time he'll leave your side is when you sleep and even then he will sleep outside your door. You have chosen to humiliate me and your family and now you leave me no alternative but to humiliate you."

Don Osvaldo usually leaves for the office every morning before 6:30, but this morning he has waited to see how young Osvaldo is dressed. At 7:30 there is still no sign of him. If he delays any longer he will be late for school. He asks Felipe to go to the boy's room and wake or roust him. Felipe goes to the room and returns. "He's gone, boss."

"Gone? What do you mean gone?" He shoves Felipe aside and goes to the boy's room. There is no sign of the boy. Only an open window tells of his departure. He looks out that second-story window. Below is a badly trampled bush. He orders for the house, the guesthouse, and the grounds to be searched. Nothing. As he looks around the boy's room again, he sees that the boy has taken nothing with him.

A YEAR passes. Still no sign of the boy. Don Osvaldo has hired private investigators and approached the police with offers of huge rewards. He has had every mercado scoured. All to no avail. Young Osvaldo has disappeared. Some of the few men that Don Osvaldo has confided in have cautiously expressed their opinions that what the boy was going through in the mercado was just a phase—something he would have outgrown. The notion haunts him. Had he been too rash? If he had only borne with that adolescent nonsense, would young Osvaldo still be home? Six more months pass. Now he is convinced that something has happened to the boy, that he has been the victim of foul play. The thought that his empire will pass on to his nitwit sons-in-law taunts him.

Then one day a business associate says to him, "Don Osvaldo, I didn't know your son was studying for the priesthood."

"What?"

"One of my sons is toying with the idea of entering a seminary. Sunday, we visited the Quiroga Seminary. I could be mistaken, but I could almost swear that I saw your son there in a black cassock with all the other seminarians."

"Are you sure?"

"If it wasn't him, it had to be his identical twin."

That same afternoon Don Osvaldo arranges a meeting with Archbishop Pérez. The following morning he meets with the Archbishop in the latter's office. "Most Holy Archbishop, I'm sure you are aware of the rather large financial contributions I have consistently made over the past several years to Mother Church in the spirit of thanks. God has blessed me with His Goodness and Mother Church has been good to me, too. However, I would not be completely honest if I did not admit that I have always hoped that God Almighty will take into consideration those contributions when it comes time for me to pass on. But now I find that even before I pass on, I am in dire need of a very earthly favor. One that is as important to me as anything on this earth. And, I must say that if you cannot grant me this one favor, then I'm afraid that it will be very difficult for me to continue with my contributions as I have in the past."

Two mornings later before the 5:00 Mass, Don Osvaldo is seated in the darkness of the choir loft at the chapel of the Quiroga Seminary when the young seminarians file into the pews alongside the altar to await the beginning of the daily Mass. The eleventh seminarian to enter is young Osvaldo. He has changed his name to Pedro Montes, but he is nevertheless Osvaldo. Of that, there is no doubt whatsoever in Don Osvaldo's mind.

Three days later, the rector of Quiroga Seminary has Pedro Montes summoned to his office. The young man does not like the somberness of the rector's mood. Theirs has been a cordial relationship. The rector has always been encouraging and approving. Now he is reluctant to look at the young man. His look instead is directed down at the letter before him as he strokes his chin with his thumb and forefinger. Finally he says, "Brother Montes, I find it necessary to ask you to leave this seminary."

The young man is stunned. He blinks, he reddens, he shakes his head. "But why? What have I done?"

The rector sighs. Without looking at the young brother, he begins speaking of the seminary's rigorous academic standards, its selectivity in making certain that those who enter the priesthood from its institution will truly be able and dedicated to working with the poor. By making this decision, he does not mean to impugn the young man's dedication or his character or his capabilities, but... "Oh, I can't do this. Brother Montes, your father is a very important man. Needless to say, we did not know he was your father. You kept that from us. Probably for good reason. At any rate, he has discovered that you are studying here. He does not want you to be a priest and he has intervened at the highest level to gain his way. I have been ordered to terminate your studies here.... If you divulge what I have just told you to anyone, there could be serious consequences for Quiroga and myself.... But I can't be concerned with that now."

They sit in silence in the dimness of the late afternoon sunlight. After a while the rector says, "Brother Montes, I think you will make a fine priest. Your affinity for the poor is real. Because of that, I have taken the liberty of speaking to the rector of St. Anthony's Seminary. He is a lifelong friend of mine. St. Anthony's is the seminary for the cloistered order of the same name. Its seminarians take the vow of silence. I have told Padre Bernardo, the rector, everything. He is prepared to accept you and let you complete your studies for the priesthood there. If you change your name, no one will ever find you there, not even your father. But I must warn you: for those who are not suited, that type of monastic life can be very difficult.

For the next five and a half years, Raoul Ortega is a seminarian at St. Anthony's. The vow of silence is not as difficult as he thought it would be. The studies and prayers at Quiroga had already required a good deal of silence. At St. Anthony's the studies and prayers are increased and there is great emphasis placed on meditation. Then too, everyone around him is committed to silence. Somehow the austerity of his living conditions seem to support the silence. His room is small and bare, having only a crude desk and chair, a lamp, and a cot. His possessions are limited to a brown habit, a pair of pants, socks, underwear, a shirt, a sweater, and a pair of sandals. His desire to become a priest and serve the poor is stronger than ever. He prays that his resolve is not being driven by anything his father has done, and he prays too that he not worry, as he often does, how he will be able to serve the poor as a member of a cloistered, silent order.

Two weeks before his ordination into the priesthood, Padre Bernardo advises him that word has come from Rome that the Holy See is seeking Spanish-speaking priests to go to America to tend to the ever-growing flock of Catholic immigrants there. The immigrants are poor and uneducated and in dire need of spiritual guidance. "Given what I know about you, Brother Raoul, I think you would be the perfect fit. Of course, it would mean leaving the order, at least temporarily. But if you're willing, I'm sure that everything can be arranged." For Brother Raoul, his prayers have been answered. God has clearly spoken.

A problem arises as he prepares to leave Mexico. In obtaining a passport, a certified copy of his birth certificate is required, and as a result he has to use his given name of Osvaldo Pedro Montes Arriaga. He balks at returning to that name, but there is no other way. "Not to worry, Padre," Padre Bernardo says, "we have ways of doing these things quietly. Your father will never know."

But a problem arises in a different context once he is in America. He reports to the Bishop's office in San Francisco and there presents all his documents. Later that day, the Bishop's secretary, a thin, nervous, pale man, says that there are certain discrepancies in the documents that he will have to bring to the Bishop's attention. The next day the secretary informs him that the Bishop is troubled by the fact that since the beginning of his seminary studies, he has used three different names. Padre Montes is convinced that once again his father has tracked him. His explanation of his father's opposition to his vocation falls on deaf ears. The secretary keeps shaking his head no and repeating that this matter will have to be looked into in greater detail. They will have to take it up with the Mexican seminaries. The last thing the Bishop wants is for an imposter to be tending to the Holy Father's flock in the Central Valley.

No matter what the nervous, officious secretary says, Padre Montes knows his father is behind this, is trying to block the assignment. For the next six weeks, he prays to God Almighty to thwart his father's efforts and to help him overcome the deep bitterness he feels for him. But each time he returns to the Bishop's office his bitterness grows stronger, and now it is also directed at the pernicious secretary there. How easy it is, he notes, to forget that this is just God's way of testing him.

"Father Montes. Or is it Father Ortega? Or Father Arriaga? Then of course, it could also be Father Raoul or Father Osvaldo. Which is it, sir?"

"It's Father Montes."

"Well, whatever it is, how many times have I told you, sir, that we would call you when we know something? We don't have anything yet, and this is the fourth or fifth time you've been in the office. Again, we will call you when we know something."

"Why is it taking so long?"

"In America, we're careful with our investigations. That may not be the case in Mexico, but it is in America."

"Investigation? What are you investigating?"

"Who you are."

"But you know who I am. You have my passport."

"That may or may not be the case. But when a person uses three different names over a four-year period, one has to wonder who that person is. Who he really is? Or even, what he's done to be using so many false names. How do we know that person hasn't committed a serious crime and isn't running from the authorities?"

"As I said, we're being very thorough in our investigation. Letters are being sent back and forth to Mexico. That takes time. We want to be certain that we know who the person is that we're putting in charge of all those Mexicans in the Central Valley."

Three weeks later in February of 1945, the secretary leaves a message for Father Montes asking him to return to the Bishop's office.

"Well, the Bishop has some reservations about you, but we're going to take a chance and assign you to the St. Teresa parish in Fresno. But the Bishop wants you to know that we'll be watching you very carefully."

✝ IV

SUMMER COMES early for Jesusita's family. In the second week of April, she pulls the kids out of school thinking that after the first year, Sergio and Yolanda had to be bigger, faster workers and that perhaps Paulina could begin working with them part of the time, depending on how much Concepcion could be left alone. All of this would mean more money and an easier winter. By July they have worked their way up to the Central Valley and on over to the coast and the lettuce harvest. In mid-July they are camped near Hollister, and Jesusita is exhausted. Each morning when she wakes, she wonders how she can get through another day, let alone another week.

It has been a difficult summer. In June, Concepcion contracted a fever that lasted nine days and finally necessitated taking her to a doctor in Visalia. Jesusita slept little during those nine days and still worked her eleven-hour days in the field. Two weeks later Paulina came down with a rash that led to many more sleepless nights. While Sergio and Yolanda helped with the cooking and washing, the brunt of that work still fell on Jesusita.

When the summer began, there had been much arguing among the kids, and often Jesusita found that they were ignoring or poorly completing the chores she had given them. In June she bought a barber's leather strap, which she was quick to use to stop the bickering and fighting or to correct failures to do the assigned chores. As soon as Jesusita went for the strap, there was an immediate silence, a stillness, or a scurrying to do or redo what had or had not been done. But it was always too late. Each delinquent received a blow; no explanation, excuse, or blame was heard or needed. If the reaction to the blow went beyond what Jesusita thought was justified, there was another blow. Jesusita had neither the time nor the patience to listen to any further squabbling or excuses. They had been told once and that was enough.

It is 7:20 in the evening and Jesusita has gotten a ride into Hollister from Pedro and Luisa Rodríguez to shop for some milk, wieners, and bread. She has known the Rodríguezes since last summer. She thinks they are silly, stupid people who talk a lot about nothing. But they have a car, so she is quiet and respectful around them. Sitting on her left in the backseat is Concha Gutierrez, a fat woman, probably less so than Agripina, but fat nevertheless. Jesusita does not like fat people. She thinks they are slovenly, piglike people who do not have much self-discipline or self-respect. She met Concha briefly last summer but has never said more than "hello" to her, and that with some effort. She doesn't care that Concha knows that. On her right is a small, dark, older woman who has been introduced to her as María de Jesus Rios.

The ride into town takes fifteen minutes with Pedro opining most of the way that last year's lettuce crop was not only bigger but more plentiful. Luisa agrees with him. In the backseat, Jesusita feels nauseous. After another hot day in the fields and who knows how many weeks without bathing, Concha is giving off a foul odor. No matter how she twists her head, Jesusita cannot escape the odor. She has shifted to her right so much that the small, brown woman there has been squished into the little car's corner. Concha is taking up more than half of the backseat because every time Jesusita has shifted to her right, Concha's large body seems to expand or decompress and stay tightly pressed against her, especially that gigantic thigh which has to be giving off some of the odor.

The car finally pulls up alongside the market. Exiting the little vehicle is a great effort for Concha who now has to slither her huge bottom, less than an inch at a time, toward the door. Everyone has exited the car except for Concha and Jesusita who is waiting behind her. When Concha finally turns in the seat and starts to raise one large leg off the floorboard, Jesusita gives up and exits on the passenger side where María de Jesus is standing with the door open, watching. When Jesusita is outside the car, the woman smiles and says, "I'm María de Jesus Rios."

"Yes, I've already been told," Jesusita answers. And she walks around her thinking, *These women are forever socializing. I didn't come here to socialize. I came here to shop. I have four kids back at the ranch to socialize with if that's what I want to do.*

In the store María de Jesus seems to be following her. Every time she stops the woman is in the same aisle a few paces behind her. At the cash register, Jesusita is the first one in line and as soon as she begins putting her items on the counter, María de Jesus comes up behind her. Outside when they reach the car, it is locked and the others are still in the store. As they stand waiting, it is clear that the woman wants to talk. She is smiling, looking at Jesusita and bobbing her head as if she is thinking of something to say. Jesusita has nothing to say and there is nothing to smile about. She is exhausted after another day in that brutal sun and just wants to get back to the ranch to get Concepcion ready to sleep, so that she can sleep too. But her aloofness doesn't discourage the woman.

"Is this your first season?" the woman asks.

The smile, the friendliness, irritate Jesusita. "Why do you want to know?"

"Oh, I'm just curious. I've seen you with your family and I have to admire you. Working like this with that little one to take care of and a family of five to feed."

The flattery makes Jesusita suspicious. *What does this woman want? What is she up to?* "Why should that make you curious? There are a lot of families working here."

"I guess it's not curiosity so much as just admiring what you're doing."

"What do you want from me, woman?" Her tone is gruff, angry.

"Nothing. Nothing, except that I want to help you."

"Help me?" She looks down with scorn at the thin, bony, frail woman who must be in her fifties or sixties. It's hard to tell with Indians. "You help me? How can you help me? Huh! You mean, how can I help you!"

"No, I'd like to try to help you. I know I can help you."

"Woman, you know nothing about me!"

"I know that you have four kids and that you're probably raising them and working for them by yourself."

"Look, I'm tired, and I'd like to be left alone. Please."

"I don't want to leave you alone. I raised four kids out here by myself just like you're doing. I know what it's like. I know what you're going through. In fact my baby, Beto, he's seventeen now and he's still out here with me. You've probably seen him around."

"So what makes you think you can help me?"

"I'm going to teach you how to pray."

"Pray! Pray! Are you..."

The others come around the corner with their groceries. Pedro is railing against the grocers. "Lousy bastards! They take one look at us and they know what we are! They know we can't buy food anyplace else so the prices go up, up! They think we can't read prices. Maybe I can't read English, but I can read prices. The numbers are the same. They don't lie. I can add. They think we don't know how they're changing the prices, but I've already added the prices before I go to them. How do I tell them in English that I know they're cheating me? I can't. I don't know how. And they know I don't know how. So what do I do? Refuse to pay, walk away from the groceries. And then what will we eat tomorrow if I do that? They know they've got me by the balls. But what can I do? What..."

The two women have stopped talking. It is a conversation that neither wants the others to hear. But María de Jesus' words have hit hard, and on the ride back to the ranch Jesusita contemptuously plays them over and over again in her mind. *Prayer! What the hell does she know about prayer! I've prayed and prayed. I've even cried as I've prayed, as I've begged, and all it's ever gotten me is more misery. There's a God for some people but there's never been a God for me. All He's ever done is laugh at me.* She turns just enough so that she can look down disdainfully at the squinched-up woman. Prayer, shit! But the woman returns her look with a smile. The smile is open, soft, friendly, which baffles Jesusita. *There has to be something wrong with that woman. She can't be all there. She saw my look, and still she smiles.*

They come to the ranch. Pedro turns off the main road onto a dirt road that leads past the ranch house out into the lettuce fields. When she can see her shelter, Jesusita says, "Don Pedro, let me off at the crossroad, would you please?" She is surprised and annoyed when the woman beside her says, "I want off there too, Don Pedro." She doesn't know where the woman's shelter is but she is certain that it can't be near hers. *Why in the hell does she want off here?*

The car stops. The little woman squeezes out of her corner, opens the door, and slips out, and then she holds the door open for Jesusita, smiling. As Jesusita gets out, she promises herself that she has done all the talking she's going to do. The car leaves. The woman looks up at her, still smiling. Jesusita walks past her into a row of lettuce toward her shelter.

"Jesusita, wait, please, I need to talk to you."

Jesusita doesn't pause or even turn around.

"Jesusita, please wait. I need to talk to you." She can hear the woman scampering after her, can hear the rattling of whatever she has in her grocery bags. She quickens her pace. The noise behind her grows louder. The woman is trying to keep pace. When she is a row from her shelter, Concepcion sees her and begins shouting, "Here comes Mama! Here comes Mama!" and ducks into the shelter. Whatever this woman wants, Jesusita thinks, I'd better hear it now rather than at the shelter in front of the kids.

"What the devil do you want?"

"I just want to talk to you. I just want to help you."

"Help me with what?"

"Help you with your struggle, with your heavy load..."

"What are you talking about?"

"I can see how tired you are. How worn out you are. The load you're carrying, no person, not even a man should have to carry. I know it's hard for you to believe, but I went through the same thing when I was your age. I would have given anything then for someone to have helped me."

She is not five feet tall. Her skin is copper brown. The richness of that color hides many of the creases around her eyes and mouth. Her thick hair is stark white and is pulled back in a single braid. Her dark eyes are open and clear, so open and clear that Jesusita can no longer suspect or distrust her.

"What is it you want?"

"I want to talk to you for a few minutes. That's all I want. Maybe I can help you. Maybe we can become friends."

"Talk to me then. Tell me what you think is so important to tell me before my kids come."

"I was maybe a little older than you when it happened to me. One day my husband disappeared, without a word, and never came back. I think it got too hard for him. We were very poor and no matter how much he worked, it never got any better. It got worse when he left, much worse. My kids were about the age of yours. My baby, Beto, was almost five. Like you, I had to come to work in the fields. It was the hardest time of my life. You see, when Beto was born, his legs were so bowed that he needed two canes to walk or even stand. Some contratistas wouldn't let us work because of him. They said he would be too much of a problem out in the field. And he was. But if we didn't work, we didn't eat. Unless we begged. And sometimes that's what we had to do—beg. You know how hard it is to beg, beg in the street with your four kids? You know what that makes you feel like? I used to wonder if it was easier being a whore. The only thing that kept me going was my kids. They needed me.

"One day we were begging on the street when a woman stopped and said that in two days people were going on a pilgrimage and that we should go. She told us about a man who had been a cripple and still worked in the fields. When people asked him how he did it, he said by praying. One day while he was working and praying in the fields, the Virgen appeared to him and blessed him and told him to throw away his crutches, that because of his great faith he was a cripple no more. He got up and walked, yelling to everybody to come and see that he could walk. Since then many people make a pilgrimage to the place where the Virgen appeared, not far from here, taking with them their young and their sick. And many people have been cured and thrown away their crutches too.

"I didn't think I could make a three-day pilgrimage, especially with Beto. But actually it was Beto who she kept looking at when she was talking to me, and she said not to worry, that there would be plenty of help with Beto and if worse came to worse, he could ride in the wagons that carried the clothes and the bedding. So we went and..."

Concepcion arrives shouting, "Mama! Mama! Mama!" clutching at her mother's pant legs, pulling her toward their shelter.

"I'm going to have to get this girl ready to sleep."

"Can we talk some more?"

"When?"

"Tomorrow after work and after everybody's eaten?"

"Yes."

Later that night, it is her readiness to continue listening that puzzles her as she lies next to her children. Why continue? What did all this talk about cripples and pilgrimages have to do with her and her family? She has no cripples, no sick or infirm. She has no interest in pilgrimages. The woman said that maybe they could be friends. She has no friends. Since Rogelio died, there's never been any time for friends. She's never wanted any friends, at least not with these people. So why did she agree to listen to her again? She doesn't know.

The next evening, just after 7:30, Jesusita sees María de Jesus at a distance, walking across the lettuce fields toward her. A man is walking beside her. She can't tell if the man is with her or just walking beside her. As they near, she can see that he is a young man, a strapping young man. When they are closer still, nodding greetings to each other, she sees that the young man is with her and that he might still be a boy.

"Jesusita, this is my son...." She pauses. Jesusita knows. "Beto."

He is a handsome boy, not much more than eighteen, if that. He smiles warmly, politely, bowing a little as he says, "Beto Ríos, señora, para servirle."

"Oh, mijo, I forgot my list. You know, the one about the pilgrimages. I know you are going to your friends, but will you run back and get it for me? Hurry, please."

The boy turns and runs, long, loping strides between rows of lettuce. María de Jesus watches Jesusita watching. Then she says, "He's the one I was telling you about yesterday."

"When did he lose his crutches?" Jesusita asks, knowing.

"That time I was telling you about. When we made our first pilgrimage."

"But I have no cripples in my family."

"When we suffer like you're suffering, when the loads we're carrying are much too heavy for us, we all become cripples. Trust me, Jesusita. I know what those pilgrimages have done for me. I've seen what they've done for others. None of us used crutches. I know how faith in God, in His Divine Will, can lighten one's load, change one's life. For the better, for much the better."

THERE IS a break of a few days between the end of the lettuce season and the beginning of the apricot harvest. For several years now, the workers there have used that time for their annual pilgrimage. The shrine is sixteen miles south. If they begin early one morning, they can be there early the next day, pray and worship until mid-afternoon and then start back, returning before nightfall of the third day.

Jesusita has decided to join the pilgrims this year. She is skeptical. Since Rogelio's death she has prayed to God the Father, the Son, and the Holy Ghost without any luck. She has implored the

Virgin Mary and the Virgen de Guadalupe with silence for an answer. She has prayed to the saints that she knew and to saints that others have told her about with no success. Add to that the thought of marching thirty-two miles with four kids, one who is five, in the hot sun and there seems very little reason to go. But thoughts and dreams of suicide and beyond have been plaguing and terrifying her. There have been times when she has been stooped over a head of lettuce, her thousandth or two thousandth head of lettuce, and thought that she can't go on, that she can't pick one more head of lettuce or one more box of apricots or crate of peppers, with no end in sight. In her dreams she is floating free, alone and free, somewhere in the night sky without the hint of a worry or a burden. True, as she floats, her wrists are bleeding, won't stop bleeding, but there is no pain and that is such a small price to pay for her release.

Just last week Concepcion woke in the middle of the night crying of a sore throat. She did everything she could to comfort her, to quiet her, so that the others might sleep, so that she might sleep. She had eleven hours of stooping and lifting in the sun waiting for her in the morning. Concepcion continued to whimper. She dreaded the thought of another sickness. Then the girl began screaming when she touched her. The child was in pain. No doubt about it. Then it occurred to her: Wouldn't she and Concepcion be far better off if she were to slice their throats or cut their wrists? Wouldn't they, really? The thought scared her, but the logic taunted her. Wouldn't they? A few minutes later Paulina said, "Mama, I can't sleep." And the logic grinned and said they would *all* be better off if she sliced all their throats and cut all their wrists and then hers. Then she wouldn't have to worry about what would happen to them if she killed herself. Eventually Concepcion dozed off. And Jesusita dozed off too, but with that thought. And it was with her the next morning, the logic taunting her in the fields. The thought of the act itself terrified her, as did her inability to refute the thought and its logic. As often as she shook the thought off, it returned. So much so that she didn't trust herself alone with her children on the ranch while the others went on their pilgrimage. As she gathered their belongings and took down the boxes, she was convinced that she had made the right decision.

As THEY near the meeting place, the point of departure, she is surprised by the size of the throng already there. It is well over a hundred. Most are not the workers she knows. Most she has not seen before. Where they have come from she does not know. All are poor. Some are in rags. Most are in small groups of families or friends. Some have a physically disabled person in their group— blind, crippled, half a stump of a man, a hobbling dwarf, a man without arms, a few with huge growths on their faces. The march- ers themselves are of all ages, shapes, and sizes. They are quiet, almost reverential, and some are already praying. What she does not see is any sign of the despair that she carries in her heart.

There are several donkey-driven carts on the side of the road loaded with an assortment of clothes, bedding, food, and drink. Some of the marchers urge her family to put their mochilas on the cart where small children are already sitting atop bundles. Her older children see friends, ask if they can be with them, and run off. She looks for María de Jesus but cannot find her in the throng. A tall, thin woman smiles and motions her and Concepcion into the line. She has a warm, friendly face. "If you go to the back of the line," she says, "you may never get there. What is your girl's name?"

"Concepcion."

"Such a pretty name. And this is my daughter. Her name is Catalina."

She has not seen the little girl who is clutching the far side of her mother's skirt. She is a badly twisted child. Her body is bent to her left from the waist down. Her left leg is raised at the knee and rests on the tip of her left foot. Her upper body is stretched to the right and her thin, long, face carries with it a permanent- ly open mouth. Jesusita shrinks from the sight of the child, then catches herself and tries to hide her discomfort. The woman has long since ignored these reactions; instead she bends a bit and says softly to the child, "Catalina, this is Concepcion. Concepcion must be about your age, don't you think?"

The march is long, hot, and arduous. After two miles Jesusita knows she'll never reach the shrine unless she rides on the carts. She has put Concepcion on one of the carts even before the end of the first mile and wishes she had stayed there with her. What keeps her marching is that everywhere she turns, there are older, heavier women who show no signs of strain or weariness. Instead there is a quiet confidence about them, a certainty of purpose. Some are quietly praying. Every now and then someone begins singing a traditional, religious song and is joined by the throng. She sneaks glances at the woman next to her. The twisted child is still marching, limping it's true, but that's probably the way she always walks. And it's also true that for brief stretches the woman has carried her. But they are still marching, mother and daughter, hand in hand, at peace with themselves and the world.

What is it, she asks herself, as the blisters on her feet begin bursting, what is it that keeps the marchers going? She knows but she won't let herself know. What do they think they'll get from this? The vast majority of them have no physical disabilities. What can they be cured of, she scoffs. She looks around for women her age. She sees some. Their dirty, ragged clothes, if nothing else, say that their lives are not easy. They can't all be fools. What do they expect to get from this? Some sort of miracle that will change their lives and make them happy forever and ever? It's never worked for her. Yet the quiet, sober, steady movement of all these people says that they believe.

Someone says they have marched almost six miles. She is limping badly. Each step is torture. She leaves the line and starts toward the carts. She climbs on the cart that carries Concepcion and other children. There is no other adult on the cart. She doesn't care what anyone else thinks of her. The pain is too great. Concepcion is asleep. She covers her to shade her from the sun. Then she falls asleep. When she wakes there are adults on that and other carts.

She thinks they must have traveled a long way. The word is that they will be stopping soon at a creek and spending the night there.

As the two donkeys grudgingly pull their cart slowly down the dirt road, she thinks how silly it was to have dragged herself and her kids on this godforsaken pilgrimage. She should never have listened to María de Jesús, who she still hasn't seen. She begins to think that after all that talk, María de Jesús didn't even come. She sees a very old couple near the end of the line about twenty feet from her. She watches them because she thinks that they may be in danger of being left behind. They are a small, stooped couple, each shuffling along with the help of a wooden staff. They look to be in their eighties or perhaps even in their nineties, she doesn't know. But old they are. She wonders if they have shrunk a great deal with age or whether they were small, indigenous people to begin with. He wears one of those stiff, white, palm cowboy hats that are common in the rancho, and she has raised part of her black rebozo over her head. Monitors come up to them repeatedly and point to the carts as they talk. Each time the couple shake their heads no. Even though they are shuffling and moving slowly, they do not appear to be struggling or in pain. She thinks of them as both admirable and ridiculous, and it troubles her that people their age would risk their health and safety to be in the march. But they believe. From time to time she loses track of them, but when the march stops at the creek she sees that they are still in line.

She gets a closer look at the couple as she and her children prepare for the night. They are indeed old, very old—milky, red-streaked eyes and he with one eye that is completely covered with a whitish film. The backs of her hands are a mirror of green veins and bones. Still, they are in mid-line the next morning when she hoists herself up onto the cart. They say it is three or four miles to the shrine, and she doubts that the couple will make it and hopes that someone other than herself is watching them. Now they walk hand in hand, her left hand in his right hand, balancing themselves with their staffs in their other hands. Not only do they remain in line, but with each passing mile they don't seem to fall behind. When the front of the line reaches the shrine, there is a roar that spreads through the throng. As the roar reaches the old couple, they straighten themselves, raise their heads, and shout with the others.

The shrine stands at the end of a dirt road deep in the lettuce fields. It is a ten-foot-wide, four-feet-deep, three-sided, roofed structure set on a two-foot platform. Against the center of the back wall is a life-sized statue of the Virgen de Guadalupe. The wall is painted sky blue, except for the golden rays apparently emanating from every part of the statue's body. The platform itself is filled with hundreds of votive jars, many empty, many still containing unburned portions of wax. From the front to the back of the line, the marchers kneel. Fresh jars of votive candles are placed on the platform and lit. Singing begins and prayers are said. The sounds of more than a hundred voices rising in unison into the clear, open air are impressive. Rows of ten people are brought to the edge of the platform and allowed to pray, meditate, or talk to the Virgen for ten minutes and then are sent to the back of the line and another row of ten take their place. A set of crutches is thrown into the air and someone screams, "I've been cured! I've been cured! I can walk!" The crowd roars. This is what they have come for. One woman screams that she can see and another that her headache of a year is gone. More roars and affirmations from the crowd.

Jesusita watches and listens intently. Her resistance, her doubt is weakening. Slowly she and her four children move toward the platform. When they reach it, the oldest are put in a row in front of her. She watches as they kneel at the platform, hoping to see some sign of effect or lack of effect. As Yolanda leaves the platform, she turns wide-eyed to her mother and nods yes, yes, yes. When Jesusita kneels at the platform with Concepcion, she doesn't know what to say or how to say it or whether she should say anything at all. At first she says and does nothing. But then feels an enormous pressure to do something. She turns to the woman on her left and sees that she is crying—but smiling too, tears of joy. The woman is nodding and her lips are moving and a stream of tears is steadily falling on her rebozo. Jesusita whispers a halting, mindless Hail Mary and then another and another before she stops and stares into the eyes of the statue and whispers, "Help me, dear Mother! Help me! I can't do this alone. Not anymore. I can't. I know I can't. I need your help!" Then she feels an influx of warm, soft air that lifts her from within and gently suspends her in its softness as a voice from within repeats, "Have faith, child, have faith. And He will help you." She too bursts into tears and believes, and she and Concepcion are led away from the altar by one of the monitors.

Later, it is a joyful crowd that she mills about in before they start back. There have been no more attestations of cures, of miracles, but there is joy on every face, including hers. And she can see that everyone has gotten what they came for and more. She sees the old couple. They are gleaming, smiling and talking to another old couple. She waits until they are finished. Then she approaches and says, "Can I talk to you for a moment?"

The two raise their heads and look up at her. "Of course," says the old man.

"Is this the first time you've come?"

"Oh, no. We come every year. We've come every year since the Virgen appeared to Jose Luis."

"Why do you come?"

"Because without God, life is too hard. No, it is impossible."
She nods.

"My child," the old woman explains, "no one can understand life. No one can understand or explain the hardships and the setbacks. But if you accept God...if you believe in Him...believe in His Divine Will...know and accept that your will is not His Will...believe that this life is but a part of His grand plan...believe that He can do no evil and therefore will do no evil. Then you will understand that everything happens for a reason, as part of His grand plan, and that in the end everything happens for the best. Live in that belief and you will see just how much easier and better your life will be, here and in the next life with Him."

People are starting to prepare for the trip back. Jesusita has no idea where her older children are, and she begins looking for them. She meets María de Jesus. Their smiles are spontaneous, big, warm. They hug. They part, still smiling.

"Are you glad you came?"

"Yes, oh yes."

"You see, I told you."

"Thank you, María de Jesus."

On the ride back, the children are no longer a burden. She understands that they have been given to her so that she can raise them to be part of His Greater Glory. Her thoughts of suicide and infanticide shame her. How far she has drifted from her main purpose in life.

It is early evening when they reach the ranch outside of Greenfield where they will be harvesting apricots for the next weeks. Finding a suitable place for a shelter as well as the needed boxes and wood for the shelter, sorting through their belongings, and setting up a place to cook and then cooking before it's too dark to see would have been unbearable just last week. But now she has God on her side. And with Him comes a patience, an acceptance that she has seldom known. They eat. The older ones help her clean up. They sleep. As she lays next to them, she knows that life will definitely be easier. *Thank you, Jesus.*

Going up and down that tall ladder the next day with buckets full of apricots and moving that heavy ladder, which by the end of the first day seems enormous, from tree to tree leaves her sore and exhausted. Sergio and Yolanda fall asleep without dinner. Paulina complains that she can't move those big ladders and that she's afraid of heights. She is surly and defiant when Jesusita scolds her. Concepcion is cranky and spills her dinner on the ground. All of that, she thinks, would have broken her a week ago. She could not have gone on in the frame of mind she was in. But now she lowers her eyes and speaks to Him and He to her, and she knows that this too will pass—that this too can and will be endured and that in the end He will make it worthwhile.

V

IN MID-OCTOBER, Jesusita and her family return to Fresno for the winter. They return to the same two rooms in Juanita Salas' home, and she returns to cleaning offices from 5:00 PM to midnight five nights a week for Mr. Jim. "Jesse, you'll always have a winter job with me. Shoot! You do the work of two women." She still doesn't understand some of what he says, but from the tone of his voice and his smile, she knows it's good. The family quickly falls into the routine they left in the spring, except that she has made an important addition. She now goes to the 6:00 Mass every morning.

St. Teresa church is less than two blocks away. If she leaves by 5:52, she is there at least a minute before Mass starts, and if she leaves the church within five minutes after Mass ends, she is home in time to wake and ready the kids for school. Waking at 5:30 each morning requires no effort: Mass and Holy Communion are a wonderful way to start each day. It's a guaranteed blessing. The October nights have turned cold and it is still dark when she walks to church. The street is empty, quiet, and peaceful. In a few weeks the tule ground fog will settle in for the winter, sometimes limiting visibility to just a few feet around her. She is not afraid. It would be ironic indeed if anything were to happen to her on her way to a visit with God. She knows that God would never permit that.

She is surprised to find that only she and the priest, whom she has been told is from Mexico, are present at the first Mass she attends, which seems to increase the size of the little church— a whitewashed, wood-framed structure with a pitched roof that bears a white cross above the entrance. Twelve pews line the right side of the center aisle; on the left side of the aisle are ten pews with a confessional behind them. A railing separates the laity from the holy works of the priest. The tabernacle on the altar is covered with a satin fabric. Above it is a statue of a crucified Jesus; to the left is a replica of the Flaming Heart of Jesus and to the right is a replica of the Virgen de Guadalupe. She is certain that tomorrow morning there will be more people there, that this is an aberration. But for the rest of the week it is only she and the priest. The priest surprises her too. He is so young-looking and so light-skinned that he could pass for an American.

They say nothing to each other during that first week of Masses. At exactly 6:00 he emerges from behind the altar dressed in his vestments and carrying a chalice. He mounts the altar steps and begins the recitation of the Mass in Latin. She follows along with her rosary and sometimes in meditation. Two-thirds of the way through the Mass, he descends from the altar to give her, as she kneels at the altar railing, Holy Communion. He blesses her with the white wafer which contains the Body and Blood of Jesus Christ and then places it on her tongue. He returns to the altar and continues his Latin recitation. Moments before the end of the Mass, he turns and blesses her in Latin. Then he takes the chalice and disappears behind the altar.

On Saturday afternoon she enters the church for Confession. The posted hours for Confession are 2:00 to 4:00. Again she is alone not knowing if the young priest is in the confessional. She goes to the confessional. It is a four-by-six-foot block of wood that takes up all but a foot of the center of the aisle on the left side of the church. It is divided in two, on one side sits the priest, on the other kneels the penitent. What separates them is a sheet of plywood that has a one-by-one-foot sliding slat that opens at face level with the kneeling penitent. The opening is covered on the priest's side by a piece of cloth. The entrance to each side is covered by a seven-foot curtain. She enters the confessional and kneels. Nothing happens. She waits. There is absolute silence. Still nothing happens. She begins thinking that the young priest is not there when the wooden slat slides open. The young priest sits on the other side. They are no more than two feet apart, but she can't see him. She begins, "Bless me, Father, for I have sinned. These are my sins since my last confession."

"What are they?"

She lists them. They are few and trivial.

"Anything else?"

"No, Father."

"Say an Act of Contrition and for your penance say a Rosary."

She says the Act of Contrition.

"I absolve you of your sins. Go in peace and may God bless you, my child." The wooden slat slides shut and there is not another sound from his side of the confessional.

She continues kneeling, wanting more, expecting more. But there is no more. She rises and stands in silence for several moments. The brevity and abruptness of the young priest has shocked her. She steps out of the confessional and starts out of the church, but stops and looks back at the sealed confessional, puzzled. "My child?" He looks more like *her child,* and she leaves.

The second week of Masses is the same as the first—the quick emergence to and exit from the back of the altar without a single word being spoken directly to her, the sole parishioner in attendance. Except for a few words, the following Saturday's Confession is a duplicate of the first. All week long she has tried desperately not to commit any sins, not even the smallest of venial sins. On her walk to church that afternoon, the only possible sins she can think of are her bouts of anger with Paulina. The girl is thirteen now, and there has been a dramatic change in her. Unlike the others, she is no longer afraid of Jesusita. Instead, she is openly defiant, scornful, and has an ever-present look of hate in her eyes.

It drives Jesusita almost mad. She's taken the strap to the girl, but that has changed nothing, except that the look of hate is stronger. The girl defies her openly in front of the others who always do as she says. She doesn't know what to do. If she loses control of Paulina, she'll lose control of them all.

"These are my sins since my last confession, Father."

"What are they?"

"At least five times this week I have become very angry with my daughter. This has been an ongoing problem and..."

"How old is your daughter?"

"Thirteen. She won't obey me. She won't do as I say. She deliberately defies me and I get angry, very angry. Sometimes I hit her. Sometimes I can't control myself. She makes me so angry."

"Those may not be sins, my child. Proceed."

The rest is the same, even another concluding "my child."

Now she is even more disturbed by his abruptness and leaves the church thinking, *Who is this man, this so-called priest, this boy posing as a man, as a priest?*

Her question is somewhat answered the next day on her way home after the 11:00 Sunday Mass with Juanita Salas, a plump, middle-aged woman who lives alone in the front part of the house and empathizes with Jesusita. Her children are gone, she works in a bakery, and there is never any mention of a man. "He came a few weeks after you left for the campo. I think it was the last Sunday of May. Before him we had no priest. We had that gringo priest, Father Gallagher, who speaks a little Spanish and who came sometimes on Sundays to say Mass whenever it was convenient for him. But I shouldn't speak badly of him. He was the only priest in the whole valley that speaks any Spanish, and he had to be everywhere.

"Anyway, right after you left, this Father Gallagher came and told us that the Holy Father Himself, the Pope in Rome, was going to send us our own Mexican priest because there are so many of us here now. What we know about this young priest, this Padre Montes, is what Father Gallagher told us. Padre Montes hardly talks to anyone. In fact, he talks to us only when he has to, and then he's often rude. And he's never said anything about himself to anyone.

"There are many things people say about him. How true they are, only he knows. They say that he comes from a very rich family in Mexico. How anyone knows that, I don't know. But it might be true because he's so white. There can't be a single drop of Indian blood in him. And everyone knows that the rich, powerful families that run Mexico are all white. If he was rich, he gave it all up because Father Gallagher said that he studied with an order that works with the poor and takes the vow of silence, which meant that he never talked to anyone there. Maybe that's why he never talks to any of us. He just doesn't—not even a little bit. He keeps to himself. He lives in that tiny, old house behind the church and doesn't have a housekeeper. Some of the women say that he's either afraid of women or hates women. I don't think that's true because he doesn't speak to men either, unless he has to. His manner has put a lot of people off. I know you've been going to Mass every day at 6:00, and I'll bet there's not many other people there."

"There's only me and him."

"See, I told you. He's got this funny thing about saying Mass every day except Sunday at 6:00. He won't say it any later during the week."

The third week begins, and still he doesn't speak to her. She's offended but has seen that he didn't mix with any of the other parishioners after the Sunday Masses either. Instead, he hurries off to his little house. They say that he keeps the church locked except when he's in it. It occurs to her that if she doesn't leave immediately after the 6:00 Masses, but instead waits, he will have to ask her to leave, he will have to speak to her. So on Tuesday she waits until 6:41 when she needs to leave to wake the children. There is no sign of him. She waits again on Wednesday and Thursday—still no sign of him and the church doors are unlocked when she leaves. But on Friday, his voice comes from behind her, "Who are you?"

He startles her. "What?"

"I said, who are you?" His face is tense, stern.

✠ 66

"What do you mean, who am I?"

"Just as I said. Who are you and what are you doing here?"

She's bewildered. She understands none of this. But his eyes are demanding an answer. "My name is Jesusita González," she whispers, "and I came here for Mass and Holy Communion."

"Where do you live?"

"I live with Juanita Salas just down the street."

"Why haven't I seen you until lately?"

He's not believing her. "I've been working in the campo for almost seven months."

"You're sure the bishop hasn't sent you?"

"The bishop? What bishop? I don't know any bishop."

"No one from the bishop's office has sent you here?"

"Why would anybody send me here? I came because I want to go to Mass and Holy Communion."

"Why?"

"Because I need to. It helps me in my everyday living."

"Why don't the others come? Why are you the only one that comes?"

"I don't know about the others, Padre. I just know about me. I come because God helps me get through the day."

"Don't you think it's a sign of disrespect for the others not to come?"

"Disrespect? No. They probably don't come because it's early and they have to go to work."

"This is winter. Many of them don't work. Do you work?"

"Yes, but at night."

"I have this Mass at 6:00 so that they can come to it before they go to work, if they're working. So that they can start their day with God.... What do they say about me?"

"Say about you? What do you mean, Padre?"

"The parishioners. They talk about me, don't they?"

"I don't know. I don't know many of them. The only one I really know is Juanita Salas. She doesn't talk about you. Only if I ask her."

"Why would you ask her about me?"

"Because I've been coming here for three weeks now and you've never spoken to me. Not once. So I have to wonder why? I have to wonder what's wrong with me."

He turns and leaves without another word, leaving her bewildered. But only for a few moments because she remembers that tomorrow is Saturday. Tomorrow there is no need to wake and ready the kids for school. Tomorrow she can wait for him as long as it takes. She can follow him out the door if need be. She will follow him to his house, sit on the steps if necessary. He will talk to her tomorrow.

He sits at his table in his miniature kitchen along the side of the window where he can watch without being seen. He watches for her to leave the church, but he doesn't see her. His mind takes him elsewhere. Has he made a fool of himself again? She doesn't look like anyone who's come from the Bishop's Office. And what she said—living with Juanita Salas, working in the campo for seven months—seems irrefutable. When the parishioners hear about this one, as they surely will, they will think he's gone mad. They most probably will report him to the Bishop, not for being an imposter, but rather for being an idiot. He's supposed to be their shepherd, their leader. Yet he runs from them every time he has to have contact with them. He has never been poor and they can sense that. He is not one of them and will never be one of them no matter how hard he tries, and they know that too. He is terribly self-conscious when he has to be with them, when he has to say more than hello to them. Four-and-a-half years of living in silence hasn't helped. True, he has learned how little really needs to be said—how much of most conversations is utter nonsense and how so much of what is said serves only to flatter oneself or to try to befriend someone or try to avoid being alone or, in his case, to try to put himself at ease. But being alone hasn't helped, it's hurt.

Jesusita leaves the church in full view, but he doesn't see her. He sees instead his father talking to the Bishop in San Francisco, just as he has seen him so many times when he has failed to deal with his parishioners. But more and more, he has had to admit that his father has nothing to do with these failures. For all he knows, his father might be dead. Today it is no excuse at all. This woman will surely tell Juanita Salas, Juanita will tell three or four others, and each of those will tell five or six others until all of the Mexicans in Fresno will know, making it all the harder the next time to calm himself, to stand still and talk to them, and to not think of how self-conscious he is.

The next morning she leaves her house earlier than usual and then wonders if she has left too early. But the church door is unlocked. He is already there. She kneels and prays, listening for him but not hearing not a sound. Minutes pass and she is beginning to think that he might not be there. Then at six exactly he appears from behind the altar in vestments and with chalice, ringing the little altar bell to announce to the congregation, which is her, that Mass is about to begin. During the Mass, each time he turns and faces the pews, his eyes are either closed or focused far above her. When he gives her Holy Communion, his eyes are closed in prayer. When the Mass ends, he is gone. But he will have to return, and she will wait however long it takes.

A full fifteen minutes pass before she hears him on the sacristy steps. He moves around the altar, genuflects, and starts down the aisle without having looked at her or acknowledged her. Yet when he reaches her pew, he stops and without looking at her says, "What do you want from me? Why do you want to belittle me again?" It is not what he intended to say because he had intended to say nothing. But what he said is irretrievable now, not unlike yesterday. He has made matters worse.

"How have I belittled you, Padre? I want only that you talk to me. I am a person—a person with many faults but a person nevertheless—a person you were sent here to guide and help."

"How can I help you when I can't help myself?" With that come the tears, loud, sobbing, convulsing tears.

She is stunned. She had seen Rogelio cry once—at his mother's funeral—but those had been silent, manly tears that dripped involuntarily from reddened eyes. Nothing like this. Nothing like the loud, coarse, convulsing sounds that fill the church. She is embarrassed for him, confused by him. She thinks it will stop; it has to stop, but it doesn't. It gets louder because now he is trying to say something through the sobbing. Finally she makes out a jumbled, "You don't understand! You don't understand!"

"What don't I understand, Padre?" Which turns the sobbing into a long, loud wailing moan. "Tell me, Padre, what don't I understand?"

Then through the sobbing comes a garbled, "They don't understand!" repeated again and again.

She reaches out to him and tugs at the arm of the black cassock, gently pulling him toward her. He steps into the pew and sits next to her. She puts her arm around him, and he rests his head on her shoulder. The sobbing quiets and the convulsing stops.

"What is it, Padre? What is it? What don't we understand?"

"You don't know how hard I've tried, how much I've tried." He is calm now, crying softly, talking quietly, his words occasionally broken by hiccupping, tears now and then falling on her hand. There is no way he can stop now. He tells her of his inability to talk to her and his parishioners. Never has he been around poor people like this. And now he lives with them and has been sent to lead them, to save their souls. But he can't talk to them. He has nothing in common with them. And the harder he tries to communicate with them, the worse it becomes. That's why the church is always empty. The more he thinks about it, and there are times when he can do nothing but think about it, the greater the fear becomes that he will never be able to talk to them. He has tried and failed so many times that now he feels paralyzed when he has to speak to one of them. He explains that his family's wealth will always prevent him from being one of them—or even like them. He tells her about his father and the Bishop too. As he speaks, she sees his hands. They are fine, delicate hands, much finer than Rogelio's. But Rogelio's hands were those of a man.

Once he stops talking, he keeps his head on her shoulder. Minutes pass. He regrets that this has happened. He's afraid to leave her because once he leaves her the consequences will begin. He has cried like a baby. His behavior has been disgusting. He has said too much. He has bared himself. He could not be more naked. As soon as they part, she will tell someone. She has to. It has all been so bizarre. He will be the talk of the town. The Bishop will be told. He will be stripped of his habit.

She has no idea how long they have been there, but her kids are surely wondering what has happened to her. If someone happens into the church and finds them like this, it will be embarrassing. "Padre, I have to go. My children are awake by now and I have to tend to them."

He lifts his head and looks at her through sorrowful, red eyes. "If you tell anyone about this, it will destroy me. The Bishop will send me back to Mexico. There they will chase me from the priesthood. Please promise me that you will say nothing about this to anyone."

"Why would I want to tell anyone about this, Padre?"

"Because it is so disgraceful."

She thinks he is about to cry again. "I promise, Padre, I will not say anything to anyone about this."

✝ VI

Juanita Salas' home is an old, wood-framed house that originally consisted of two bedrooms, a kitchen, a living room, and a bath. Years ago someone added two rooms behind the kitchen. It is these two rooms that Jesusita sublets. The two rooms are connected to the front house by a door that's been cut through the kitchen wall. Juanita shares the kitchen and the bath with Jesusita's family. One of the two rooms has two beds. The three girls sleep in that room. The other room has a table and chairs. It is used as an all-purpose room. The family eats their meals there, visitors sit there, and the children do their homework there. At night Jesusita and Sergio unroll mats and sleep on the floor of that room. The entrance to these rooms from the outside is through a door that opens onto the backyard.

As Jesusita returns from Mass that Saturday morning, she hears shouting and, what has to be Concepcion, howling coming from the back of the house. It angers her. The closer she gets to the back door, the angrier she becomes. She can't leave them alone for five minutes without them fighting and disturbing Juanita. She flings the back door open, and silence falls over the room—but only for a minute, because Concepcion begins howling again, now adding, "Mama! Mama!" to her tears. Standing next to Concepcion is Paulina. Yolanda is watching from the doorway of the other room, and Sergio is sitting at the table eating breakfast.

"What's going on here?"

"Concepcion took my..." Paulina starts.

Concepcion screams, "Paulina hit me! Paulina hit me!"

"Why did you hit her?"

"She's lying. I didn't hit her."

"Yes, she did! She hit me!"

"Why did you hit her? Stop looking at me like that!"

"Why do you always blame me for everything? You never believe me."

"I said stop looking at me like that!"

It is a look of hate. One they both know well. One that digs deep into the mother. One the daughter can see how deep it digs. She wants it to dig deep. She needs it to dig deep.

The slap to the face comes as it always does, openhanded but hard—hard enough to turn the girl's head to one side. The girl doesn't cry. She never cries, no matter how hard the blows are, because she knows that that too infuriates her mother. The girl straightens herself, and the look of hate is that much fiercer. She juts out her chin, daring her mother to hit her again. There is no hint of fear, remorse, or hurt. Just hate. The room is still. Concepcion has stopped howling. For several moments there is absolute silence. They are all afraid of Mama, always afraid of Mama. Except Paulina. And when Mama gets like this they are even more afraid. Except Paulina.

"I said take that look off your face!"

From the doorway of the other room Yolanda pleads, "Mama, she didn't do anything. I swear, Paulina didn't do..."

"Shut up! Unless you want some of it too!"

Sergio shudders. Yolanda is more of a man than he. As always he's strapped with fear and doesn't know what to do or how to do it.

This time the blow is closed-fisted to the girl's cheek, knocking her to the floor. From there, even before she starts to get up, she looks up at her mother with that hate, clear-eyed, not a hint of tears. There is a swatch of redness on her cheek. Slowly she rises, without a word or a sound, hating, fixated on hate. Again she juts out her chin. Her mother turns and starts for the belt.

"Paulina, stop looking at Mama like that!" shouts Sergio. It's the most he can do.

They all know where the belt is, and when Mama starts for the other room, they know what will follow. They look at Paulina, pleading with their eyes. *Stop, Paulina, stop!* They have seen it too many times. But the girl stands stiff and erect, watching her mother approach the closet.

Trembling, Jesusita turns from the closet, belt in hand. The others watch. It is the three-inch-wide, barber belt that they have all felt. It seems as though they have never seen Mama so angry or Paulina so obstinate. As Mama starts across the bedroom, Concepcion whines. Yolanda screams, "Paulina, stop it! Stop looking at her like that! Please, Paulina, please!" But the girl stands calm and resolute, hating, knowing that this will infuriate her mother all the more. Yolanda runs to her sister and grabs her, pressing her fingers into those bony shoulders. "Stop, Paulina! She'll really hurt you!" Paulina looks past her sister with a look that couldn't be more fixed, more hateful, at her oncoming mother.

"Move, Yolanda, unless you want some of it too."

Yolanda steps back.

"I said stop looking at me like that!" The woman is shaking, her eyes are wild with rage.

The girl stares defiantly at the woman. If anything, the hate has increased. The woman lunges forward. The belt lands hard, knocking the girl down. On the floor the girl shakes her head a few times before looking up. The look is still one of hate. There are no tears.

"I said don't look at me like that!" The woman's eyes seem about to burst. Her mouth is open, taut, breathing hard.

Prone, the girl's look has not changed.

"I said..." Yolanda throws herself on her sister and the next blow strikes both girls. Concepcion screams. The woman's body is one of convulsions. "Shut up!" she hisses. She looks down at the stricken girls and shouts, "Get her out of here, Yolanda, before I kill her!"

The woman has lost all control. The girl sees that and knows that she has gone as far as she can. For the first time she looks away from the woman. Slowly she rises and follows her sister past the frenzied, raging woman into the bedroom where Yolanda closes the door behind them.

She will remain in that room for days until her mother decides that she can come out again. All the while the door will remain closed and the shade will be kept down. She will eat her meals alone in that room and will not be allowed out even to use the bathroom. She will use a bedpan which Yolanda will empty whenever necessary. The siblings assume that Paulina's confinement is just part of her punishment. Jesusita has other reasons. She does not want the neighbors to see the signs of the beatings—worse, the teachers at the school. Last year, one of the teachers noticed welts on Paulina's legs and sent home a note asking to talk to Jesusita about them. Jesusita did not answer. When a second note came, she had Yolanda tell the teacher that her mother didn't read, write, or speak English. She heard nothing more about the welts. Later in the year, there were notes about Paulina's repeated absences, often for a week or more. On these occasions Yolanda was instructed to tell the teacher that Paulina was home sick in bed.

When the teacher had asked if Paulina had been seen by a doctor, Yolanda had answered the next day, "We don't got no money for doctors."

For the rest of the morning and into the afternoon, Jesusita is a shambles. She spends most of the morning outside in the backyard in the early November cold, away from her kids, alone with her thoughts. The hate in Paulina's eyes won't leave her. Where has it come from? How is it possible that her own flesh and blood, the child she carried for nine months, the child she brought painfully but so willingly into this world and then nurtured, raised, and loved, can hate her so much? This has to be God's way of testing her. But testing her for what? Hasn't she been tested enough? Her whole life since Rogelio died has been one big test. The other kids don't hate her. She has raised them all the same—has given no preference for one over the other. Yet one hates her, hates her with a venom that could kill some mothers. Yes, she is strict. Yes, she is a disciplinarian. They would not have survived if she hadn't been. Hate! Is this what she gets in return for all the sacrifice, the years of working herself to the bone day and night? *Oh God, don't let her hate me! Help me through this!* That look of hate has so consumed her that not once does she think of any resulting bruising or welts.

Now it is he who comes early, half an hour before the confessions are set to begin. He needs to talk to her—contain the damage if he can. The likelihood is that she has already said something to someone. Maybe he can defuse that. One or two persons may not be insurmountable, but if it goes beyond today, beyond this morning and this early afternoon, it will probably be too late. As he sits in the confessional, he wonders if he shouldn't be more visible, be out there somewhere in the body of the church. She might come early and not see him and think he's not there and leave until 2:00—or not return at all. But others might come and wonder what he is doing sitting in a pew or standing at the altar without his vestments on. Better to remain in the confessional and listen for sounds in the vestibule and then step out of the confessional and let her see him. But he hears nothing. Minutes pass without a sound. His glances at his watch fail to produce any sounds either. Maybe she's not coming. Not after this morning.

How pathetic he was. He has to change. He has to communicate with his parishioners. He can't continue to leave them unattended. In fairness to them, if he can't change, he should leave, he should go back to Mexico where his father will surely have him defrocked. She may be able to help him, if only she hasn't revealed too much of what happened this morning. On second thought, after this morning, she may have lost all respect for him and won't come—will find it too difficult to bare her soul to him. But she has nothing to bare. She has had no sins to speak of. All the more reason for her not to come. If only he can speak to her this afternoon, convince her that he's committed to change, has to change, will change, and therefore there's no need to tell anyone about this morning.

Two o'clock and she hasn't come. Will she come? At 2:04 he thinks not. At 2:07 he's convinced that she won't, yet clings to the hope that she will. At 2:09 he sees no reason why he can't go to Juanita Salas' house and speak to her there. But he will have to wait until 4:00. Confessions are from 2:00 to 4:00. He can't wait until 4:00. It might be too late by then. If he goes now... He hears sounds in the vestibule. He peeks out. It's her. He sighs a great sigh of relief. He peeks again. Good, there is still no one other than them in the church. They can talk before she confesses. But how best to begin? With his apology or with his commitment? She enters the confessional and kneels. Just as he is about to slide the slat open, he hears more sounds in the vestibule. Two women are standing at the entrance to the church. Now he sighs a sigh of frustration. For weeks no one but she has confessed, and now this. He slides the slat open.

"Bless me, Padre, it has been a week since..."

"Shhh. Lower, please." They will hear. He listens.

"Bless me, Padre, it..."

"Shhh!" He listens but he hears nothing. He peeks. No one. He pushes the curtain back and leans his head out. No one. They must have gone. Now they can talk. "Señora, about this morning..."

"Father, I have no sins, but I do want to talk about this morning, if you'll let me."

"Please do."

"Like I said, I have no sins. If anything, I have been sinned against. One of my children, a child mind you, hates me and shows me in every way she can that she hates me. And this is a girl of thirteen. Do you know what it feels like to be hated by your own flesh and blood? Do you have any idea how hard I've..." Now it is she who is crying.

This is not what he had in mind. He looks out again. No one.

She describes the looks, the hate, and how undeserving she is. But for her, the girl would be an orphan out in the street. She's at her wits' end. She doesn't know how to make the girl stop hating her. When she calms down and is crying quietly, he asks, "Who have you told?"

"I have told no one but you, Padre. Do you think I want people knowing that my own daughter hates me? That I must be such an evil person that my own daughter hates me? What have I done to deserve this? Tell me, Padre, I ask you, what as a mother have I done to deserve this?"

She goes on for several minutes. She has gotten loud. Twice he looks out. Still no one.

When she quiets down, he's more specific. "Have you told anyone about this morning?"

"Do you really think, Padre, that I could tell anyone about what she did to me this morning? You must think I'm proud of that. Put yourself in my shoes. Would you tell anyone that your daughter hates you, hates you the way my daughter hates me?" Now she is crying loudly.

It is hopeless, he thinks. In her condition he will never be able to talk to her. He begins thinking of ways to get her out of the confessional. Someone is bound to come in and hear and see her and wonder what he's done to her. Then it occurs to him that it may not be hopeless after all. Again he waits until she quiets down. Then he asks, "When did all of this start?"

"This morning."

"When this morning?"

"After I left you."

"And it went on all morning?"

"Yes, I haven't been able to do or think about anything else."

"It went on even this afternoon?"

"Yes, Padre. I was such a mess that I almost didn't come to confession. I only came because I needed to talk to someone. I needed to talk to you."

It is not hopeless. "And you did nothing to provoke this girl?"

"Oh no, Padre. Like I said, I just came home from church. They were fighting and she started in with her hateful looks."

"How long did it last?'

"The hate went on all morning and into the afternoon." There is no mention of the beating. It is not relevant. The hate was there. It's always there. It preceded the beating.

We will get there yet, he thinks. "There is absolutely no reason at all for anyone, especially your daughter, to hate someone as close to God as you are. I am your confessor. I know the condition of your soul. I see you at Mass and Communion every morning. No one in this town is closer to God than you."

"Then why is He permitting this?"

"Sometimes God works in strange ways, ways that to our feeble minds are incomprehensible. This much I know: He is testing you. Just as God tested Abraham with his son, God is testing you with your daughter. You must bear up under this hardship. It too will pass."

"And until it passes, how do I deal with her? Help me, Padre!"

Be patient, he thinks, *the more patient and considerate you are with her, the more she will have to be with you.* "Well, you must try to avoid situations that give rise to her bouts of hatred."

"How do I do that, Padre? There are five of us, myself and four children, living in two rooms. I can't turn around without seeing her."

"Surely you must have some idea of what leads up to these bouts of hatred?"

"No, Padre, not really. Like I said, when I got home this morning the children were quarreling. I asked what happened and she turned on me. That was it. I did absolutely nothing to provoke her. How can I avoid something like that? How could I have expected that?"

He doesn't answer. She waits. He shifts in his seat. "It is a difficult situation."

"So what do I do, Padre? Let her disrespect me whenever she feels like it? My other children are watching. It does not set a good example for them. This morning I sent her to the other room. She wouldn't go. It took her older sister to coax her. How do I deal with her until this passes? Do I let her do as she pleases, whenever she pleases? Hate me in front of the others whenever she chooses? Lose the respect of my other children? Give up the discipline that they need? Let her run the household?"

"No, you can't do that. You can't let that happen. She can't be allowed to get away with that type of behavior."

"So what do I do?"

"In those situations she must be punished."

"How?"

"Spare the rod and spoil the child."

"I have no other remedy, do I?"

"It's your duty as a parent."

There is nothing more to say. She feels relieved. He welcomes her silence. He waits. It continues. Now he can talk about the morning openly, frankly. He parts the curtain. There is still no one there.

"Earlier, you told me that you were without sin?"

"Yes, Padre."

"So what we have been talking about has not been a confession?"

"No, Padre."

"Of course if you are without sin, there is no need to confess."

"If you say so, Padre."

"Do you want to confess now?"

"No, Padre."

"Fine. And you needn't worry that I would say anything to anyone about what you told me here this afternoon. Because I won't. Had you told me those things as part of a confession, then of course my lips would be sealed and I could never repeat any of that to anyone. But not to worry. I won't say a word to anyone about the terrible situation you have in your home. Any more than I hope that what I said and did this morning after Mass, you will not repeat to anyone."

"Why would I tell anyone about that?"

"Have you?"

"Oh, no, Padre."

"Will you?"

"No, of course not. Never."

"I'm so ashamed of what happened in church this morning. But it's brought me to my senses. I have to change my ways or I can't stay here. I want to stay here, but not like I have been... Will you help me?"

"Yes, Padre."

THE 11:00 Mass on Sunday is the most-attended Mass of the day. The following morning is no exception. It is packed to overflowing. All the seats are taken, and the latecomers are standing three and four deep in the vestibule. When Padre Montes turns at the altar to give his congregation the first blessing, he forces himself to look down at them with his eyes open instead of looking up at the ceiling with his eyes closed as has been his custom. As he turns back to the altar he wonders if anyone has noticed. There are two more blessings, each he makes looking at his congregation rather than at the ceiling, each progressively easier. On the last blessing he makes eye contact with a few but can't tell what effect, if any, it has had. His sermon deals with man's imperfect nature and the Christian need to try to understand and forgive our neighbors' failings. Again he makes eye contact but is baffled by the seeming lack of response.

When the Mass ends, the church empties rapidly. Many will remain outside socializing in the church's entryway for five or ten minutes. Today when Padre Montes leaves the altar, he doesn't disappear behind it. Instead, he stops at a side table and deposits the chalice and serving plate there, taking his time, waiting as the church empties, until all those still in it have their backs turned to him. Then he goes to and through the altar railing and meets Jesusita who is waiting for him beside a front pew. Together they start down the center aisle toward the church doors. She thinks that he is striking in his green and gold vestments and cannot understand why it is so difficult for him to talk to his parishioners. Why is he so afraid? As they move toward the doors he mumbles about the heat when in fact this has been the coldest fall morning yet. He mumbles about installing a cooling system.

She sees the tenseness in his face and says, "Padre, they are just people—poor, working people."

The words resonate and become, "Papa, they are just people. They are people just like you and me." Shame washes over him. Who is he? What has he become? How could he have drifted so far from these people?

They are at the doors, two steps past the doors when she stops, thinking: *They can all see us from here, but no one can hear us from here.* A hush comes over the crowd. The conversations had been lively and friendly, and now there is a ripple of silence as people point, gesture, poke at each other, and whisper about the two standing just outside the church doors.

"Talk to me, Padre," she says in just above a whisper. "Don't think about them. Don't worry about them. Just look at me and talk to me. Say anything you want. It doesn't matter. They can't hear you. They won't hear you."

When he continues looking at her with a blank stare, she says, "At least shake your head or nod as if you're listening to me and agreeing or disagreeing with me. You've got to do or say something, Padre. Please. Remember how much you told me you had to change? This is where the change begins."

He nods, stiffly at first but then more naturally. "Good. Now talk to me again, like you were in church, about that cooling system, about anything." He repeats the need for a cooling system and how much he thinks it will cost. He does so haltingly at first, stumbling at times but with every few sentences more and more at ease. She asks him about his family, and he answers without hesitation about his mother and sisters. She turns and looks out at those who are watching, and without exception, every group that she looks at turns away as if they hadn't been staring, as if they hadn't been whispering, and they begin makeshift conversations.

He is comfortably talking about the Quiroga Seminary when a small, dark, Indian woman wearing her best apron approaches him and says, "Padre, it's so good to see you out here with us. We thought you didn't like us, that we weren't good enough for you."

For a few moments all he can do is blink. Then he swallows hard, bends, and reaches down and hugs the woman and in a voice that all can hear says, "Oh, no! That's not true! That's not true!"

✝ VII

"WHAT HAVE you done?" Juanita asks. "Everybody's talking about you!"

It is still Sunday, just after 1:30. The two women are standing in the doorway that leads from the kitchen into the two rooms that Jesusita is renting.

"What do you mean, what have I done?"

"I've had three women here since the 11:00 Mass asking about you."

"Asking about me?"

"You were talking to Padre Montes after Mass?"

"So?"

"That's a big thing here. He's talked to no one since he came. A lot of women have tried. Even some men. But he has had nothing to do with anyone. Until now, until you. I wasn't at that Mass, so I didn't see any of it. Were you talking to him?"

"Yes."

"What were you talking about?"

"Oh, I don't know. About the church. About his family. About how he likes it here."

"And he was talking to you about these things?"

"Yes."

"And you came out of the church with him?"

"Yes."

"And you were standing with him on top of the steps where everybody could see you?"

She's annoyed. Why should she have to recount coming out of the church with Padre to anyone? "Yes."

"How did you start talking to him?"

"I've been talking to him a little after Mass in the mornings and after confession on Saturday." She's upset. Since when does she have to be explaining herself to anyone? "What's all the fuss about?"

"Well, you're new here. I mean new to the church. People here really don't know you. They know that you live in my house, and they know that you work nights cleaning offices. Some have seen you around the campo chino. But they say that you never talk to them. Hello and goodbye, maybe. But that's it. That's all you ever say to anyone. And you never went to church last year when you were here, when the gringo priest used to come. And now all of a sudden you walk out of the church with Padre like you're old friends."

"Look, I talk to him a little in church during the week when nobody else is there. I don't see anybody else going to the 6:00 Mass or confessing on Saturdays. Maybe if they did, they'd be talking to him too."

"Well, they want to know about you. Whether you're married? Where's your...?"

"Wait! Wait!" She can feel herself getting angry. She turns, and, just as she expected, all her kids, except Paulina, are in the room behind her, motionless and listening. She closes the door and steps into the kitchen. "Go on."

"They asked where your husband was and if all those kids were yours by the same man? They wanted to know where you came from. How you got to Fresno. Why did you choose it? They wanted to know why you didn't go to church last year when the gringo priest used to come. And why all of a sudden you're this big saint, always in church, never leaving Padre alone?" *Who are these women stirring up this filth? Let them come to me with all their ugliness.*

"I'll be honest with you, Jesusita, they were hinting around at it and one finally came out and said it, 'Is she having an affair with the Padre? Is she his whore? Is that why he doesn't have a housekeeper, so that she can sneak in and out of his house whenever she wants to?' That same woman wanted to know if I thought one of your kids was Padre's. If Padre ever came over to visit you and one of the kids? One of them said that you were just like him, not talking to anybody, not wanting anybody to get too close to you—probably so that no one would find out what was really going on with you and the Padre?"

Now Jesusita is clearly angry. But instead of answering, she turns and pushes open the door to the two rooms, hitting Concepcion in the forehead in the process. The child whimpers, then cries. Just as she had expected, her kids were listening behind the closed door. "I want all of you to go to the bedroom now and close that door!" They turn immediately; they know the anger in her voice. "And Yolanda, get this crybaby out of here, now!" She watches as they go into the bedroom. Once that door is closed, she closes the kitchen door and turns again to Juanita. "Who are these women?"

"They are the women who, when the gringo priest used to come, were in charge of the church. They used to clean and decorate the church, put up flowers on Saturdays for Sunday Mass, get the church ready for holy days. All those things."

"Who put them in charge?"

"They put themselves in charge."

"Who are they?"

"One is the Señora Álvarez. Another is the Señora López and the third one is the Señora Retana. I'm sure you've probably seen them at Sunday Mass. They've all seen you there and at the mercado and around this side of town. They say that you barely say hello and act like you think you're superior or something."

"What do they look like?"

"The Señora Álvarez is short and stocky, not fat, just stocky. She's the leader. She wears skirts down to her shoes. They all do.

Like if they're still in Mexico. Her blouses are loose and dark, and sometimes she has a big, brown, wood rosary hanging from her waist. The Señora López is really dark. It's not for nothing that they call her 'la negra.' If she had kinky hair, you would think that she was a 'negra.' And she's real skinny. The Señora Retana is actually very pretty. You wonder what she's doing with the other two. She's light-complected and has very fine, long, brown hair. She always wears black—like a nun or something. Maybe just trying to fit in with the other two. Do you know who I'm talking about?"

"No. But why are they saying these awful things about Padre Montes and me?"

"Probably because when Padre Montes first came, he kicked them out of the church. What I mean is that he said that he didn't want them doing anything anymore in the church. They say that he said that God didn't need no flowers or fancy fixtures—what God needed was clean, healthy souls. They say he said that he didn't want the church looking like a house of disrepute. I don't believe he said that, but that's what they say. Now he has a crippled old man who cleans the church and the churchyard."

"Did you tell them that it wasn't true?"

"What wasn't true?"

"What they're saying about me and Padre Montes."

"No...no, I didn't."

"Why not? You see me every day. You know what my life is like. You know none of that's true. Why didn't you say something?"

"I wasn't in church this morning. I didn't see what happened."

"I'm not talking about this morning. I'm talking about what they said about me and Padre Montes. You know that's not true. Why didn't you say something?"

"I...I don't know. They were so excited, so convinced of what they were saying.... I guess I didn't want to start arguing with them in my own house."

Jesusita turns and leaves, slamming the door behind her. From the bedroom comes Concepcion's voice, "Mama, can we come out now?"

"No!" she shouts. "You stay in there until I tell you to come out! And I don't want to hear a peep out of any of you!"

She sits at the table rubbing her face in her open hands. Yesterday it was Paulina, and today it's this. It's always something. Juanita's words won't go away. "What have you done? Everybody's talking about you." She wants to cry but won't. "Everybody knows...," flits in and out of her mind. *What do they know? What do these simple, silly peons know about anything? They're incapable of knowing anything.* She would have had nothing to do with them in Mexico. Rogelio might have let some of them clean out the pig pens. That was the most they would have had to do with them in Mexico. She thinks of returning to Mexico. But to what and where? They sold or gave away everything when they came to the United States. At least she can provide food and shelter for herself and her children here. "Everybody is talking...."

She sits with her thoughts until Juanita opens the kitchen door, without knocking, and says in a hushed voice, "They're coming."

"Who's coming?"

"Those three women."

"What three women?"

"The three women that came earlier. The three I told you about. They're back. This time they came to see you."

"Me?"

"Yes, you. They thought you lived in front with me. I told them you lived back here. I..." There's a knock at the back door. "That's them." Juanita closes the kitchen door and is gone.

Jesusita goes to the curtained window and looks out. It is the three that Juanita has described. The short, stocky one knocks again. There's a stronger fit of anger in Jesusita now. She takes a broom and goes to the door. She opens it and stares. They are standing behind a screen door.

"Yes?"

"Señora González. We're from the church and..."

"What do you want?" Firm, hostile.

"We want to talk to you."

"I don't want to talk to you."

"Oh, I'm sorry. I can see that you're cleaning. Can we come back at another time?"

"I'm not cleaning. But if you don't get away from my door, if you don't get away from me, I'll clean all three of you with this broom."

"What?"

"You heard me. Now get!"

"This is no way to..."

"I know what you've been saying about me. Now get!" And with that she kicks the screen door open and takes a swing at the stocky one, narrowly missing her. She steps outside and raises the broom again, and the three run. She chases them, swinging the broom, shouting, "Get out of my house! Get out of my life, you no good witches!"

WHEN PADRE Montes comes out from behind the altar the next morning. He says, "Señora González, I would like to speak with you for a few moments after Mass."

She nods. Her mind is a jumble. She has not slept well. She doesn't want to speak to him. She is too embarrassed to speak to him, to repeat the vile, sacrilegious image of him, God's priest, having an affair with her. She knows that she can't possibly face him and repeat those words. The Mass passes in one big blur. It is only talk, she tells herself. But "everyone is talking." The truth will win out. But lies sometimes win too. How can people listen to those sinful words? But they are listening. She is leaving when she hears him behind her. "Señora, I know you have to get the children ready for school, but I just want to express my thanks."

She turns and he is beaming. "The woman who came up to us yesterday morning on the church steps, the woman I hugged, and I have only you to thank for that. You made that possible. That same woman, Amelia Rocha, came to the rectory yesterday afternoon with her husband and her brothers and sisters and their children. There were sixteen of them. They brought food and drink with them, and we ate and laughed and talked until it got dark.

It was wonderful. Two other families have invited me for dinner this week. It seems like everything has changed, turned around, and I have only you to thank.... What's the matter, señora, what's troubling you?"

"I'm not feeling well, and I have to get the kids off to school. That's all. So if you'll excuse me, Padre. I should be going."

"Yes, of course. Thank you so much for yesterday."

"You're welcome, Padre."

Now MORE than ever, especially after being chased by a broom, Dolores Álvarez is bound and determined to reveal the real relationship between *that woman* and Padre Montes. She asks Lupita López and María Elena Retana to meet with her in her home the next night. And after speaking with her uncle, Felipe Domínguez, she asks him to come as well. The two women arrive early. "The more I learn about it, the more I think about it, the more I'm convinced that we have something very big here, something that should be reported to the Bishop in San Francisco. That's why I've asked you to come here tonight, even though we've already spent so much of the day together. I've asked for my uncle to come too because I think he can be very helpful." Dolores Álvarez pauses, brings an index finger over her closed lips, and looks as if she is in thought, nodding to herself, underscoring the seriousness of the matter. There is no doubting her fervor. "We have a man and a woman living in sin right before our very eyes. Of course, there are men and women everywhere who are not married and yet fornicate, choosing to live in sin. But our situation is very different. This man is our parish priest. This woman suddenly and mysteriously appears in our church. She has four children, but no man. The fact that none of these children resemble each other tells us that there have been, more than likely, several men in her background. You might think that this practice between a priest and a woman is not uncommon in Mexico—that there are priests there that have fathered children, some even with different women. But this is not Mexico, this is America, and that is not the accepted practice here. Think for a minute about what we're dealing with here. This priest fornicates with his whore on any given night. Early the next morning, while he is still in the state of mortal sin—because where else and in front of what priest could he have possibly confessed himself before Mass the next morning? Anyway, the next morning he blesses the host and wine, changing them, or so he wants us to believe, into the Body and Blood of Jesus Christ, and then gives the host to us as that. Do you for one moment think that this sacrilegious man can, given the state of sin he's in, change that wine and host into the Son of God? I don't." She pauses for a moment and looks first at Lupita until she softly shakes her head, and then at María Elena until her eyes are full in agreement. "One more thing: How can this same man forgive our sins in the confessional when he himself is steeped in sin?

"One more thing: Innocent people don't attack well-meaning people, who come to ask questions about ugly rumors. We don't even know the woman and she chases us away with a broom. Do either of you think that an innocent person would have reacted the way she did this afternoon?"

The other two women exchange a glance—who to answer first? Lupita López doesn't hesitate. "I don't like the woman. I never have liked her. I don't trust her and I wouldn't put anything past her. I have seen her a few times at the mercado, and she will not speak to me. I said hello to her the first two times, and she just looked at me as if I were trash, as if I was one of those negra women from Panama or Central America, even though she could tell from my Spanish that I wasn't one of them, that I had to be a Mexican. I don't talk to her anymore when I see her. But she still gives me that look, as if she's so much better than me. It doesn't surprise me that she's been the only woman in the church who's been able to get near Padre Montes. She's the kind of woman who would do anything to get next to him."

Then María Elena says, "I've been wondering how any woman would want to risk the special punishment God Almighty must have reserved for the woman who tempts one of his consecrated priests. It's been hard for me to believe that. But to see them on the church steps this morning, so happy together, and she a stranger in this town, after Padre Montes has turned his back on all the rest of us—well, that changed my mind. And then after what she did to us this afternoon, that pretty much convinced me. No, there has to be something going on here between them."

"When you hear what my uncle has to say, I guarantee you, you will have no doubt at all."

WHEN FELIPE Domínguez arrives, he gives each of the women a light kiss on the cheek, mumbles a few nice things to them, and then he is escorted by his niece to an armchair in the living room where the women take seats around him. It is Dolores Álvarez who questions him.

He is a sixty-six-year-old cripple who somehow made his way into the United States during the 1910 Mexican Revolution. He was born with his right leg several inches shorter than his left leg. He has always worn a shoe that has a sole and a heel six and a half inches thicker than the other. Despite the shoe, he limps heavily. He lives in a shed in the backyard of a house that abuts the church property. When the three women were in charge of the church, he had helped them by taking care of the churchyard.

"Tell the ladies, tío, what you just told me a few hours ago."

The old man is not accustomed to being the center of attention. He begins slowly, softly, self-consciously. "A few days after the Padre told Dolores that he didn't need you taking care of the church anymore, I went to see him at his house. I knocked on his door for a long time, but he didn't answer. I knew he was there because I had seen him go in there from my house. I kept knocking until I knew that he did not want to answer. I started to leave, and he opened the door. He looked mad—like maybe I got him out of bed or something. But he didn't say anything, nothing. Didn't ask what I wanted or who I was. Nothing. Just stared. That made me real nervous, and I started mumbling and stumbling about did he need anybody to clean the church and take care of the yard. And him just shaking his head no. I started walking away, and he let me go almost out of his yard and then he called me back. I guess he saw me limping and saw my leg and felt sorry for me."

"That man wouldn't feel sorry for a leper. Did he talk to you then, tío?"

"Not really. He just asked if I cleaned and took care of yards before, and I told him yes. And then he asked me how much I charged, and I told him whatever he wanted to give me was fine because it was for the House of God and I didn't want to take advantage. He said he would pay me three dollars a week for cleaning the church on Saturdays and taking care of the yard two times a week. He said that the money would be in an envelope that he would leave it in one of the collection baskets at the back of the church on Saturdays. I took that to mean that he didn't want me bothering him at his house anymore."

"Can you see his house from your house?"

"Oh, yes."

"And can you see the church too?"

"Yes.

"All of the church, the front and the back?"

"Yes, all of it."

"Have you ever gone to the 6:00 Mass since Padre Montes came?"

"Yes, right after he hired me, I went for about a week. I guess I wanted to show him what kind of a person I am. I would have gone longer except he never spoke to me. He walked right by me in church without even saying hello. It was like I was bothering him, intruding on him. The only thing he ever said was after the first Mass. He walked past me and two women, and when he got to the doors he said, "Time to leave. I'm locking up.""

"Did those women stop going too?"

"Yes, they did. Well, see, I'm an early riser and from where I sit and drink my morning coffee, I can see the comings and goings of people to the church. After I stopped going, it wasn't too long after that that nobody went to the 6:00 Mass except the Padre."

"Is anybody going to the 6:00 Mass now?"

"Oh yeah. A few weeks ago that new woman started going. I don't know her, but I've heard her called Jesusita."

"Tell us about that."

"It must have been about three weeks ago because I've seen her at three confessions. Anyway, one morning, I'm sitting there having my coffee and I see this woman going up the steps into the church. I can't tell who it is because it's still dark. But from the streetlight I can tell that it's a woman. I wonder to myself how long she'll last because nobody's lasted more than a few weeks. She's there every day that first week, and on Saturday afternoon she goes to confession. I'm working in the yard then, and I see her go in and come out. She's not in there very long, and I can plainly see that she's the one who's been going to the 6:00 Mass."

"Did she come back the next week?"

"Oh, yes. She came every day last week and every day this week, and my guess is that she'll come every day next week too."

"Why do you say that?"

"Because there's something going on between those two."

"What do you mean?"

"The second week she came every day the same as usual. But toward the end of the week the Padre started going over to the church earlier and earlier. I didn't think much about it at first, but it kept getting earlier. She came a little earlier too, but not like him, and I didn't connect the two. Not then. That Saturday she went to confession, in and out."

"And this week?"

"That's when all the strange things happened. He kept going over there earlier and earlier until finally he was there by 5:30. What he was doing in the church by himself, I don't know. She was coming earlier too."

"Did you ever think that maybe he wasn't even saying Mass on those mornings?"

"No, I never thought that. I never went over to the church to see if he was saying Mass, but I think he was."

"Tell the ladies what happened this week."

"Until Friday, everything was pretty much the same. He got there at 5:30 and she got there maybe ten minutes later. What they were doing before Mass started, I wondered a little bit about, but I didn't know. Then at 6:39 on Friday morning, because I did look at my clock, I guess after Mass was over, I saw him climb out of the sacristy window and..."

"Wait a minute. Wait a minute. Tell us what you mean by sacristy and why a window and not a door."

"OK. The sacristy is where the priest gets dressed before he says the Mass. It has all the fancy stuff he wears for the Mass. And the gold chalice is down there too. The sacristy in our church is in the basement. You used to be able to use a side door down there and go up some steps to the outside. But the lock on that door is broken. It's been broken since before Padre Montes came. You can't open that door, so you can't go outside through that door. You have to go upstairs through the altar and go out of the church that way. Anyway, on Friday after Mass he climbed out of a window down there, then went along the side of the church to the front steps and into the church that way. Why he did that, I'll never know. And what they did once he was in there, I'll never know either, except that they were in the church for quite a long while. They came out together, and she waited while he locked the church. Then they had what seemed like some serious words up there before she went on her way. He got real close to her, and I think he might have even kissed her."

"Tell them about what happened yesterday afternoon, tío."

"I was getting to that. I was working in the yard when he went over to the church for confessions. Confessions are supposed to be from 2:00 to 4:00, but it was 1:30 when he went over to the church. Now I was really suspicious. So twice I snuck up there to see. The first time I couldn't see anything and thought he must have been down in the sacristy. The second time I heard him cough in that confession box. There was nobody else in the church either time.

"But just then, she came. It was a little past two. When she went by me, I could see that she was upset, probably because she thought she had missed him. I watched her go up the stairs, and when she was in the church, she turned right which meant that she was going to the confession box. They were in that box a long time, more than half an hour. Twice I snuck up there again. They were in that box all right. But I couldn't tell if they were on separate sides or on his side real close together. I say that because there were a lot of strange sounds coming from that box. She was moaning and making funny noises, but I couldn't tell if they were sounds of pleasure or sounds of pain. It had to be pleasure because she could have easily walked out of there if it was pain. It was one of the most disgusting..."

"Stop! Stop, Mr. Domínguez!" María Elena pleads. "I know what you're telling us is true. You have no reason to be lying to us. But my church, my religion means too much to me, and I'd rather not have to judge these pathetic creatures. They will have to answer to God. I'd rather not dwell on these horrible acts. Let God deal with them."

"Well," Dolores says, "just keep in mind what we saw this morning on the church steps. The two of them in a world of their own, happy, not sad. And she wasn't the least bit afraid of him. And when have you ever seen him like that with anyone other than her? What does that say about what my tío has just told us?"

WHEN THE others have gone, Dolores Álvarez says to her tío, "It pains me to say this, but I do believe that he's sleeping with her, and I feel obligated to prove it for the good of our church and all the church members. And there's only one person that can help me prove it. That's you, tío."

"I've told you all I know. There's nothing more I can tell you."

"No, but you can do more."

"Like what?"

"Like watch who comes and goes from his house at night."

"Nobody comes and goes there at night."

"How do you know? Have you ever watched to see who comes and goes from his house at night?"

"No. I'm an early riser. But I go to bed early too. I'm in bed by 8:30 every night."

"What would it take for you to change those hours, just for a week or two?"

"What do you mean?"

"I mean that I would like for you to stay up until eleven with your lights out to see who comes and goes."

"I can't do that."

"Why can't you? Sleep as late as you want the next day, but stay up watching at least for a week or two, if you see what I think you're going to see. It is so important to all of us Catholics here that I will make it worth your while."

"What do you mean?"

"How much does the Padre pay you?"

"Three dollars a week."

"I will double that. Six dollars a week for two weeks no matter what you find or don't find."

IT TAKES two days, but by Wednesday Felipe Domínguez's tale is in full swing in the Santa Teresa parish. The gardener has *heard* them having sex in the confessional. By Thursday it is the gardener has *seen* them having sex in the confessional. Fortunately for Padre Montes, because of the Sunday evening dinner he had with the Rocha family, he is invited to dinner at a family's home every night of that week. The reactions to his visits through Wednesday night are overwhelmingly positive. The vast majority of people find him to be a warm, gracious guest—shy at first, but once he gets past those first few minutes, joyous and yet humble and sincere. But on Thursday and Friday nights, some of the receptions are stiff and even cold. Unbeknownst to him, the ugly story has begun reaching his hosts. But he is confident and at ease now, and the genuine affection he has for the host families and their friends shines through. He leaves converts and at worst doubters. Then on Saturday just before noon, the teenage son of the woman who is to be hosting dinner for him that night comes to his house and says that his mother is very ill and the dinner has to be cancelled.

DOLORES AND her uncle have agreed that the surveillance will begin on Monday night. Early Tuesday morning, she is at his house.

"Did you see anything?"

"No. Nothing." But he isn't looking at her.

"You saw no one come to the house last night?"

"No." Still there is no eye contact.

"You're sure?"

"Yes."

"Look at me, tío.... Did you stay up until eleven like we said?"

Now he looks at her, but it is a squeamish look. "I don't think so."

"You don't think so? What does that mean?"

"It means that I fell asleep in the dark looking out the window, and I don't know when that was."

She leaves disappointed, but she is back early Wednesday morning. "What time did you go to sleep *last* night, tío?"

It is an embarrassed look that he gives her. "I don't know, but it was late. A lot later than Monday night."

"Did you see anyone come or go?"

"No."

"Tío, this is very important. Our souls, our eternal happiness depend on it. Tonight set your alarm clock. Set it for 9:00 and then for 9:30 and then for 10:00 and 10:30. That way, you'll stay awake. Can you do that?"

"Yes."

"Tío, I had said that I'd give you six dollars a week for two weeks. But this is so important, that I'm going to raise it to eight dollars a week for two weeks."

"Eight dollars!"

"Yes."

On Thursday morning she begins by handing him four crisp, new one-dollar bills. "This is half of what I'm going to give you this week. I'm giving it to you now so that you'll know that I mean business."

He takes the bills, shakes his head, fingers them, and admires them.

"Did you see anyone come and go last night?"

"I saw someone come."

"About what time?"

"It was after 10:30."

"Did you see who it was?"

"No, it was too dark."

"Did you see her leave?"

"No, it was after eleven."

"You're not looking at me."

"Yes, I am."

"And you're sure you saw someone come?"

"Yes."

His look is steady. She wants to believe him but she's not sure. "Look, tío, if you can tell me that you saw her come and go at least one time, even as soon as tomorrow, I'll give you the twelve dollars then, and you won't need to watch anymore. All I need is one time."

On Friday morning when she asks, he says, "Do you have the twelve dollars with you?"

"Yes, I do."

"Can I see them?"

"See."

"Yes, I saw her come and I saw her go."

"You're sure?"

"Yes."

"Positive?"

"Yes."

"What time did you see her come?"

"It was close to eleven."

"How do you know that?"

"I looked at my clock."

"Like you're looking at me?" It's a much better look.

"Yes."

"How did you know it was her?"

"The wind was blowing, and the streetlight was swinging enough so that I could see her. And I saw her."

"When did she leave?"

"Real late."

"And you were still awake?"

"No, I had fallen asleep, but she tripped on the steps when she came out and that woke me up."

"Are you sure?"

"Do you have the money?"

"Yes."

"Yes, I'm sure."

"Would you be willing to tell other people this, just like you're telling me, looking at them just like you're looking at me?"

"Yes.... And where's the money."

JESUSITA THINKS the lies have died, have come to nothing. Each morning Padre tells her about another family he has dined with and how well it went. But on Saturday morning Juanita convinces her that the lies are still very much alive and circulating. That afternoon she enters the confessional at exactly 2:00. He knows it is her, and he's glad that she has come. But he is not prepared for what she has to say.

"I have not come to confess myself, Padre. I have come to warn you."

"Warn me?"

"Yes, warn you. They are spreading ugly lies about us and a lot of people are believing them. They plan to attack you tomorrow morning at the 11:00 Mass."

"What lies? What are you talking about?"

"They're saying that last Saturday afternoon we had sex in the confessional. They're saying that every night, late at night, I'm going to the rectory and sleeping with you."

He is stunned. "You're joking?"

"It's not a joke, Padre. People are believing it. They're taking it very seriously. Some of them are planning to do something to you at tomorrow morning's Mass."

"Who's saying these things?"

"Dolores Álvarez and her friends. The ones you wouldn't let clean the church anymore."

"Have they told you this?"

"No."

"Who's told you this?"

"Juanita, the woman I rent from, told me this morning."

"She's heard it?"

"Yes."

"How can they say this? Where are they getting their information from?"

"They're getting it from your gardener, the man who's working outside right now. He's telling everybody that he saw us having sex here in the confessional last Saturday and that he has seen me going to your house late at night."

"They're lies! But why is he lying?"

"He's Dolores' uncle. Didn't you know that?"

"No. But that doesn't give him the right to lie. Are people believing him?

"Yes, according to Juanita."

"What's this about tomorrow morning's Mass?"

"She said they were going to bring it up tomorrow morning at Mass. What they will do then or say, I don't know."

"And you say everybody knows, everybody's been told?"

"I don't know about everybody, but Juanita said a lot of people know."

He doesn't know what to say. After a while he mumbles about now knowing why his dinner tonight was canceled. Then he is silent again.

"I have to go, Padre. He saw me come in, and I don't know how many others he's got out there watching. We *were* in here a long time last Saturday."

"Who saw you come in?"

"Your gardener. The same one who's spreading the lies. I saw him when I came in right now. He was acting like he was watering. When he saw me looking at him, he turned away."

"Are you coming to the 11:00 Mass tomorrow morning?"

"I don't know, Padre. I've been through so much these past few weeks, when all I've been trying to do is communicate with God. It's been too much."

"I need you to come. Without you, I'm just one voice against all of theirs. If you don't come, they'll say that you didn't come because what they're saying is all true."

"I don't know, Padre, I don't know."

SHE DOES come. She arrives at 10:30, seating herself in the front row, thinking that in this way she will have fewer people to see, to answer to. He is the second to enter, fifteen minutes later. When he sees her, he moves to her side of the aisle. When he reaches her, he puts his hand on her shoulder and pauses long enough to say softly, "Thank you for coming. It means a lot to me." Then he continues down to the sacristy where he kneels and prays before donning the all-white vestments that he has chosen for this morning.

As he climbs the sacristy steps to the altar, he decides to strike first. When he comes out from behind the altar, instead of stepping up onto the altar, he goes directly to the pulpit, climbs its three steps, and looks about the packed, surprised church as the hushed murmurs grow louder and says, "Where are you, Felipe Domínguez? Felipe Domínguez, where are you?" Half of the congregation turns to the far left corner of the church. He sees Felipe Domínguez shirking in his seat, and he cries out, "Come forward, Felipe Domínguez! Come forward! This is the House of God! You will be safe here!"

Felipe Domínguez sits with his chin tucked into his chest, shaking his head no. Now there are people near him urging him to go forward.

"There is nothing to fear, Felipe, God is here! He is the Protector of the innocent and the Curse of evil, lying men! So unless you have something to fear, something to hide, come forward!" Padre Montes spreads his arms wide as if waiting to embrace Felipe.

Felipe continues shaking his head. Two men have pushed their way to either side of him.

"Go up there, Felipe, go up there. If you don't, people will think you're lying. All of us are depending on you. So long as you have been telling us the truth, and we believe that you have, nothing will happen to you. Don't let him get away with yet another outrage."

"Come forward, Felipe! God is watching! He knows what's in your heart!"

More people make their way to Felipe, Dolores Álvarez among them. Everyone is watching. Skepticism is increasing. "Tío, you have to go up there. You have nothing to fear, nothing to hide. We are all here to make sure that nothing happens to you. The truth will always win out."

As he starts down the center aisle, Felipe is trembling and limping badly, alternately lifting and dragging his club foot. Fear masks his face. The sight of his exaggerated, twisted body slowly moving down the center aisle and the sound of the dragging club foot have silenced the congregation. They all watch with apprehension and growing disbelief.

"Come," Padre Montes says calmly, soothingly, beckoning Felipe Domínguez forward with his hands. "Come and stand with me before our God."

The closer Felipe gets, the more profusely he sweats. His eyes are leaping about and his body is quivering as Padre Montes reaches out to bring him past the altar railing to the foot of the altar. When Padre Montes touches him, Felipe slithers away.

"There, there, Felipe. If my touch bothers you, I will no longer touch you. All I ask is that you join me for a moment in looking at the tabernacle, the House of God. Just be calm and look." Padre Montes turns and slowly, gently, extends his right arm toward the tabernacle. His voice is soft, kind, soothing.

The congregation looks on in silence. Felipe's body twitches. He doesn't look. He can't look.

"Now I want you to turn and look at the woman in the first row. Señora Gonzales, will you please stand? Look at her, Felipe. That's it. Is this the woman you have been telling people that I have been sexually involved with?"

For a few moments the church is absolutely silent. Then Felipe Domínguez lets out a long, loud moan and falls to his knees, bringing his head down to the foot of the altar and in a loud, plaintive voice bellows, "Forgive me God! Forgive me! I have lied and lied and lied! Please forgive me, God!"

Padre Montes stands over him watching, resplendent in his immaculate white vestments as the broken man begins to weep. "Why did you lie, Felipe?" he says quietly.

"Because she paid me! She gave me money to lie!"

"Who gave you money?"

"My sobrina, Dolores."

Everyone turns to where Dolores Álvarez has been sitting. But she has gone.

OUTSIDE AFTER Mass, Padre Montes and Jesusita are surrounded by well-wishers. "What a horrible thing to have done to the two of you."

"I heard something but I just couldn't bring myself to believe it, Padre."

"How could anyone say these things about a man of the cloth?"

"And about a woman who daily receives the Sacraments."

"They will have to answer to God, and I would not like to be in their shoes."

"Padre, señora, I didn't believe a word of it."

And so it goes until Padre Montes leans toward Jesusita and quietly says, "My, how quickly the damned have risen."

She's not sure what he said or meant. When she looks at him, puzzled, a woman says, "What was that, Padre?"

He thinks for a moment and then says, "Oh, I was just mentioning to the Señora González how quickly the fortunes of this parish have changed. With the kind of interest and support I have seen over the past week, I'm convinced that we can do many things that have never been done here before or, for that matter, have never been tried here before."

A woman says, "What we really need here, Padre, is a Guadalupana Society."

"I agree. But I am leaving that entirely in the hands of the Señora González. I'm convinced that she's the kind of a person that can put together the kind of organization that this church badly needs."

There are "yeses" from several of the women.

Later, four women walk Jesusita home. They are all interested in the Guadalupana. Jesusita is beaming.

"What are your plans for the Society?"

"Well, I don't know. This comes as a surprise to me. Padre Montes and I have not talked about this. I will have to think about it."

"How many members will you have?"

"I don't know. I'll have to talk to Padre Montes to see what he has in mind."

"With four young children, how can you manage to be at Mass and Holy Communion at 6:00 every day of the week?"

"Believe me, it is worth every sacrifice or effort that it takes. I get so much in return. It makes my day-to-day life so much easier."

"I suppose that's true when you've really found God."

"Yes, it is."

When they reach Juanita's house, one of the women says, "Would you mind if we came in for a few minutes to talk about the Guadalupana a little more?"

"No, not today. The house is really a mess." It is better for now that they not see how the five of them live.

"Well then, why don't we go over to my house? It's just two blocks away."

"I can't, really. I've been up since before 6:00 and have been gone most of the morning. It's time that I look after my kids, especially the little one. Besides, I really should talk to Padre, see what he wants, what he expects before we go any further."

"Will you contact us as soon as you've talked to him?"

"Yes, yes. Of course."

She watches as they leave. The respect, the deference, they have shown her has buoyed her. She can't remember how long it's been since she has felt this good. As she walks along the side of Juanita's house, she notices for the first time that it is a clear, crisp, beautiful autumn day. She can hear Concepcion playing in the backyard, screeching with laughter. It is times like this that make life worth living. When she reaches the backyard, Concepcion sees her and screams, running toward her. She takes one side of her mother's skirt and reports, "Sergio's at a friend's and Yolanda is watching me. She just went inside for a minute. Mama, can Paulina come out now? She's been in that room a long time now. Yolanda says she's been in there for eight days now."

Paulina.

A big, black tarp falls over everything, wiping out her wonderful day. She stops and thinks. Not once has the girl asked to be let out. Not once has she said that she's sorry. Twice in those eight days their eyes have met, quite by accident, when one of the others has left the door open. She has looked, even though she knew as she did that it was best not to—looked and met Paulina's eyes. They were sullen and hateful eyes that gave nothing, relented not one bit. And Jesusita had looked away. The girl has lived in that room for eight days. She has eaten there, slept there, defecated and urinated there, coughed there, and farted there. Jesusita has constantly yelled at the others to keep the door closed because when it is open she can smell Paulina's foul stench. She would have let the girl out days ago if she had only asked to be let out or said that she was sorry as she had in the past. But this time isn't like the past. This time the girl hasn't asked, and Jesusita somehow knows that this time the girl won't ask. Times have changed. And for the first time ever, Jesusita hints to herself that the girl intimidates her, yes, maybe even frightens her.

Yolanda meets her in the backyard. "Mama, you've got to let Paulina out. Our two rooms stink of her. I have tried cleaning our front room, opening the door and window, but the smell won't go away. She has been in there too long. You said to keep the window and shade down in the bedroom, so the smell has only one place to go. It's gotten so strong that I think even Juanita can smell it. What are you going to tell her when she asks what that smell is? Please Mama, you have to let her out."

Times have changed. *The girl will die in there rather than ask or apologize. And if one of those women, or some of them, or anyone comes to visit uninvited and smells the stench... Oh, my God!* "Let her out then. But I don't want to see her, not until she apologizes. I don't want to look at her. Take her straight to the bathroom and bathe her. Change the water twice. When that's done, open all the doors and windows and tell her that I said that she has to stay outside until it gets dark. I don't want to see her. I hate to think of what I might do if I see her." Times have changed, and Jesusita knows it only too well.

✝ VIII

"TAKE GOOD care of your little brother," his mother said. "I'll be right back." She didn't come back. But Felix Bocanegra never forgot what she said. He was twelve and his brother was four. They stood and then sat on the steps of the Fresno County Hospital until one of the nurses took them inside late that night. They spent the rest of the night at the County Shelter for Children.

Over the next four years, Felix and his little brother Ralph are placed in six foster homes as wards of the courts. Given Felix's odd ways, Ralph's age, and their social worker's determination to keep the brothers together, permanent placement was getting more and more unlikely. The spoken reasons always have to do with Felix. "There's something wrong with that boy. He's slow. And the way he stares at you when you first tell him something. It's like he's looking right through you. Those are strange eyes." "We just can't give him all the time and special attention he seems to need. We've got too many other kids here." "He seems to understand everything you tell him but it usually takes a while to sink in, and then, lots of times, he just can't seem to follow through." "He's just too big a problem at school. They say he needs special tutoring. Well, we don't have much schooling ourselves, and we can't afford special tutors—not with what the county pays us."

After the sixth placement fails, the brothers remain in the shelter for more than three months. The social worker has exhausted the few Mexican foster homes as well as the white foster homes that are willing to take Mexican kids. One foster mother has said that she might be willing to take Ralph but not the two of them. The social worker continues to hope for a single placement for the two brothers.

Then one afternoon Elmer Jensen, a young rancher who owns 110 acres on Manning Avenue, seven miles southwest of Fresno, comes into the agency office. He is wiry and impatient. When there is no one at the front desk, he stomps his heavy boot on the floor thinking that will bring someone. No one comes. He stretches his sinewy neck in every direction, and his face reddens, emphasizing the white band across his brow where his hat usually sits. Still no one comes. He paces the small reception room raising one bony shoulder after the other as he does so. Then he runs fingers through his dirty blond hair trying to decide whether to stay or go. He can't go. He has to stay, and that irritates him all the more. He raises his arms; stretches and twists his long, thin body; and holds that stretch and grunts loudly. Someone comes. Irritated, he tells the receptionist that he is wanting to place an older, teenaged boy on his ranch. He says he wants the boy to work two hours a day after school and eight hours on Saturdays. In exchange the boy will be given a home with a good Christian family and a little spending money to boot. What he doesn't say is that the ranch has gotten too big for him to work alone. He has four kids, but they are much too young to be of any help to him now. The only boy in the shelter to fit that description is Felix. While the social worker doesn't want to break up their family, it is beginning to look like this might be the only way to get the boys out of the shelter. Besides, every indication is that once Felix is eighteen, his sole means of support will be manual labor. This ranch might just be a good training experience for him.

"The boy I have in mind is a Mexican."

"What's that got to do with anything?"

"Frankly, some white folks wouldn't feel comfortable taking a Mexican boy into their family."

109 ✠

"That's not gonna be a problem for us."

"He's also not too smart in school. A little on the slow side."

"I never was too smart in school myself. Just went to the fifth grade. That's never held me back. I got 110 acres of good ranching land. What I got now is a lot more than most folks who finished school will ever have, and I intend to get more."

Three days later, Felix Bocanegra is dropped off at the Manning Avenue ranch with a brown-paper bag of county-issued clothes. There in the dirt driveway, Elmer Jensen sizes up the boy: about five feet, ten inches—tall for a Mexican. A little on the thin side, but rangy and capable of a good day's work on the ranch. He's a little slow to answer and sometimes his eyes seem to get stuck when he looks at you, but he'll do just fine.

They go around to the back porch door. When they reach the steps, the screen door swings open. "I'll take that," Lois Jensen says, extending her arms to the paper bag and blocking the door as she does so. The boy is surprised, not knowing who the woman is or where she's come from. But he returns her look, set and unwavering. "Give me that bag." There are no introductions, no greetings, no words other than those. The boy hands up the bag. The woman takes the bag, turns, and in the same motion brings the screen door behind her, latches it and is gone. Felix goes to work that morning. There is no mention of school.

Later, after the kids have gone to bed, Jensen and his wife talk in the kitchen.

"I don't want him in the house."

"I didn't bring him in the house."

"You would have if I hadn't been there. If I hadn't stopped you. How many times do I have to tell you that I don't want him in the house?"

"I thought we agreed that he could stay in the back porch."

"Not after the way he looked at me."

"How did he look at you?"

"He's evil. Those eyes are evil. I don't want him around my daughters."

"What's he gonna do to Millie and Bonnie? They're five and six."

"Don't tell me you've never heard of child molesters."

"What makes you think he's a child molester?"

"I don't care what he is. I don't want him around my daughters. What other family out here has a Mexican living with them in their house? And us with two little girls, too."

"He's not in the house. He's out on the back porch."

"And that's not part of the house?"

"I've already told him that he's going to stay in the porch and that he's going to use the wash trays out back."

"And where's he going to eat?"

"Not with us."

"Did you tell him that?"

"Not exactly. What I told him was that his meals would be put in the back porch for him. I suppose I could have told him that after he picked them up, he had to go outside and eat them in the dark.... I think we're getting pretty silly about all this."

"I'm not silly. I'm just certain that I don't want a Mexican living with me in my house."

"Lois, where else am I gonna put him?"

"That's your problem. You're the one who ran down to the county looking for an orphan kid."

"I did it for us. I did it for all of us. For you and me and the kids. I can't work this ranch by myself. It's too big for one man."

"No one told you to go ahead and buy another sixty acres. We were just fine with fifty acres. But no, you had to have sixty more. Now we're broke, and I've got a Mexican living with me!"

FOR THE first several months, Elmer and Felix work together digging furrows and building berms for the irrigation of the vines. They tie vines and weed around the vine stocks. They thin and irrigate in the fruit orchards. After two weeks, Elmer is completely satisfied with the boy's work. He does the work of a full-grown man and probably better than some. What is odd, and at first was annoying, is the boy's difficulty in beginning a conversation with anyone. Once he has begun, his speech is pretty much normal except if he is being prodded or hurried—or thinks he is being prodded or hurried. Begin a conversation with him, and the boy's head will cock to the right and his eyes will fasten onto yours as if the words he is searching for are written there. It is a look that lasts for several seconds. It is not a threatening or hostile look. Rather, it is a plain, calm, open look—not a stare, yet one that after a few seconds becomes disconcerting, almost as if he is looking into the deepest part of you. His eyes add to the strangeness. They are a bright brown which often during the look seem to turn a bright orange-yellow.

After the first weeks, Elmer devises a way to work around many of those beginnings. "Son, if I ask you something that can be answered yes or no, don't even try to talk to me. Just shake or nod your head no or yes. We got a lot of work ahead of us and it's not going to do us any good to stand around waiting for you to say yes or no. Just nod or shake your head and we'll carry on."

Sometime later, Elmer asks the boy, "You like it here?"

There are several quick, vigorous nods.

"You want to stay here?"

More nods.

"Instead of working with me, you want to go to school?"

He shakes his head for several seconds.

"That woman that brought you out here, your social worker, she said she'd be back in a few weeks to check on how you're doing. She expects that you'll be in school. If she finds out that you're not in school, that you're out here working with me instead, she's liable to take you back to the shelter. Is that what you want?"

Another continuous shaking motion.

"So when she asks you what school you're going to, you'll say what?"

The boy takes his long look at Elmer and finally turns away shaking his head.

"You forget already?"

The boy nods.

"Ok, let's try it again. Washington High School. Say after me: 'Washington.' "

His eyes set. "Wash."

"Washing."

"Washing."

"Ton."

"Ton."

"Now, all at once, Washing-ton."

"Washing-ton."

"Ok. Now, high school.... No, no. Just high, like you're saying hi to somebody. Washington Hi."

"Washington Hi."

"Good. Good. Now what grade are you in?"

"Ninth."

"Great!" Elmer thinks of continuing but thinks better of it. It's been a long day, and he and the boy are tired. And no matter how much they practice, there is no telling what the boy will say when the social worker comes.

It is two months before the social worker visits the ranch. He is not the social worker that Felix has had for four years. When he asks Felix, "How's school?" the boy begins his search as Elmer holds his breath. Finally he answers, "I don't go to school." Elmer groans.

"Of course," the social worker says. "I almost forgot. It's summer vacation. There is no school right now. You like it here, son?"

Elmer tightens. The boy's eyes set on the social worker again.

Damn, you looney bastard, Elmer rails within, *all you've got to do is say yes. What's so damn hard about that? Yes! Yes!*

"Did you hear my question, son?"

Felix nods vigorously.

"You like it here?"

More vigorous nods.

"Good."

When the social worker is shown the back porch and the cot in the corner, Elmer says, "I was gonna fix it up, close it off by putting paneling over the screen, but with this heat I thought Felix would be a lot more comfortable without it until the nights get cold in October or November."

"Sounds good to me," the social worker says.

Lois Jensen is standing apprehensively in the kitchen doorway when the social worker turns to her and asks, "How's Felix fitting in here with your family, Mrs. Jensen?" Just two nights before, Elmer stormed out of their bedroom saying that if she doesn't stop bitching about that boy, he was going back to Missouri and let her see what she could do with the ranch by herself. "Oh, he's fine, sir," she says. "He fits in perfectly. We couldn't ask for a better boy. Thank you for letting us have him."

Then, a few minutes after he arrived, the social worker leaves, and Felix wonders where his little brother is and why the social worker didn't tell him. Worse, why he didn't ask.

SUNDAY IS the Sabbath and nobody works on the Sabbath. The preacher in the little Pentecostal church in tiny Easton has two ways of saying it, "...and on the Sabbath, He rested..." and "no God-fearing man works on the Sabbath." Elmer Jensen is a God-fearing man. So every Sunday morning at 9:00, the Jensen family piles into their Ford pickup and drives to Easton for Sunday service, not to return until 2:00 or 2:30 that afternoon. The house is locked, including the back porch, and Felix is left behind.

Sunday is the worst day of the week for Felix. There is nothing to do. He has asked Mr. Jensen if he can work on Sundays, but Mr. Jensen just says that God-fearing men don't work on Sundays. Once he has dressed and eaten his breakfast, he is not allowed in the porch until dark. That is not a problem on weekdays because he and Mr. Jensen usually work until 7:00; dinner is on the porch at 7:30 and not long after, it's dark. On Sundays there is nothing for him to do except stay out of the sun. Most Sundays he spends either in the apricot or plum orchard, sitting or lying down. He has thought about everything there is to think about—mostly Ralph—too many times. He doesn't have a watch, but he can get an idea about what time it is by watching the sun's shadows. But the shadows on Sunday move slowly, too slowly. Mr. Jensen has started paying him five dollars a week, but there is nothing to spend it on. There's a little store in Easton, but that's five miles away and Mr. Jensen doesn't want him walking off the ranch because a lot of the ranchers don't like or trust Mexicans. They'll think he's up to no-good, and "some of them might could even shoot at you." He has started putting his five dollars in a tin can and burying it behind one of the water pump sheds because on Sundays after church, he can hear the Jensen kids playing in the porch, jumping up and down on his cot, and going through his things. He thinks they must do that during the week, too, when he's working. He always misses little Ralph, but on Sundays he seems to miss him more because there's nothing else to think about. He promises himself that the next time the social worker comes, he's going to ask him where Ralph is.

Then one Sunday afternoon when the Jensens come home from church, Mr. Jensen finds him in the apricot orchard. He is mad.

"Felix," he says, irritated, "where in the hell do you keep that damn money I've been giving you? I know you haven't spent any of it 'cause there's no place around here where you could spend it…. Don't look at me like that. I'm not gonna take it from you. It's your money. You earned it. But now I've got to buy you some Sunday clothes with it. We've got some real nosy people around here who know you're living with us. They've told our preacher about you, and him and a bunch of them think I'm responsible for your soul too, not just your body. So now I've got to bring you to church with us on Sundays. Hell fire! I never signed up for saving your soul when I went down to that Welfare Department and got you. I just said that I'd give you a damn good home and I have. Right?" He nods, waiting for Felix to nod, and Felix nods.

They drive to Fresno late on the following Wednesday afternoon. The temperature has been in the low hundreds for weeks, and Wednesday seems to be one of the hottest days. All the windows in the pickup are rolled down, but the rushing, burning hot air gives no relief. They park in front of the Salvation Army Store and enter. The store is empty and dark. Every window has been covered or partially covered to keep out the heat. Yet the compressed, stale air inside is no less oppressive than the heat outside. The two stand looking about the empty darkness until Jensen says in a loud voice, "Anybody home?" A thin, small, white-haired woman steps out from behind a counter and says, "Can I help you?"

"Yes, ma'am, I sure hope you can." As Jensen moves toward her, she looks at them quizzically. Then she wrinkles her brow, turns to Felix, smells, and steps back. Elmer looks at Felix and sees what he has become accustomed to seeing: an unwashed face, a sweat-stained shirt and straw hat, filthy overalls, and cracked, worn shoes. There is also that sharp, offensive smell, like rotting cheese. He knows what he has always known but never considered until now: Felix doesn't bathe. He's embarrassed but reminds himself that he is not Felix. He changes his clothes twice a week, and today he changed his shirt and boots before they came into town, and he bathes once a week.

The woman, who is wearing an immaculate, starched and ironed, flowered, cotton dress, says again, but now hesitantly, as if she really doesn't mean it at all, "Can I help you?"

"Yes, ma'am, the boy here needs some Sunday clothes."

"Are you two related?"

"Oh, no, ma'am."

"I mean, how are you two related?"

"Well, see ma'am, I'm a rancher. I have 110 acres of grapes and apricots, peaches and plums out on Manning Avenue. This here boy's a Messicun who lives and works with one of my neighbors out there. When our preacher found out about this boy, he told my neighbor that he had to bring him to church on Sundays. I'm sure you can imagine, my neighbor was very upset. I offered to help by bringing the boy into town for some Sunday clothes."

"So by Sunday clothes, you mean clothes for church services on Sunday?"

"Yes, ma'am."

"I don't think I've got too much of that, but I'll show you what I got."

They follow her to the back of the store where it is darker still. She turns on a light and shows them some slacks and shirts.

"I don't know what size he wears. Maybe if he could just try on..."

"No, no. I'd rather not. Even though all our clothes are donated and are second-hand, we still have them all washed and cleaned. I would just rather not have him try them on."

"Well, that's OK, but I think he'll be needing more than a shirt and slacks. We dress-up pretty good out there for our Sunday church. He'd be needing a coat or maybe even a suit. You got any suits?"

"I have two. They're down here in the corner. I'm not sure they'll fit him, but we can take a look." She moves to the back of the room.

Elmer follows her and then sees that Felix has not followed. "Felix, come on over here.... You heard me. Come on. You've got to go to church on Sunday, and you can't go dressed the way you are. Now get on over here."

Felix doesn't move. The woman is watching.

"Now Felix, you heard me. Don't make me come over there and get you."

Felix takes several slow steps toward Elmer, stopping a few feet behind him.

"I have this gray suit." She holds up a hangered jacket. "But I think it might be too small for him."

"Oh, that's way too small. Looks like a little boy's suit to me."

"The only other thing I have is this black suit. Now this might be too big for him. And I want to warn you. It's a heavy wool suit. Much too hot for this heat. You might be able to wear it here in Fresno from October to April, but not now. It's a wool flannel suit. Here, hold it. See for yourself."

Elmer raises the suit up and down and hands it back to the woman. "I'm not too worried about the heat because our Sunday services start early in the morning and are usually over before the heat really sets in. I'm more worried about whether it'll fit him or not. Could he try on just the jacket? My wife could fix the pants."

"No, I wouldn't want to do that. Like I said, all our clothes are washed and cleaned before we put them up for sale, and we want them to stay that way until they leave the store. Here, take the jacket and hold it up to him. That ought to give you a pretty good idea."

Holding the black jacket by the shoulders, Elmer turns and says, "Step on over here for a minute, boy."

Felix doesn't move.

"I don't know what's got into you, boy, but I'm not going to put up with it much longer. Now step on over here."

This time Felix shakes his head no.

"Alright then, I'll step over to you." As he does, Felix folds his arms across his stomach, bends over, and squats down so that he is no more than two feet tall. Elmer reddens, anger stirring as he stands next to Felix with the bottom of the suit coat an inch above the boy's head.

"Now I can see why your neighbor didn't want to bring this boy in himself," the woman says, adding fuel to the fire.

"I'll tell you what, ma'am. I'm gonna take this suit, and he's gonna wear it on Sunday come hell or high water. My wife can sew anything. I'm gonna need a white shirt and a necktie too. Got any of those?"

"I sure do."

On the drive home, Elmer says several times, "What in hell got into you in that store, boy?"

Felix doesn't answer.

"Well, you know you're going to church with us on Sunday, don't you?"

Still no answer.

IX

SANTIAGO HAS been waiting. He doesn't like waiting. In fact he came fifteen minutes early, hoping that Angie would be early too. Instead, she is late. He has been there for twenty minutes and there is no sign of her. He is angry, but desperate too. What if she doesn't come? He left the others in a frenzy. All week long he has told them about her. They had given up hope of any female pleasure in their lifetimes, and he had reignited it—uncontrollably so. What if she doesn't come? What will they do to him?

Then she emerges from the alley. As she walks toward him, he examines her to be sure. There are mounds on her chest and her legs are firm and full. Hips are forming. They will like her. He relaxes. And once relaxed, he thinks of his pleasure. First his pleasure. Before he gives her the quarter, he says, "I told my friends I would bring you. They're waiting. When we finish in the show, I will leave. Wait a few minutes and then you leave too. I will be waiting for you at the corner in front of the Louie Kee Market. When I see you come out, I will start walking toward my house. It's a white house. Follow me, but stay a half a block behind me. I don't want people to see us together. They will not like it if they see a Mexican girl with a Filipino man."

She does as he says. She follows a half a block behind. She thinks she knows where the white house is. Since she has been meeting him at the Ryan, she has heard the girls at the playground say that there are a bunch of Filipinos living in the white house down the street. Those girls are always making fun of the Filipinos. They say they sound like turkeys when they talk. They say they are ugly little men, uglier than Chinamen. They say the men stare at them whenever they pass by the house, and that makes them nervous. One girl said that she told her father about the way they were staring at her. He got mad, but not at them. He got mad at her and told her not to be walking by their house anymore. If Angie ever believed what those girls said about the Filipinos, she doesn't anymore. Not since Santiago told her that she could make a lot of money with them.

She sees Santiago turn into the white house's front yard, walk along the side of the house, and then disappear behind the house next door. He is waiting for her at the back of the house. "They're all inside. They want to meet you real bad. I'm going to put you in my room. I told them they can each have ten minutes in there with you for twenty-five cents."

"Twenty-five cents for what? What do I have to do?"

"The same thing you do with me in the show. They can touch you or you can touch them."

"Either one but not both for twenty-five cents?"

"Yes."

They enter the house through the back door. She can hear movement in the kitchen. When she enters the kitchen, the movement stops. All six are standing. None of the chairs are occupied. None of them look at her. Two seem to be having a low conversation. "Boys! This Angie!" Only one glances at her. The others look toward her but not at her. All of them are neatly combed and in their Sunday clothes. Their shoes are shiny. "I'm going to put Angie in my room. You boys decide who goes first and line up."

The room is small and unadorned except for the four beds that have been squeezed into it with just enough room to sidle between them. "Sit down," Santiago says. "This is my bed," patting a bed. She sits and looks about at the barrenness as he goes to the lone window and pulls down the shade blocking the mid-afternoon sun. "I'm going to let them in one at a time. I'll be standing out-side the door. When their ten minutes is up, I'll knock and come in. If anybody gives you any trouble, and I don't think anybody will, just yell out my name and I'll be in here."

The first one is waiting at the door when Santiago opens it and comes in as Santiago leaves, closing the door behind him. Then they're alone. She can hear him breathing. He takes two steps to-ward her and then stops. He is still two beds away, and she thinks how much easier this had been at the Ryan. There she couldn't see him, couldn't see it. There she could watch the movie and touch and be touched until he groaned and stiffened, and then she left without ever having to see him or it. Here there is no movie, no darkness. She will see him and it and everything. But the man doesn't move, doesn't come any closer as the minutes pass. She turns and looks at him and sees that he is nervous and scared. Mo-ments later there's a knock at the door. It opens and Santiago says, "Ten minutes." And the first one leaves confused and dejected.

She looks at the second man as he stands looking, not at her, but about the room as if he had never been in it before. He looks like the first man: short, small, dark, his black hair slicked-back, his dress slacks belted well above the waist. After a mounting silence, he comes and stands beside her and speaks to her softly with words that she can't understand. Then he strokes her hair, gently, until Santiago knocks.

The third man paces back and forth along the foot of the beds, stopping every third or fourth time he has paced the width of the room to study her from behind, sighing loudly before he begins pacing again, studying her from behind again and again until there is a knock at the door. The next man sits next to her on the bed and fidgets with his hands until he says that she reminds him of his sister. He asks her if he can kiss her and she nods and he kisses her on the cheek. He tells her about his life as a boy in the Philippines, pausing every so often to ask if he can kiss her, each time kissing her on the cheek. She is not interested in his life in the Philip-pines and instead counts and recounts the number of fruit boxes stacked in the doorless closet from the floor almost to the ceiling. Twenty-one, no twenty, no twenty-one. Each box has clothes and other things stacked in it. She tries to make out what those other things are. When the knock comes, he takes a hurried kiss without asking and leaves.

The fifth man sits where the fourth man was sitting and immediately puts his arm around her, turns to her, and cups each of her breasts with each of his hands. It is the first time anyone other than herself has touched her breasts which are now noticeable under her clothes. They are definitely growing, and each day she looks in the mirror to see how much more noticeable they are. It is odd and offensive to have a man's hands on her breasts. But he has paid to do it, and the knock will come soon. He starts to breathe heavily, and she wonders if just her breasts can make him groan and stiffen and leave. She hopes the knock will come soon. He asks, "Will you touch me?"

"If you pay me more."

"How much more? How much do you charge?"

"I charge twenty-five cents to touch me and twenty-five cents more if I touch you. Fifty cents."

"Twenty-five cents more?"

"Yes."

"But I already gave Santiago thirty-five cents."

"Thirty-five cents? No, he's only supposed to charge you twenty-five cents to touch me. You've already done that. So if I touch you it's twenty-five cents more."

The man drops his hands, straightens himself, and looks around the room angrily. Just then the knock comes. He springs from the bed and is at the door as Santiago opens it. "God damn you, Santiago!"

"Hey! Hey! Come on out. Let Pedro get in there. He's been waiting a long time. Come on out here. Let's talk about whatever's bothering you out here."

She watches the two men squeeze past each other in the doorway. The door closes with the next man standing just inside it. She turns back and waits for him to come to the bed. This is the last one, and so far it's been a lot easier than she thought it would be. "My name is Pedro Fuentes." She doesn't turn even though this is the first one to introduce himself. He will come to the bed soon enough. But after a while when he hasn't come, she turns and sees him still standing just inside the door smiling uneasily.

"What's the matter?"

"Nothing."

"Why are you just standing there?"

"I'm thinking."

"Thinking? What are you thinking?"

"That maybe I don't want to do this."

"Do what?"

"Touch you."

"Then why did you come in here?"

"Because the others would laugh at me if I didn't."

She can hear loud voices on the other side of the door. Someone is arguing. Probably the man that just left and Santiago. "Are you just going to stand there?"

"Maybe not. If Santiago opens the door and I'm still standing here and the others see me, they will laugh.... Can I sit by you?"

"Yes."

He sits at the far end of the bed. They sit in silence waiting for Santiago's knock. She can hear men shouting in the kitchen. She can hear words but she can't understand them. "What are they yelling about?"

"They're mad at Santiago."

"Why?"

"Because he told us that we had to pay thirty-five cents just to... you know...touch you. Now one of them is saying that you said that if they paid twenty-five cents they could touch you, and you would touch them for another twenty-five cents—when Santiago said that if we wanted you to touch us it would be another thirty-five cents."

"Santiago said that to you too?"

"Yes."

"Did you give him thirty-five cents to touch me?"

"Yes, everybody did."

They sit silently. She is angry, and he is worried that if they come to blows in the kitchen, Santiago might forget about knocking. The shouting continues. Then there are sounds that sound like scrapings.

"What was that?"

"I don't know," not wanting to alarm her, not wanting to tell her that he thinks someone might have picked up a chair.

They sit for a while longer.

"Are you going to touch me?"

"No."

"Why?"

"I don't know.... I guess it's because I don't know you and you don't know me. How could I touch you?"

"DON'T LIE to me, Santiago! They told me!"

They are in the backyard. She is leaving. He has given her a dollar and fifty cents. "Please, let's not talk about it here. They're all watching. Let's go into the garage and you can talk all you want to talk."

She follows him into a small dark garage that has more stacked fruit boxes filled with an assortment of things. "You told me that you were going to charge them twenty-five cents to touch me, but they told me they paid you thirty-five cents."

"Wait a minute! Wait a minute! I told you I would give you twenty-five cents if you let them touch you. No, I never told you what I would charge them for my work too. That's *my* business, not *your* business."

"It's my business too. I had to tell him how much I charge if I touched him. And I told him twenty-five cents, but you charged him thirty-five. And then he got mad."

"Yes, but he didn't get mad at you, he got mad at me."

"How did I know that? When he got mad, he got mad, and I sure thought it was at me then. So it's my business too."

"First of all, I let them and you use my room and bed. You could never get six guys to touch you in the Ryan in one afternoon. And I had to talk you up to these guys, tell them that you were real nice and clean and pretty and not some old whore. That took a lot of talking. Then I had to stand guard by the door the whole time you were in there with them. Do you know what could happen to you if I just let six, real hard-up Filipinos have their way with you in the house alone? I was standing outside that door protecting you, making sure none of them got nasty with you. Yes, I charged them thirty-five cents. Twenty-five cents for you and ten cents for me. And if they wanted you to touch them, another thirty-five cents. Twenty-five cents for you and ten cents more for my work. What's wrong with that?

"What's wrong with that is that I have to know what you're telling them so they don't get mad when I tell them something different."

"I probably should have charged more. But I don't like to be greedy. I know you've never had a dollar fifty in your life before now. And for what? For sitting on a bed in a room for an hour. Pretty good, huh? And that doesn't even include what I gave you at the show."

THE FOLLOWING Sunday the room is dark. A blanket hangs over the shaded window, and strips of cardboard have been tacked around the doorway cutting out the slices of light that had filtered in before. The room remains darkened for the many Sundays that follow. Touching gets bolder and bolder. Soon all six are paying seventy cents every Sunday. Pedro Fuentes does not touch her. He sits next to her, mostly silent, sometimes telling her about the Philippines and listening to her tell about her school.

Inevitably, touching is not enough. The men want more. They say that they want to fuck Angie. Santiago says that he doesn't know if she is willing but that he will talk to her. But first things first, how much are they willing to pay? One of them says a dollar.

Santiago guffaws, throws his head back and then shakes it. "Don't be ridiculous! This is a young virgin. There are men who would pay a hundred times more for this opportunity." Then they are at two dollars. Everyone is willing to pay two dollars. But how much can Santiago skim off the two dollars? Not much. He acts as if he is giving the two dollars considerable thought. "No," he shakes his head. "She'll never go for that. We've talked a little bit about it, enough for me to know that she'll never go for that."

"Two fifty," one of them says, "and I won't pay a penny more."

"That's all I can pay," another adds.

Two fifty means two dollars for her and fifty cents for him. He's pretty sure she'll take two dollars, but fifty cents for him is just not enough. "You guys still think you're in the Philippines. How long has it been since you've had any pussy? None since you left the islands, and how many years has that been? If you want to keep beating your meat every night, that's alright with me. But you know, the beds squeak, and I wish you'd go a little easier on yourselves because you keep waking me up."

There are a few crooked smiles and some hostile looks.

"Let's talk real. All of you know that the whore house here in Fresno won't take Filipinos and niggers. So you can't go there. And even if you could, from what I hear they charge three to five dollars depending. And you two guys are telling me that you won't pay three dollars here. That's ridiculous. I know she'll do it for three dollars. But it's got to be everybody or nobody. And if you two guys want to keep the other guys away from pussy for fifty cents, then there's not much I can..."

"Ok, ok! Three dollars! But that's it!"

THE NEXT Sunday outside the Ryan, he says, "We're not going to the movies today. We've got to talk. There's going to be a change, a big change. I know you'll like it. But we have to talk about it."

"Ok, talk."

"Not here."

"Where, at your house?"

"Not in the house. In the garage. I'll wait for you there."

For weeks now, she no longer follows him to his house. Instead, she takes a circuitous route that he has devised that takes her blocks out of the way but ends up in the alley behind his house. In the garage Santiago tells Angie what "the boys" want to do, repeating the twelve dollars it will mean to her.

"It's gonna hurt."

"No, it won't. Not if you use this jelly. Rub it in there real good and you won't even feel a thing."

"Sometimes they hurt me just with their fingers."

"Have I ever hurt you?"

"No. But I've seen some of my mother's boyfriends' things. Those things are huge."

"Is my thing huge?"

"No."

"Alright then. We're not talking about your Mama's boyfriends. We're talking about six little Filipinos. Their things are small, not much bigger than their fingers. Heck, you know that. You've touched them. Believe me, I know that. I live with them. I see them in the mornings when they wake up and their things are hard. Not much bigger than their fingers."

"I don't know, Santiago."

"Listen to me, listen to me. Would I lie to you? Have I ever lied to you?"

"Only when you told me that they would pay twenty-five cents to touch me and you got thirty-five cents."

"But I didn't lie. I just didn't tell you I was charging them ten cents more for my work. Not telling you something isn't lying. Is it?"

"I don't know, Santiago."

"Look, just think about this for a minute. You're almost as tall as Fidel and Francisco, aren't you?"

"Yeah."

"I bet your Mama's boyfriends are two times as big as you?"

"I guess so."

127 ✠

"Do your Mama's boyfriends have bigger arms, hands, feet, and heads than Fidel and Francisco?"

"Yeah."

"So you know they have to have a lot bigger peckers than Fidel and Francisco, don't you?"

"I guess so."

"Believe me, Angie, if you use the jelly like I tell you to, you won't feel a thing." He spreads two blankets on the dirt floor. "Lie down."

"Why?"

"Because I'm gonna show you that it won't hurt, not with the jelly. Take off your underpants and give me the jelly."

"Why?"

"Like I said, to show you that it won't hurt. Now hold still while I put some jelly in there. And I'm not paying you for this because it's for you, not for me—so that you can make a lot of money.... Ok, now lie down.... Open your legs.... Remember, I'm not paying you for this. In fact, you should be paying me.... Does it hurt?"

"A little."

"But not a lot, huh?"

"A little."

"Is that little worth twelve dollars?"

"Maybe.... I don't know."

"There, I'm finished and it didn't take no ten minutes. And I bet some of those guys won't be in there more than two minutes. A dollar a minute. You couldn't get that anywhere, Angie.... Hey, why are you crying? Did I hurt you?"

"No."

"Then why are you crying?"

"I don't know."

"I can't take you in the house like this, not with you crying. And those guys are in there waiting. They've been waiting all morning. You can't keep on crying."

"I know."

"Then stop."

"I can't."

Santiago sees his six dollars floating away. "Do you want to go in the house?"

"I don't know."

This will never work. He's already warned those guys any number of times that if anyone finds out what the girl is doing there, if the police find out, they'll all go to jail for a long time. Now the girl comes in crying and they're supposed to fuck her? That will scare the shit out of them and make them madder than hell at him. And if she can't stop crying and cries even more when they do it to her and goes back home crying? Then for sure the police will come....

"Maybe we should wait a week, not do anything today.... Is that better?"

"I think so."

"You think so! You think so! This is not a game, Angie. Those guys in there are going to be mighty mad at me if we don't do it today. They've been waiting all week for this. Now I'm going to have to go in there and tell them you're not going to do it, that they'll have to wait another week. And you think so! If we don't do it next week, they'll probably kick my ass. So are you coming back next Sunday?"

"Yes."

"And are you going to let them do it?"

"I think so."

ALL WEEK long "I think so" haunts him. If she doesn't come, if she doesn't do it, that probably means the end of his business. Six dollars a week for standing by the door for maybe half an hour. It doesn't get any better than that. And free pussy to boot. Although he has to be careful about that: not to get her before they get her, but after. They were mad, really mad when he told them. One of them threw his coffee cup at him. Missed him by an inch.

"She got sick and had to go home," he had told them.

"Sick, my ass. She got sick after you fucked her in that garage.

You think we're stupid or something? You got yours and left us hanging, hurting here in this goddamn house. You didn't give a shit about us. You just fucked the shit out of her, got her sick, and here we were like idiots, waiting."

For Angie it was the twelve dollars that gripped her. For twelve minutes, she could make as much as her mother made in a week cleaning toilets and mopping floors down at the train station. The things she could buy for twelve dollars! And no one would know. With the jelly it hadn't hurt that much, no more than the fingers. In a month or two she would be rich! By Saturday, her biggest concern was where she would keep all this money.

When she meets him in the garage on Sunday, she seems scared, worried, preoccupied. His shoulders sag. What's he going to tell them now? They're watching from the kitchen and if he dallies too long with her now, they'll think he's fucking her again and come busting into the garage. "What's the matter?"

She looks away and sighs. Finally she says, "But where will I keep all that money?"

"What?"

"Where am I going to keep the money? I can't take it home. If my mother finds it she'll think I stole it, and I can't tell her how I got it. She might even call the police. If my brother finds it, he'll spend it first, then tell my mother."

She's going to do it! She's going to do it! "Don't worry about a thing. I've got a metal box here in the garage that I keep my money and papers in. It has a lock and you can use it too. I'll give you a key for it."

"But what if I lose the key?"

"I'll have a key too."

"But then you can steal my money."

"Angie, listen to me! Those guys are waiting inside. You're just going to have to trust me. I'm not going to steal your money. I'm not..."

LATER, IN the dark room, she hears, "Angie, it's me, Pedro. I'm not going to do anything. Can I sit next to you?"

"You're not going to do anything, Pedro? Why, don't you like me?"

He shuffles his way through the darkness to the bed. "You know I like you, but I can't.... You're crying. Did they hurt you?"

"A little bit. They stink and they're heavy and they made funny noises and two of them laid flat on top of me the whole time. But that's not why I'm crying."

"Why then?"

"I guess because I feel ashamed."

"You know you don't have to do any of this?"

"I know."

The weeks become months, and soon she has almost two hundred dollars saved in the metal box. She worries that Santiago might steal it, but more and more she is finding that there is no place to spend it. Twice she has paid a street woman a dollar to go into King's—the only dry goods store in Chinatown—with her, and each time she has had the woman pay for a dress that she likes. On their third visit to the store, she discovers that one of her mother's friends works there, and she runs from the store leaving the puzzled street woman with the unearned dollar.

The dresses sadden her. She can't wear them to school or anywhere other than at the Filipinos' on Sundays. She keeps them in a fruit box in the garage. She changes into one of them as soon as she arrives but doesn't dare go into the house before the appointed hour because the Filipinos will begin pawing her. Her body is filling out more and more, and she would love to wear the dresses out in public, somewhere, anywhere. Instead she contents herself with pacing back and forth in the garage looking at herself while Santiago watches, knowing that he will never touch her then because he wants to get her into the house as soon as he can. They're worse than hungry animals in there. Sometimes he does it to her after the others and before she leaves. But before he does, he always tells her that he's not going to pay. Those times are less and less. He just doesn't seem to want to. He likes the money better. Once in the house she takes a minute before letting the first one in. She has learned to undress herself rather than let them undress her. A tear on one of the dresses has taught her that. For an hour at most, she lies naked on the bed. After, she is finding it more and more difficult to put the dresses on. Except for the men in the kitchen, she would walk back out to the garage naked. Finally one afternoon, she takes the dresses to a raging incinerator behind Louie Kee's Market and tosses them in. The next Sunday, she walks into the Filipinos' kitchen in the same worn, stained dress that she wears to school almost every day.

She buys and brings so much candy and sweets to school that by the end of the day she gives much of it away. It isn't long before one of her teachers asks, "Angie, where are you getting the money to buy all that candy?"

"I'm not buying any candy."

"Well, where's it coming from?"

"A friend of mine's father owns a store."

"And he gives you all this candy?"

"No, I work at the store after school and that's how I get the candy."

After that, she gorges herself on candy and sweets before and after school and takes only what she can consume to school.

WEEKS PASS and one Sunday afternoon Angie says in the garage, "Today when Pedro is the last one in there with me, I don't want you to knock."

"Why?"

"He'll come out when he's ready."

"Then I should charge him more?"

"No."

"Why?"

"Because I need to talk to him when we're through. That's why."

"The other guys aren't going to like this."

"I don't care what the other guys like."

"Yeah, but I have to deal with them, not you."

"You want me to quit?"

"Quit! What're you talking about?"

"Then let me talk to him. He'll come out when we're finished."

"What is this with you? Do you like him or something?"

"I don't know."

"Don't let the other guys think that.... What do I say to them?"

"I don't care what you say to them."

Months have passed and not once has Pedro touched her. On this Sunday afternoon, more than anything she wants him to. The others mean nothing to her. More often than not, they disgust her. For sure it is their money that keeps her letting them. But there is something else. It is the need and want they have for her—the way they look at her when she first walks into the kitchen on Sunday afternoons. It makes her feel important, something she has never felt before. Seldom does it take more than four or five minutes, and usually a lot less, for them to relieve themselves. Then she listens as they secretly try to wipe themselves in the dark, as they carefully slip on their pants and tiptoe out of the room long before Santiago knocks, almost as if they have done something wrong.

Pedro has been different. He sits next to her in the dark, and never has she felt so much as one of his fingers on her. But then, maybe he doesn't like girls? Maybe he's one of those maricóns that Saul and his friends are always laughing about? She hopes not. He talks to her. He listens to her. He is always asking if "one of those idiots," as he calls them, has hurt her. He cares about her. Lately he has been trying to convince her to stop coming on Sundays, to stop letting them. They are abusing her, he says. All week long she has been thinking how good it would be to have him in her while her arms and legs hold him there for as long as they can.

When Pedro's turn comes, she is ready. She waits until he sits on the bed. "Wait a minute," she says as she stands. She turns on a light and stands before him. No, he is no maricón. "Excuse me," she says as she sits on his lap and rubs her breasts on his face. His breathing is loud. He's no maricón. She fondles him. He is definitely not a maricón. Long after he has come, she clings to him.

"I've got to go."

"Santiago hasn't knocked."

"It's been a long time and the others will know. Santiago will know. He'll want more money and the others will watch to make sure I pay more."

"Don't worry about Santiago. I'll even make him give you back what you paid today because this is something I wanted to do."

"Don't do that. The others will really get angry."

"Isn't it nice just lying here like this?"

"But where's Santiago? It's been more than ten minutes. Did he go somewhere?"

"Enjoy this, Pedro. Santiago will tell us when it's time."

On the succeeding two Sundays, Pedro takes her as strongly and lovingly as she wants. There is no talk of her stopping her Sunday visits. On the third Sunday, he isn't there.

"Where's Pedro?" she ask Santiago.

"He's gone."

"Gone?"

"He didn't want the others to see you on Sundays anymore. He got in a fight with two of them, and then the others jumped on him too. They beat him up pretty bad. Then they threw all his things out in the street. He's gone."

A FEW weeks later Angie's mother says, "You're pregnant."

"What?"

"I said you're pregnant."

"Pregnant?"

"Yes, pregnant. Don't play with me, young lady. You're pregnant and you know it. I've been hearing you in the bathroom in the morning. There hasn't been any blood in your underwear for months now. And look at your stomach. Who is he?"

"Who is who?"

"I said don't play with me. Who's the boy that got you pregnant?"

"I don't know."

"What do you mean you don't know? How can you not know who got you pregnant?"

"I don't know what you're talking about."

"What do you mean you don't know what I'm talking about? You don't know who stuck his filthy thing in you? I've told you and I've told you: you'd better not get pregnant on me. I've told you and I've told you what men and boys are like! All they want to do is put their thing in you! That's all they can think about! That's all they are! But this little fucker you opened your legs for isn't going to get away with this! Your father and your brother's father got away with it. But not this little fucker. Not this time. Who is he? Who is he?"

Angie stares at her mother.

As the moments tick by, the woman's anger mounts. Her rage is not just for Angie and her little fucker but also for the two little fuckers of long ago. "Who is he? Tell me!"

"I don't know."

The first blow is to the girl's cheek almost knocking her over. "Who is he?"

"I don't know."

Another blow but to the mouth, and, as Angie doubles over, the woman kicks at the girl's stomach but hits the girl's ribs instead. The girl falls to the floor, crying, her arms wrapped around her stomach.

"Cry all you want, but I've told you forever that I didn't want you bringing me a baby into this house." She's not shouting now. She's conciliatory now. She's explaining her anger, easing her guilt as she watches the girl now rolled into a ball on the floor, sobbing. "You don't know what you're doing to yourself. I was your age when I had Saul. That was not a picnic then, and it won't be one now. I let his father and your father have their fun with me and then run when I got pregnant. Left me with all the pain and headaches and hard work of raising you two, and I'll be damned if I let the bastard who got you pregnant get away with it, too."

Moments pass. The girl lies rolled up on the floor, crying, saying nothing.

Her mother waits for an answer, but there is no answer. The rage returns, mounts. "Who is he?"

"I don't know."

"You liar! You know damn well who he is! Who is he?"

The girl shakes her head.

The woman grabs the girl by her hair, trying to pull her up to kick at the girl's stomach. But the girl is clutching her knees, remaining a ball, protecting her stomach. And the woman kicks and kicks until she can kick no more. Then she shouts, "Get the hell of out here! And don't come back until you're ready to tell me who he is! I mean it! Get out! Get out!"

It is dark when the Filipinos come home from work. They find Angie on the back porch steps crying. She tells them that she is pregnant, that her mother knows, that her mother wants the name of the father and won't let her return to the house until she tells her. She says that maybe they're all the fathers. She doesn't know. Santiago puts her in his room and then holds a meeting in the kitchen. They speak in Filipino. He tells them that he has seen cases like this before. If the girl, who is not yet fourteen, tells her mother or anyone that any one of them could be the father, they will all go to jail for a very long time and then be deported. After much discussion, it is decided that the girl should live with them. After all, the baby is most likely one of theirs.

It is a difficult five months. She sleeps on the couch in the front room of the four-room house. School is out of the question. She doesn't want anyone to know, and Santiago has convinced her that anyone just looking at her will know. She doesn't leave the house alone. It's as if she's in hiding. Santiago has told her several times that if the police see her on the street in the daytime, she will end up in the young people's jail. She spends her days reading comic books and romance magazines and listening to romance serials on the radio. She's certain that if Helen Trent can find romance after thirty-five, there is plenty of time for her after the baby comes. But there are only so many romance stories she can read and listen to, and the days drag by slowly.

Twice she has tried to return to her mother's house but each time her mother has yelled, "Out! Out! Get out of here before I call the police! How dare you come back to my house with that load of shit that you're carrying in your belly! Get out! Out!" Neither time does Mama ask for the boy's name.

Angie only leaves the Filipino house after dark—and then only to go to Chinatown with two Filipinos walking behind her but keeping enough of a distance so that no one can associate them with her. When she asks Santiago why they do this, he answers, "Just to be safe."

"Safe from what?"

"Just to be safe."

Six days a week Angie has the house to herself. Every morning except Sunday, the men leave before sunrise and return after dark. She can sleep as late as she wants, do whatever she wants in the house, and need not deal with the Filipinos at all. But loneliness gets the best of her, and most days she waits to eat dinner with them and talk to them afterward. At times she senses a hostility on their part that she can't understand. There is some grumbling among them that because she is living there now and receiving free room and board, she should drastically reduce her Sunday rates or not charge at all. Santiago is quick to refute this. "I've talked to her about your feelings," he tells them—although he hasn't. "And she told me that she won't do it for less, that she would rather go back to her mother's and you all know what could happen then." There is no reduction in her rate.

By the seventh month, the men are hurting her so she stops. The men are quick to raise it with Santiago. "We're not getting anything on Sundays anymore, and she's living here for free and eating our food. The way we see it is that we should at least be charging her something. She's made a lot of money off us. We haven't seen her spend any of it. She should be paying us something."

Santiago has his eye on the future. In three or four months she'll be able to work again. "Why should she pay to stay here when she can live with her mother for free? She doesn't want to because then she'll have to tell who the fathers are. Is that what you want?"

The baby is born on a cold, foggy December night. Before that, Santiago has looked frantically and desperately for a midwife. He finds one two weeks before the birth on a ranch near Dinuba. He pays her the unheard sum of fifty dollars on the condition that she not breathe a word of this to anyone. When the old woman comes to the house, the only thing she says to them is, "I want you all to stay in the kitchen until I tell you to come out, and that could be tomorrow."

When they hear the baby's first cries, the mood in the kitchen changes dramatically. They jump for joy. Their baby is born. Gone is the dread, fear, and sense of inconvenience they had worn just moments before. Hearing their reaction, Angie decides to name the baby girl "Elena" for the mothers of two of the men and the sister of another.

The men love the baby. She is the first thing they go to when they come home from work. They hold her, they kiss her, they jostle her. They argue among themselves that whoever happens to be holding the baby is not holding her correctly or has been holding her too long—that others would like to hold her every bit as much. Each thinks, and even says aloud, that the baby looks like him or someone in his family. They argue about this too until someone points out that since they were all with Angie on the Sunday that the baby was conceived, the baby logically has to favor every one of them or someone in their families. One thing is sure—she is a Filipina girl. Her nose and her skin and her eyes and her mouth and her hair. She is one of them. She is theirs. She is one of the many women and girls they left behind in the islands.

Within days of the infant's birth, they say that the baby and her mother need their own room, their own bedroom. They move two of the three beds out of the smaller bedroom into the front room, leaving one of the beds for the mother. One of the men sleeps on the couch. They buy a crib and a cradle and a bathinette. They buy clothes and booties and blankets for the infant.

In their exuberance over the baby, Angie begins slipping out of the house some nights when they come home from work. When they complain that the baby needs her mother, Santiago is quick to defend her. "What do you care if she goes out for an hour or so at night? She's been with the baby all day. She needs a break. We're the fathers. We should be with the baby some of the time. Besides, she's not pregnant. No cop is going to stop her now. And don't forget Sunday afternoons. She says she'll be ready in two Sundays. And have you noticed how much more like a woman she looks like now?"

Angie has noticed. Not so much in the bathroom mirror but rather in the way men look at her when she walks down the street. Those are not the looks they used to give her. She is buying clothes now, not only in Chinatown but downtown, clothes that fit her, show her off. Men's eyes tell her that she is a full-fledged woman. And she loves it.

She begins going to dances. Saturday nights at the Palomar and Sunday nights at the Rainbow. The baby is in good hands. She is looking for romance. She soon learns that she can have as many men as she wants every night of the week. But she chooses only those where there is a chance of romance. Except for that hour on Sunday afternoon, she can sleep off Saturday night and be fresh Sunday night. On Mondays she sleeps whenever the baby sleeps and sometimes when she doesn't sleep. The Filipinos' lust for her ripe body is greater than ever, which makes them more timid and compliant. Whenever there is a chance of romance, she invites whoever that young man might be to her home during the day while the Filipinos are at work. But romance never blossoms. The only thing young men are interested in is sex. At least a few of the older Filipinos show some care for her.

Still she continues her Saturday- and Sunday-night searches until she is pregnant again. When she discovers this pregnancy, she tells the Filipinos that it is their child. She plods on with her search until one of the other girls at the dances says to her, "Honey, we can see the baby moving. Don't you think it's about time you started staying home."

She has another girl whom she names "Fifi"—after the heroine in one of her romance magazines. The Filipinos are beside themselves with happiness until the police swoop in and jail all of them and place the infants in the county shelter and Angie in Juvenile Hall.

There are several attempts to place Angie in a foster home, but she is incorrigible—sneaking out, jumping out, breaking out of her room to go to Saturday- and Sunday-night dances. Finally she is committed to the Juvenile Hall itself where she remains until she is seventeen. Released to her mother's custody, she remains in that custody until they have walked three blocks from Juvenile Hall. Alone and with no visible means of support, she turns to the only work she knows—full-time whore at the Valley Rooms— hoping that there she might meet him at last.

X

THE GUADALUPANA is a huge success. The church has never looked better. It has become a social center. There have never been so many church-related activities. The success of that organization is attributable to the hard work and ideas of Jesusita González. No one questions that.

The Guadalupana spends half the day on Saturday readying the church for Sunday services. They meet every Sunday afternoon in the church. They have held jamaicas and games of chance on the church premises to raise funds for the purchase of religious paintings and statues and for the repainting and decoration of the church. Jesusita has limited the membership to ten, saying that a greater number is unruly. There have been mumbles of resentment and envy from those excluded, but never loud enough to challenge the respected one.

And she is respected. Some even consider her saintly. The incredible devotion she has for daily Mass and Holy Communion after working until midnight five nights a week and raising four kids is proof enough of her closeness to God. Then too, there is the absolute confidence and reliance Padre Montes has in her, confiding in and consulting with her on almost everything that concerns the church. But not everyone likes her or is willing to call her saintly. Her fierce determination, discipline, and energy can intimidate. With the exception of Padre Montes, she has allowed no one to become close to her. She can be brusque and demeaning and too often a course of action has to be her way or no way at all.

Still, she has heard the whispers and words of others. The words have been repeated so often, that before long she begins to give them credence. *Maybe I am a saint.* And at other times: *I am a saint.* The few times others disagree or oppose her, she has reasoned that it has to be difficult for the average lay person to understand the ways of a saint.

She finds it beneficial to cultivate that image. She lets it be known that given her rising responsibilities in the cleaning of office buildings, she is the last to leave work, usually after 12:30 in the morning. Then she must walk from downtown to her home on the west side, Fresno's high crime area, at one point passing through the unlit area of loading docks, storage plants, and the tracks of the Southern Pacific Railroad. When asked if she's afraid, her answer is always the same, "Trust in God and may His Will be done." She makes it clear that on those nights she sleeps at most four and a half hours and yet is unfailingly at the 6:00 Mass and Communion later that morning. She has taken to wearing all black at the weekday Masses. Nor is it odd for her to enter the church on some mornings, when others are in attendance as there sometimes are now, and crawl on her hands and knees from the doors of the church to the front pew, apparently as saints have been known to do. She fasts every other weekend, drinking only water on those Saturdays and Sundays. She has twice collapsed, and members of the Guadalupana have explained away some of her strange behavior at the Sunday meetings because of the fasts.

Her weekly Saturday confessions always begin with, "Bless me, Padre, for I have sinned. It has been a week since my last confession." From there she recites one or two trivial transgressions that she has committed during the week. "I became very angry with one of my workers for her sloppy work and shouted at her in front of the other workers."

"That is probably not a sin, my child. In certain circumstances anger may be wholly justified."

Or, "Coming home from work on Wednesday night as I was

crossing the tracks, I heard a man coming up closer and closer behind me. I prayed and prayed but the man got closer and closer. I became very frightened and for several moments I lost complete faith in God. I despaired. And I've heard you say that despair is one of the great sins."

"Did the man harm you?"

"No."

"Did he disturb you in any way?"

"No, he turned off once we passed the tracks."

"That is not a sin, nor is it despair, my child. That is a reasonable fear, and fear is a human emotion. Most anyone in that situation would have been fearful."

Or, "This morning I committed the sin of sloth. As we were cleaning the church, I assigned all the work to the other members, and I went down to the sacristy and hid and rested."

"My child, given all you do for this church and the parish, you deserve to rest. What you did this morning is not a sin. You are striving for perfection. That is admirable. But as I've told you many times, we are human beings and by nature not perfect. Even the saints, when they were on this earth, were not perfect. Think of Mary Magdalen. Go in peace and may God bless you."

BUT THEN, there is Paulina.

Jesusita never talks about Paulina, never mentions her. To avoid talking about her, she never talks about any of her children. When the other women talk about their children, she is quick to move the meeting to church matters. The other women are not offended. They understand that Jesusita's undying commitment is to God and His Church. Once a member asked pointedly about Paulina. "Your daughter, Paulina? My son is in her class. He says she's always absent. I hope there's nothing seriously wrong with her."

She has the answer ready. She has repeated it to herself many times. She has kept Paulina out of school many times because of the welts and bruises the beatings have caused. In the campo she had heard of a father who was jailed and the kids taken away from him and the mother because a teacher had reported a student's condition to the police after a parental beating. "Oh, no. She's always been a sick, frail child. Just growing pains."

"Have you taken her to the doctor?"

"Yes, before we came to Fresno. He said the same thing—growing pains. He said she should be fine once she stops growing."

She doesn't know what to do with Paulina. The girl is always taunting her. It's as if she wants to be beaten. She avoids looking at the girl because more often than not, the girl will return her look with one of hate. She avoids giving the girl chores. The slow, deliberate, slipshod way she does them too often leads to a confrontation and a beating. She would avoid giving her chores altogether except that the other kids are very aware of how few she now gives Paulina. To give her none would show the others that Paulina has won, beaten her in her own way, and, worse, let them think that she might be afraid of Paulina.

In fact, she is afraid of Paulina. It is no longer a hint. It is real. Something that she can no longer hide from herself. But she can't let the others see. Afraid, especially since the story has been circulating about in the community for the past few weeks about that thirteen-year-old girl in Selma who set her house on fire while her mother was sleeping. This is something that she wouldn't put past Paulina. She hopes that Paulina hasn't heard the story, but there is no way she couldn't have. Still, none of the kids, not even Paulina, have mentioned it. Yes, but none of the other three would dare mention it in her presence. Why then hasn't Paulina? Probably because Paulina thinks that to do so will only put her on notice—on guard against the fire that Paulina has already planned. As it is, Jesusita has slept badly for the past two weeks.

At other times, Jesusita is convinced that Paulina is possessed by the devil, that God has permitted the devil to enter the girl's body to test Jesusita's commitment to Him. The lives of the saints are replete with tests, obstacles that God has placed in their path to Him. This is God's will. It's happening. He's permitting it to happen. But she has not heard of any saint having to deal with

Satan himself. She doesn't know what to do. How can she tell anyone that she, Jesusita González, has a daughter who is possessed
by the devil? She asks Padre if there are still people who are possessed by the devil.

"Oh yes, by all means. Do you know of anyone or have you heard
of anyone like that?"

"No, Padre. I only ask because some time ago you talked about
people who had been possessed by the devil, and it made me wonder if those things still happened."

"Yes they do, and Mother Church has definite, proven ways of
chasing the devil from those poor unfortunate people."

"Do you do that?"

"Yes, I can."

"How do you do it?"

"First of all there have to be certain things that are happening
to the possessed person or that the person is doing. Those things
have to be reported to the priest. If that person lived in this parish,
then to me."

She stops listening. What would she tell him? That Paulina
looks at her with hate, won't do what she says, and that she beats
her? If those that didn't like her heard that, they would laugh. She
could just hear them. "Saint Jesusita says she has a daughter who
is possessed by the devil just because she hates her and won't do
what she says. Can you believe that?"

"THE TRUANT officer came this morning," Juanita says.

"What's a truant officer?" Jesusita asks. They are at the door in
the kitchen.

"He's the police for kids that don't go to school. He wanted to
talk to you."

"Talk to me? About what?"

"About Paulina. He was saying that she misses a lot of school."

"What did you tell him?"

"I thought you might be sleeping so I told him you weren't here.
They all think you live with me. It's the same address. Not too

many people know about this place in the back."

"What did he say?"

"He started asking me about Paulina."

Jesusita puts her hands up in a jerking motion and looks at the closed bedroom door. "Shhh! She's not feeling too good. She's probably asleep. Let's go into the kitchen and talk." They step into the kitchen and she closes the door behind them and says, "So what was he asking you about Paulina?"

"He wanted to know if Paulina was here and if I knew why she was missing so much school."

"What did you tell him?"

"I don't like to tell the gringo police nothing. Especially the gringo police that wear suits. So I acted like I didn't know too much English and didn't know what he was saying."

"What did he do then?"

"He left but he said that he would be back. You wait and see, he'll come back with that Charley Montemayor who thinks he's so much better than us because he talks a lot of English and the police always use him to trap us."

"Did he say when he would be back?"

"No, he didn't. But he'll be back with that Montemayor stooge, you watch. And this time I'm going to have to tell him where you live."

"I know. I know. But what do they do when a kid has missed a lot of school?"

"Well, when my kids were still living here, I had a lot of problems with my youngest son, Christian. He would never go to school. He wasn't like Paulina, sick at home all the time. No, he would say that he was going to school, leave, but never go to school. They finally caught him—that same guy that came this morning, that guy in a suit, and they took him downtown to the jail for kids. He was there for three weeks. I had to go to court with him, and the judge kept asking me stuff through that Montemayor guy, about why he didn't go to school. And I kept telling him that I didn't know, that he was leaving the house every day saying that he was going to school but never went. They finally turned him loose, and he still didn't go to school. After that, I think they just gave up on him. Because they never came to the house again and they never bothered me again."

"When your boy was in jail, did he wear his own clothes or jail clothes?"

"What a silly question. Why do you want to know that?"

"I'm just curious. Did he?"

"He had to wear jail clothes just like the other kids."

"Oh." If they take Paulina down there now, the bruises and welts will still be there and they will see them.

THE TRUANT officer returns early the next morning, just as Juanita said he would, with Charley Montemayor. This time they come to the back door. Jesusita watches them from behind the curtain, the big white man in a black suit, tie, and hat and the little, fat Mexican with a sport coat and slacks. The white man knocks hard and then harder. The little Mexican is shifting his weight from foot to foot all the while mumbling something to the white man who keeps nodding as he knocks. She is scared, but angry too at being scared in her own house by strangers. More scared than angry. The knocks are now a pounding, and she worries that Paulina might open the window in her room and tell them that they are there. And what will she do then? Beat her some more? No, the beatings have to stop. As soon as the bruises disappear, Paulina has to go back to school—the sooner the better.

The two start toward the window. She drops down on the floor beneath the window and stretches out against the wall. They're standing above her at the window talking in English. She can catch a few words but not enough to understand. They are trying to look through the curtain.

Even if they do see anything, they won't see her on the floor. She hopes that the shade in the bedroom is down. She has told the kids over and over again to keep it down. But it would be just like Paulina to pull it up when she heard the knocking and the talking. She hears them moving toward the other window and she holds her breath. But in a few moments, they come back and leave.

She is still scared. She knows they'll be back soon, and the bruises will still be there. It will be days before she can let them see Paulina. If they drag her and Paulina down to court before then, everybody will know about the beatings. And those that don't like her, that are jealous of her, will be happy. "Saint who!" they will shout. If they come back in the afternoon after all the kids are home from school, how will she keep all of them quiet? And how long will Paulina keep quiet?

They return in early afternoon, just minutes after Concepcion has come home from school. Concepcion has said several times that she is really hungry, and Jesusita is about to go into the kitchen to fix her a taco when there is a knock on the door. They have come quietly, taken her by surprise. She cups the girl's mouth with one hand, lifts the child, and goes to the window where she again lies on the floor, pressed against the wall with the gagged child.

The knock becomes a pounding after a minute or two goes unanswered. It is Charley Montemayor who speaks in loud Spanish. "We know you're in there, señora, and we think the girl's in there, too. We need to talk to the girl and to you too. All we want to know is why she's not going to school. It's not like we're going to take you and the girl to jail. We just want the girl back in school."

She doesn't answer and waits with dread knowing that Paulina will answer. But the girl doesn't answer.

"Alright, if you and the girl don't present yourselves down at the Juvenile Center at L and Tulare Streets by 4:00 tomorrow afternoon, the next time we come, we won't knock. We'll have the police with us and they'll kick the door down and we'll take both of you down to the Juvenile Center ourselves."

SHE WAITS for Padre Montes the next morning after Mass. She is still in the pew as he approaches.

"What is it, my dear? I could tell all during the Mass that something is bothering you."

She is near tears. "Padre, I need to talk to you."

"Of course. Let's go outside."

"No, no. Can't we just talk here? There's nobody here."

"What is it, my dear?"

The tears start. "I think you know, Padre, how much I love my children and that I've tried very hard to be a good mother."

"Everyone knows that. There can be no doubt about that."

"Paulina, my thirteen-year-old, is a very sickly child. I know I've already mentioned that to you. Before we came here, I took her to the doctor and he said she would always be frail and sickly. I keep her at home when she is sick—which has been a lot lately. And now..."

He has nothing but admiration and respect for this hardworking woman who is as close to God as anyone he knows. He listens and watches with great empathy. At one point, he asks himself, *Lord, God, how much more can you want from this poor woman?* Her account of the truant officer and Charley Montemayor offends him.

"...I can't take her down today like I'm supposed to, Padre, because she's been very sick. Maybe next week, but not today."

"Do you know this Charley Montemayor?"

"No, Padre. I've never seen him in church."

"He's one of the few who doesn't come to church. I think he thinks he's risen above us. But his mother and wife come to church. I will speak to them, and I will also speak to Father Reilly, the pastor of Good Shepherd Church. He may know someone who can help."

The next morning before Mass he steps out from behind the altar and goes to the front row of the otherwise empty church and says, "There is no need to be worrying about the truant officer or Mr. Montemayor. Nobody will be breaking down your door. The matter has been taken care of. But try to get the girl to school as much as you can."

"Oh, yes, Padre."

Paulina returns to school the following week. When she comes home from school that first day, Jesusita has instituted a new rule.

Whenever Jesusita is home, Paulina is to remain in the bedroom with the door closed. Whenever Jesusita leaves the house for work or for any other reason, the girl is free to move about the two rooms and the yard. It is the only way, Jesusita believes, that she can make it to May without any further beatings and without the school learning about the beatings. Come May, and the earlier in May the better, they will leave for the harvest in the southern part of the state. There she will work Paulina to the bone. All the girl will want to do when they meet at the end of the day is eat and sleep. She won't have the energy or the desire to taunt her.

But she taunts her still. Every time someone opens the door to the bedroom, it seems like Paulina is standing there with that look of hate until Jesusita turns away. And she is quick to turn away and stay turned away. Then too, Paulina says that she has to leave the bedroom to go to the bathroom at least five times a day. She's tempted to use the bedpan again, but the stench is too strong and somehow seeps into the other room as well. Worse, every now and then a Guadalupana member finds some excuse to come knocking at her door. No, the stench is too noticeable. So she keeps her back turned, letting the others see that their sister has done to her what none of them can do. And Paulina stretches those trips out of the bedroom for as long as she can, finding every reason or distraction to stay out of the bedroom. It is almost as if Paulina has guessed that she can't hit her, won't hit, her while school is on. With the girl's fourth or fifth trip to the bathroom on any given day, Jesusita, with her back turned, feels ready to explode. The new rule will never get her to May. Then Sergio mentions that in two weeks there will be a ten-day break between semesters. Jesusita begins to wait and think and plan.

It is the Friday afternoon after the semester has ended. One by one they come home from school. They will not have to return to school until a week from Tuesday. She knows that Juanita will be leaving for work at 3:40. She waits. At 3:45 she goes into the kitchen and calls, "Juanita! Juanita!" Juanita is gone. She goes back into her room and locks the kitchen door. She calls everyone, except Paulina, into that room. She tells them that they are to wait outside until she says they can come in. Looks of apprehension abound. The two older ones know, and the younger one senses it. They go outside and she locks the door behind them. She sits at the table with her back turned to the bedroom door and waits. Paulina has yet to come out. Usually by now she has come out of the bedroom at least twice to go to the bathroom. Paulina knows. She waits.

She has the belt rolled up and tucked under her sweater at the waist. The longer she waits, the more she shakes with spasms of nerves. She could easily go into the bedroom and begin, but she would rather wait. She'd rather have Paulina saunter out of that room, nonchalantly, as she has for weeks now and say in that surly voice with those hate-filled eyes, "I have to go to the bathroom." Repeating it once, twice as she stands behind her, mocking her until she forces a "Go!" An acknowledgment from the back-turned woman. No, she would rather wait until the girl comes out in that same mocking manner. Then she will give the girl an aborted trip to the bathroom that she will never forget.

Twenty minutes pass. Thirty minutes. She knows. She has to know. Forty minutes. She may have to go in there. It's getting colder outside. Soon it will start to get dark. Soon Concepcion will start howling that she wants to come in. She grits her teeth to stop the shaking and is about to go in the room, when she hears the door to the bedroom open. This time there are three quick steps and a hurried, "I have to go to the bathroom."

"What?" without turning.

"I have to go to the bathroom."

"I can't hear you. Come closer."

The girl doesn't move, doesn't answer.

"I said, come closer."

She hears feet shuffle and then turns, springs, and, before the girl can react, the belt comes thrashing down on her neck and shoulder. The girl hunches and the next blow lashes across her back.

"You want to go to the bathroom! I'll show you how to go to the bathroom!"

The girl turns and runs, and the woman follows swinging—hitting as often as she misses. The girl throws herself into a corner of the bedroom and curls herself into a ball. Now with a stationary target the woman does not miss. She catapults every ounce of force that she has into each blow. The girl cries and screams in pain. Outside Concepcion wails. Yolanda runs to the bathroom window and screams, "Stop, Mama! You'll kill her! Stop, Mama!"

It is Yolanda's screams that register, that tell her that the neighbors will hear or have already heard, that she has to get them inside to stop their screaming. She runs to the door and pulls on it. It doesn't open. She unlocks it and, barber belt in hand, hisses, "Get in here! Get in here! And stop your screaming unless you want some of this too!"

The next morning she slips into the bedroom and close enough to Paulina's bed, without awakening anyone, to see that the welts and bruises on the girl's legs and shoulder and neck are big and widespread with deeper shades of yellow, purple, and red. At the edge of her ribs is a long line of dried blood. Never has the girl bruised so badly, and never before has she broken the skin. She worries that the welts and bruising won't be gone by a week from Tuesday.

Maybe the girl has learned her lesson. Because in the days that follow, before the dreaded Tuesday, whenever the girl leaves the bedroom, it is with Yolanda. And it is Yolanda who speaks, who says, "Mama, Paulina needs to go to the bathroom." The first two times she turns and sees that it is Yolanda who is looking at her, that Paulina's head and eyes are downcast. Thereafter she no longer turns to the bedroom door when she hears it. And thereafter Paulina no longer looks at her when she comes out of the bedroom. Maybe she has learned her lesson.

The awaited Tuesday arrives. The bruises and what are now marks are still visible. She tells Yolanda to dress her sister in Yolanda's turtleneck sweater and long blue dress. As they are all leaving,

Jesusita stops them at the door and reminds them, but now more sternly than ever, that if any of them mention anything to anyone about the punishment she has been forced to give Paulina that they will first answer to her, and then the police will come and send them all back to Mexico. In Mexico, she will never be able to earn enough to keep them together and they will each have to go their separate way.

AT SCHOOL, the teacher leans over Paulina's desk and quietly asks, "Are you feeling alright, Paulina?" The girl does not look at her but nods several small nods. "You're not sick today?" The girl hesitates and, again without looking, shakes her head. "Good." She fights back tears until the teacher leaves. She wants badly to tell and show. But the fear of being in Mexico, trying to survive alone, is too great.

At church on Sunday after Mass, she and Yolanda and Concepcion are standing near the sidewalk waiting for their mother who is busy on the church steps talking to a group of women who have surrounded her. Only Padre Montes has more people crowding around him. The women are a happy group, and Paulina watches as her mother laughs and talks and turns from one woman to the next.

An old woman approaches and excitedly says, "Oh, you girls are so lucky to have the mother you have! The woman's a saint! Her place in heaven has already been reserved for her, and for you too. Because I'm certain she'll take you with her. What I would have given, as a girl, to have had a mother like yours."

Now for the first time in years, Paulina is afraid of her mother. The pleasure she derived from taunting and daring her mother, of watching her lose control, has been submerged in fear. It was that moment when her mother turned on her in the kitchen. The look on her mother's face was unlike all those other times she had lost control. The rage as great, or greater, than any she had ever seen or felt. Her eyes were set upon destroying her. She had run from her as never before. Crouched in the corner of the bedroom, she had heard the deep, gasping breaths before the blows and the grunts that came with the blows. Blows that had hurt as never before. She would have killed her had it not been for Yolanda's screams. Now as she stands there on that Sunday morning, watching her mother charming the women on the steps, she asks herself again and again, *How is it possible that no one, except me and my siblings, cannot know who this woman really is?*

Once school begins, it is understood, although no one has said as much, that Paulina is free to come and go as she pleases in the two-room home. But now, whenever Jesusita is home, she stays in the bedroom of her own accord with, as often as not, the door closed. When she comes out of the bedroom to use the bathroom, she never looks at her mother. She keeps her eyes averted when Jesusita speaks to her and answers in a subservient, deferential tone. A few times when she has somehow said something that has annoyed or offended Jesusita, the woman is quick to say, "Let me remind you, Paulina, that Easter vacation is just a few weeks away."

JUST AFTER Easter vacation, Mr. Jim offers Jesusita the position of head cleaning woman at the office buildings. It is a steady, year-round job that would pay her far more than she could earn in the campo. But it will not pay her nearly what the family as a unit could earn during those months. She is about to refuse the offer when Pedro Rodríguez suggests that Sergio, Yolanda, and Paulina can accompany them through the harvest season. "They are old enough," he says, "and able to match many of the adult efforts. They will only have to pay for food. Other than that, whatever they earn is theirs."

Jesusita likes the idea. It will mean a considerable increase in the family income and, just as importantly, she will be free of Paulina for six months. While there are no longer the looks of hate, the hate is still there and it is an awful unspoken burden for a mother to carry around. At times the girl's subservient manner underscores the hate more than ever. She knows that any effort to humor the girl will change nothing.

They leave on May 2nd. They will not return until the end of October. The little car is crammed with possessions and there is a three-foot stack tied down on the roof. Luisa and Pedro are already in the car. Jesusita is standing on the footpath in front of Juanita's house, facing the car with Concepcion at her side. Sergio, Yolanda, and Paulina are on the other side of the footpath with their backs to the car. Jesusita looks at Sergio and opens her arms. He takes two steps toward her and she hugs him and says, "Take care of yourself and your sisters, mijo. This is your little family now. I'm putting you in charge. And you girls, obey him! Hear!" Then Yolanda comes forward and she hugs her and says, "I'm going to miss you so much, mija. Take care of yourself." She looks at Paulina and opens her arms, but the girl looks down and doesn't move. She glances at the front of the car and isn't sure if Pedro or Luisa have noticed. She moves across the footpath and hugs Paulina. The girl stiffens and the mother hugs her tighter and then kisses her on the cheek. The girl pulls her head away. The mother's lips follow and she kisses the girl again, this time whispering, "I love you, Paulina. You have to believe me, I love you." The girl tilts her head even further, so that her opposite cheek is touching her shoulder. Embarrassed, Jesusita straightens herself and steps back across the footpath glancing again at the front of the car as she does. Luisa couldn't have seen and Pedro is looking straight ahead. Maybe they didn't see. But whether they did or didn't, it is the hug that she will never forget.

WITH ONLY Concepcion to care for, she is able to put more time and effort into church activities, and her stature continues to grow. After Mass on Sunday the number of people seeking her out at least matches those who want to talk to Padre Montes. Her daily devotion to God is recognized everywhere. It has been said that she is waiting only until her children are grown to die and take her rightful place in heaven next to God. She is so admired and respected that when an old couple decide to return to Mexico to die, they offer to rent her their house.

It is an old but well-kept house with three bedrooms, a living and dining room, a kitchen, and a bathroom, and it is a block closer to the church. When she sees it, she wants it. Besides the wonder of the space, Paulina also comes to mind. The back bedroom has two doors, one that opens onto the bathroom and one that opens onto the kitchen. She would put Paulina and Yolanda in that bedroom. Sergio will soon be eighteen and deserves his own room which will be the middle bedroom. She and Concepcion will take the front bedroom. The living room and dining room will be used primarily for Guadalupana activities. She will see Paulina mainly at meals, and, given her work schedule, those will be few. But there is the sobering matter of rent.

"I like it very much, señora, but I'm not sure I can afford it."

"How much are you paying Juanita?" the woman asks.

"Twenty dollars a month."

"You can have it for that."

"No!"

"Yes. You have done so much for the church and are so close to God that I want you to have it."

It is the 28th of October. The little car seems to be loaded down with even more possessions than before. Jesusita watches from behind a curtained window. Sergio and Pedro have gotten out and are beginning to untie the things that are crammed on the roof. Sergio is darker and he seems bigger. Yolanda gets out and stretches. She too is darker but otherwise appears to be the same. Another girl, or young woman, gets out of the car on the other side, and Jesusita wonders who she is and how Pedro got four persons into the backseat of that little car. She's been watching for Paulina, but Paulina doesn't get out. And she thinks that it's just like Paulina to stay in the car, to show Pedro and Luisa that she doesn't want to get out, that she doesn't want to be with her mother anymore. Who knows what she has told them about her over the summer? It doesn't matter. No one will believe her. Everyone knows how close she is to God. Still, Paulina won't come out of the car. How embarrassing. She doesn't dare go out on the front porch.

Then she sees that the young woman is Paulina. She looks again. It is Paulina—three to four inches taller and many pounds heavier and now with the body of a woman. She hurries out onto the front porch with Concepcion trailing behind her. Paulina has changed so much. Maybe the hate has gone too. For one brief step, one brief moment, she starts toward Paulina but goes instead to Sergio with open arms. She hugs him and tells him how happy she is to see him and how much she has missed him, but she is thinking of Paulina, wary of Paulina, hoping. She turns to Yolanda and hugs her too and repeats what she has just said to Sergio. But her eyes are on Paulina. She is a big, beautiful girl-woman. Has the change included the hate? Then, just as she is about to leave Yolanda, Paulina moves past her, holding Concepcion's hand, and goes into the house. No, nothing has changed.

She sees little of Paulina because Paulina is always in her new room with the door closed. When she calls her out for a meal or a chore, there is often the hope of having some positive contact with her. But she is increasingly and, at times, bitterly disappointed. The girl no longer averts her eyes and they are no longer hate-filled. They are blank, void of emotion. Her voice is flat. The girl speaks to and looks at her mother only when her mother speaks to her—and then it is as if the mother is speaking to a mute or the wall. After two months, Jesusita believes that the girl is slowly driving her crazy, wants to slowly drive her crazy.

One Saturday morning, Jesusita calls Paulina into the kitchen. Paulina answers with that same blank stare. They are alone in the kitchen.

"I want you to cut up this tripe for me."

Paulina looks at her mother for a moment, says nothing, and then starts for the drawer where the knives are kept. As she passes Jesusita, Jesusita lunges at her, grabbing her by the arm with one hand.

"Look at me! Look at me! I'm a person! I'm somebody! Look at me like I'm somebody not like I'm the wall!"

The girl looks at her with that same blank look. Rage seizes Jesusita. "I said...," raising her arm to hit the girl. But Paulina is quick to grab the arm and force it back and downward until the woman cries out in pain. With that same blank look, the girl says, "Don't you ever try to lay a hand on me again. Because if you do, it will be a lot worse than this. Do you understand?"

The woman, bent back and down in pain, looks up at the bigger, stronger girl and with her eyes pleads for forgiveness and for love too. But the girl only stares with that same blank look. Finally Jesusita says, "Yes."

From that moment on, Paulina does as she pleases. Jesusita does not confront her. She is afraid of a scene. She knows that Paulina wants a scene so that she can show the others who really rules in that house. She is sure that Paulina has already bragged to the others about the last scene. She ignores Paulina—or tries to. Yet every time that Paulina comes into the kitchen and she is there, whether alone or with the others, there is an awkward, tense silence. She turns from Paulina, no matter what she might be doing, or leaves the kitchen if the tension becomes too great.

Now Jesusita is harsher, more rigid, controlling, and demanding of the others. The older two are still afraid of her. For them, their size is not relevant. Concepcion has long since learned to tread lightly around Mama and is more frightened than ever when she has done something to incur her wrath. That too changes, if only in appearance, when one afternoon Jesusita is yanking a screaming Concepcion by the hair, pulling her to the kitchen door to show her her muddy footprints, still pulling and now slapping. Paulina rushes from her room shouting, "Stop it! Stop it!" and pushes Jesusita so hard that the woman falls on the floor. To the startled, prostrate woman she warns, "You're not going to do to her what you did to me!" Thereafter Jesusita is careful how and when she disciplines Concepcion.

When Jesusita says, "I want everybody to get in here and start eating. Dinner is getting cold," Paulina waits until everyone is five minutes into their meal before entering the kitchen. When Jesusita names only three for dinner, wanting to blot out Paulina's disobedience, Paulina still enters five minutes later anyway. When Jesusita says that it is cold and everyone should wear a jacket to school, Paulina leaves the house without one. Before Jesusita learns to stop making casual remarks, she might say, "It looks like it's going to be a beautiful day," only to have Paulina say, "I don't think so." Jesusita soon reaches the point where she can only hope for May to come.

EACH SPRING the snowfall in California's majestic Sierra Nevada Mountains melts and roars down into the Central Valley. Before they were dammed, the San Joaquin and Kings were mighty rivers that flowed north and south of Fresno to become smaller and smaller streams that ultimately disappeared in the valley's great western wasteland.

It is the first Sunday in May. The older three will again be leaving for the harvest in Southern California on Tuesday. Jesusita has decided to have a picnic, as many Mexican families do, on the banks of the San Joaquin River just north of Fresno. Sergio has borrowed Pedro Rodríguez's car and drives the family over the steep, windy, bumpy dirt road that leads down to the river. It is Concepcion's first ride in a car, and she is excited. Yolanda has warned Sergio several times to be careful, but it has had no effect on him. Jesusita is sitting in the front passenger seat with Sergio saying nothing during the drive, thinking instead of the other silent presence in the car, Paulina, hoping and wishing that there is some way that she can at least lighten the girl's hatred for her before they leave. When they reach the picnic area, Paulina is the first one out of the car. She kicks off her shoes and runs the remaining thirty yards to the river. None of them can swim and Jesusita wants to yell out for her to be careful but checks herself. She has learned her lesson well. She watches as Paulina pokes her feet into the icy water and jumps back several times. She sees Paulina stand ankle deep in the water, look back at them, and then begin to walk along the river's edge, raising her dress to her knees but wading no deeper than her ankles.

As the others unload, Sergio discovers that the tamales have been left behind. It is assumed that Sergio and Yolanda will have to return to the house to steam and retrieve the tamales. Concepcion jumps up and down, pleading to return to the house too, because today, she says, will be the only chance she will ever have to ride in a car again. Jesusita sees an opportunity to be alone with Paulina and says that of course she can go back with Sergio and Yolanda. After setting up a picnic site, the three leave.

Alone, she watches the girl from the picnic blanket, trying to think of the best way to approach her. But approach her she must. Once the others return, there will be no other chance. Tomorrow is a school day and they will be leaving early Tuesday morning. *Just be nice,* she thinks, *and don't get mad, don't lose your temper. Most people will be nice if you're nice.* She walks slowly, nervously down to the river. The girl doesn't see or hear her coming. When she is a foot behind the girl, she says, "Paulina, we have to talk."

Pauline turns. The river is loud. The look on her face says that she hasn't heard.

She raises her voice. "I said we have to talk."

The girl shakes her head. "I don't want to talk to you."

"Paulina, I'm your mother. We can't go on like this."

"I don't care. Leave me alone."

"I won't leave you alone. We're going to talk." She takes Paulina by the arm. The girl jerks free and moves just far enough into the water so that her mother can't touch her.

Now the mother is angry. "If I have to yell, I'll stay here and yell! We're going to talk!" She steps into the water and again reaches for the girl.

The girl moves farther away. The water is up to her thighs.

The mother inches closer and then lunges at the girl grabbing her arm. "We have to talk! We have to talk!"

The girl pulls free and stumbles.

"I hope you drown!"

Stumbling again, the girl loses her balance, falls, and is swept away.

She sees the girl's head and dress bob up once at mid-river about fifty yards away.

Then the girl is gone.

Sixteen days later and twenty-seven miles away, a hunter comes across Paulina's body at the edge of a stream.

✝ XI

THE SECOND police interrogation is unlike the first. It occurs eight days after the body is found and takes place in the district attorney's office. The first had taken place at the river on the day of the drowning. A lone patrol officer had made his way down to the picnic site long after a crowd had gathered. He had asked the sobbing woman in English what had happened and had to rely on several younger Mexicans, including Sergio, for a translation of her broken, tear-filled account in Spanish. It was what she had said to others several times before and had heard repeated by others to latecomers. She had come to the river with her family for a picnic. After they had set up a site, everyone except she and Paulina had returned to their home to retrieve forgotten tamales. Paulina was wading at the edge of the river. She was sitting on the blanket watching the river and Paulina and from time to time calling out to her to be careful because she couldn't swim. Either Paulina didn't hear her or didn't want to hear her because she kept wading farther and farther out until the water was above her knees. Then all of a sudden Paulina was gone. She hadn't seen her slip or fall. She was just gone. Moments later she thought she saw Paulina's head and dress come up far down in the middle of the river and then disappear.

Those words, that version, made Sergio uncomfortable. There was something about it that puzzled him, that he didn't want to pursue.

When he and Yolanda and Concepcion returned with the tamales, they found their mother flat on her back on the blanket, kicking at it, screaming up to the sky, "No! No! Oh no, no, no! Please God, not this!" Tears were streaking down the sides of her face, matting her hair, and wetting the blanket. Sergio had never seen his mother like this. Yolanda ran to her.

"What is it, Mama? What is it? Tell me!"

It was moments before the woman could spout out, "Paulina! Paulina! Oh, my Paulina!"

"Paulina what, Mama? What did she do to you? Did the two of you fight while we were gone?"

"No, no," shaking her head.

"Tell me what Paulina did. Please, Mama, tell me."

"She drowned. She's gone. She's dead."

"What? Where?"

"In the river."

"Where? Were you there?"

"No, no, no, no."

"Where in the river?"

Jesusita pointed to the river.

Yolanda leaped up. "Oh, my God!" And she ran toward the river, screaming, "Paulina! Paulina!" with Concepcion crying and screaming behind her.

Sergio could see other picnickers standing and staring. He knelt by his mother. "Mama, what happened? Did you and Paulina fight?"

"No. Oh, no, no, no!"

"Were you at the river with her?"

"No, never."

But he had noticed her mud-caked feet. He looked at her feet again. "Did you go down to the river looking for her?"

"No, I never went to the river. I was up here telling her to be careful because she couldn't swim. And then she was gone."

Sergio had never confronted his mother about anything, and he couldn't bring himself to begin then.

When Yolanda returned, several people followed her. As word of the drowning spread, more people came. Kneeling, Yolanda was able to coax a set of facts out of her mother that was to be repeated again and again that afternoon and told to the deputy sheriff that came on the scene. No one challenged those facts. But then, there was no reason to challenge this saintly, church-going mother's account of what had happened. Sergio kept to himself. It was not for him to question his mother openly if he couldn't privately. But when the patrol car drove up and the few remaining onlookers turned to the officer, Sergio took a towel and wiped his mother's feet.

"What are you doing, mijo?"

"I'm cleaning you, Mama."

Within days, Sergio had accepted his own version of the facts: given his mother's distraught condition, she had forgotten or didn't realize that she had gone down to the river looking for the vanished Paulina.

WHEN THE coroner first saw Paulina's badly decomposed body, his thought was that the cause of death was obviously drowning. He planned but a cursory examination of what remained of the body until he saw a series of open lines, wounds maybe, across the back and thighs of the girl. They were too neat and straight to be the work of an animal feasting on a dead body. Instead they appeared to be lines caused by a rope or a wire or even a belt. Probably not inflicted after death. Most likely before death. But when? Just before the drowning? If that were so, then the girl had been the victim of foul play and there was criminality here. He made his suspicions known to the police, who asked themselves, *Had the girl been abducted, assaulted, and tortured before the drowning and then dumped into the river?*

The police called in Charley Montemayor. What had he heard in the Mexican community about the drowning of the González girl? Nothing, other than that she had been swept away by the river when she was wading in it. Had he heard of any other possible eyewitnesses other than the mother? No, not that he knew of. But other Mexican families were picnicking on the river that Sunday. How to reach those families? There was a Spanish-speaking radio program that was broadcast every evening from 6:00 to 6:30 that was listened to by almost all of the Mexican families within a forty-mile radius of Fresno.

FELIPE DOMÍNGUEZ is hunched over a small radio on his bed trying as best he can to listen, over the static, to that Mexican program. He is the caretaker-watchman on a large grape ranch seventeen miles southeast of Fresno. He lives in a ten-by-ten-foot room, which is the base of a water tower forty yards from the main house. The summer heat has already arrived, and he has the sole window and door cracked a few inches to draw what is hopefully cooler air from the outside while keeping out as many flies, gnats, and mosquitoes as possible. In a few minutes the cook will ring the bell on the porch and set his food and drink there.

He is a devoted listener to the half-hour program, and at times, for weeks, it is his only contact with the outside world. He admires the announcer's strong, smooth voice and often imagines him as a handsome, rich man with a wonderful life. The announcer turns to the local news. "The Fresno police are asking that anyone who witnessed the drowning of the daughter of Jesusita González to contact them." He stiffens. Jesusita González. Is that the same woman? He listens intently. "The drowning occurred on Sunday, May the 4th around 2:30 in the afternoon on the San Joaquin River. Anyone with any information is urged to..." He was there. He saw them. "The girl is described as fourteen years old, tall, and appearing..." He thinks back to the bank of the river that Sunday afternoon. He was thirty yards or less away from them. "...is urged to contact the police." If it was the same day and time, and he thinks it was, that must have been the girl that drowned.

He had gone fishing with his nephew and a friend of his nephew's that morning. Early that afternoon, they were leaving. In fact, his nephew and the other man were already up at the car. He had been untangling his line and was gathering his things when he turned and saw Jesusita. It was her. No doubt about it. She was the woman who had ruined his life, driven him out of Fresno. He would never forget that face. She was standing behind the girl who was standing at the river's edge. She was saying something to the girl. She grabbed the girl by the arm, and the girl broke free, a step or two more into the river. She reached for the girl again, but the girl moved deeper into the river. He left then, turned, and went up the hill to the car. He didn't want Jesusita to see him. He was still embarrassed about what had happened at the church. As he thinks about it, he can't tell if they were arguing or playing.

The next morning, his niece, Dolores, comes out to the ranch. "Tío, did you hear on the radio yesterday that the bitch's daughter drowned?"

"Was that her daughter?"

"Oh yeah. She was the middle one."

"I wasn't sure."

"Anyway, Frank and I were talking and we were thinking that you guys were out there right around the time this thing happened. You know, the police are investigating this now, and Frank thinks that means that they're not buying her story. She's been telling everybody that the girl slipped and fell and the river took her and drowned her."

"I didn't know she was saying that...I didn't even know the girl drowned."

"Well, I haven't seen you since before this thing happened. All I had heard was that the girl drowned. I didn't know it was the same day and time that you guys were out there, 'til I heard it on the radio.... Did you see anything, tío?"

"I saw them."

"You did?"

"Yes, I saw them down on the bank of the river."

"Where were you?"

"I was down there too, at the edge of the water, maybe thirty yards from them."

"You keep saying 'them.' Did you see both of them? Were they together?"

"Yes, they were together. I saw both of them."

"You're sure it was the two of them? Because she's told everyone that the girl was wading alone in the water, and she was telling her to be careful from where she was sitting, and the girl must have slipped and was taken by the river and drowned."

"It was her. How can I ever forget that witch? It was her and she was with a girl—I guess the girl that drowned."

"Are you sure?"

"Yes, I'm sure."

"What were you doing down there?"

"We went fishing. We were leaving. They were already up at the car. My line had gotten tangled, so I was still down there getting my stuff together when I saw them."

"What were they doing?"

"The girl was in the water. I mean her feet were in the water and that witch was behind her, right behind her, talking at her. I think loud, but I couldn't hear. She wasn't in the water but she was close enough so that she could reach out and grab the girl, which she did."

"What do you mean 'grab'?"

"She grabbed the girl's arm but the girl broke free and moved a little deeper into the water."

"Then what happened?"

"The witch moved closer to the girl. I don't know if she was in the water or not. Anyway, she reached for the girl again and when she couldn't grab her, she pushed her."

"Pushed her? Are you sure, tío?"

"Yes."

"And they were together at the edge of the river, and the witch, as you keep calling her, wasn't sitting somewhere away from the girl?"

"No, they were together."

"What did the girl do when the witch pushed her?"

"She kind of slipped and then straightened herself."

"Then what happened?"

"I don't know. Because I left then."

"Why?"

"Because I was afraid that she was going to look over and see me. I guess I'm still pretty embarrassed about what happened in Fresno. So I left."

"And this is the truth this time, tío? I mean all of the truth?"

"Yes."

"When Jesusita grabbed her and pushed her, were they playing or what?"

"No, they weren't playing. The witch was mad about something and the girl was trying to get away."

"Could you tell that from where you were standing?"

"Oh, yes."

"You're sure?"

"Yes, I'm sure,"

"And you'll tell this to the police?'

"Yes, I will."

IT IS Charley Montemayor who comes home boasting to his wife, "Well, they got that saint of yours now. The cops have a witness who saw your saint push her daughter into the river just before she drowned."

It is the wife's mother who goes to Padre Montes and tells him, "They're going to arrest her, Padre. They're saying that she drowned her daughter."

It is Padre Montes who whispers to her before Mass begins, as four others in the church watch, "When Mass is over, I want you to go straight home and lock the doors and do not open them for anyone, and I mean anyone, until I've had a chance to talk to you."

"But why, Padre?"

"We can't discuss this here and now. What time do the kids go to school?"

"Seven-thirty."

"I'll be there at 7:35. This is important. Do as I say."

"Yes, Padre."

Jesusita bursts into tears and a series of mournful groans when he tells her. "The police say they have a witness who says that he saw you push Paulina into the river on the day she drowned."

"No! No! No!" is all she can say for several minutes. When she is able to speak, she says, "It's not true, Padre. It's not true."

"I know it's not."

"You have to believe me, Padre. It's not true."

"I believe you."

"Who is it that is saying this?"

"I don't know. The Señora Vargas told me, and her daughter, the wife of Charley Montemayor, told her. Montemayor, I'm sure, got it from the police. But she didn't say who it was that was saying this."

"Since then, I have confessed to you three or four times, Padre. You know that I would have confessed that to you if I had done it, don't you, Padre?"

"Yes. You've always confessed everything to me, and the great majority of the time what you have confessed are not sins."

"And I've gone to Holy Communion every morning since then. Do you think for one moment I would receive Jesus into my body if I was filthy with that sin? I would burn forever in hell if I did that."

"I know. I know. Believe me, I know it's not true."

When he leaves, she leaves with him. Since it happened, she finds it difficult to be alone. Now it will be impossible. She asks if he can unlock the church so that she can visit with God.

"Yes, of course. I'm sorry I brought this news just when it seemed that you were beginning to put all this behind you. But I thought it would be better if you heard it from me before the police came."

"Thank you, Padre." If only he knew what these almost four weeks have been like.

She has kept Sergio and Yolanda with her in Fresno until she can cope with Paulina's death. She hasn't slept much. Every time she tries, she hears the river. It is loud and gets louder and louder. She presses her hands against her ears but she can still hear it. She pulls her pillow over her head but she can still hear it. Then she sees Paulina again, in the river, trying to get away from her. Furious, she screams, "I hope you drown! I hope you drown!" She doesn't touch her, but her voice is her agent. It is angry and evil and damning. Paulina loses her balance and falls. No, it wasn't a touch or a push. It was her voice and all the evil in it. And Paulina is forever gone. She need not be sleeping or trying to sleep to hear the river. She can hear it at any unguarded moment no matter who she's with or where she's at. Anywhere she is, anytime, day or night, she sees Paulina without warning standing in the river, stumbling, falling. It was her voice, but, as God is her witness, she did not intend for that to happen. Twice Mr. Jim has sent her home. "Go, Jessie. Get some rest, get some peace of mind. You're no good to me here. This thing is driving you crazy." And it is. The only place she can find any peace, any calm, is in God's Home, in His Church. Because there she knows that He knows that she never intended what happened. She would gladly cut out her tongue if only she could have those terrible words back.

The following afternoon, Jesusita goes to the rectory. Since the episode with Felipe Domínguez and his niece, she has avoided visiting the rectory. But this can't wait. When Padre Montes answers the door, she entreats him, "They just came, Padre! The police just came to my house with that Montemayor! I have to go to the district attorney's office tomorrow afternoon or they will arrest me. They want to question me. Help me, Padre! Help me!"

Padre Montes goes to Father Reilly who then visits his friend, the district attorney. "John, this woman is considered a saint in her own community. The damage you might do in that community by accusing her of murdering her own daughter might never be repaired."

"But Father, those people don't vote," the district attorney answers, smiling.

"That's not the point, John."

"I was only kidding, Father. What you don't seem to want to accept is that the police have a witness who says that he saw her push the girl into the river. I have to question the woman."

There are concessions made. Padre Montes will be allowed to be present at the questioning. While Charley Montemayor will be the official interpreter, Jesusita will be allowed to bring an interpreter of her own choosing to aid her with any difficulties or misunderstandings she might have with Montemayor's interpretations.

IT IS 12:44 when she comes home from work. She enters through the back door and stands in the kitchen for several moments, listening. She hears nothing. Carefully she takes off her shoes and socks and then plants her bare feet solidly on the old wood floor, feeling for any movement in the house. There is none. She moves cautiously in the darkness, not wanting to wake the girls, avoiding those parts of the floor that will squeak until she reaches Sergio's room. She is mindful to close his door behind her lest Yolanda hears. She shakes him, gently. "Sergio! Sergio!" she whispers. "Sergio!" He groans. "Shhh! Sergio!" More groans. "Sergio!" She shakes him harder.

"What, Mama?"

"Shhh! Be quiet! I don't want to wake the others."

"What is it, Mama?"

"I need you to come to my room."

"For what?"

"Never mind for what. Just come to my room. Now, quietly, and don't turn on any lights. I don't want to wake the others."

She is standing at the door in the darkness when he enters. She closes the door and in a hushed voice says, "We need to talk—but quietly. You know how Concepcion is the next day if she doesn't get her sleep." She takes him by the arm and leads him to her bed. She has decided that it will be easier to talk to him in the darkness. They sit. She says, "The police came here this afternoon."

"For what?"

"They want me to go to the district attorney's office this afternoon."

"Why?"

"To question me."

"About what?"

"They say they have a witness who says that he saw me push your sister into the river before she drowned."

"What?"

"Yes."

They are silent. He feels his heart and his head pounding. Since it happened, he has been able to set aside, if not forget, her mud-caked feet by telling himself that she was too distraught to remember that she had gone down to the river. Yet, unknown to anyone, he has returned to the river, to the place where they were on that Sunday, and gone down to the river, waiting to see when the river's mud will envelop his feet. It happens only when he is at the river's edge. As he sits with his mother in the darkness of the room, he sees her mud-caked feet again and his mud-caked feet, too. And now someone says he saw her push Paulina into the river. His head hurts. He is thankful for the darkness. Somehow he has to return to his room without her seeing the look that has to be on his face.

"I need you to go with me this afternoon."

"Where?"

"To the district attorney's office."

His heart beats faster. He can't go with her. He won't go with her. He won't lie for her. He can't lie for her especially now that someone has seen what she did. "I have to go to school."

"Forget school. This is much more important than school."

"Why me?"

"Because they say that I can bring my own interpreter, and I don't know anybody that speaks English as good as you."

"Yolanda does. She speaks English way better than me. Take her."

"You're eighteen. You're a man. She's a girl. They'll listen to you a lot better than they will her."

"I won't be eighteen for two more weeks, and I don't know how to interpret."

"Yes you do. All you have to do is listen to their interpreter and make sure that he's saying it right."

"Mama, I don't want to..."

"I don't care what you want. You're going with me and that's it."

They sit in silence again. She chides herself for getting angry. She might have woken the others. He repeats to himself that there is no way he can lie for her, especially now. She breaks the silence. "You better get back to bed. Morning will be here soon enough. And remember: You are not to tell anyone, not Yolanda, not anyone, that I had to go to the district attorney's office to talk about your sister. Nor about this crazy who's telling all these lies."

As THEY approach the district attorney's office, Padre Montes says to Jesusita, "You have nothing to worry about, señora. You are innocent. Almighty God knows that. We know that. You have only to speak the truth and this whole nasty affair will end."

She does not hear him. She is thinking, *I have worked so hard just to come to this. As God is my witness, I did not intend for her to fall in the river. But if this witness is a white man, they will never believe me.* She searches those moments at the river again and can't remember seeing anyone near them.

Sergio is thinking, *If I tell the truth, she will go to jail. Then what will we do? Concepcion is so young.*

When they enter the office, the woman behind the desk looks up startled. Padre Montes smiles and says, "Hello," but that doesn't change her look. *She must know,* Sergio thinks. It doesn't matter what he or Mama or anybody says, *Mama isn't going home with us today.*

For Jesusita, she has entered offices thousands of times. But never like this. This is where her life as she knows it will end.

"Can I help you," the woman says uneasily.

Padre Montes steps forward and is about to speak and then thinks better of it and turns back and says, "Sergio." The woman's attention shifts to Sergio, and she repeats, "Can I help you?" Sergio looks to either side before fully accepting that he must speak. "My mother's supposed to..."

"I'm sorry, I can't hear you. You'll have to speak up."

He moves closer. "My mother's supposed to talk to the police or somebody here."

"What is your mother's name?"

"Jesusita González."

"Again, please?"

"Jesusita González."

"And who is she to see?"

Sergio looks around him as if hoping to find a name until Padre Montes says, "Meester Toe Mass."

"Alright, have a seat. I'll let Mr. Thomas know you're here."

As they wait, people that work there come and go, many giving them quizzical looks. Sergio sees how clean and well-dressed those people are. It makes the shabby, soiled clothes that he and his mother are wearing seem even shabbier and more soiled. Under her blouse, Jesusita is fingering her rosary. Her lips have begun that tiny, almost imperceptible movement. Praying, talking to God is the only way she's going to get through this.

A pleasant, red-faced, white-haired man opens another door, smiles, and standing half-way in a hallway says, "Father Montes, Mrs. González and...and..."

"Sergio González," Padre Montes adds.

"I'm John Thomas. Will you please come with me?"

Jesusita pinches her rosary bead harder. Sergio doesn't trust the man. *Yet he is the first person who smiled at them, and the smile seemed real. But if it was real, what are they doing here?*

They follow the man down a dark hallway. Padre Montes is mindful of Father Reilly's words. "John Thomas is a good man, Padre. He's honest and fair. He's a Catholic, and his wife is, too." Jesusita wipes the sweat from her brow with her free hand and talks directly but silently to God: *Help me, dear God, help me. You know I'm innocent, you know I never intended this to happen.* Sergio is wondering how he would ever be able to find his way out of this place.

They enter a long, bare, narrow, well-lit room. Windows take up much of the opposite wall, and a long, narrow table with several chairs take up much of the space. Three men stand when they enter, two on the opposite side of the table and one at the end of the table. John Thomas motions the three in Jesusita's party to take seats on their side of the table and then moves around the table to stand between two of the men. "Why don't we all have a seat and then let everybody introduce themselves." He gestures with an open hand to the man on his left—"I'm Sheriff Fred Williams." To the man on his right—"I'm Deputy Sheriff Paul Summers." To the man at the head of the table—"I'm Charley Montemayor, the interpreter."

"I've already introduced myself. So, why don't we start with you, Mrs. González?"

She has heard those words and Montemayor's interpretation, but they have meant nothing to her. She sits mute. She is there and not there. Sergio leans over to her and says, "Mama, they want you to say your name." Neither do those words register. Padre Montes tries. No response. Sergio pleads a second time. Nothing. They wait. She sits motionless, her eyes fixed at mid-table.

John Thomas says, "Mrs. González, as I see it, you have two options. You can cooperate with us and answer my questions and go home with your son and Padre Montes once this interview is completed. Or, we can keep you here next door for however long it takes for you to decide that you will answer my questions. This is an investigation and only an investigation at this time. I won't be making a decision on how to act until I have examined all the facts in this case. I have at least one other witness to interview before I do anything."

Montemayor adds "in the jail" to "next door," but Jesusita just sits and stares.

John Thomas tries again. "Gentlemen, why don't the four of us step outside for a few minutes and give the Father here and her son a chance to more carefully explain to Mrs. González, in a more relaxed way, what her options are."

They leave. Sergio leans over and puts his arm around Jesusita's shoulder and says, "Mama, look at me. Please look at me." She turns. There are tears in his eyes. She does what she has not done for too long to remember. She reaches up and touches his hand and strokes it and nods. "Mama, we need you at home. Concepcion is still little. She really needs you. Yolanda and I need you. What will we do without you? It won't be our home anymore. Please answer his questions. Please." She is no longer nodding but she continues to stroke the back of his hand. She says nothing, just looks. Tears are running down both sides of Sergio's face. "Please, Mama. We need you."

Padre Montes leaves the room. He is gone for a short time. When he returns, he says, "I have the district attorney's promise—and I trust him—that if you answer his questions, no matter what the answers might be, you will be going home with us this afternoon."

"Please, Mama, please."

"I will answer his questions."

Padre Montes leaves the room again. When he returns, the others are with him, and the questioning begins.

"Mrs. González, do you recognize the young man seated on my right, Deputy Summers?"

Jesusita is exhausted. But she is going home after this is over. She looks at the young man intently, thinks, and begins shaking her head. Sergio doesn't understand the question. Why would Mama have seen him before?

"Is that a no, Mrs. González?"

"No."

"On that Sunday afternoon at the river, after you daughter Paulina had drowned and while you were sitting on a blanket, do you remember talking to a police officer?"

She looks back on that afternoon. Did she talk to a policeman? It is not clear. For Sergio it is instantly clear. Now he knows this policeman. He sees the police car pull up above them. He takes a towel and rubs away the mud.

"No."

The District Attorney pauses, looks at notes and says, "You don't remember or no?"

Sergio thinks, *Maybe she really doesn't remember after all.*

"I remember everything about that afternoon. I didn't talk to the police."

The deputy shakes his head and says something to the district attorney. Sergio silently moans. Jesusita waits for the next question.

"Alright, can you tell us in your own words what happened that Sunday afternoon?"

She doesn't hesitate. She has told this story many times. There is nothing about this retelling that is disturbing. It is only when she is alone that the events of the afternoon plague her. She says it calmly, matter-of-factly, without any show of emotion. It is a version that Sergio has heard her tell several times.

"We went down to the river for a picnic. When we got there we remembered the tamales. Everybody went back to the house to get them. Except for me and...and...Paulina." She pauses. "I was sitting on a blanket on a hill above the river, and she was down at the river wading. I told her a few times to be careful because she couldn't swim. I would watch her and then not watch her. Then, when I looked one time, she wasn't there. She was gone. I looked up and down the river, and for a second I thought I saw her head and dress in the middle of the river far away. I never saw her again."

This time his mother's words shame Sergio. He keeps his eyes fastened on the wood grain before him. How can she remember so many things about that afternoon and not remember that she had been down to the river itself?

"You were sitting on the hill watching her?"

"Yes."

"How far were you from her?"

"Far."

"From the end of this room to the other end?"

"No, a lot farther."

"Mrs. González, why don't you step around the table to the window behind us and point out how far away your daughter was from you?"

She does not want to go to the window. She asks Sergio in a low voice if what Mr. Montemayor just said is what the man wants her to do. Sergio nods. It was not what she was hoping for. She asks again. Sergio nods again. Slowly she begins to stand, placing both hands on the table, using her arms to lift her. Her arms tremble. Sergio can see this without raising his eyes and is certain that everyone in the room sees this too. They must be asking themselves why she is trembling so badly if she is telling the truth. Slowly, she moves around the table and stops as she reaches Montemayor and looks back at Sergio and motions for him to accompany her. Sergio looks the other way. The district attorney says, "Sergio, your mother wants you to come over here with her. Please help her."

She goes to the window. Sergio follows. She studies the outside for a good while. Sergio watches. He sees her head lift and her eyes go farther and farther out. He sees the deputy shaking his head again. She points to a young eucalyptus tree near the Sheriff's office. "It's over there by where that tree is." *No, Mama, it wasn't nearly that far. No one will ever believe that.*

The deputy sheriff says something to the district attorney. "That's sixty or seventy yards away. Are you sure you were that far away from your daughter, Mrs. González?"

"Yes," she nods.

"Are you sure?"

"Yes," she repeats, still nodding.

"Thank you. You can have your seat."

They return to their side of the table.

"How many times did you tell her to be careful because she couldn't swim?"

"Three or four times."

"And you were sitting on your blanket when you said that?"

She nods.

"That's a yes?"

"Yes."

"What would she do when you said these things?"

"She would turn and look at me and not pay any attention to what I said."

"Did she hear you?"

"Oh, yes."

"How do you know that?"

"I could see that when she turned to me."

"Were you screaming?"

"No."

"Shouting?"

"Not too much."

Sergio can hear the roar of the river and doesn't like her answer. *How can she not understand what she's doing?*

"You're sure she looked back at you and heard you?"

No, Mama, please.

"Yes, I'm sure."

"Think about the next question, Mrs. González, before you answer it. Think about it very carefully.... Did you ever go down to the river while your daughter was wading in it?"

Sergio sees his mother's mouth quiver and her eyes blink. He sees her mud-caked feet, and he lowers his head and eyes as she says, "No."

"Are you sure of that, Mrs. González?"

"Yes, I'm sure."

"My guess is that you've been told that we have a witness who says that he saw you push your daughter into the river?"

"That's not true." Tears run anew. "It's not true."

"Why would anyone say such a thing if it wasn't true?"

"I don't know. But it's not true."

"You're sure you never went down to the river?"

"I'm sure."

The district attorney pauses. The mud-caked feet will not leave

Sergio's mind. The district attorney's look is fixed squarely on his mother. His mother does not return the look. Instead, she has her head bent. Her lips are moving in that almost imperceptible motion of the rosary.

Finally, the district attorney says, "Mrs. González, I have a few more questions that I'd like to ask you. But before I do, would you please look at me?"

Montemayor repeats the request. Jesusita's lips stop. Slowly she raises her head. Sergio watches, thinking, *She's lying, has lied, and is about to lie some more, and everybody in the room knows it. Where or how can I hide? If they see my face they will know for sure that she is lying.* He brings his hand to his forehead and begins rubbing it, masking his eyes.

"After your daughter's body was found, it was examined by the coroner. We routinely do that in these kinds of cases to establish the cause of death. Initially we all thought the cause of death to be drowning. But after examining the body, the coroner is not so sure. He found a series of lines of what appear to be wounds on your daughter's back and thighs. He thinks these may have been there *before* your daughter was swept away by the river and might have contributed to her death. Do you know anything about these lines or marks or wounds?"

Padre Montes interrupts, "Lines? Marks? Wounds? What does the district attorney mean by that? What are we talking about?"

The District Attorney continues, "My understanding is that these are like open wounds or sores. The body was in a great deal of decay when it was found. It had been exposed to the sun, wind, and water for many days. There are rodents and small animals that may have come upon the body. There are a lot of those out there on the west side. All of that makes it extremely difficult to tell what these wounds, if they are wounds, are, where they came from, or what or who caused them and when. The coroner has pretty much ruled out rodents or small animals because of the straight lines. He thinks that these lines could have been caused by a rope or wire or something else."

A long, loud howl fills the room. When it stops, Jesusita's face is buried in her arms on the table. "Oh no, no, no! Paulina! No, Paulina, no!" The tears and cries go on for several minutes.

Then John Thomas says, "I think it might be better if we stop now and come back tomorrow."

Padre Montes answers. "Let me and Sergio talk to her for a few minutes. My guess is that she'll want to finish this today."

Once again the four leave the room. While Padre Montes talks to her, Sergio sits stunned. *Those are belt marks. Did Mama beat her again before she pushed her into the river?*

Padre Montes says, "Your mother wants to finish this today. I'll tell the others." He leaves the room. Sergio can't look at her. He sits looking the other way. He can't speak to her. But then, Jesusita won't look or speak to him either. The four return.

The district attorney continues his questioning. Jesusita's answers are short, tearful and hushed. Sergio hears neither the questions nor the answers, convinced not only that his mother has drowned his sister but also that she beat her for the final time before that.

"Mrs. González, do you know anything about those lines or marks or wounds on your daughter's body?"

"No."

"When is the last time you saw your daughter naked?"

She shrugs. "A long time ago."

"Do you remember about when?"

"No."

"When is the last time you bathed her?"

"Years ago when she was still a little girl."

"Have you ever seen any marks or lines or wounds on her back or thighs?"

"No."

When the district attorney concludes his questioning of Jesusita, Padre Montes asks, "Can you tell us who this mystery witness is?"

"No."

"Never?"

"I haven't talked to him yet. Once I do and reach a decision as to how to proceed with this case, his name will be given to Mrs. González."

As they rise to leave, John Thomas says, "Sergio...young man, I want you to stay. I have some questions for you. Father, you and Mrs. González are free to leave. I may be a while with Sergio. So I suggest that you take Mrs. González home. I'm sure that Sergio can find his way home once we're finished."

The district attorney walks out with Jesusita and Padre Montes. Sergio sits with his chin touching the top of his chest. He knows that the others are looking at him but he can't return the looks. The district attorney re-enters and takes his place on the other side of the table. "Sergio, how old are you?"

There is a long pause. He knows how old he is. He tries to say it. But he doesn't know how to say it, how to begin. The word for it in English has disappeared. He knows it but now he doesn't know it. He searches for the word in Spanish.

"How old are you, Sergio?"

The pause continues. Montemayor asks him in Spanish. He answers in English, "Eighteen."

"You speak English?"

He nods, barely raising his chin from his chest.

"You're nodding. That's a yes. Please look at me."

He looks up haltingly. "Yes."

"Good....You were here when we questioned your mother about the Sunday afternoon your sister drowned?"

"Yes."

"You know that we have a witness who says that he saw your mother push your sister into that river?"

"Yes."

"I want to be frank with you, Sergio. Because I really believe that it's in the best interest of your mother if we are frank. Do you understand me? We can use Charley here to interpret for us if you want."

"No. I understand. Except for the word 'frank.'"

"That means honest. Oĸ?"

"Oĸ."

"Your mother did not help herself here this afternoon. In fact, I think she may have hurt herself. From all the good things I had heard about her, I had expected much better."

"What do you mean?"

"I mean I don't think she was very honest."

He looks away.

"I couldn't help but notice your reaction to some of her answers to my questions. You weren't happy with some of those answers either, were you?"

He looks back at the district attorney as calmly as he can. "Happy? What do you mean 'happy'?"

"Not satisfied. In other words, you knew she wasn't telling the truth, didn't you?"

"I don't know what you mean."

"Oh, come now, Sergio, you know exactly what I mean. You knew she was lying and you showed it, didn't you?"

He doesn't answer. He can't answer.

John Thomas stares for a moment and then moves on. "You were at the river that Sunday afternoon, weren't you?"

"Yes."

"Once you got there and before you went back to your house for those tamales, did you do anything?"

"Yes."

"What?"

"We fixed our picnic place."

"That's right. You put down a blanket and put a lot of things on and around it?"

"Yes."

How far was the blanket from the river?"

His heart beats faster. "I don't know."

"You were with your mother when she came over to this side

of the table and pointed out how far she was from the river. Out to the eucalyptus tree some seventy yards away. Was the blanket that far from the river?"

A no is a betrayal. A yes is a lie. He can feel sweat forming on his forehead. "I don't know."

"You don't know! Well, maybe we can help you know. You remember Deputy Summers, don't you?"

"Yes."

"He went down to your picnic site that afternoon, didn't he?"

"Yes."

"Did he talk to your mother?"

A yes is a betrayal. A no is a lie. "I don't know."

"How could you not know?"

"I wasn't there all the time."

"Where did he park his car?"

"I don't remember." He thinks that this too has to be a trap for his mother.

"Did he park his car below the blanket and closer to the river, or above the blanket and farther away from the river?"

He can still see the car above them as he wipes her feet clean. "I don't remember."

"Let's see if we can refresh your recollection. Deputy Summers, did you park your patrol car above or below the blanket?"

"Above it, sir."

"How far were you from the river?"

"Forty, forty-five yards maximum, sir."

"How far was the blanket from the river, deputy?"

"Twenty, twenty-five yards at most, sir."

"Now, Sergio, how far was the blanket from the river?"

He bites his lower lip. He shakes his head. Twenty-five yards makes her a liar. Seventy yards makes her a liar too. "I don't know."

"You do know, Sergio. You do know.... Let me tell you something. In two days I will be interviewing the man who says that he saw your mother push your sister into the river. After what I've heard today and probably what I will hear on Friday, I will be asking the grand jury to file a charge of murder against your mother. Do you know what a grand jury is?"

"No."

"It is a group of people from the community who will listen to the witnesses I have and then decide if they should charge your mother with murder. One of the witnesses I will present to the grand jury will be you. You will be sworn to tell the truth, and if you lie before the grand jury and say you don't know like you're doing here, I will file a perjury charge against you. Do you know what perjury is?"

"No."

"It's lying in court after you have been sworn to tell the truth. Do you know what happens to people who commit perjury?"

"No."

"They go prison for a very long time.... Now let me tell you something else. You and your mother probably think you are helping her by lying. But you're not. Once she's been convicted and is front of the judge for sentencing and the judge knows that she's been lying, just like everybody in this room knows it, he's not going to reward her for lying. Her sentence to prison will be a lot longer than it would have been if she had admitted her guilt and says she was sorry. Do you understand what I've just said?"

Shamed, Sergio's eyes are focused on the long lines of wood grain that he does not see. He doesn't answer.

"Did you hear me, Sergio?"

"Yes."

"Did you understand me?"

"Yes."

"Yesterday, Deputy Summers and I went down to that place where all of you were on that Sunday. The river is still very full and very loud. You'll agree with me, won't you Sergio, that the river must have been very full and very loud on that Sunday?"

He doesn't know where the district attorney is going. But it can't be good. He doesn't answer.

"Sergio, was the river loud that day?"

"Yes."

"Very loud?"

"Yes."

"With all that noise, do you think your sister could have heard anything your mother said from here to the eucalyptus tree that's some seventy yards away?"

The answer he wants is all too clear now. "I don't know."

"Alright, let me ask you this. You know that your mother went down to the river just before your sister drowned, don't you?"

He is caught in mid-breath. For a moment, everything stops. He feels a sharp pain in his upper chest. How can this man know? How can he know?

"Sergio, answer my question!"

Had the deputy seen him wiping her feet?

"Sergio!"

"How could I know? I wasn't there. I went home with my other sister Yolanda to get the tamales." He has to get rid of those shoes.

"What do you know about the marks or wounds on your sister's body?"

He shakes his head a little. "Nothing."

"Get him out of here."

HE WAITS until long after she should have gone to work before he goes home—so that he can do what he has to do without dealing with her. It is after eight when he enters. Yolanda has begun to get Concepcion ready for bed.

"Where have you been?"

"Seeing a man about a job."

"Where?"

"In the campo."

"Are you hungry?"

"No, I already ate," he lies. But he is not hungry.

He goes to his room and closes the door and starts to do what he has to do. He can hear Concepcion protesting that it's too early to go to bed and thinks that this is the last time that he will hear that. After a while there's a knock on his door. "Just a minute." He covers what he is doing. "Ok, come in." It's Concepcion. She's in her pajamas. She comes to him and he bends down and she kisses him on the cheek. "Goodnight, Sergio." His eyes water.

A few minutes later he finds Yolanda in the kitchen. "Goodnight. I know it's real early but I'm real tired. I'm going to bed."

"Where were you this afternoon? How come you weren't in school?"

"Like I told you, I was seeing a man about a job."

"Who?"

"Shorty Espinoza. You don't know him. He's a contractor. Me and two other guys were tracking him down all afternoon."

"Is he gonna give you work?"

"They're working in El Centro and he says he can use us."

"How will you get there?"

"He'll drive us. They have a camp down there."

"Have you told Mama?"

"No. But we need the money. She won't care."

Back in his room, he checks everything once again. He's ready. He lies down and for a moment is afraid that he might fall asleep before she comes home. But he feels the tension running through his body and knows that there is no danger of falling asleep. He thinks of all the years he has spent with her, of the many things he has endured because of her. Now it is over. It should have been over long ago, but he didn't have the courage. Now courage is not a consideration. What must be, will be. He is aware of Yolanda in the bathroom next to him. Then the house is silent and dark. He has no idea what time it is. There is a clock in the kitchen and one in her bedroom. He has no need to know the time. She will come, and he is ready.

There is no pattern or structure to his thoughts. They are a rambling review of his years with her. Incidents, words, beatings, pain, fear, dependence, hate, anger, need, and respect too. It is a moonless night, and he thinks of her crossing the railroad tracks on her way home, small, vulnerable, and courageous. But for her, where would they be? That is not a consideration now. She has crossed the line. It is over.

He hears her at the back door. He jumps to his feet. She will be in the kitchen in seconds. He has planned to wait until she is passing his door to call her into his room so that Yolanda and Concepcion won't hear. Because they must stay with her. Why make it any more difficult than it already is and will be for them? But he can't wait. He can't hold back and he rushes from his room and is in the kitchen before she can finish locking the back door. He turns on the kitchen light and startles her.

"You killed her!" he shouts. "You murdered Paulina! You murdered my sister! They know you did! They know you lied! They know I lied for you! They know!"

The shouting startles her again. When she sees and hears him, she sits down at the table and places her forehead in her open hand, shielding her eyes with the bottom of that hand, exposing only the top of her head. Her shoulders sag and her back is bent.

Yolanda comes out of her room. "What's going on here?" Concepcion comes running. "Mama! Mama!"

"What's going on here? I'll tell you what's going on? That woman there, I can't call her my mother anymore because I can't! That woman there murdered Paulina, murdered our sister! That saint! That holy woman who goes to church every day of her life murdered Paulina!"

"Stop it, Sergio! Stop it!" Yolanda shouts.

"Stop it? Why should I stop it! Look at her! Do you see her denying it? Do you even see her shaking her head no? Do you see her crying? No! She knows what she did!"

Concepcion, crying, runs up to Jesusita. "Mama! Mama!" Jesusita doesn't see or hear the child. Concepcion grabs her mother's thigh, puts her head on her mother's thigh. The woman remains motionless.

"Mama," Yolanda says softly. Jesusita doesn't answer, doesn't move.

"Just so you know, Yolanda. The police have a witness who saw her push Paulina into the river before she drowned. She and I and Padre Montes were at the district attorney's office this afternoon answering questions. She lied, and I lied for her. They're going to send her to prison for murder and me for lying. Look at her! Is she denying any of this? Is she calling me a liar?"

"How could it have happened?"

"I'll tell you how. When we came back here for the tamales, she went down to the river. She probably got mad at Paulina like she always did. She beat Paulina, like she always did, because they've found all these wounds on Paulina's back. Then she pushed her into the river. She's been telling everybody that she was seventy yards away from Paulina the whole time we were gone and never went down to the river. You know how far seventy yards is...? It's far. She's lying. When we came back with the tamales and I saw her feet full of mud, I knew she had been down to the river. I knew then that she was lying to everybody. When I saw the police coming, I got scared and wiped the mud off her feet so the police wouldn't know that she was lying. Ask her if I'm lying.... Go on, ask her!"

Yolanda looks at her bent, motionless, silent mother.

Sergio glares at her before he says, "Saint Jesusita, I hate you! I hate you! I hate all the ugly things you ever did to us! But most of all I hate you just like Paulina hated you!" He turns, leaves the kitchen, and goes to his room.

Moments later Yolanda hears the front door slam shut. She does not see Sergio all the next day, and when she goes to his room that night, she sees that he has gone.

On Thursday afternoon when Yolanda comes home from school, she finds Jesusita sitting in her room next to a side window, staring out into space. She doesn't answer Yolanda. The bed is made and she wonders if Jesusita has slept at all. She does not come out of her room for the dinner that Yolanda has prepared. Yolanda and Concepcion eat their dinner silently and somberly, very much aware of the woman who will not come out of her room or speak to them. It is 5:40 and Jesusita does not leave for work. At

5:45, Yolanda knocks and then opens the door and asks Jesusita if she is going to work. Jesusita is sitting in the same place and in the same position. She does not answer. Concepcion watches, scared.

When Yolanda and Concepcion leave for school the next morning, Jesusita still hasn't come out of her room. She sits in the same chair, in the same place and position, staring out into the same space. She doesn't answer Yolanda who stands at her door until she can see the blouse around Jesusita's waist move ever so slightly and then again and again. The longer Jesusita continues in this state, the more it confirms Sergio's accusations. Now she's afraid of her mother as she has never been before. But she doesn't know what to do. If she goes to the police and tells them about Mama's muddy feet and the beating, what will happen to her and Concepcion?

When she comes home from school, Concepcion is in their room with the door closed. She is very quiet. "What's the matter? Why are you in here with the door closed?" Yolanda asks. She knows, but she asks anyway. Concepcion doesn't answer.

"Are you hungry?"

Concepcion nods.

"Then go in the kitchen and make yourself a taco. Go on. I have to use the bathroom. I'll be out in a minute." When she comes out of the bathroom, the girl is still in her room with the door closed. Yolanda opens the door and steps into the kitchen. She listens. She hears nothing. She looks in the direction of Jesusita's room and sees nothing. But she is reluctant to go there. "Come on," she says to the girl behind her, "let's make some tacos."

In the sink she sees some dirty dishes. *She's up,* she thinks. *I'd better go say something to her. It'll be worse if I don't.* She knocks. There is no answer. She opens the door. Jesusita is asleep on the bed, sound asleep. Let her sleep. Later, as Yolanda prepares dinner, she has still not seen or heard her mother, and she begins to have a new and different worry. If Mama misses work again, will she lose her job? Then how will they eat? How will they pay the rent, the gas, and the electricity? She tries to wake her mother but can't. After dinner she tells Concepcion that she has to go downtown to tell

Mr. Jim that Mama is sick and can't go to work. The girl says that she wants to go too, that she's afraid to stay home alone.

"But you won't be alone, Mama's here."

"That's worse," Concepcion says.

"No, no, I'm not going to talk business with Mr. Jim and have a little girl with me."

Concepcion starts to cry, a loud, wailing cry.

The two of them meet with Mr. Jim in his office.

"What's wrong with her?"

"I don't know. She's in bed and can hardly get up."

"Have you called a doctor?"

Yolanda shakes her head and says nothing, embarrassed to say that they never call a doctor, that they don't have the money to pay for a doctor.

"Well, it probably wouldn't do much good. It probably has to do with your sister's drowning. She's been real upset about that lately."

Concepcion's eyes widen.

"Yes, she has," Yolanda says.

IT IS late Saturday afternoon when Padre Montes knocks. "Is your mother home?"

"Yes, she is, Padre, but she's asleep."

"Is she alright?'

"She's been sick, Padre."

"I thought maybe that was the case. I had to go to Bakersfield and just got back last night. She wasn't at Mass this morning and didn't confess this afternoon. That's the first time that's ever happened. What's the matter with her?"

"I don't know. She just stays in her room and sits or sleeps and doesn't say anything. We eat, and she doesn't eat. I've only heard her go to the bathroom two times and then she goes through Sergio's room and doesn't see us."

"Where's Sergio?"

"He's working in El Centro."

"El Centro! Did he tell you that the district attorney might want him to be a witness in court?"

"No."

"When did he leave?"

"Thursday."

"And he left just like that, without saying anything about being a witness in court?"

"We need the money, Padre. What my mother makes is not enough to support us for the whole year."

"Where is he in El Centro?"

"I don't know. But I'm waiting for him to send me a telegram telling me where he is so I can join him."

"And what about Concepcion?'

"We'll do like we did last summer. My mother took care of her while me and Sergio and Paulina worked in the campo. I was think-ing of going as soon as I hear from him. School's almost over and I'm not going to pass, so what's the difference? But with Mama sick like this, I don't know. I can't leave Concepcion with her.... Maybe I'll just take her with me. She's been out in the campo lots of times."

"When did your mother get sick?"

"Thursday."

"Right after we met with the district attorney?"

"I guess so."

He thinks for a moment. Yolanda waits. "I better talk to her. Will you wake her, please?"

"I think it's better if you try to wake her, Padre. She hasn't been paying much attention to me."

He knocks on Jesusita's door. There's no answer. He enters. The shades are down and the room is dark. He sees the lump of her. He goes to that side of the bed. "Jesusita, it's me, Padre Montes."

She opens her eyes immediately. There are no signs of sleep.

"How are you feeling?"

She nods.

"Yolanda says that you've been very sick. What's the matter?"

"I'm just tired, Padre, very tired. I don't have the strength to do anything. More than that, I don't *want* to do anything."

"Yolanda says you're not eating. You won't have any strength to do anything if you don't eat."

"What did the witness say, Padre?"

"What witness?"

"The one the district attorney was going to talk to yesterday."

"I don't know. I've been gone since Thursday. But I wouldn't worry about anything that man says if I were you. We both know that you had nothing to do with the drowning. The truth will win out. Anyone who knows you, who knows how close you are to God, wouldn't give this so-called witness a second thought."

"But what if they believe him?"

"No one's going to believe that man."

"Who is he?"

"I don't know. But I'll be seeing Father Reilly on Monday, and I'll know a lot more about this then."

"But if they believe him, what will happen to me and my family?"

"Jesusita, you're worrying yourself sick over this. You've already worried yourself sick over it. You have to stop worrying. You'll drive yourself crazy if you don't."

"Will they send me to jail? For a long, long time? What will happen to my kids?"

As he leaves, he says to Yolanda, "Don't worry. In a few days she'll be a lot better. Mark my words. In a few days she'll be her old self."

"Then I shouldn't call anybody?"

"Call anybody? Who were you going to call, my child?"

"I was thinking of calling the Señor Núñez. He used to be a chiropractor in Mexico. Lots of people go to him. They say he's better than a doctor."

"And cheaper."

"Yes."

JESUSITA IS not at Mass on Sunday. But after the 11:00 Mass, when all the admiring crowd has left him on the church steps, Charley

Montemayor's wife approaches. "Padre, do you know who the se-
cret witness is in the drowning of Doña Jesusita's daughter?"

"No, who is it?'

"You have to promise me that you will not tell anyone that I
told you."

"I give you my word. Who is it?"

"Felipe Domínguez."

"No!"

"Yes."

"Are you sure?"

"I'm positive."

"Tell everyone! Spread the word!"

"I can't. Charley would kill me if he knew I told even you."

"That's not a problem. I will tell people, and no one will know
that it came from you."

That afternoon as the Guadalupana members wait in the church
for Jesusita to convene their meeting, Padre Montes begins it instead. He tells them that Jesusita is still sick. Then he tells them
about Felipe Domínguez and his latest accusations. The women
are aghast. He asks them to go door-to-door in the parish that afternoon and tell everyone who will listen about these new lies. He
tells them to invite anyone who is willing to see God's will and
justice done and willing to swear to the lies that Felipe Domínguez had previously told to meet him there at the church that evening at 6:30.

"PLEASE JOHN, in all the years I have known you, I can honestly
say that I have never inserted myself, or tried to insert myself, in
any of your prosecutorial duties. But this is very different."

"As I've already said, Father, I met with the man and found him
to be credible. Oh, I've had better, more sophisticated witnesses.
But one must remember that he's a simple man who's worked in
the fields all his life. He's not accustomed to having to come forward like this. Given that, I think he'll do just fine in court."

"John, before you file those murder charges, will you please take a few minutes to talk to these other people who want in the worst way to talk to you about your witness?"

"How do they know who my witness is?"

"I don't know. But they'll be at my rectory this evening at 7:00. Please, just a few minutes."

When John Thomas drives up to Father Reilly's rectory at 7:10 that evening, he sees thirty-four Mexicans congregated in front of it and thinks, *I'm not talking to all those people and I'm not staying for any demonstration.* Once inside, Father Reilly's housekeeper who speaks Spanish and basic English assures him that he will only be speaking to a few of the people outside. One by one the Mexicans tell him, through the housekeeper, how Felipe Domínguez spread lies throughout the community about nightly sex and sex in the confessional between Padre Montes and Jesusita. And how he later admitted in church before the congregation that he had lied because of the money that his niece, Dolores Álvarez, had paid him. It isn't until the fifth person repeats the story that John Thomas realizes that it was Dolores Álvarez who brought Felipe Domínguez to his office on Friday. Looking out the window at the waiting crowd, he asks that fifth person, "Will they tell me the same thing about Mr. Domínguez?"

"Yes, sir."

It is then that he says, "That's enough! I've heard enough!" and leaves.

The next day he has Deputy Summers go to Selma and bring Felipe Domínguez to his office. When John Thomas tells Domínguez what people had said the evening before, Domínguez becomes mute. He speaks not another word to anyone, no matter what is said to or asked of him. Murder charges against Jesusita González are never filed.

☦ XII

TWO DAYS after Jesusita returned to work, eleven days
after Padre Montes told her that there would be no
criminal charges filed against her, Yolanda and Concepcion left. She did not know when exactly they left because she
had not only lost all contact with Yolanda and Concepcion, but
all interest in them as well.

Nine days after Padre Montes brought the good news, Yolanda
came home from school to find her mother fully dressed, sitting
at the kitchen table. "I'm going to work tonight," she said, not to
her specifically but to whomever or whatever she was staring at in
the kitchen. The three sat together for dinner for the first time in
two weeks. Nothing was said. Jesusita sat hunched over her plate,
at times mumbling to herself, picking at her food with her fork,
occasionally bringing that partially filled fork to her mouth, and
then slowly, deliberately chewing on food that had to be tasteless,
while the little one watched, too frightened to eat. Jesusita had lost
a lot of weight. Her neck was turkey-like in a dress she had worn
for years but now looked two sizes too big. Yolanda wondered if
she had enough strength to make the walk across the tracks, let
alone work. Still, it was better that she go, that she try, that she
get out of the house. And she wondered too, now that Jesusita was
up, how long it would be before she became aware of how much
she and Concepcion feared her.

When Mr. Jim saw her, he tried to send her home. She wouldn't go. There was no way he could restore her to the position of head cleaning woman, not in the condition she was in. Instead, he assigned her the work of a new cleaning woman, three floors in the Power building, regretting that assignment as he made it, certain that she would never finish it and if she did, that it would have to be redone early the next morning. But finish it she did, sometime after three in the morning, and made her way home just as she had worked: by sheer rote and willpower and the need to survive. Once at home, she collapsed on her bed, fully clothed, with all the bedding beneath her.

Yolanda woke her just before four that afternoon. "Mama, are you going to work tonight?"

"Yes," she answered, rising, straightening her dress, and combing her hair with the same need and resolve that she had worked and walked the night before.

They ate together again. It was to be the last time. Except for a few words from Yolanda, it was a duplicate of the night before. Some mumbling, picking and staring down at her plate, now and then bringing food to her mouth, and then mechanically chewing as Concepcion sat and stared, wide-eyed and scared, fork in her hand that seldom went to her mouth. "Mama, please eat. You have to eat if you're going to work." Wasted words. Jesusita gave no indication that she heard or cared.

Then, long before she usually left, with most of the food still on her plate, Jesusita stood and said, "I have to go," left the table, went to her room, and then out the front door. It was the last time they saw her.

IT IS Padre Montes who wakes her. "I'm sorry. Did I wake you?"

"I was sleeping. But it's late. I have to go to work."

"It's Saturday, Jesusita. You don't work on Saturdays."

"Is it?"

"Yes. Where's everybody? I've been knocking and knocking."

"I don't know."

"Did they go to the store?"

"I don't know."

"Yolanda hasn't left for El Centro yet, has she?"

"I don't know."

"What do you mean you don't know? Surely you would know if your daughter's gone to El Centro and taken Concepcion with her."

She doesn't answer.

"Jesusita, you've got to get over this. Paulina's dead. You had nothing to do with it. The police and the district attorney have admitted that. Felipe is a born liar. The whole world knows that. You are falling apart. You have to get over this. It is over, ended, finished."

It will never be over, she thinks. *For me, it will never end.*

"You haven't been to Mass or Communion or Confession in more than two weeks. This is not you. Everyone is wondering what has happened to you. Everyone is worried about you."

She doesn't believe him. No one is worried about her. They all suspect. They were sure she'd be convicted. They were disappointed when she wasn't.

He is waiting for an answer, but she doesn't answer. She is looking away to one side. He waits until he becomes exasperated. "When Yolanda comes back, tell her I want to talk to her. Tell her that I'd like her to come over to the rectory." He pauses. Gently he puts his hand on her shoulder. "Jesusita, you have to put this behind you." Then he turns and leaves.

The house is silent. Now she wants them to be there even though she knows they are gone. She listens, hoping. Nothing. What is this about El Centro? There is an emptiness in the house that she has never felt before. She listens some more. Nothing. She looks about for signs that they are still there. She sees none. But she is in the front room and what signs would she see there? She steps into the dining room. Sergio's door on her left is closed. It's been closed since he left. Will Yolanda's door be closed? She reaches the kitchen. Yolanda's door is closed. But that could mean anything. She looks carefully around the kitchen for some sign that they are still there. None. That doesn't necessarily mean that they have gone. Yolanda is very neat, clean. She always picks up after herself and everyone. She looks at Yolanda's door. It says nothing. For all she knows, the two of them might be sitting quietly in there, not wanting to wake her. She listens. She can't tell if they're in there or not. She goes to the door and raises her fist to knock, but stops and listens again. She is sagging; hope is running out. She doesn't knock, not wanting anyone to not answer. She opens the door. There is no one in the room. She thinks, eyeing the bureaus and the closet, that they could have gone to the store, that they could be in the backyard. Maybe she should wait, not mess up their things until they come back from the store, or until she goes and looks out in the backyard. But her mind, like her eyes, is on the bureaus, on the closet door. She knows what she is going to find when she opens them, but until she opens them, she doesn't know. It is not yet a fact.

She opens them, every last one of them. They are gone. Without a single word to her, they are gone. She is neither surprised nor saddened nor disappointed. After Paulina and Sergio, she expected this. What she is, is beaten.

ON WEDNESDAY afternoon, Padre Montes knocks on Jesusita's door. He is concerned. Jesusita still has not been to Mass and Communion even though they say that she is working again. They say she is acting strangely. On the street and at work, she talks to no one, even when she's spoken to. It's not as if she doesn't know they're there, because she looks right at them at and doesn't answer. Then too, Yolanda has not come to see him, and several parishioners have told him that Yolanda and the girl have not been in school.

Jesusita opens the door, looks up at him but says nothing.

"Can I come in?"

She unlatches the screen door. He opens it and steps inside. She doesn't speak.

"Is Yolanda here?"

"No."

"Did she go to El Centro?"

"Yes."

"Did the little one go with her?"

"Yes."

"When did they leave?"

"Two days ago."

"You're alone now?"

She nods.

"You're working again?"

"Yes."

"But you haven't been to Mass and Communion?"

She doesn't answer. Her eyes turn bland—blank.

He returns the following day and the day after that. She doesn't answer the door. He knows she is home. The talk is that she only leaves her house to go to work and buy groceries. The shades are drawn; he can't feel any movement in that old wooden house. He is determined to speak to her, not let the situation get worse. He waits a block from her house one afternoon. When she passes on her way to work, he comes out from behind a tree.

"Jesusita, what has gotten into you? Why are you doing this to yourself?"

She doesn't answer. She walks on.

He follows. "Jesusita! It's me, Padre Montes! Answer me! Don't you understand that I want to help you! I care about you, Jesusita! It pains me to see you this way!"

She doesn't answer, doesn't break her stride.

"Jesusita, you've..." He is shouting. Children run out of their yards to stare at him. Women push aside their curtains or open their doors. But when they see that it is Padre Montes and that he is annoyed with them for looking, they retreat. After a block and a half, it occurs to him that he is doing more harm than good.

He meets with Mr. Jim.

"I don't know what to tell you, Padre. She won't talk to anybody. Not that she and I ever talked much.... Because of the language I mean. But I could usually make myself understood and she always did exactly as I asked. And she still does. She never said much to me before but she says less now. But that's OK. She's still one of my best workers. But I couldn't keep her as my head cleaning woman, not in the condition she's in. So I just let her work alone."

"How is her work?"

"Well you know, she has three floors over in the Power building. Everybody's supposed to be finished by midnight and everybody is—except Jessie. Some nights I'll double back to check. Some are already gone and the rest are definitely ready to go. But I'll look over at the Power building, and I can tell by the lights that she still has a long way to go. I don't know when she finishes. Anywhere from one, two, or three in the morning. I could care less because in the morning those three floors are spotless. If I had three more like Jessie, I wouldn't have a worry in the world."

He talks to José López, the grocer.

"There have been a lot of changes in her, Padre, a lot. She used to come in here two or three times a week, plus sending her kids a time or two. Since this thing at the river, she only comes once a week. And that's early Monday morning, every Monday morning. You know people do most of their shopping on the weekend. There's never anybody shopping here early Monday morning. She knows that. So she comes Monday morning. I open at 8:00 and she's here by 8:02, buys what she needs, and is usually gone before the next customer comes in."

"What's she like when she's here?"

"She doesn't talk anymore. Not even 'buenos días.' She just gets her things, puts them on the counter, pays for them, and goes. Doesn't say a word. And she doesn't buy like she used to. Of course, everybody says she's alone—that the kids are gone. So she doesn't need a lot like she used to. But even then she buys very little for the week, even for one person. She's lost a lot of weight. She's real skinny. She's not eating much. It's not for me to say, Padre, but there's something really wrong with her."

THE RUMORS begin immediately.

"Have you heard?"

"No, what?"

"About Jesusita."

"I've heard some things. What have you heard?"

"She's not going to Mass every day, not going anywhere near the church. Given up on the Guadalupana."

"She's been sick, hasn't she?"

"Yes. But she's well again and she's working and still not going to church. And she's acting real strange. Won't talk to anybody."

"My kids told me that her kids aren't in school anymore."

"Yes. Nobody knows what happened to them. Even the little one is gone. Remember last year? The little one stayed with her when the big ones went to work with Pedro."

"That's right. I hadn't thought about that."

"Something weird is going on over there."

Those who don't like Jesusita rush to judgment.

"You know, I know that he can't be trusted, but maybe Felipe Domínguez was telling the truth this time."

"What do you mean?"

"Charley Montemayor believed him. He thought Domínguez was telling the truth. And he was there three times when they questioned him. He says the police believed Domínguez, but it was the district attorney who said no. He says that you have to remember that the district attorney is a Catholic. He's a good friend of that priest over at Sacred Heart. He says that Montes went crying to that priest who got a hold of the district attorney and that was it."

"Charley Montemayor says all that?"

"Yes, he does."

"And you believe him?"

"Don't you...? I mean, it all makes perfect sense. Domínguez tells the truth. The police call her in for questioning. She gets sick. Wants everybody to believe that she's real sick. Doesn't go to church for the first time in years. She's working now and still doesn't go to church. Is that what a saint would do? She won't come out of her house except to go to work. She won't talk to anybody. Her kids disappear. They probably saw what she did at the river and she's afraid they'll tell the police. All of a sudden, they're gone. She's hiding. Her neighbors say she keeps the shades down and won't answer the door for anybody, not even her big friend Montes. It's all pretty strange, isn't it?"

"Yeah."

Even the Guadalupana members are quick to question.

"Something's not right there."

"I agree."

"First she's sick or says she's sick. Now she's working. And this whole time she hasn't worked once with us in the church or come to one of our meetings which she herself organized. And no Mass, no Communion, not even on Sundays. That's a mortal sin, you know?"

"I know. If she can work, she can sure go to Mass on Sunday. I hate to say this, but I don't think she's as holy as everybody thought."

"I think you're right."

THERE ARE those who still believe in her, but they are fewer and fewer. They remain with her mainly because of Padre Montes. "We must not judge Jesusita harshly. She is not well. Paulina's drowning has taken a great toll on her. Hopefully with our prayers, God will see fit to return her to us. In the meantime, we must be patient and understanding and nonjudgmental. As for those who make much of the fact that she is now alone, pay no attention to those ugly rumors. Yolanda herself told me, before she left, that she and the little one would be going to El Centro to join Sergio in the campo and that she would be taking the little one with her because of her mother's condition."

But the scoffing continues throughout June and into July. No one considers Jesusita to be saintly now. Even Padre Montes has shied away from talking about her in saintly terms. Then in the third week of July, Pedro and Luisa Rodríguez stop in Fresno for two days on their way to the coastal crops. The first people to greet them ask about Jesusita's children. They have not seen any of them. Are they sure? Yes, they're sure. Not in El Centro or Arvin or Delano? No, nor in Taft or Wasco either. The word spreads. Some of the more ardent scoffers prevail upon Pedro and Luisa to talk to Padre Montes. He is taken by surprise.

"Are you sure?" he asks over and over again.

"Yes, we're sure. Why would we lie, Padre?"

"Could they have been working in other campos, campos that you didn't work in?"

"Of course, Padre. But why would they go to campos that they're not familiar with, especially with the little one with them?"

Pedro and Luisa move on, leaving a furor behind them. Charley Montemayor relates the disappearance of Jesusita's children to the sheriff and his deputies. "They're not here. They disappeared two months ago. That woman has been telling everyone that they went to work in the fields with the folks that just left. Lies. Those people have been working in the fields all over the state since May and have not seen them anywhere. Those people are the same two people that her kids worked and traveled with all last summer. Where are those kids now? The Mexican community is up in arms. They smell foul play. They want something done."

The sheriff and his deputies had believed Felipe Domínguez. To them, Jesusita's strange behavior since the disappearance of her children has borne them out. The sheriff would have filed murder charges against her had it been up to him. Only the district attorney has that power, and he was unduly influenced by his priest friends. But the sheriff and his deputies have long memories and the next district attorney election is only nineteen months away.

Speculation runs wild in the sheriff's department. The prevailing view is that the woman's children all knew that she had drowned their sister and were threatening to go to the sheriff. To stop them, she has murdered them too. There is a big dirt basement under her house, and she could have easily disposed of their bodies there without anyone being the wiser. She also has a big backyard and could have, without much effort, dug shallow graves out there for the two younger ones. The sheriff goes to the district attorney seeking a warrant to search Jesusita's home and premises. John Thomas has already been second-guessing his original decision not to file murder charges against Jesusita. He has heard about all the rumors and speculation circulating in the Mexican town. Now that the kids' disappearance has been confirmed, he has no alternative but to issue a search warrant, which he does, hoping against hope that the sheriff finds nothing and making a point to constantly remind himself never again to give Father Reilly the kind of attention that he gave him in this case. As he drafts the search warrant, he counts. There are only eighteen months until his next election.

Two nights later, Jesusita returns home from work just after 2:30. She is shocked to find the screen door open and pushed flat against the front wall. She looks again in the dark and finds the front door wide open. She is scared as she steps into her home. Her couch has been moved into the center of her front room. Her hutch has been overturned and there are broken dishes everywhere. One of the shades has been torn from its window. In her room her mattress and box spring stand on edge pushed into the window shades. Her bed's wooden slats are nowhere to be seen. Her bureau has been shoved away from the wall and all the drawers are open and empty. Two of the drawers lie atop a pile of clothes on the floor. There is another pile of clothes and shoes on the floor near the closet. In the dining room there is a broken chair, and the table and other chairs have been moved over by the windows. The door to Sergio's room is open. His bed has also been disassembled, and the clothes and other things he has left behind are in a pile on the floor. In the kitchen, there are broken dishes and glasses everywhere. Pots and pans are strewn on the floor. The cupboards and cabinets are open and empty. The icebox is open and the ice has melted. The mattresses and springs from Yolanda's room line the kitchen wall. The room itself is littered with everything that Yolanda did not take with them.

The kitchen door is wide open. Jesusita closes it and then pushes against it with all her weight to make doubly sure that it is closed and locked. She remembers that the front door is also open. She closes it and leans against it as she locks and relocks it. Next to it, she sees for the first time several sheets of paper nailed to the wall. Each page is filled with typewritten words of which her name is the only one she understands. She starts to turn out the lights but thinks that whoever did this might still be in the house. Terrified anew, she begins a room-by-room search looking at every space where someone could be hiding, tentatively at first and then boldly once she is reasonably certain no one is in that space. There is no one but her in the house. She returns to the front room, turning out the lights as she goes. She sits on the floor with her back against the front door. Sleep does not come.

Daylight appears. It has been there for some time before she realizes it. She goes to the back door. Opening it, she sees that bushes along the fences have been broken and bent and two uprooted. The basement door is open. She has nothing down there except a few yard tools and jars of preserved fruit that she has canned resting on crude shelves she made. The tools are untouched, but the shelves have been overturned and some of the jars are broken, making a muddy, mushy, sticky dirt floor in places. She wants to cry but can't and doesn't.

As she closes the basement door, Petra, the nosy, old, next-door neighbor whom she never talks to, is standing outside watching. "It was the police. I saw them. They came yesterday after you went to work. It was the police. They went in and out of your house, and I heard all that banging and breaking and I kept yelling, 'Stop! Stop! You can't do this! You're not supposed to do this! You're the police!' And you know what they told me? Or rather what that fat little Mexican who's always with them and doesn't think he's a Mexican anymore told me? 'Shut up, old woman! Shut up! Before we arrest you and search your house too!' Can you believe that? He's not even a police and he's going to arrest me? But I shut up anyway. Because you never know what could happen these days."

It takes Jesusita weeks to rid herself of the debris. Each day on her way to work, she takes only what she can carry concealed under one arm under her shawl and then surreptitiously dumps it at various places along the railroad tracks. She does this so that the community won't know about her and the police. But the community has long since known. The next-door neighbor's words spread like wildfire. The day after the search, Padre Montes knows. He goes to Father Reilly, pleading with Reilly to intercede with the district attorney to stop this police harassment. John Thomas refuses to discuss Jesusita's case anymore with Father Reilly. Padre Montes tries to visit Jesusita, going to her house on two successive afternoons, but she will not answer.

OVER THE next two months, the community's interest in Jesusita wanes. But when the school year begins in late September and the González children are not there, a new stirring begins.

"Were the González girls in school today?"

"No."

"That means that they haven't been in school all week. And remember, they were there for the beginning of school last year."

"I know."

"What are the police doing about it?"

"I don't know. Montemayor says that he thinks the sheriff is going to try to get the district attorney to talk to Felipe Domínguez again. But he doesn't think the district attorney will."

A month later, Pedro and Luisa Rodríguez return to Fresno for the winter. They report that not once have they seen the González kids in any of the many ranches they have worked at in the last three months. They also say that they asked everyone they met if they had seen or heard of the González kids working in the campo. The answer was always no. Now the community is angry. They demand that the sheriff and the district attorney do something. The common cry is, "If these kids were from a white family and not poor Mexicans, they wouldn't be standing idly by as they are now. They would be busy bringing the responsible person to justice." The sheriff announces that he will be conducting an investigation into the disappearance of the González children and that the person or persons responsible will be brought to justice.

Padre Montes is concerned for Jesusita's safety. What has happened to her? If she would just be herself, none of this would be happening. Has she despaired? Has she committed the greatest sin there is: despairing in God? Is that why she has given up Mass and Communion and Confession? He does not like thinking those thoughts. But how else can one explain what has happened? On the other hand, she is not well. Everybody understands that. And people who are not well cannot be held accountable like the rest of us. He tries to visit her, but she won't answer the door. One night, he goes to the Power building and waits for her in the park across the street. The early November night is much colder than he expected. He curls up on a park bench but falls asleep. When he wakes it is past two, and he is certain that he has missed her.

A few hours later at the 6:00 Mass when he turns to give the first blessing, he sees a lone woman, covered by a black shawl, kneeling in the last row. As he continues with the Mass, the woman is foremost in his mind. At first he has no idea who she is and then begins to think that it might be Jesusita. When he turns for the second blessing, he sees that it is Jesusita kneeling as far from him as possible and almost hidden by the black shawl. Each time he turns from the altar she is kneeling; she never sits or stands. When the time comes for the reception of Holy Communion, she remains kneeling in the last pew. He thinks of speaking to her but decides that it would be better to wait. At the conclusion of the Mass as he steps down from the altar, he says, "Jesusita, I need to talk to you. It is very important. Let me change out of these vestments and I'll be right back." She doesn't answer or move. When he returns she is gone. Maybe she hasn't despaired, he thinks. Or maybe she has but is now reaching out to God in her own way.

The next morning as he turns to offer Holy Communion to a church empty save for her, he says, "Jesusita, please come forward and receive the Body and Blood of Jesus Christ. I know you are without sin. I doubt that missing Mass on Sunday is a sin in your case. But if it is, I absolve you from it now. Come receive the Body and Blood of our Savior." For the first time she stands and steps out of the pew. Instead of moving toward the altar railing, she turns and leaves the church. *No, it is not a matter of missing Mass on Sunday,* he thinks. *Perhaps she has despaired.*

The following morning as he begins the Mass, he hears her entering the church. He turns. "Jesusita, I must speak to you. Please wait until..." She is about to enter that last pew; instead she turns and leaves. Either she is sicker than he thought or she has despaired completely.

She is there the next morning, entering just after he has begun the Mass and leaving as he recites the last prayer. He does not attempt to speak to or acknowledge her. It is better that way. Let her come to terms with God in her own way. For the next two weeks she comes to Mass every morning except Sundays—there is no 6:00 Mass on Sundays. On two of the mornings, there are two other women present. On a Saturday morning after Mass, as he is about to start down the stairs to the sacristy, he hears shouting outside the church. He puts down the chalice and rushes to the front doors. Four women have Jesusita pinned against the church fence and are hitting her, shouting that she is a murderer, a sinner who has no right to be desecrating their church. He yells at them to stop. When the women see him, they run. Before he can get down to the bottom of the steps, Jesusita is also gone.

The next day, he gives an impassioned sermon at the 11:00 Mass. The church is filled. He relates what he has seen over the past two and a half weeks and yesterday. He compares Jesusita to Jesus being stoned on his way to Calvary. "She is not well!" he shouts. "But she is the holiest person I have ever known! Not only as a priest but in my lifetime! Those of you who committed those atrocious acts, who beat her, and those of you who condone those atrocious acts have sinned not only against Almighty God and His Church but against her and me! She is the holiest of women, I tell you!" He pauses and surveys his congregation.

"She is a murderer," someone says. "She killed all of her children," another seconds. "Stand and identify yourselves, you non-believers! I dare you to stand and say that before everyone here to Almighty God in His Church!" Four people stand. They say nothing. They leave. Three more follow. "They will have to live with their heresy before God!" he bellows. His face is red and his eyes are fierce. "Don't be afraid! The rest of you nonbelievers stand and identify yourselves! Leave now! You are not welcome in the House of God!" No one else leaves.

The next afternoon, Montemayor is summoned to the sheriff's office. "Charley," Sheriff Williams says, "I've been in touch with the sheriff of Imperial County down in El Centro. He says that the González kids are alive and well and living together in El Centro. The reason no one has seen them working in any of the ranches is because the boy and the girl have good jobs in town. The younger girl is in school there and doing well. So I'm terminating our investigation as to the whereabouts of the González children. I want you to make that known to the Mexican community."

Montemayor is reluctant to carry that information to his community. He remains silent, shaking his head.

"What's the matter, Charley?"

"I think it's better if you tell them, Sheriff. They'll believe you more than me."

The next evening Sheriff Williams addresses a crowd of sixty-eight people from the church steps. When he is finished, someone asks, "How do we know that they're really working in town?"

"Well, you have my say-so. But if you want to see for yourself, you can go down there. You'll find Sergio González working for the city and county down there as a Spanish-speaking interpreter. Yolanda González has a good job at Kroger's, the biggest grocery store in the county. Apparently their English is a real asset to the folks in that border town."

"Where are they living?"

"In one of El Centro's better neighborhoods, and the young girl is attending El Centro's best elementary school and doing very well."

As the crowd disperses, someone says, "That still doesn't explain why those kids went to El Centro without her and why they haven't even come back to visit her."

Another answers, "I don't know and I don't care. I've heard enough about Jesusita and her kids."

Still another says, "Me too."

THE DAYS turn into weeks, the weeks into months, and the months into years. By then, to most in the community, she has become that weird, crazy woman who leaves her house every afternoon to clean offices until one or two in the morning, who goes to the 6:00 Mass every morning but never receives Communion, who buys her groceries once a week on Monday mornings. She speaks to no one but has never been known to hurt or bother anyone. She shies away from children wherever she might see them. She is unpleasant to be around, and that probably explains why her children never visit her. A few continue to insinuate that she is this way because she drowned her daughter.

Padre Montes still maintains that she is the holiest person he has ever known. He prays for her every day, asking God to let her be well again for His Own Greater Glory. Just after the sheriff's announcement, he establishes a Sunday 6:00 Mass. No one misses the implication, but Jesusita no longer misses Mass. Again and again he tries to speak to her but she always turns and leaves—and she never answers her door.

It is Charley Montemayor who comes to the rectory and says that the sheriff is asking that Montes come to the jail to help settle a dispute. Sheriff's deputies have arrested two Mexican men who were creating a disturbance and trying to break into Jesusita's house. They tell Padre Montes that they are the sons of the owners of the house who have died and left the house to them. They have come from Mexico to reclaim the house and evict the current resident, but she will not answer the door even though the neighbors say that she is in the house. Padre Montes answers that if their parents are dead, then the house is now the property of the church because before their parents returned to Mexico they executed a will, which he has in the rectory, leaving the house to the church and he is not about to evict the current resident.

After much discussion, the men say that in any case Jesusita owes them many months of rent that she did not pay when their parents were alive. Padre Montes answers that that is preposterous. But Sheriff Williams thinks there could be some truth to it. When one of his deputies spoke to Jesusita's boss, Jim Morrison, he said that in the last couple of months her work record has been spotty and that she hasn't worked for the past week. In fairness to these men, Sheriff Williams says his deputies ought to at least speak to Jesusita, but she won't open the door to anyone.

Padre Montes accompanies two deputies and Montemayor when they kick Jesusita's front door in. All the shades are down and despite a bright, sunny afternoon the house is dark. The house seems more sparsely furnished than before and it has a musty, stale smell. Jesusita is in bed. From the dirty dishes and soiled clothes that are stacked around the bed, it appears that she has been in bed for some time. The deputies try talking to her through Montemayor, but there is no indication that she hears him or them. She doesn't answer. Her eyes are fastened on Padre Montes. There is a supplicant look to those eyes. One of the deputies says, "Father, talk to her."

"Jesusita, these men are the police. They have questions to ask you. It is very important that you answer them. They have men claiming to be the sons of the owners of this house. They say that their parents died and they want this house. They want you out of the house. They also say that you have not paid the rent for months and they want that money as well."

She doesn't answer. But her eyes are still with him, open, supplicant.

"Jesusita it is very important that you answer."

She blinks, searching for words. Then she says in a low voice that is difficult to hear, "I know nothing about the owners' deaths. I have paid all the rent except for last month and this month too.

I have the money. That's not it. My back hurts so much that I can barely walk to Mass. I haven't worked for more than a week. I can't bend down to do that work anymore. It hurts too much, and I can't make the walk there anymore. It's too far. Something's happened to my back. It hurts more and more, and now it hurts all the time. I haven't paid the rent for two months because the Western Union is too far away. It's not that I don't want to pay it or don't have the money to pay it. It's just that it hurts too much to walk that far. The only time my back doesn't hurt now is when I'm lying here in bed."

The deputies have heard and seen enough. One of them says, "Let's go."

Padre Montes is not so ready. "I will not leave, Jesusita. I will stay here all night and all week if I have to, until you tell me that you will let me have a doctor examine you."

Her eyes remain the same, supplicant, pleading. "Yes," she nods.

"You won't lock me out?"

"No."

"You'll let the doctor examine you?"

"Yes."

"You'll give me a key so that I can bring the doctor, so that I can look in on you from time to time?"

"Yes."

The doctor says that Jesusita has a dislocated disc in her lower back. Surgery is an option but is costly and not always successful. If she continues to rest and refrains from all heavy or extended physical movement, she can reduce the pain significantly. Returning to her job cleaning offices is out of the question. It will cause further damage and continuous pain. Padre Montes sees her daily until she is able to get out of bed and move around the house without pain. He waits until that time to ask what he has been obsessed with asking for years. Finally he says, "Jesusita, why won't you receive Holy Communion?" Tears fall, her body bends, she sits down and hides her face in her crossed arms. "I am not worthy, Padre. I am not worthy. Please don't ask me anymore. Go. Leave me. Please."

✝ XIII

THAT NIGHT, Elmer gives Lois a full account of what happened at the Salvation Army store. When he is finished, Lois says, "Well, all I've got to say is that if he's going to live here, he's going to have to go to church with us on Sunday. And he can't go dressed the way he is here every day. Which means that he's got to wear that suit and shirt and necktie. Can you imagine what a laughingstock we'd be if he showed up dressed like he is?"

"What do you mean 'if' he's going to live here? I can't work this place by myself, and we don't have the money to hire a grown man."

"That's not my problem. I'm not the one who went out and bought sixty more acres when we were doing just fine with fifty. And I told you from the beginning not to do it. But did you listen to me? Oh, no, you had to be a big-time rancher."

"Please Lois, let's not go through that again. We got a serious problem here."

"No, *you've* got a serious problem."

"What'd you mean?"

"I'm not taking him to church smelling like he does, suit or no suit. He needs a bath. Probably hasn't had one since long before he got here."

"How's he gonna take a bath if you won't let him in the house?"

"He doesn't need to come into the house to take a bath. He can take one in the wash trays down by the barn."

"He can't fit in those trays. They're divided and he's damn near as tall as me. Hell, I couldn't get half of me in one of those trays."

"Who says you have to get all of you or him in one of those trays?"

"What're you talking about?"

"There's nothing that says that he can't stand in one of those trays with water up to his knees. Then he can kneel in it with water coming up to his stomach. Next, sit him in it with his legs hanging over the trays' edge. That'll bring the water up to his neck. Get him out and have him dunk his head in it up to his neck. Do those things any way you want. Just make sure that you change the water every time you put another part of him in and he'll get him a good bath."

"There's no hot water out there."

"Who says he needs hot water in this weather? Shoot, after a day in that sun he'll be as happy as anyone can imagine to get in that cold water.... So you better start washing him, so I can start measuring him and sewing. Believe me, I'm not getting near that boy until he's been bathed. I don't have much time 'til Sunday, and I don't want to look like a darn fool on Sunday with him in a suit that's three sizes too big for him. And you can tell him for me that if he doesn't take a bath real soon, he's out of here."

Elmer Jensen does not sleep well that night. The following morning as they're gathering their tools, he says, "Listen to me, Felix. Listen to me real good because I mean what I say. On Sunday, you have to go to church with us. And before that, you have to take a bath out here in the trays and get measured for and wear that suit and white shirt and tie I bought you at the Salvation Army to go to church. If you don't want to do all those things, I'll have to take you back to the shelter on Monday. You gonna go to church with us on Sunday all clean and wearing that suit?"

"Why did you tell that woman yesterday that I live with one of your neighbors and work on his ranch?"

Felix's response surprises and angers Elmer Jensen. *That silly, stupid bastard. I should have whacked him a good one in the store yesterday. That would have straightened him out good then, and I wouldn't* have to be dealing with *this silly shit now.* "I asked you a question, boy, and I want a goddamn answer now!"

But Felix doesn't answer. Instead he stares at Elmer with pitiful orange-yellow eyes.

I'd better control myself. Better not start beating on the boy. God knows where I'd stop once I got started. And if the Welfare people ever hear about it, I'd be working this place by myself. I'll be damned! I take this pathetic idiot out of the shelter when family after family didn't want him. I give him a good job here with decent pay, more money than he's ever had, and I give him a home here...

"You know I live with you and work with you here. You know this is my home."

His home! His home! The sorry son of a bitch ain't never had a home! His home.

Now it is Elmer who doesn't answer. He simply stares at Felix, not knowing what to say or do.

"So why did you say those things when you know they weren't true?"

Sorry son of a bitch, is all that enters his mind as he continues staring. *Sorry son of a bitch.* Finally, he says, "Look, that was a slip of the tongue, boy. It won't happen again. You're right. You live and work here too. This is your home."

Felix's eyes water. He looks away. He has nothing more to say. Elmer Jensen looks away too, letting those moments pass. After a while, he says quietly, awkwardly, "Well, we'd better get started..."

There isn't much for Felix to think about. He has seen the orchards blossom, their green pods grow and ripen into delicious fruit. When he came, some of the vines had tiny leaves, some none at all. Now all the vines are miniature trees with huge leaves that he can lie under away from the sun. He has watched the first tiny green clusters form on those vines and grow and grow into luscious bunches of grapes. And he knows that he and Mr. Jensen have made it all happen. No, there is no place else for him to go, least of all the shelter. And this is his home, too.

He bathes late that afternoon in the wash trays by the barn with

Mr. Jensen holding up a large towel in front of the trays so that he can't be seen from the house or the road, and then changing the water before he assumes each of the different positions. He has no underwear, and Lois insists that he wear some of Elmer's clean underwear before she measures him, which she does in the back porch in the presence of her husband, after the children are in bed. The last measurement and fitting takes place on Saturday night. At 10:40 she returns to the porch with the suit and shirt for the last time. They're a loose fit but she says she sewed them that way so that he would have room to grow into them in the years to come. Felix dons the clothes, and as he turns from side to side for the last time in the open, screened-off porch, he begins to sweat, first lightly, then profusely. "It's hot," he says. "This suit is real hot."

"Well, I've done quite a few things with that suit and shirt," Lois says. "But the weather is in God's Hands."

The next morning the Jensen's leave earlier than usual for Sunday service. The four kids have piled into the front seat of the small pickup. Elmer Jensen sits behind the steering wheel with the engine idling. Junior has already pressed himself against his Dad. Millie has taken her place on Bonnie's lap and Freddie is sitting in Mama's place waiting for her with the door open. Felix sits outside in the pick-up bed with his back against the cab. He is dressed in his black suit, white shirt, and tie and wears his sweat-stained straw hat against the sun.

When Mrs. Jensen reaches the pickup, she goes to its bed and says, "When we get to the church, I want you to sit in the back in the last row. We're going to be sitting in front. Since you're not really a member of our church, it wouldn't be right for you to sit up there with us. I don't want you talking back there with anyone or being a distraction to anyone. All of that will just reflect poorly on us.... Take off that hat! Give it to me! It's your work hat! You can't wear that to church! It's stinky, smelly, and dirty! What will people think?"

She returns to the house with the hat. Again they wait. Felix begins sweating heavily. Just a few minutes before, the hat's band had absorbed or diverted much of the sweat. Now his sweat drips down freely onto his black suit which feels like it's roasting him. The white shirt has pasted itself on his upper body. Although it is not yet nine o'clock, the sun seems hotter than ever. *It has to be the suit,* he thinks. Millie and Junior begin rapping on the back window. Felix turns, grinning, just as Mrs. Jensen returns. "Stop banging on that window! You know I don't want you talking to him, especially you girls!" Finally the pickup moves and in minutes the rushing hot air dries and cools Felix.

They are the first people to arrive at the church. It is a small church. The doors are open, and Mrs. Jensen begins pointing to the last row even before they can see it. Felix takes his seat as the others move forward. He has not been in many churches, but this is by far the smallest and the plainest and the hottest. Sweat begins streaming down the sides of his head and forehead almost immediately. Others begin arriving. They look at him curiously, whisper among themselves, and then move past him. He has never been among so many white people in his life. Sweat is gluing the heavy wool to his upper legs. He picks at the pant legs, lifts them, squirms, and shifts in his seat only to see that the space he has vacated is wet. Embarrassed, he moves back, covering the damp. Bonnie and Junior turn in their front row and grin back at him. Bonnie receives a slap and Junior a yank. They don't turn again.

The preacher appears. He stands on a raised platform. He wears a suit, but a light one. He begins by talking, then shouting about God and Jesus and the Devil, and about Heaven and Hell. Felix has heard some of this before. So he knows that God is good and the Devil is bad. If you're good, you go live with God when you die. If you're bad, after you die you'll burn in Hell with the Devil forever and ever. Felix hears him. You'd have to be deaf not to, but he doesn't listen. For one thing, he doesn't understand a lot of the words that the preacher is using—but the main thing is, Felix doesn't think he's bad. How can he be bad when he works all day, most every day, and his work makes good things? The only person he talks to is Mr. Jensen, his boss, and he always does what Mr.

Jensen tells him to do. So how could he be bad? If anyone is bad, it's Mr. Jensen when he lied to that woman in the store in Fresno. He knows why Mr. Jensen lied. He's always known why he lied. Even if Mr. Jensen won't say so.

When the preacher stops shouting, a woman up there starts playing a piano and a man sitting next to her starts beating on drums. People start singing and clapping their hands. It gets loud in there, real loud. He can't make out most of the words except that he can tell that it's mostly about God and Jesus and Heaven. Some people seem to be shouting rather than singing. They're throwing their hands and their arms up when they clap. He's never been in a church like this.

Then the music stops and the preacher starts shouting about God again, but mostly about Jesus. Then people go up to him and he talks to them and they kneel before him one at a time. And he puts his hands on their heads and prays. When he's finished, the people come down smiling and happy. The music starts up again. Singing joins in. Felix thinks about Ralph. Where is he? Does he have to go to a church like this one? After a while, people go up on the platform again and tell their stories, mostly about them and Jesus. He doesn't listen. He is soaked with sweat and his butt is hurting from so much sitting. He wishes they could leave. He sees a woman leave the preacher and come down the aisle with her eyes closed and her hands folded, smiling. She looks happy. He looks around and sees others with their eyes closed and thinks it's a good idea. He closes his eyes and the next thing he knows is that an old man is leaning over him shaking his knee saying, "Better wake up, son. Everybody's leaving and you keep on sleeping and you're liable to be left behind."

For the next two days whenever they're together, Mr. Jensen tries to convince Felix that he, Felix, enjoyed the Sunday service. Felix won't answer, won't agree. Finally, frustrated, Mr. Jensen says, "Well, you damn well better start liking it. Because, unless you go back to the shelter, you're going there with us every Sunday."

Now Felix answers, "Why did you tell that woman in the store that I don't work here, that I don't live here?"

"Are you gonna start that again?"

"I just wanna know. Why?"

"I'm not gonna talk about that anymore."

"If I'm gonna go to church every Sunday, I need a hat."

"A hat?"

"Yeah. Mrs. Jensen won't let me take this hat to church. She said it's too smelly and dirty. So she took it away from me on Sunday and I sweated all over my new suit. Now my new suit smells."

"If you promise me that you'll stop talking about that woman in Fresno, I'll get you one. I've got to go over there on Thursday, and I'll see what I can do."

"I need a hat."

The next morning, Mr. Jensen comes out to the barn with a piece of string. Taking one end of the string between his thumb and forefinger, he presses it against Felix's forehead. "Hold still." Then he winds the loose end around Felix's head until it meets his thumb and forefinger. "Ok, I got it," marking the string with a pencil. The next afternoon he says to Felix, "Ok, mister, I've got to go to Fresno. You're in charge here. I know you can do it." The boy nods seriously.

On Friday morning, Mr. Jensen walks into the barn holding a dark gray fedora. "Try it on. Try it on." The boy is surprised and pleased. The hat fits. He turns in every direction while Mr. Jensen admires him with the hat on. "My God, with that suit and tie, you're gonna look just like a lawyer." The boy grins.

Over the next year and a half, Felix Bocanegra does not miss a single Sunday service. Little changes except for the increase in the smiles the Jensen children flash at him every chance they get, both in church and in the pickup—sometimes not without a slap or a pinch to the kids, and a warning from Mrs. Jensen. "I'm telling you for the last time, boy, stop smiling at my girls."

Three times during the first six months, the preacher calls Felix up to him. "Come on up here, son. Come on up here and meet Jesus," while everyone stares and some shake their heads in disbelief. The boy does as he is told. Respectfully he walks down the center aisle neither too fast nor too slow and carefully climbs up the platform's two steps. "Come on over here, boy." He goes to the preacher who gently puts both hands on his shoulders. "Now tell me, do you want to meet Jesus? Do you want to meet your Savior?" The boy stands mute. From the front row Elmer Jensen can be heard to be saying softly, "He's slow, preacher. He's slow." The preacher gently guides the boy down on his knees. He puts both hands on the boy's head and cries out, "Dear Jesus, help this poor boy. He's not very smart, Lord, so You're gonna have to help him more than You would the next person. Bring him to You, Jesus! Bring him to You!" The boy kneels silently, knowing that this too will pass if only he can remain motionless and mute. While from the front row can be heard, "He's slow, preacher. He's real slow."

After the third time the preacher says, "Yes indeed, he *is* slow. Very slow. But he understands that Jesus is here because he comes every Sunday, doesn't he? He wants to come every Sunday, doesn't he? He asks to come every Sunday, doesn't he?"

"Yes, he does, preacher. Yes, he surely does."

"Well then, that's a good sign, that's a true beginning. It shows that despite his limitations, he knows, he understands. I'll bet he begs to be here. So keep on bringing him. Because Jesus will show him the way. And remember, 'The meek shall inherit the earth.'"

IN THE last days of January, tule fog has hung over the valley for weeks, making the days dark, cold, and gloomy. Elmer and Felix are pruning in the apricot orchard when Junior comes running. "Daddy, Daddy, there's a man at the house and Mama says that you and Felix better come now! And to hurry!"

"Who is it?"

"I don't know."

"She wants Felix too?"

"That's what she said. 'And tell your father to bring Felix. Hurry!'"

As they half-walk, half-run, Elmer Jensen is worried. Just two

Sundays before, after church, he heard that Fred Wilson had gotten into trouble with the sheriff over a sixteen-year-old Mexican boy, an illegal immigrant, who didn't speak a word of English, who had been working twelve to sixteen hours a day, seven days a week on the Wilson ranch for food and shelter. As the house comes into view, Elmer keeps thinking about the vast differences between Felix and that boy. But he is still worried.

When they reach the house, Elmer and Junior go in. Felix waits outside in the driveway. The man introduces himself as Brian Maddon of the Fresno County Welfare Department and then stops short. "Where's Felix?"

"He's outside," Junior volunteers.

"It's very important that he be present. I need him here."

Elmer looks nervously at Lois who tells Junior, "Go get him. Tell him to come in here. Tell him that *I* said he should come in."

Once Felix is in the front room, the social worker begins again. "Felix, in three and a half weeks, on February 23rd, you'll be eighteen and you will no longer be a ward of the court. What that means is that then you will be an adult for most purposes, a person who can come and go as he pleases. You can work anywhere you want and live anywhere you want. But you will also have to work to support yourself. The Jensens here and the county will no longer be obligated to provide you with food, clothing, and shelter. On February 23rd, you can walk away from this ranch or stay here as you see fit."

Elmer Jensen asks many questions regarding what their obligations are to Felix if he decides to stay and what his are to them. When he is finished, the social worker asks Felix if he has any questions. "Only one. Where's my brother Ralph?"

"He's back in the shelter again. And as an adult you can see him any time you want. Visiting days are Sundays from noon to four."

THAT NIGHT there is a heated discussion in the Jensens' bedroom.

"I don't want him in the house. It's as simple as that. And the porch is part of the house. Not only is he filthy and bad smelling, but I see the way he looks at the girls. And they think he's so nice. Him sleeping in the porch is too close for comfort as far as I'm concerned."

"Lois, I've never seen him look at the girls any different than he looks at everybody else. He does the work of two men. He's working fifty and sixty hours a week now and it's winter. There's been times in the summer where he's worked eighty hours a week. I can't run this place by myself, and I can't afford to hire full-time help to replace him. All I give him is five dollars a week and his room and board and he's satisfied."

"You should have thought of that when you went out and bought those extra sixty acres."

"Please don't start that again."

THE NEXT morning Elmer says, "Well, let me put it to you this way, boy, are you gonna stay here with us or are you gonna move on?"

There is that long pause before Felix begins, which today Elmer finds irritating. "I'm hoping to stay, Mr. Jensen, if you folks let me. I got nowhere else to go. I don't know nobody else. This is the only work I've ever done. You heard the man say that I have to start supporting myself. I like the work here. You folks have been real good to me. I want to stay."

"Well, that's good to hear."

But even as Elmer speaks, he knows that that is only half the battle. Lois didn't talk to him this morning when they got up. She didn't say a word to him as she fixed his breakfast, and once she served him she left the kitchen without eating and still not a word for him. She's not going to change her mind. Come February, Felix must be out of the porch. Where to put him? The barn is too big and drafty and to make a separate room in it would be too costly. Besides, it still would be too close to the house, and Lois would have the same complaint: "That boy is still too close to those girls." He thinks about it all day and a good part of the night, but there is just no place to put the boy.

The next day just after lunch, as he goes over to the McCutchen

acres, as he still calls the sixty acres he bought from old man Mc-
Cutchen, Elmer Jensen finds himself looking at his answer: the
chicken coop—an abandoned ten-by-twelve-foot structure that
McCutchen had once used for chickens. It is still in good condition, and there is plenty of old lumber lying around the ranch that
he can use for siding. A kerosene lamp will be all the light Felix
will need, and there is an old wood stove in the barn that is still
plenty useable.

"I don't understand what your problem is, Lois."

"There's no water over there, no toilet."

"He hasn't had water or a toilet here. He's used the trays out
back to wash up and bathe, and he's always used a shovel to bury
his waste. So how is this going to be any different?"

"So where's he going to cook and eat?"

"Lois, be reasonable. You've cooked for him and we've fed him
all this time for next to nothing extra, and it doesn't take a heck
of a lot more work to cook for seven instead of six."

"That's easy for you to say. You're not the one doing the cooking."

"Please Lois, do you know how much we'll be saving by keeping him?"

"Where's he going to eat? I don't want him eating in the barn
anymore. I'm tired of seeing those big fat rats running in and out
of the barn after every time he eats. It won't be long before we
have those rats in this house. And I'm telling you right now, Elmer
Jensen, I just won't stand for it."

"He can eat in his chicken coop."

"That's at least two city blocks away."

"You've said over and over again that you don't want him near
the girls."

"And I don't. Come February, I don't want him coming around
this house not even to pick up his food."

"Junior can take his food over to him."

"Junior! Are you out of your mind? Do you think I want my
son associating with that boy every day? Have you any idea what
kind of bad influence that boy can have on your son? Remember

what that social worker said the other day? Your trusted worker was in seven foster homes in five years before he came here. What does that tell you about him? And you want your son associating with him? Not me. No sir, not me."

"I'll take his food over to him."

"What! We're a family, remember? We sit down and eat together. You mean to tell me that me and the children will be sitting down to our dinners alone while you're busy feeding that...whatever you want to call him? No sir! Not if I have anything to say about it."

"So I'll take his food out to him *after* we eat. This ain't no restaurant. He doesn't need to have piping hot food."

Then they are silent. Lois Jensen thinks while Elmer Jensen hopes. Finally she says, "Well Elmer, I hope you know what you're doing."

There is still more talking to do, and Elmer does it the next morning.

"Felix, you know I'd like very much for you to stay on here. You're like my right-hand man." He waits for the boy to answer.

"Thank you, Mr. Jensen."

"But there is a problem."

"What's that, sir?"

"Come February, you're gonna be eighteen. You'll be a man then, son. And I'm just not comfortable with a grown man sleeping in somebody else's back porch."

"I don't mind it."

"Well, you should. Because a grown man needs his privacy. Needs to be able to come and go as he pleases without worrying about the folks in the other part of the house. He needs a place to keep all his own things, like his Sunday suit. Who knows, you might even want to have a girl or two come and visit."

Felix reddens.

"I mean, you know, just visit. Like one of those girls from church. Or it could be a man friend."

"I don't have any friends, Mr. Jensen."

"You will. Wait and see, you will.... What I've been thinking is fixing up that chicken coop on the McCutchen acres. With a little siding and some paint and the old stove in the barn plus a kerosene lamp, it could be pretty nice. Real nice. And..."

The boy listens, nodding more and more. When Elmer Jensen stops, he says, "I like your idea, Mr. Jensen. I like it just fine."

"Good. Now there's one other thing. You've worked out pretty good. And like I said, I consider you to be my right-hand man. I've left you in charge of the ranch many times when I've had to go into town, haven't I?"

"Yes, sir."

"So I'm here and now raising your wages from five dollars a week to seven dollars and fifty cents a week. Seeing's how you only work six days a week, that's way more than a dollar a day."

"Thank you, sir."

"There's one other thing you should know. This here ranch is a business, and one of the main rules of businesses is that you don't talk to anyone outside the business about business money matters. In other words, what I pay you is just between you and me. It's nobody else's business. If I was to find out that you were out there talking to people about what I pay you, I would be mighty offended. Have any problem with that?"

Their eyes meet. In Elmer's mind the search takes longer than it should. He doesn't like it. But Felix finally says, "No, sir."

"Good. Then we'll start in on that coop tomorrow. Who knows, we may have you in there before your birthday."

JUST AFTER eight o'clock on the Sunday following Felix's eighteenth birthday, Bonnie runs into the bathroom crying, "Daddy! Daddy! Felix is out on the road going somewhere!"

"What road?"

"The Manning road! And he's all dressed up too!"

"Where's he going?"

"I don't know, but not to church."

"Not to church and all dressed up?"

"He's going the other way, not the church way, and he's in his Sunday suit."

Elmer Jensen gets in his pickup and overtakes the boy on Manning Avenue. He has always taken long, loping strides, but now on the asphalt road, the strides seem even longer and faster.

"Where you headed, boy?" he says through the open passenger window.

"To see my brother."

"I thought your brother's in Fresno?"

"He is."

"Fresno's seven miles away."

"I know. That's why I'm leaving early."

"You're not going to church with us then?"

"Nope."

"What'll I tell the preacher?"

"I don't know.... Just tell him the truth. That I went to see my brother."

"How you getting home?"

"The same way I'm getting there. Walking."

"You sure you can make it?"

"I'm gonna make it."

Make it he does. Almost every Sunday for the next two and a half years, whatever the weather is, or how early or how late it might be, or wherever his brother is in Fresno, that strange, dark, young man in a black suit with a red tie against a white shirt that is frayed and crust-brown at the collar and a battered, gray fedora can be seen hurrying along Manning Avenue with those giant strides on his way to or from Fresno. Twice in those first months, deputy sheriffs on patrol stop that strange young man in a black suit walking around in ranch country only to have him answer with bewildered eyes that he is coming from visiting his brother and insisting that he lives and works on the Jensen ranch. Twice they drive him to the Jensen ranch and talk to Elmer Jensen as the young man sits proudly in the backseat of the patrol car and listens to Elmer Jensen say, "Yes, he lives here with us and works for me."

†XIV

PADRE MONTES obsesses over Jesusita's inability to do manual labor. The house she lives in belongs to the diocese, and he is accountable for managing it. He can reduce the rent only so much. But that is only the rent. How will she pay for utilities? More importantly, how will she feed herself once her savings are gone? It is Father Reilly who refers her to the Fresno County Welfare Department and arranges for an interview and provides several recommendations. Ultimately, she and her home are qualified as a foster care facility for Spanish-speaking children. Then Shirley Tate, a bright, young social worker who speaks Spanish, sits with Jesusita in her kitchen and explains the terms and conditions of the agreement with the county that she is about to sign.

"The department is thinking of starting you off with three or four children. You certainly have the space and furniture, not to mention the experience, for that number of children. Is that agreeable with you?"

"Yes."

"Good. You understand that your work, really your only work, will be to provide a good, healthy, nurturing home for the youngsters we send you? But having raised four of your own children and given the wonderful recommendations you have, I don't think..."

The repeated referral to her as a good mother makes Jesusita uncomfortable. Though it has been some four years now, how can they not know about Paulina. It is hard to keep eye contact with the young woman. She turns her head a little. When will the young woman mention Paulina? And then, what will she say?

"This is a full-time job, Mrs. González. Twenty-four hours a day, seven days a week. You will be expected to be here full time for and with the children. But then the county pays pretty well, especially for women in your situation. When I say..."

She doesn't have to say anything. The money is good. More than she can make anywhere else, and she knows it. She can live very well on what they will pay her for three or four kids.

"...Another thing. Most of these youngsters will have family members who will be wanting to visit them."

"I thought they were orphans."

"Some of them are. But even orphans have brothers and sisters and uncles and aunts that will be wanting to visit with them. However, more than half of them are not orphans. They are children who have been abandoned by their parents and children who have been taken away from their parents by the court because of poor parenting. Those children still have parents, and some of them will want to come and visit their children. It is the department's policy that those visits should take place here in the home—or at least begin here in the home."

"You mean these people are going to come and visit these kids here in my house?"

"Yes."

"Every day?"

"No, no. Not every day. Basically only on weekends."

"You mean every weekend?"

"Well...yes, if they want to come every weekend. But that's not been our experience. Most of these folks come and visit once or twice a year or a few times more a year. But you do have to open your home to them when they do come."

"I didn't know that."

"It's really nothing to be concerned about. At most you'll get a family visiting three or four times a year. I'm sure you can handle that."

She doesn't like it. But how else can she earn money?

"One last thing. The department expects to be making your first placements here in about three weeks. You're free 'til then, but after that you'll be pretty much tied down here. If you have any people you want to visit or places to go, I suggest that you do it now."

The morning after signing the county's agreement, Jesusita waits in the rear pew after Mass for Padre Montes. As he comes up from the sacristy, it is enough of a surprise to see her still there that he stops for a moment and looks again. He can count the number of times over the past years that she has waited for him after Mass. Though she has seldom missed the 6:00 Mass, she has always sat in the last pew and left the church as soon as he started his descent from the altar on his way down to the sacristy. On the few occasions when she has waited for him, it has usually been a problem of catastrophic proportions, at least in her mind, that has kept her there. A problem usually, that he has succeeded in setting aside simply by talking to her. Today should be no different. After all she has just entered into, or is about to enter into, an agreement with the county to care for children. That should give her a good measure of peace of mind, at least financially.

Maybe, he thinks, she has come to tell him that she is ready for Confession, ready to receive Holy Communion. *Stop! Don't raise it. Don't even think it.* How many times has she turned and run from him at the first mention of either? Once she even fled from her own house, inadvertently locking him in and making him climb out a window. What a pity. There is not another person, he is certain, in the entire diocese as devout as she. How the woman has suffered. He prays for her every day, prays she will once and for all dispel that insane notion that she is not worthy of the Holy Sacraments. Barring that, he prays that he will be there to administer the Last Rites to this saintly but disturbed woman to insure that she makes her way directly to Heaven. But what sin could she have possibly have committed that needs absolution?

"Buenos días, Jesusita."

She looks at him. Her eyes are clear. Her skin is clean, smooth, pure. And yet she says that she is not worthy. Who could be more worthy? *Oh Lord God, it is time that You lift this awful burden from this woman's shoulders.*

"Buenos días, Padre. I just want to thank you for all you've done for me. Yesterday I signed the papers. Because of you I can take care of welfare children. I can earn money again."

"First of all, you deserve it. Secondly, it was Father Reilly who made all the arrangements, not me."

"But Father Reilly doesn't even know me. It had to be you who made him do whatever he did for me. So please, thank you."

They look at each other for a moment before she becomes uncomfortable. He thinks, *There is nothing wrong with this woman's mind. What is it then, Lord God, that makes it impossible for her to walk away from this illusion that she is not worthy?* She is self-conscious now, and he does not want to end these positive moments with awkwardness. "When do you begin caring for these children?"

"The lady from the Welfare said it would be three weeks."

"And then you will be bound to them probably like you have never been before?"

"That's what she said."

"Now would be a good time to visit your own children in El Centro, wouldn't it? Have you heard from them lately?"

A frightened look returns. She shifts in three different directions to get out of the pew, but can't until he steps aside. Then she leaves.

But the thought will not leave her. Should she go to El Centro? It's been four years since she's seen them. Now with the Welfare kids coming, she may never have another chance. She could die and not see them again. Still, Sergio is always in the kitchen with his mud-caked shoes screaming, "You killed her! You lied!" Yes, she lied. Who would have believed her if she hadn't? "I hope you drown!" Did she touch her, push her? Felipe said she did. Did she? She was so angry, she could have. Maybe Felipe was telling the truth. After all these years, she doesn't know. What she does know is that she never hoped that Paulina would drown. What she said was in anger. God knows that. Not even the district attorney believed Felipe. She was never arrested, and now the County wants her to take care of its kids. How much more proof do you need, Sergio?

Early the next morning, Jesusita is on a bus headed for Los Angeles. There she will transfer to a bus going to El Centro. It is the last Saturday in October, and as the bus heads south through the central valley, stopping at small town after small town, workers are still harvesting grapes in the fields. That life seems so far removed now. As the bus rises out of the valley onto the treacherous Grapevine, she tries to think back to the last time she traveled over it. That, too, seems so long ago.

She arrives in Los Angeles in midafternoon. The depot is at the edge of downtown. There are Mexicans everywhere. She learns that she has missed her bus to El Centro and must wait some six hours for the next one. She walks about aimlessly looking into store window after store window. After more than an hour, she tires and is about to start back to the depot when she sees a church. She approaches. A schedule is posted in Spanish, listing the Sunday Masses. She enters.

The church is dark and cool, and her eyes take a few moments to adjust. It is huge, much larger than she thought. There are people, mostly women, sprinkled about, kneeling, like her, in prayer. After a while she notices movement on the left-hand side of the church. She watches, thinking and then knowing what it is. Confession. Something she has avoided and will always avoid as long as Padre Montes is there. He was there with Sergio and the district attorney when she lied. Like Sergio, he will think that she murdered Paulina if she confesses the truth. Can he forgive murder? Would he forgive murder without going to the police? Would he... But it is not Padre Montes who is hearing these Confessions, who is sitting in the confessional to her left.

She sits and thinks. A half hour passes before she rises and takes her place in the Confession line. Her heart beats faster. Once in the confessional she stumbles through her first words, saying that it has been four years since her last Confession. She pauses. Then she confesses a litany of sins she has committed over those past four years. The sins of missing Mass on Sunday, of sloth and jealousy, of lying, and of taking change from her grocer that was not hers.

"Is that all?"

"No Padre, there is something much more serious that has plagued me for all these years."

"That is?" Curious now for the first time.

Without a pause or interruption she hurriedly tells him about going down to the river, about arguing with Paulina, about grabbing her and having the girl break free, about reaching for her again, and, if not pushing her, then most certainly causing her to fall. She tells about shouting, "I hope you drown!" and ends with, "and she did."

There is a long pause before the priest asks, "Why did you wait four years to confess this?"

"Because I was so afraid that in the eyes of God I might have caused my daughter's death."

"Did the police investigate the drowning?"

"Yes, Padre."

"Did they question you?"

"Yes, Padre."

"Did they arrest you?"

"No, Padre."

"Did they ever charge you with a crime or take you to court for this?"

"No, Padre."

"They never accused you of any crime for this?"

"No, Padre."

"Then why are you coming to Confession? To, I take it, confess this as a sin?"

"Because I've always been afraid that I might have caused her death. And if I did, is that not a sin?"

"Not necessarily. When you pushed her as you say you could have, did you intend that she drown?"

"Oh no, Padre."

"When you said, 'I hope you drown,' was it your intention to drown her?"

"No, Padre, no."

"What did you mean by that?"

"I was angry. I was hurt. The last thing I wanted was that she drown. What I wanted was that she love me the way I loved her."

"You're certain of that?"

"Yes, I'm certain."

"Then I find no sin. Nothing to confess there. Now, unless you have something else to confess, let me absolve you of all the sins you've told me about and tell you to go in peace, my child. May the Lord be with you."

"And I can receive Holy Communion?"

"Of course you can."

It takes her but moments to decide. She exchanges her El Centro ticket for one to Fresno. El Centro can wait. There is too much to be done in Fresno. The first bus leaving for Fresno that night is at 8:00, and it is a slow bus again—one that stops at every little town along the way. That doesn't matter. So long as it arrives in Fresno before 11:00 the next morning. She tries sleeping on the bus but is too excited to sleep. The closer she gets to Fresno the more excited she becomes. The bus arrives at 2:35 in the morning. The late October nights have turned cold, and she has a valise that she must carry almost a mile from the depot to her home. That doesn't matter. She has walked those streets late at night, hot or cold, a thousand times, and the valise could never be lighter.

It is three minutes after three when she steps into her kitchen. If she goes to sleep then she can get seven-and-a-half hours of sleep before the 11:00 Mass. But she can't sleep. After staring into the darkness for more than an hour, she gets out of bed and paces about the house until it occurs to her that she hasn't eaten anything since breakfast the day before. She fixes herself a quesadilla and a cup of hot chocolate, but after a bite and a sip decides that she isn't hungry or thirsty. She sits at the kitchen table visualizing how she will enter the church and what the reaction will be. Many of the images send shudders through her. It is almost five. Now she worries that if she doesn't sleep soon, she might collapse when she reaches the church or even on the way to the church. She goes back to bed. She tosses and turns, which is more torturous than sitting or pacing about the house.

There is one book in the house, *Don Quixote de la Mancha,* which was left there years ago by the house's previous owners. She has tried to read it several times but has found it so tedious that most times she has fallen asleep with it in her lap. She goes to the kitchen drawer where she keeps it with towels and washrags and retrieves it. She goes back to her bed with the book prepared to sleep. But the silliness and repetition of a grown man traipsing around his neighborhood in a metal suit on a broken-down horse this time annoys her rather than bores her. Now she will never sleep. That is her last thought before she wakes later that morning. Alarmed that it might be past 11:00, she jumps out of bed and hurries to the kitchen—10:07. Relieved, she begins to worry about what to wear and how best to cover her head.

It is seven minutes past eleven when she leaves her house. Anyone going to the 11:00 Mass will be in church by then. She sees no one on the street and no one sees her enter the church. She stands in the vestibule next to the holy water urn, to one side of the inner doors. From there she can hear the recitation of the Mass and peek without being seen. The church is packed. She waits. Her moment will come. The longer she waits, the more she trembles. Maybe her moment will never come.

She has been to thousands of Masses. Listening to Padre's blessings, listening to the intonation in his prayers, she can tell exactly where he is in the Mass. Still she peeks. Finally he takes Communion himself and blesses the smaller hosts. Two lines form. They are long lines, and Jesusita thinks that some in those lines are probably not capable of receiving the Body and Blood of Jesus Christ.

Slowly the lines shrink. When there are but two persons in each line, she starts down the center aisle to the altar railing. There are gasps, stirrings, and loud whispers as she passes the back pews, so much so that others in pews closer to the altar turn and see her and the reaction becomes louder. Padre Montes is about to administer the Sacred Host to the last communicant when he sees her approaching, slowly, her hands clasped in prayer and her head bent in reverence. The sight stops him for a moment, but then he nods and smiles.

Once Jesusita receives the Host, she turns and walks slowly back down the center aisle, seemingly ignoring the stares and hums, back to the vestibule and out of the church before anyone can approach her. Later she tells him, "I am worthy now, Padre. He has made it clear to me. I am worthy now."

She becomes a daily recipient of the Host once again, and when asked, her answer is always, "I am worthy now." But by the end of the week she begins rethinking her Confession in Los Angeles. Had she told her confessor exactly how she had lied to the police and everyone, would he have forgiven her? It is a worry that she shakes off as silly, and she continues with her daily reception of the Host.

SHE HAS known that they are coming. She has rearranged the rooms: Sergio's room will be the girls' room and Yolanda's will be the boy's room. She has fully expected them and yet somehow has not expected what she sees before her on that Tuesday morning. Three young, brown faces standing awkwardly next to Shirley Tate with three cardboard valises and a bag of books. She has become unaccustomed to children, has avoided them wherever she goes, has found nothing cute or interesting about them even while facing their cooing parents. She is also unaccustomed to having so many people, even if they are children, in her house. The three bring back painful memories of Sergio, Yolanda, and… and…yes, Paulina. Memories she had not anticipated, or at least not as strongly as these.

"Mrs. González, this is Ralph," Shirley Tate says, indicating the boy standing next to her. "He's ten and in the third grade. Ralph, say hello to Mrs. González." The boy twists and turns and for a moment looks up at Jesusita from the tops of his eyes and then twists and turns some more but says not a word. "Ralph's very shy. But he'll get over it once he's been here for a little while. And standing next to Ralph is Elena." Jesusita is not interested in Elena. Instead she is looking intently at the girl next to Elena. "She's nine and she's a very smart little girl. She's also in the third grade. Say hello to Mrs. González, Elena."

The girl looks up, full-eyed, and says, "Hello."

But it is the girl next to her that has Jesusita's attention, that has been looking all about the living room and the dining room with no apparent regard for what is being said. It is she that she's trying to compare.

"And this if Fifi. She's eight, and she's Elena's sister." Even though her name has just been mentioned, the girl is still looking about the two rooms, not in the least interested in the social worker's comments. "She's in the second grade. Fifi, say hello to Mrs. González.... Fifi..." Now the girl looks to the social worker. "Say hello to Mrs. González." The girl looks up to Jesusita and with a sudden, big, bright-eyed smile says, "Hello," and returns to looking about the rooms. For Jesusita the smile is enough. There is no comparison.

"Now you kids go out and play in the backyard. Mrs. González and I have to talk." Fifi darts for the open kitchen door. Elena follows. But the boy moves just a few feet from the social worker. "Ralph, outside," Tate points, and the boy moves slowly into the dining room. "Outside, Ralph." He moves into the kitchen toward the back door. She waits until she hears the back door close. "He's a bit scared. This is his sixth placement in eight years."

"Scared of what?"

"That you won't like him and won't let him stay."

"Why would I do that?"

"There's no reason that you should. He's a good kid. Most of the placement changes came early on and were more due to his older brother than to him. But he's been in and out of homes so much that I think he's afraid that this will be another one. But he really won't be a problem."

"Where's his brother?"

"He's an adult now. He works on a ranch. He will be coming to visit Ralph."

"Here, in my house?"

"Yes."

"Do I have to let him?"

"Yes. We talked about that. Remember? But the visit doesn't have to be here. They can go to the park or the movies or wherever, just so long as Ralph is back here by 5:00. Still, if they want to stay here and visit, they can."

"How often does he come?"

"That one comes pretty regular. On Sundays. Not like the girls' mom. She comes once or twice a year, if that."

"Do I have to let her in too?"

"Yes, but like I said, she'll come once or twice a year. So that shouldn't be a problem."

"The girls have parents but the boy doesn't?"

"The boy and his brother were abandoned by their parents. We don't know much more than that."

"Do the girls have a father too?"

"As far as we know, there's only a mother."

"If they have a mother, why does the Welfare Department take care of them?"

"Well, because the judge found her to be an unfit mother."

"Why, what did she do?"

"I can't speak to that. The Department's policy is not to discuss the details of any case with a foster parent or anyone. The most I can tell you is that she was found to be unfit by the court."

"For how long will she be unfit?"

"We don't know that."

"Like next month? So that I have these girls for a month and then I don't have them? And then I have to start over with some other kids?"

"No, no. That's not likely. As far as I can tell, they'll be here for a long time."

JESUSITA WATCHES from the side of the kitchen window. The social worker has been gone for more than a half hour, and still she watches. It is the young one she watches—the lanky, thin one. The boy has been sitting on the basement door with his face buried in his propped-up knees. The older, solidly-built girl is not nearly as well-coordinated as her skinny sister and has been following the younger one around the yard trying heartily, but without much success, to match her sister's limberness. The younger one is now on the second highest branch of the apricot tree talking down to her sister, who is standing on the ground with her neck strained upward. This is causing Jesusita some concern, but she is more intent on making a comparison.

No, Paulina could never climb that tree at that age or any age. Nor was she ever that skinny. And now that she can see under the girl's dress, see the usually covered thighs, this girl is light-skinned. Something Paulina never was.

The girl reaches for the highest limb and Jesusita's breath catches. She goes to the back porch concerned and angry. But stops. *This is how you always handled it before. And look what all that yelling and anger got you. Calm down. At least walk out there and talk to the girl calmly.* From the porch she sees that the girl has actually gone down a branch and is sitting there talking once again to her sister below. She chides herself for being so preoccupied with the girl. And yet it somehow seems that the match between these three and Sergio and Yolanda and especially Paulina might not purely be an accident.

She returns to the kitchen window and then pulls herself away. *Let them be. You are looking for things that aren't there. In an hour it will be time for lunch. They probably haven't eaten all day. Fix them a nice lunch. It will be your first time alone with them. Let it be a good start.*

She busies herself cleaning her clean house until it is time to prepare quesadillas and caldo. At five minutes to twelve she goes to the back porch. The boy is still sitting on the basement door but is now looking out toward the girls who are half hidden by a giant cactus. The younger girl is scraping at something at the base of the nopal and her sister is bent over watching her.

"Lunch is ready. Come and eat," she calls in a soft voice. Ralph slides off the basement door and heads to the back porch door. She was right. He's hungry. They probably haven't had anything to eat all day. Elena looks up from her bent position. "Come and eat. Lunch is ready," louder but still softly. Elena starts across the yard but Fifi keeps scraping. Anger wells up in Jesusita. She is about to go out to the nopal and bring the girl in, but stops. *Calm yourself. This is what you always did. And look what it got you.* She stares out at Fifi. Elena reaches the door. "What's she doing?"

"I don't know."

"Go wash your hands in the bathroom and then wait for me in the kitchen. Lunch is ready."

"Ok."

She looks out at Fifi again and says, "Lunch is ready. Come and eat," louder but still restraining herself. The girl keeps scraping, doesn't look up. Jesusita kicks the screen door open, steps down on the cement block and onto the backyard dirt all in one motion. *This is too much! Enough is enough!* But another thought passes through. *You have to calm down. You can't begin like this. You know what happened with the others.* She stalks on. *You can't begin like this. You'll regret it if you do. Haven't you learned?* She reaches the girl. "What are you doing?" she asks, as controlled as she can possibly be.

The girl, who is on her knees with a pointy stick in her hand, looks up with that same big, bright-eyed smile and says, "I'm digging."

The woman's shoulders sag. Her anger and emotion evaporate. It is the smile. She stands there watching the girl dig. It is a while before she asks, "What are you digging?"

For the first time, the girl stops digging and turns to the woman. "I'm trying to find out where the needles are coming from." And she begins digging again.

"Where the needles are coming from?"

"Yeah. They stuck me and if I can find out where they're coming from, I can kill them and then they won't be able to stick anybody again."

"That nopal is very, very old. It's been here for a long time. If you keep digging, you might kill the whole plant."

"That's OK. Then it won't stick anybody anymore."

She wants to tell the girl to stop digging, but can't. Instead she watches in silence, confused and tired. Finally she says, "Lunch is ready. Come and eat."

The girl turns to her again, smiles and says, "But I'm not hungry," and continues digging. She watches the girl for a while longer. Then she turns and walks slowly back to the house. Now she is only tired.

As the three eat, Ralph asks, "Where's Fifi?"

Elena answers, "She's outside."

Turning to Jesusita he asks, "How come she's not eating with us?"

Jesusita looks at the boy for a while before she answers. "She's not hungry."

"Does that mean that every time we're not hungry, we don't have to eat with you?"

Jesusita doesn't answer.

She comes in long after the other two have been sent to their rooms to "read books for school tomorrow." She finds Jesusita in her room and says, "I'm hungry now."

"I'm sorry but we ate all there was for lunch. Now you'll have to wait for dinner."

"What did you eat?"

"Quesadillas and caldo."

"Oh, I like quesadillas."

"I'm sorry."

The girl turns, sad-faced.

"Maybe you should take a bath?"

"No," she says as she leaves.

Jesusita's impulse is to grab the girl, shake her, and say loudly and clearly, "You're going to do as I say, young lady! You're taking a bath!" But she doesn't.

Moments later she hears rattling in the kitchen. She hurries there and finds the girl lighting the stove. "What are you doing?"

"I'm making quesadillas."

"What!"

"I'm making quesadillas. You said you guys ate all the tortillas and cheese, but I found lots of them in the icebox. Look." She points to the counter.

"I'm sorry, but you're going to have to wait 'til dinner."

"Why? You said I couldn't have anything to eat because you had eaten it all. But you haven't eaten it all. Look."

Jesusita is starting to tremble. Her fists are clenched. The barber belt is still in her closet. That's exactly what this one needs. None of her children would have dared do this to her. *And where are they now?* The thought taunts. *One is dead and the others have left, hating you.* "No," she says through gritted teeth.

"Ok," says the girl nonchalantly and leaves the kitchen and goes outside in the direction of the cactus.

In her room she talks to God. *Why have You sent me this one, Dear Lord? Is it to punish me or remind me or both? Haven't I paid enough for what I've done? How much more do You want from me? If You're trying to show me that all that I did as a mother led up to the drowning, I know that. Forgive me, please. Your priest in Los Angeles forgave me. Shouldn't that be enough? If I don't watch myself, this little girl will drive me crazy or worse. Is that what You want?* She waits in vain for an answer even though she knows full well that answers only come later in whatever happens.

The day isn't over. At the dinner table Jesusita says, "Fifi, after we wash the dishes, I'm going to give you a bath. You're very dirty."

"I can take a bath by myself."

"No, I'll give you a bath."

"No, my Mama said to never let anyone see me naked. Didn't she Nena?"

Elena looks up cautiously at Jesusita and nods.

"And where's your mother?"

"She's traveling. She has a big business. She makes a lot of money. She's rich. She wears a fur coat. That's why we don't see her very much. Right, Nena?"

More wary nods from Elena.

"I wouldn't worry about that. I'm a girl too. I know what we look like. I'll give you the bath myself. Nobody else has to see."

"No, you won't. I won't let you. I won't let you see me naked."

Jesusita closes her eyes and takes a deep breath. She rubs her forehead back and forth. She is about to implode. Ralph and Elena watch her, frightened. Fifi sits across from her with a crooked little smile. Suddenly Jesusita bolts straight up, turns, and goes to her room. Minutes later she hears the old water pipes dumping water into the bathtub. She clenches her teeth. *How can this girl be so much unlike Paulina and yet so much like her? No—worse.*

The next morning the children go to school. She has had as little contact with them as possible, waking them, leaving their breakfasts on the kitchen table, and saying goodbye to them from her room. This is her plan: have as little contact with them, but mostly with the girl, as possible. This is the only way she can survive that little girl. And survive her she must. Because without them, how else can she pay her rent, how else can she eat? They'll be home sometime after 3:30. She'll be in her room then. They'll have an early dinner. It'll be dark then, and she'll have them do their schoolwork and then go to bed. Simple: the end of the day and tomorrow is another school day just like today. *But what of the weekend?* she worries.

They come in through the back door as they've been instructed. The boy says, "We're home."

"Good," she answers from her room. "Change your clothes and

you can go out and play until I call you." *That was easy enough,* she thinks. But before she knows it, there stands Fifi in her doorway with her hands on her hips.

As soon as the girl sees her looking, she stamps her feet on the floor. "I hate school! I hate school! I hate school!"

Jesusita is startled. She watches. The more she watches, the more the girl stomps.

The girl starts to cry, still stomping, still saying, "I hate school! I hate school!"

Jesusita says nothing. In fact, she guards against showing any kind of concern or interest. She is enjoying watching the girl's frustration and doing and saying nothing.

The girl gets louder. She stomps harder, stomps so hard that she hurts her foot. "Oww! Oww!" she hobbles about crying. And when she gets no response says, "Don't you even care? Don't you even care?"

Jesusita doesn't answer, keeping her look as bland and blank as she can until the girl turns, crying, and leaves.

The next morning she hears them at the back door leaving for school. She waits to hear the back door close before going out of her room. But it doesn't close. Instead she hears one of them coming. Fifi again. She braces herself. No, it's the boy. "Jesusita, Fifi says she's not going to school. She says we can't make her go to school and neither can you."

"What!"

"That's what's she's saying. You better come."

The girl is sitting on her bed with her books next to her.

"Get up and go to school."

"I'm not going to school."

"You're not going to school?"

"No."

"Why?"

"Because I don't want to."

Jesusita swells with anger. She twitches. The doctor has warned her that she has high blood pressure and she should avoid getting overly excited. She doesn't care. This is outrageous. She walks hard and fast to her closet. She retrieves the barber belt. She rushes back. She stands over the girl, fuming, belt in hand. "I said get up and get to school!"

The girl looks up at her, looks squarely and calmly at her and says, "You better not hit me. You better not hit me with that."

"What!" Hoarse, a loud whisper.

"You hit me and I'll tell. I'll tell Shirley. I'll tell my Mom. I'll tell everyone down at the shelter. They all told me to tell if you hit us."

"Who told you that?"

"They all told me that. They said that you like to hit kids and for me to tell them if you did."

"What!"

"That's what they said."

She's hot with embarrassment. *They know!* The heat blurs everything except that they know. *The police knew. The district attorney knew. Now everyone knows. They know where the marks and welts on Paulina came from.* She is prickly hot. Her mind is in a panic. The three children are watching. She has to get out of that room. "Go to school," she manages to the two standing next to her. They leave and she leaves.

In her room she is awash in shame. *Everyone knows. Yes, but the priest in Los Angeles forgave me everything. That's what you think. How could he forgive the beatings when you didn't mention them? But those beatings weren't sins. If those beatings weren't sins, then why did the police keep asking about them? Would you have been arrested if you had told them, yes, the marks and the welts were from your beatings? Of course you would have. You knew that. That's why you kept denying knowing anything about them. That's why you just said "lying" to the priest in Los Angeles. Why didn't you tell him when you lied, why you lied, and what you lied about? Holding back the truth is lying, you know. He couldn't really forgive you if you were lying to him right there in the confessional, could he? And you've been going to Communion every day since then, even though you lied in your confession. That's why the girl is here. That's why God has sent her. To punish you. To let you know that He knows that you're going to Communion even though you're in sin. And yes, to let you know that everyone knows how you beat your children.*

The thoughts taunt her through the morning, leaving her in a state of exhaustion. For a long while she sits in her room staring into space. Then she hears noises in the kitchen, and she remembers that the girl is in the house too. She stands and then sits back down. *What to do with this girl? She has to be disciplined, but how? You dare not hit her, not after what she said this morning. You lock her in her room and take away privileges and she will for sure say that you hit her. So what? The girl is bound to provoke me so much that I'll end up hitting her anyway...* Several times Jesusita starts to leave her room but doesn't. It's better not to be in the house alone with her. Better to wait until the others return.

Just after 1:30, there's a knock at the front door. She looks out the side window and her heart sinks. It's the truant officer and Charley Montemayor. *What could they want? It's too early for them to know that the girl missed school today. School is not even out yet. Do they know too?* She can't answer the door. Not with the girl in the house. What would she say? Fifi's not in school today because she didn't *want* to go to school. They'll take the kids away from her for sure then.

There is more knocking, louder. She sits motionless. At some point, if she's just patient and calm, they'll stop knocking and leave. Then she hears the front door open and hears the girl's voice followed by the truant officer's voice, both in English. The girl speaks again, and then Jesusita hears Montemayor's voice loudly asking in Spanish, "Where is she?" She can't tell if the girl answers and she holds her breath. Her door opens, and the girl says, "Somebody's here and they want to talk to you." Jesusita sighs. *What now?*

The man in the suit speaks, and Montemayor interprets. "Good afternoon, Mrs. González, do you remember us?"

She nods, looking at neither man.

"I understand that you've become a foster-care mother for the Welfare Department."

More nods.

"I also understand that you've had three children placed in your care—school-aged children? The young lady standing next to you, her older sister, and a ten-year-old boy?"

Slight, almost imperceptible nods.

"I'm sure the Department has advised you that as a foster-care mother, you're obligated to give these children the same standard of care that you would give your own children."

She doesn't nod. Not that she agrees but rather that she's had enough for today and wants them to do whatever they're going to do and leave.

"One of the obligations you have is to make sure that these children attend school. Educating them is as important as feeding them. You understand that, don't you...? Is that a yes...? Mrs. González, you have to answer me using your voice. Is that a yes?"

"Yes."

"Why isn't this little girl in school today?"

She hasn't made eye contact with either man. Now she looks down and doesn't answer.

"Mrs. González..."

"She was sick."

"Sick! She doesn't look sick to me!" Montemayor interjects.

The truant officer looks over at Montemayor reproachfully, "Charley, please don't."

"Ok, ok, I'm sorry. I won't do it again."

"What was she sick with?"

"I don't know. She just said she was sick."

"She's lying! She's lying!" the girl says, pointing at Jesusita. "She's lying! I never said that."

"Well, why weren't you in school then?"

"Because she wouldn't let me go to school. I wanted to go to school but she wouldn't let me."

Jesusita shakes her head, her mouth set in a tired little smile.

"Why wasn't she letting you go to school?"

"Because she said I was bad. Because I was trying to take needles out of her cactus in the backyard. I want to go to school. I ran out the back door with my books, but she caught me and wouldn't let me go."

Jesusita continues shaking her head. The tired smile is gone.

"Well, I don't think that either one of you is telling me the truth, and I don't like it. I'm out here now because the boy you take care of, Ralph...Ralph...I forget his last name. Anyway, Ralph told the teacher that you didn't go to school today because you said you didn't want to go, and Mrs. González said that was OK that you didn't have to go. I want you to understand something, young lady. Unless you're really sick, you go to school. Understand? It's not up to you to decide whether you're going to school or not, and it's up to Mrs. González to make sure you go to school. The law says that you should be in school every day that you're not really sick, and I'm here to enforce that law."

"But she said I didn't have go to school."

"I don't care what she said. You go to school. Do you understand?"

Fifi nods. Now she too is downcast.

"Go get your books, I'm taking you to school."

"Right now? I'm all dirty. Besides, school's almost over now."

"I said go get your books. You're going to school. And just re-member this. The next time you do this, you're going back to the shelter. Go get your books."

The truant officer turns back to Jesusita. "Once I drop her off at school, I'm going over to the Welfare Department to file a report. If this happens again, I'm going to ask the Welfare Department to take these kids away from you. Am I making myself clear?"

She nods, and Montemayor adds, "He not only means it, he'll do it."

She watches from the window as the girl gets into the car. *Who is this girl, and why was she sent to me? One thing is certain, she's a liar, a vicious liar. Where did those lies come from? I was punishing her. She wanted to go to school, but I wouldn't let her. She ran out the door with her books, and I stopped her. Her mother is rich. She wears a fur coat. She's traveling. That's why they never see her. The people at the shelter know that I beat kids. How are they going to know that? Who told them? The social worker never said anything about that. Not a thing. Lies, pure lies. But her lies are evil, sinful. Does she even know what a sin is? Probably not. There's no telling where the girl has lived before. She has no sense of right and wrong, no sense of good and evil. Don't forget, the boy lied too. Yes, but his was nothing compared to the girl's. And he could have simply been mistaken. You lied too. That was different, very different. It was meant to try to protect us. Hers were malicious, calculated to hurt me, do me evil. There's no doubt the girl needs religious training. Why haven't you started? They've only been here two days, and the social worker told me that foster mothers shouldn't try to change a child's religion. How can you change something she's never had? That's true, and an eight-year-old would have a better sense of right and wrong if she had religion.* She goes to the kitchen. It's four minutes past two. They won't be home until after 3:30. There's time.

She goes to Chinatown and buys as many candles as she can find. From her basement she brings up the planks and fruit boxes and bricks that she has been using for shelving. She takes large, framed holy pictures from her bedroom and the living room and hangs them in the dining room on the wall directly across from the girls' room so that each time Fifi comes out she will see Jesus with His Flaming Heart flanked by the Virgen of Guadalupe on His Right and Mary and Joseph with the Infant Jesus at the Bethlehem stable on His Left. Under the holy pictures, she uses the planks, boxes, and bricks to construct an altar and covers it over with white sheets. On the altar she places and lights candles of every size and shape imaginable.

Afternoon shadows have already darkened the house when the children come home from school. They whoop and holler when they see the candle-lighted altar—two of them, that is, because Fifi remains in the doorway of her room, watching with a frightened look. When Jesusita sees the fear on the girl's face, she forgets her renewed resolve to stay away from the girl and instead goes up to her and says, "Come, look at our altar." The girl stiffens and shakes her head no, which makes Jesusita all the more intent. She takes the girl by the arm. "Come and look at our altar."

The girl's eyes widen and she plants her feet. Jesusita's grip tightens and she pulls, slowly sliding the frozen girl over the wooden floor toward the altar. What can she possibly be afraid of? As they reach the altar, the candles flicker and blow away from them as if in a draft, startling Jesusita who drops her grip, allowing the girl to run to her room. As soon as the girl breaks free and turns, the flames straighten themselves and burn strong and bright as before.

Jesusita looks in every direction. The windows are down and the doors are closed. She looks back at the candles; they're burning straight and strong. Did she really see what she thinks she saw? Ralph and Elena are a few feet from her, still fascinated by the altar.

"Did you see that?"

"See what?" the boy asks.

"Did you see the candles?"

"Yeah, I've been looking at them since we came."

"Did you see them almost go out?"

"They never went out."

"I know they didn't. But did you see them almost go out, like they were going out?"

"I don't know. Elena, did you see the candles go out?"

"They never went out."

"No, Elena, that's not what I asked him. I asked him if he saw the candles *almost* go out. Did you see them *almost* go out?" Frustrated, Jesusita gestures toward the candles with a pointed hand.

"When?"

"A little while ago when I brought Fifi to the altar."

"You brought Fifi to the altar? How come I never saw her?"

"I don't care if you saw Fifi or not. All I want to know is if you saw the candles almost go out a little while ago?"

"I don't know. I was looking at the man with the hole in his chest. You can see his heart, and it's on fire, and he's pointing to it. But it doesn't seem to be hurting him because the man's not crying or anything."

"That's not a man, stupid! That's Jesus," says Ralph, disgusted.

"How should I know? And don't call me stupid. If you're so smart, how come you're ten and I'm nine and you're still in the third grade with me?"

"Stop it!" she hisses. "I don't want to hear any more of it! Go to your rooms!"

The children are surprised, but they hear the anger and do as they're told. She remains there, watching, hoping that she will see it again, so that it won't be what she thinks it has to be, too terrified to deal with it, or know how to deal with it. It doesn't happen again. The candles burn, uninterrupted, straight and strong.

She fixes an early dinner and watches the girl. The girl won't look at her—which makes it all the easier to watch her. She watches to see if the girl is really eating. Watches her chew her food. Watches her throat to see if she is really swallowing her food, but isn't able to tell. Yet, with the third and fourth forkful she has to be swallowing. She can't hold that much in her mouth and not swallow. She stares down at the girl's hands and fingers, the way she holds her fork. The hands and fingers appear to be normal, those of a child, not unlike those of her sister or Ralph. And she's holding her fork just as they are. No, she's a child. Besides, someone in the other homes she's been in or someone at the shelter would have noticed by now if she wasn't and would have reported it. But that doesn't mean that Satan couldn't have entered her, couldn't have possessed her. That's why the girl won't look at her. He won't let her. He must know that she knows, and that she'll be all the more certain if he lets the girl look at her.

She sends them to bed early and goes to her room and prepares for the night. She places her rosary around her neck over her scapular and holy medals. She moves a small table next to her bed and props a crucifix up on it and lights an all-night candle before it. She goes to bed but can't sleep. She's more convinced than ever that she saw those candles almost blow out. But she's not completely sure what that means. She needs to talk to Padre. She needs to be sure. If it weren't so late, she would go to the rectory. But the last thing she needs is someone else saying that she's been at Padre's house late at night. It's all too possible that Satan could be lurking just a few feet away from her. Why has God permitted this? Is it the ultimate of all tests, like Abraham and his son? Or is it a form of punishment? For what? For what sin? What is she guilty of? The Los Angeles absolution creeps up again and the reminder that she has received Holy Communion too many times after it. No, she didn't lie to the priest. In fact she confessed that she had lied. After such a long time between Confessions, could she be expected to remember the details of every lie? Finally, she wakes. It's still dark. She couldn't have slept more than an hour or two.

On the way to Mass in the morning, the question taunts her anew: Should she be receiving Communion given the way she confessed in Los Angeles? There was nothing wrong with her Confession. She told the priest she had lied, and he forgave her. And if she ever needed the Body and Blood of Jesus Christ in her, it is now.

She waits for him after Mass. "Padre, I need to talk to you."

"What is it, my child?"

"Padre, I keep dreaming that I'm a girl again in Mexico and that I think my sister is possessed by the Devil. That frightens me so much, that I can't sleep."

"In your dream, why do you believe that your sister is possessed by the Devil?"

"Because she won't pray or go to church and seems to be afraid to do anything involving God."

"Is that all that leads you to believe that she's possessed by the Devil?"

"No. When we go to church, when my parents make her go to church, if she gets too close to the altar, all the candles get blown out even though all the doors and windows are closed. When that happens, she runs out of church."

"Yes, those all could be signs of someone possessed by the Devil, someone who cannot bear to get too close to God. But why are you afraid in this dream?"

"Because she's my sister, and in my dream she lives with me. She's close to me all the time. Wouldn't you be afraid if someone possessed by the Devil was that close to you?"

"Not if I was in the State of Grace and, as far as I can tell, you're always in the State of Grace. A person in the State of Grace is a Tabernacle of God, and the Devil can never get close enough to harm that person. It torments him, punishes him when he's that close to God. So before you go to sleep at night, remind yourself—and your dream—that you are in the State of Grace and that the Devil can never harm you or even get close to you."

"Thank you, Padre. There is one more thing."

"Yes, my child?"

"One of the three children that the Welfare Department brought me is a ten-year-old boy who made his First Communion almost four years ago. He has not been to Confession or Communion since. We've talked about his going to Confession again, and he's afraid that if he does go, his sins won't be forgiven."

"Why?'

"Because he says that there are many sins that he can't remember, so how can he confess them?"

"My dear, if an individual comes into the confessional and honestly can't remember the number of times he has committed sins or the specifics of those sins, it is enough if he simply identifies the sin, such as 'missing Sunday Mass' and says 'many times.' However, if that same individual deliberately conceals a sin, for whatever reason, he has committed a new sin and makes it far worse if after that confession he receives Holy Communion, taking the Body and Blood of Jesus into the filthiest of places, a sin-infested soul. That is a sacrilege, blasphemy, and in my opinion the worst of all sins.... As to this boy, what types of sins could he at that age have been repeating?"

"Lying."

"Oh well, in that case a general description of 'lying' and 'many times' would be more than sufficient to grant him absolution. Tell him not to worry. Tell him to come and confess to me, and he can with a clear conscience receive Holy Communion the next morning."

Jesusita goes home convinced that her sins had been absolved in Los Angeles. Had they not been, she would have since committed a number of sacrileges and would have certainly felt the punishments for those sins by now. When the children come home from school, she asks them to join her at the altar for the saying of the rosary. Ralph and Elena follow her to the altar, but Fifi goes to her room instead. She finds the girl sitting on her bed. "Won't you come and say the rosary with us, dear?" She watches the girl curl and writhe away from her. Just as she might have expected. How much more proof does she need? And she has nothing to fear: she is in the State of Grace.

As they say the rosary, Jesusita hears the girl go out into the backyard. Later, when she looks out the kitchen window, she sees the girl digging in the farthest corner of the yard. Ralph says she is making her own garden. The girl is no longer disrespectful. She comes when she is called, except when she asks them to pray. She does as she is told but always keeps her distance, always staying as far away from Jesusita as she can and never looking at her. On Saturday, the girl does as she's told but avoids the altar, slipping away any time she thinks Jesusita is going to take them there. But tomorrow is Sunday, God's special day, and Jesusita, with God on her side, is prepared to teach the girl, and whatever might be in her, some lessons that she will never forget.

XV

SUNDAY MORNING. 5:30. Jesusita is up at that hour as she is almost every morning. As she brushes her teeth, she's careful not to swallow a drop of water and break her fast. This morning of all mornings she must receive Holy Communion because today she is about to exorcize whoever or whatever is in that girl, and it is absolutely necessary that she have the Body and Blood of Jesus Christ within her. She welcomes the challenge; she's excited. On her way to Mass, the Los Angeles absolution is at it again, but she quickly dispels it with the logic that if she had been committing sacrileges since then, God would have surely struck her down by now, punished her severely in one way or another. She receives the Host with a gentle, relaxed opening of her mouth. The Host melts in her mouth. So much for the curse of sacrileges.

She lets the children sleep and takes great pains with the preparation of their breakfast, making a creamy chocolate atole and buñuelos to go with their avena. It is important to win over the other two. There is no telling what the girl's reaction will be, and the others mustn't turn against her. This could get back to the social worker, and she will need them to overcome any of the girl's lies. Luckily, the Welfare is closed today, and the girl should be a different person by tomorrow. She has heard that once a devil is expelled, his victim is physically exhausted and takes a few days to recover. She looks forward to the coming week. Sometime then, the girl should be forever grateful.

She watches as Ralph and Elena wolf down the buñuelos and have second helpings of the atole while barely touching their avena. Twice she gently says, "Children, you have to eat some of your avena too." Fifi eats all of her avena but only one buñuelos and one cup of atole, without once looking at Jesusita. It is what Jesusita suspected might happen.

After breakfast she decides that it's too early to start the process. Teaching them how to wash and dry dishes, clean the house, and make their beds should, she thinks, give the other two another level of respect for her. She is amiable as Ralph and Elena blunder through their attempts to imitate her, and suspicious at Fifi's perfect imitations. Time after time she bends over and actually touches Ralph and Elena as she leads them through their attempts. The few times she approaches Fifi, the girl automatically takes a step or two away from her, and as she demonstrates she senses the girl inching still farther away.

It is almost eleven when Jesusita takes the broom from Ralph and says, "That's enough for cleaning. We've had a good morning, haven't we?" She waits until the two nod. "Good. Now we've had a good breakfast, which takes care of our bodies. And we've learned to clean, which takes care of our home and health. Now we must learn how to take care of our souls. Now we must learn to pray."

Fifi's eyes meet hers for one of the few times in days. They are frightened, mistrustful eyes.

"Two of you have already prayed with me, and that is good. Now I must teach all of you how and why to pray. Come with me to the altar."

Fifi rushes past them, goes to her room. and closes the door. The three stop. Ralph and Elena look up at Jesusita. Elena is uncomfortable.

"What's the matter with her?" Ralph asks Elena, making her more uncomfortable.

"I don't know. She just doesn't like to pray."

"Why? What's wrong with praying?"

Elena is red-faced. She avoids Jesusita's eyes. "Nothing. I like to pray."

"Then what's wrong with her?"

"How should I know?"

"You should know. She's your sister, isn't she?"

Elena bites her lower lip and doesn't answer.

Jesusita is at a loss. She didn't expect the girl to run to her room and close the door. "Let's go to the altar, children," she says. But her mind is neither on the altar nor on the children. It is telling her, repeating, that the girl can't get away with this. She kneels at the altar, and Ralph and Elena follow. They wait for her to begin. She knows they are waiting, but it is the girl and the closed door that won't let her begin. Ralph turns and looks over at her. She stands and says, "Stay here. I'll be right back." She has enough presence of mind to say as she goes, "I'm going to bring Fifi here. She's going to pray too. And I want you to watch so that she can't later say that I hit her."

She pushes hard on the door. So hard, that the door flies open and she stumbles and almost falls. Now she is also angry and embarrassed. The girl is sitting on her bed. "Get up! We're going to pray! And this time you're going to pray with us!" The girl doesn't move. Jesusita has expected some sort of writhing or convulsions, but there are none. She takes three steps closer, stops, and watches. Still no twisting or squirming. The girl is still, motionless. For an instant she wonders, doubts, but just as quickly decides that Satan is far too clever to expose himself now. Still, she's in the State of Grace, she's a Tabernacle of God. Satan should be struggling to free himself. But the girl hasn't moved. She has to stop thinking; she is only confusing herself. She lunges for the girl, grabs her, picks her up, wraps her arms around her, and brings the girl face to face with her. The girl is writhing, kicking, screaming, and crying, just as Jesusita expected. She tightens her hold on the girl, and the girl screams louder, kicks harder. Slowly she makes her way to the altar with the writhing, screaming child, convinced that once they reach the altar, the Devil will flee and the girl will stop, exhausted. When they are a few steps from the altar, the girl bites Jesusita hard on the cheek. Jesusita screams and drops the girl, who runs to her room and slams her door shut again. Elena and Ralph let out moans of fear as Jesusita, teeth clenched, starts back to the door again. This time the girl leans against the door with all her strength. When Jesusita feels the resistance, she gives the door a mighty shove, knocking the girl back and down. She enters and stands over the girl breathing hard but saying nothing. As the girl rises, Jesusita stoops and in one motion doubles the girl over her shoulder and stands.

The girl screams, cries, and pounds Jesusita's back. "Put me down! Put me down!"

"No. No, my little devil! We're going to the altar. You're going to pray with us. And I guarantee you that whatever's in you won't be there very long."

They are midway across the dining room when Jesusita hears a pounding on the front door. She stops. Only then is she aware that the girl's screaming has been so loud that it must have brought the neighbors or, worse, the police. She covers the girl's mouth with her free hand, but the muffled screams are still loud. She takes the girl back to her room, drops her on her bed, and hurries out of the room, closing the door tightly behind her. The pounding continues. Could it be the police? Petra's too little to be knocking that hard. She motions for Ralph and Elena to be still and quiet. Cries are still coming from the girl's bedroom, but not nearly as loud as before. She doesn't think they can be heard outside, but she's not sure. She doesn't know what to do except stand still and be quiet. If they are still and quiet and the girl's cries are muffled enough, maybe whoever's at the front door will leave. The pounding starts again. Whoever he or she or they are, they have heard the screams and know that they are there. She tiptoes to her bedroom and from behind sheer curtains looks out on the front porch. They are out of sight. She stands frozen in her room, all too much aware of the girl's continued cries. If she can hear them in her room, then whoever's out there can hear them too.

She hears shouting. "Open this damn door before I go to the police! I know you're in there! I heard you! So open this goddamn door before I go to the police!"

It's a woman. Her voice is young and strong. Who could it be?

"Alright, I'm leaving! But I'm coming back with the police! I know you're in there and I know what you're doing to my kids and why you're not opening the door!"

She hears the woman leaving. "No, no, not the police. Please not the police," she mumbles and rushes to the front door. "I'll open," she shouts, "but not the police! Please!" In her anxiety, she turns the lock and the key and the handle in inconsistent ways, locking and unlocking herself in, turning at the handle again and again but unable to open the door.

The woman has approached the door again. "Open this goddamn door!" The woman is standing on the other side of the door. The door opens. A dark, young woman in a fur coat and high heels, heavily made-up with a huge black pompadour, stands there.

"Who are you? What do you want?" Even as she asks she knows. It is the fur coat.

"What do you mean, who am I? You goddamn better well know who I am. I'm the mother of the two girls you're beating up on in there. What do I want? I want to go down to the police station and file charges against you for beating my girls. I want to go down to the Welfare and make those silly bastards move my girls out of your place. That's who I am and that's what I want."

"Please don't curse here. Please don't take God's name in vain here."

"Don't give me that holy shit, you old bitch! I've heard all about you. So holy on the outside and so evil on the inside. Charley's told me all about you. I know what you did to your own daughter and I'll be goddamned, did you hear me, GODDAMNED, if you'll do the same to mine! Now open this fucking door!"

"It's open."

"I'm talking about the screen door!"

Jesusita unlatches the screen door. The woman yanks it out and takes another step forward. The two women are standing inches apart.

"Where's my girls?"

"I'm here, Mama," answers Elena who, along with Ralph, is standing a little behind and to one side of Jesusita.

"Where's your sister?"

"Mama! Mama!" comes a running, crying Fifi, leaping to and hugging her mother's side. "I hate it here, Mama! I hate it here! I hate her!"

"Why are you crying? Was that you I heard screaming? Was she beating you?"

"Yes, Mama, yes. She was beating me. She always beats me. Hard."

"I didn't beat her. I wasn't beating her. I was just trying to get her to pray with us."

"Pray? Pray, shit! Since when is this a goddamn church?"

"Elena, was I beating or even hitting your sister?"

Elena's eyes widen. Fifi stops crying and turns and looks at her sister. Elena looks at her mother, then at Jesusita. Back at her mother.

"Don't be afraid, sweetheart. Mama's here. You can tell me. Mama's here. There's nothing she can do or even try to do. I'm here."

Elena stands there as if thinking. Then she nods once...twice... several times. "Yeah, she was beating her. She beats her all the time."

"That's a lie," Jesusita yells. "They're both lying. Ralph, you were there. You saw. Did I beat her, was I hitting her?"

"I don't know. I couldn't see."

"You couldn't see? You were at the altar across from her room. The door was open. You saw me bringing her to the altar."

"I couldn't see. You made us kneel. So I couldn't see."

"They're lying. They're all lying. I have not mistreated them in any way. As God is my witness, I have not hit her or any of them."

"You holy people never do anything wrong, do you? Elena, go get your jacket and your sister's too. I'm taking you girls down to the police station. She can't get away with this.... Ralph, you better get your jacket too and come with us. I don't trust her alone with you."

They stand there inches apart. One with anger and hate in her eyes and the other with confusion and pleading in hers. "You God-fearing people are always so righteous on the outside and so fuck-ing rotten on the inside. But you won't get away with it this time."

Ralph and Elena return with the jackets. "Put them on, kids, and let's go. The next time you see us, lady, will be with the police."

She stands at the door watching as the woman in the fur coat and high heels, holding one daughter with one hand and the oth-er daughter with the other and with the boy trailing, heads in the direction of the police station. She stands there in the brisk November morning, dazed and shocked, still absorbing what has happened and trying to understand why it has happened.

The woman and the children have dropped out of sight when she hears, "Jesusita, Jesusita." It is Petra, for whom she has little regard and has never refrained from showing it. Petra is standing in Jesusita's front yard several feet from the front porch, which is as close as she will come. She is not welcome here and she knows it. Jesusita is still at the door and once she turns to Petra, once Petra knows she has Jesusita's attention, she says, "Aren't those two girls and the boy the kids you're taking care of for the Welfare?"

Jesusita doesn't answer. Instead she looks down scornfully at the woman.

"I mean, what are they doing with that woman?"

"What are you doing in my yard?"

"I'm just trying to help you."

"How are *you* going to help *me* with anything?"

"Maybe you don't know who that woman is."

"What woman?"

"The woman those kids are with, the kids you're supposed to be taking care of."

"I know who she is! What business is it of yours who she is?"

"Plenty. I know who she is and I don't think you really know."

"Tell me who you think she is and then get out of my yard."

"She's one of the whores at the Valley Rooms."

"What?"

"You heard me. She's one of the whores down at the Valley Rooms, you know, the whorehouse on Kern Street in Chinatown."

"You don't know that."

"Yeah, I do."

"How do you know that? Do you go down there and sweep up after they're finished for the night?"

"No, I've never been in that whorehouse."

"Then how do you know that?"

"My brother used to go down there all the time until they threw him out for beating up one of the whores, the same one that's walking around with your Welfare kids. He went to jail for it. She went to court and testified against him. I was there in court. I saw her."

"You're lying."

"Why would I lie to you about my brother and her? I'm just trying to help you because I know you shouldn't be letting those kids be with her. If the Welfare ever found out..."

"Get out of here! Get off my property! Now!"

"OK, OK, I'm going. But if you don't believe me, just do one thing when she brings the kids back. Tell her to take off that fur coat. I'll bet you anything that she won't. You know why...? Because under it she's naked. From now until March when the cold stops, she wears that coat out on the street whenever she leaves the whorehouse. But she's naked underneath. If she won't take it off when you ask her to, then just open it up or lift it real quick, and you'll see and you'll know that I'm not lying—that I'm just trying to help you. What decent woman walks around the streets of Fresno naked under a fur coat except a whore?"

"Get out! Get out of my yard!"

In her room she waits for the police to come. She will be going to jail and lose her work with the Welfare. How will she support herself when she comes out of jail? She doesn't know. Nor does she know how all this came about. First, she was sent a girl possessed by the Devil. Then it turns out that the girl's mother is a whore. To be a whore, to do what a whore does day in and day out, surely Satan has to have some control over that woman as well. Why has God permitted it? Is it because of Paulina? Or her confession in Los Angeles? Or both? She no longer defends herself. She no longer denies wrongdoing. The message is clear: one pays for one's sins not only in Hell but also here on earth. She tries to pray but can't.

She waits. She's lost all sense of time. All that exists is this nightmare. His punishment for all her sins. She hears, sees, and feels nothing except His punishment. A sound breaks through. For a moment it stops the pain. She listens. Someone is knocking. *Is it them? Are they back already?* She listens. There are no sounds, just the knocking. *Would the whore knock? Is the door locked?* She can't remember. If she doesn't answer, will they go away? Not her, not them. They know she's there. The knocking continues, soft but steady. Not the way she knocked. *Could it be the police? The whore said she was going to the police.* She remembers what the police did the last time they came. She sneaks up to the door. She puts her ear to the door and listens. No sounds or movement from the porch except the knocking. She opens the door and screams. "Oh my God! Oh my God! No! No! Go away! I know who you are! Go away! I know who you are! Go away! Please go away! I don't need any more! I know what I've done!"

On the other side of the screen door is a tall, dark, thin man in a black suit and a grey hat.

She tries to shut the door, wants to shut the door, but can't. It's as if she's paralyzed. "Go away! Please go away! I know who you are! Go! Please go!"

The man says nothing. He simply stares with eyes that are bright yellow-orange. He opens his mouth as if to speak. He's wearing a white shirt and tie which doesn't fool her. She knows who he is. She's never seen eyes like that or a look like that before. She slams the door shut, hurries back to her room and props the chair against the doorjamb. He must not have seen the open window or he would have come through there. Can eternal damnation be worse than this? She doesn't know. The knocking continues. It won't stop. Will it ever stop? But then it stops. She listens. For whatever reason, he has stopped knocking. Maybe he's gone. She tiptoes to the front room and the front window. She strains to her left against the curtain to see. Her heart sinks. He is still there with his head a little downcast as if listening. Listening for what?

She watches him, spellbound and frightened. Who would have thought that he looked like this? And wearing a suit and white shirt and tie. She's never seen a Mexican dressed like that. So who does he think he's fooling? And that hat. White men don't even wear hats like that. But aside from those clothes, he looks like a regular man with arms and feet and hands and shoulders and a head. But he must be able to look like anything he wants. So why is he dressed like this? So that she won't suspect. But those eyes gave him away. And that stare too. And he didn't talk. He knocks again. Why is he bothering to knock? If he can possess and live inside a person, get past their skin and bones, why couldn't he walk right through that door. He could, but he's trying to fool her. When he turns in her direction, she jumps back from the curtain with her heart beating strongly, hoping that he hasn't seen her.

She slips back into her room and, closing the door, jams the chair under the door knob. She listens for any sound from the porch. She hears none, and now he isn't knocking. He hasn't heard her. She lays on the bed with her heart still beating rapidly. If she lays still, he will have no way of knowing that anyone is in the house. But he knocks again. She covers her ears and vows to keep them covered, until from her window, she can see him reach the sidewalk and leave.

After a while, one of her hands falls from an ear, and she realizes that the knocking has stopped. But she hasn't seen him on the sidewalk. He's still on the front porch, and now she's almost certain that the front door is unlocked. He can come in any time he chooses. She makes sure that the chair is tight under the doorknob. When the knocking starts again, she sees him again, almost as if he's in the room with her—those bright, yellow-orange eyes staring at her, that mouth open as if to speak but doesn't. She wants to scream but doesn't dare. That might be what he needs to come in.

She's shivering. The November early afternoon shadows and the cold are coming through her open window, but she has to keep it open. He's still on the porch, and if he gets in the house, the window is her only way out. When the knocking begins again, she wraps a pillow around her head and watches the sidewalk. But she can still hear the knocking. Where has that woman taken those kids? If she doesn't bring them back today, the Welfare will know tomorrow. And how will she explain it? What will she say? Paulina and the Los Angeles confession return. She shakes her head, but they won't leave.

Then she hears them on the porch. The whore is talking to him in English. He answers, and they keep on talking, just like the old friends they have to be. The kids are talking too, laughing and giggling. They come into the house, and the whore tries her door. It doesn't open. "Open this motherfucking door before I kick it in!" the whore shouts.

Jesusita rushes to the door and removes the chair. The whore and the man are standing in the doorway with the kids behind them. She moves to one side to see as little of him as she can. She looks at the front of the fur coat, but it reveals nothing.

"We're gonna stay here tonight and tomorrow night, and there's not a damn thing you can do about it. I don't trust you with these kids and neither does the boy's brother here. Those asshole police won't help me. But the Welfare will on Monday. I wouldn't go make a big fuss about me staying here if I was you. I know too much about you. Charley's been telling me…"

"Charley who?" Jesusita asks.

"How many Charleys do you know…? Your old friend Charley Montemayor. Who else? He's told me a lot about you, stuff that only the police know. He says you're real secretive, that you try to hide from everybody. But I'm warning you, you make a big deal about me being here and those Welfare people are gonna know a whole lot more about you than they do now. When I get through telling them, I guarantee you, you'll never take care of another Welfare kid as long as you live. Do we understand each other?"

She nods. She understands. She's afraid, and she's tired too. Who else? What else? How much more? As she nods her eyes are on the fur coat.

"What are you looking at?"

"Nothing."

"You're staring at my coat, aren't you?"

"No."

"Why are you staring?"

"Isn't it too hot in here to be wearing that?"

The woman stops. Looks down at the youngsters and says, "Why don't you kids go outside and play. I got a few more things I've got to say to Grandma here."

The children leave, and the woman steps into the room, leaving the man in the doorway. She is angry. "Now look, Grandma, whether I'm hot or cold is none of your goddamn business. Understood? That's my business. I decide whether I'm hot or cold, not you. And whether I want to take off my coat is my business too, not yours. If I want to keep it on, I'll keep it on. If I want to take it off, I'll take it off. In other words, none of that is any of your goddamn business. Understood?"

"Please don't take the name of the Lord in vain in this house."

"I'll say whatever I fucking please here. I'll say whatever the fuck I want to say in this fucking house. Understood?"

She doesn't answer. Petra was right.

"One last thing. There's five of us and only one of you. We need a hell of a lot more space than you do. So you stay in here. I'm gonna close this door, and we'll use the rest of the house."

She can hear them in the girls' room. They're running and jumping, probably off the beds, laughing and screaming in pleasure. She resents it. But there's also the taunting thought that there has never been so much joy in her house.

After a while, the woman opens her door and enters without

knocking. "Grandma, I need to borrow one of your nightgowns. One of those heavy flannel ones that you old women wear."

Jesusita goes to her bureau and takes out a white cotton nightgown whose flannel has been washed away long ago. "This is the only one I have," she says, handing it to the woman. "The other one's in the dirty clothes."

A few minutes later, Jesusita hears the back door and then stillness and silence in the house. She waits before going to the kitchen window. They're all outside and the woman is wearing the white nightgown. They are all at the big cactus. Fifi is at the base of the cactus, digging again as the others watch. Strange how the littlest of them can command so much attention. Not so strange when you consider what has to have happened to her. She's going to kill that poor plant. When the boy turns, she ducks down. Has he seen her? Did he see her? She had better get out of the kitchen. As she passes the girls' room, she sees the fur coat on Fifi's bed and pauses long enough to make sure there isn't another stitch of clothing to be seen anywhere. There is none. Petra was right.

Why, dear God, why? What have I done to deserve this? Paulina and Los Angeles return. She closes her eyes and shakes her head as she returns to her room.

It is dark when the whore opens her door. "The kids are hungry. I'm going to fix them something to eat. Can I make something for you?"

The voice is soft, gentle even. *What does she want?* There is money hidden in her mattress. *Is that what she's after?* "No, I'm not hungry."

"Have you had anything to eat all day?"

The voice is caring. *What is she up to? She's not caring. She can't be. What does she want? Don't open yourself.* "I've eaten and I'm not hungry."

"Are you sure?"

"Yes."

The woman leaves. She hears them in the kitchen. They are laughing, talking loudly, jumping, chasing each other, screaming with laughter. She would never have permitted that. *It will get out of control. One will fall and start crying. They will fight.* The merriment continues. Her kids never laughed like that. It doesn't matter. *Kids have to be disciplined from early on. These kids have no discipline. But if the girl is possessed, how can she laugh like that? All that laughter has to be part of the plan to seduce and possess the other two. How can they be so happy around that whore and him? That's part of the plan too. She's orchestrating the whole thing.* The laughter, the chasing continues. *It can't be real.*

It is a while before they quiet down. She hears them eating. She's hungry. Her stomach is growling. At some point, she is going to have to go out there, no matter what the whore says, and fix herself something to eat. *When? As soon as they leave the kitchen.* She listens. They are laughing at the table. *When will all this pretending end?* If they stopped laughing and ate the way they're supposed to eat, they'd be finished by now and she could eat. Finally, she hears the kids going to the girls' room. *Is the whore still in the kitchen?* She doesn't know. *Is she cleaning? How can she clean? How can a whore clean?*

Her door opens again. "I brought you some eggs, potatoes, and beans. That's all I could find to cook. I know you must be hungry. I brought you some milk too."

"I'm not hungry."

The whore turns on the light.

"Turn off the light," she says angrily.

"I don't want to spill any of this."

"I told you, I'm not hungry. Turn off the light."

"If I turn it off, I'll make a mess."

"Turn it off. This is still my house."

"Whether it is or it isn't, you still need to eat something." She steps across the room toward Jesusita. The closer she gets, the farther back Jesusita leans in her chair. The whore sneers. When she reaches Jesusita, she says, "Here hold the glass while I bring that little table over here." Jesusita keeps her hands on her lap. "I said hold the glass." Jesusita remains motionless. The whore bends and moves the glass of milk down to Jesusita's lap. The back of her hand touches the back of Jesusita's right hand. Jesusita gasps, jerks up in her chair, and pulls her hand back as far as she can.

The whore sets the plate and the glass on the floor and turns to the frightened, backward-leaning Jesusita. It is a sad, yet angry look. "What's the matter? Are you afraid to let me touch you? Am I so filthy, so rotten, so evil in your eyes that you're afraid that I'll contaminate you? Dirty you, rid you of your saintly cover? Yes, I'm a whore. You must know that by now. I saw your neighbor come over here when we left. That makes me a horrible sinner, doesn't it? The lowest form of life that you can think of, right? Scum, shit. That's me. Judging me is a very simple thing for you to do, isn't it?

"Well, let me tell you something. What I do, I do to make money. And I don't do it alone. I do it with men. Men that you know. Men who went to your church this morning with their wives and kids. Men that the priest will give, what do you call it, Holy Communion, to right alongside you. Some of these men have been coming to me for years. One of them has told me over and over again that I'm a real problem for him. He says that his wife expects him to go to that Communion with her every Sunday. But before he can do that he must confess his sins to the priest and be forgiven. Almost every week I'm one of his sins. He says that to be forgiven, he has to promise that he won't sin again. He's been coming to me for years. His wife won't give him any. Now that she's had her kids, she sees no reason to. So there he is, telling the priest how sorry he is and that he won't sin again, when he knows goddamn good and well that before the week's over he'll be aching, dying to fuck me. So besides judging me, Miss Judge, how do you judge your fellow churchgoer? And how do you judge his wife, as long as you're in the business of judging people?

"It isn't just your church people who are and have been my customers. I've had doctors and lawyers and the chief of police and some of his men as my customers. I've even had your neighbor's brother as a customer. He was in love with me. He loved me so much that he beat me because I wouldn't stop working, because I wouldn't stop fucking other men. He's married, isn't he? Kids. A real family man. Yes, I've fucked these men. All of these men and more. But you know what's so funny about all this..."

"I don't want to hear. I don't want to hear." Jesusita starts to get up out of her chair but the whore shoves her down again.

"You're gonna hear, Miss Judge. You're the one who chose to judge. So now sit, listen, and hear, and really judge for a change.... The strange thing is that probably more than half of these men don't just want to fuck me, they want to do weird things to me or they want me to do weird things to them. Some don't want to fuck me at all, some just want weirdness. Some want me to tie them up and beat them. Tie them up naked, kneeling on their knees and elbows with their butts sticking up high in the air, begging me to hit them harder. What would all you churchgoers have done if you could have seen me beating your naked, tied-up ex-chief of police, his ass beet-red and him still begging for more? I know what you would have done. Put me in jail and say that I had drugged the poor man because no respectable man in his position could have ever done such a thing. But let's say that I hadn't drugged the ex-chief, that he was at the whorehouse under his own free will, that he was begging me to keep beating his naked ass of his own free will. How would you have judged him, Miss Judge?

"What, no answer, no judgment? Well, let me tell you about the man who always wants to dress up in my underwear and have me chase him around the room with a dildo until he accidentally falls and me and my dildo catch up with him. Do you know what dildos are, Miss Judge?"

"Please, no more. Please, I can't take any more."

"No, you're going to listen to me just the way I have to listen to you people every time I step out on the street. 'Look at her,' all of you say. 'Look at that slut. Has she no shame?' I can hear you even when you're not talking. I can see what your eyes are saying. I can hear how much you enjoy laughing at me. Why do I keep on whoring, you ask? Because I refuse to clean toilets and mop floors in the train station the way my mother had to all of her life for slave wages. Because I refuse to spend seven months out of the year, like so many of you, stooped over on some white man's ranch picking fruit with slime, sweat, and dirt stuck all over me. I'd rather see that white man close up in my little whorehouse room with his pants down, see the ache and hunger in his eyes rather than in mine."

"Please, let me go to the bathroom. I think I'm going to vomit."

"Go ahead and vomit. You can just as easily vomit here as in the bathroom. I'd like to make you vomit. I'd like to see you vomit, knowing that I made you vomit with the truth for a change."

"Please. I really..."

"Sit down and shut up! You're going to listen to everything I have to say, just like I listen to all the things my customers tell me. Of course, they pay me to listen and I'm not going to pay you a penny. The curious thing is that after all these years, these men pay me more money just to listen to them than for all the weird and everyday sex that they have with me. If they fuck me, that just takes a few minutes. The same if they want me to put my mouth to them. A little longer if they want to put their mouths to me. A lot longer if dressing up or tying up or playacting is their thing. On their first visits, they usually leave right after they've come. After a few visits, they start to stay afterward.

"They want to talk. And by talk, I mean they talk and I listen. The talks get longer and longer. My boss doesn't care because the longer they talk, the more they pay. They tell me things that I'm pretty sure they don't tell anybody else. I think they feel free to tell me anything because in coming to me and doing whatever they want to do with me, they probably think that they've gone down as far as they can go, so there's no reason to hide anymore, no reason to lie. They talk about their wives a lot, usually about what a sad marriage they have. They talk about problems they're having with their kids and, a lot of times, about how much their kids hate them. They talk about the problems they've had with women, starting with their mothers and on up to now. Lots of them are afraid of women. Some want to hurt women. Lots of them say they don't know why they're telling me these things. Some say that they've never told anybody these things. They're so open that sometimes I start to think that they're my friends. Then I'll run into one of them on the street and he won't even look at me, he's ashamed of me, won't even answer my 'hello,' doesn't know me. So I'm one thing to them in my little workspace and something real different out there in public. Fucking, weak-kneed hypocrites. I wonder..."

"Mama! Mama!" Elena's at the door. "Come! Come! Fifi's hurt herself real bad!" The whore rushes from the room.

Jesusita can hear the girl crying in the next room. She's hungry but hunger is minor compared to the dread and fear that the whore will return. She props the chair under the doorknob again. She sits on the bed just a foot from the open window. If the chair doesn't hold, she'll jump out the window and run toward the church. The cold night air is chilling the room, but that doesn't matter. She starts to shiver and thinks of wrapping herself in a blanket but decides against it because it will take that much longer to get out of the window if she has to. Better to shiver.

She waits, but the whore doesn't return. She can hear voices in the next room, quiet voices but nothing strange-sounding. The whore and the girl have probably focused their attention on Elena and Ralph. She thinks of the whore's ranting, but doesn't believe any of it. What weighs on her most is why God has permitted this. She asks again and again but never receives an answer. She wakes sitting on the bed shivering. She doesn't know what time it is or how long she has slept. The house is silent. She goes to the door. The chair is still propped tightly under the doorknob. She listens intently. Not a sound. Do devils sleep? Maybe they pretend to sleep to dissuade anyone from thinking that they're devils.

She is freezing and exhausted. She climbs into bed on the side nearest the window, a side that she never sleeps on. She shivers under the blankets. Once she begins to warm, she realizes that her head is still exposed to the cold and slides completely under the blankets. When she wakes, it is still dark and now Los Angeles can't be silenced. And she knows only too well why all of this has happened.

She climbs out of her window to go to Mass. But then she realizes that it is far too early for any Mass. She must go back in before anyone sees her out in the front yard at that hour. Maybe some of the neighbors, besides Petra, have already seen the whore and him at the house and already know what's happened. She starts to lift the screen but decides to return to the sidewalk to see if anyone is coming from either direction. None. Back at the screen, she thinks that she best first listen for cars. None. She lifts the screen and hoists herself up to the window ledge. Her upper stomach is resting on the ledge, but she is stuck there. She doesn't have the strength to lift herself any farther. She is hanging there with the screen sharp against her back. One car passes and then another. She tries again and again to lift herself but can't. She wants to cry but fights it. If someone were to come and see her crying as she hangs helplessly trying to get into her own house through a window with a whore inside, she could never live that down.

Frustrated, she lets herself slide down. Her breasts scrape hard against the ledge. Her chin bangs against the ledge, and the screen frame slaps the back of her head. On the ground again, she looks around to see if anyone has seen. She sees no one but is convinced that the people across the street must have seen. She fights back tears. On each side of the window are two large macetas with huge geranium plants in each. If she can twist and rotate them over until they are under the window, they should give her enough height to get over the window ledge. If she does that, she will probably damage the plants and once inside the macetas will remain under the window and the whore will know what she has been up to and become angry. Why should she care if the whore becomes angry? She doesn't know, but she does care.

She rotates the macetas into position. She steps down on the geraniums and boosts herself up and over the window ledge. Woefully, she looks back at the crushed plants. One look and the whore will know that she has left her room. She checks the chair. It's still in place. She listens for voices, noise. Nothing. She doesn't think devils sleep—they have been damned to eternal damnation and not sleeping must be part of that damnation. But possessed people must still sleep—they're not dead yet. That accounts for the silence in the girls' room.

Hunger reappears, now in the form of a dry ache in the pit of her stomach. She chides herself for not being able to eat in her own home, but she's afraid to face the whore again, afraid that the next time she will lose her mind. She looks at the window and then at the mattress, at the side of the mattress where she has hidden her money.

The hunger hurts. She doesn't know what to do. Nor does she even know what time it is. The clock is in the kitchen. Now she is thirsty and has to go to the toilet too. But water is in the kitchen and the toilet opens onto their bedroom. She thinks she can hear them in the kitchen. She goes to the mattress and takes all the money her hands can find. Then she takes her coat and, hurrying to the window before the whore comes back, jumps out.

It is three days before Padre Montes learns more about Jesusita's disappearance, how she left the girls with their mother and the boy with his brother. It is Reyna Oaxaca and Manuelita Mosqueda, two members of the Guadalupana, who come to the rectory to report to him. It is Reyna Oaxaca who last saw Jesusita at the bus depot on Monday morning.

"I was on my way to Mendota to visit my sister and her family when I saw Jesusita sitting by herself in the far corner of the depot. I had to look twice to make sure it was her because she looked so strange. She was curled up on one of those depot seats with her coat covering her, looking in every direction. When I bought my ticket, the ticket man saw me looking at her and asked me if I knew her. I said yes, and he said that I should try to talk to her, try to calm her down because she was acting very strange. He said that he had sold her a ticket to Los Angeles, but the whole time she kept looking around, very scared, saying, 'They're coming after me.'

"After I bought my ticket I went over to where she was sitting and tried to talk to her. She had brought her feet up on the seat; her knees were up at her neck. She had covered herself with her coat. Only her face was showing. The whole time she kept looking around, mumbling something to herself that I couldn't understand. When she did look at me, her eyes were as big as balls. My bus came and I had to leave. In all the years I've known her, I've never seen her like that.

"Today, Manuelita and me went back to the depot to see if she really got on that bus to Los Angeles. I talked to that ticket man and he said yes, that he and the bus driver, with a lot of trouble, got her on the bus."

For years, Padre Montes remembers Jesusita in his daily prayers. But he never sees or hears from her again.

ABOUT THE AUTHOR

Ronald L. Ruiz is the author of a memoir, *A Lawyer* (2012), and three previous novels—*Happy Birthday Jesús* (1994), *Giuseppe Rocco* (1998), and *The Big Bear* (2003). Born and raised in Fresno, California, Ron was educated at St. Mary's College, California, University of California, Berkeley, and University of San Francisco. He practiced law from 1966 to 2003 as a Deputy District Attorney, a criminal defense attorney, and a Deputy Public Defender. He was appointed to the California Agriculture Labor Relations Board by Governor Jerry Brown in 1974 and later served as the District Attorney of Santa Cruz County, California.

THE TYPE

Jesusita is set in Espinosa Nova, a revival based on the types used by Antonio de Espinosa, the most important Mexican printer of the sixteenth century and likely the first punchcutter anywhere in the American continent (1551). His books are considered the highest point in the history of ancient Mexican printing. However, there wasn't a version of his type that enabled contemporary use.

Cristóbal Henestrosa began the first sketches of Espinosa Nova in December 2001 and invested nine years of research, writing, drawing and redrawing into his digital interpretation. In 2010, it was awarded two certificates of excellence: one by TDC2 (Type Directors Club Typeface Design Competition), one by Tipos Latinos (Biennial of Latin American Typography).

Titles and initial capitals are set in ITC Golden Cockerel. It was originally designed by Eric Gill for Robert and Moira Gibbings' Golden Cockerel Press, England. Most notably used in *The Four Gospels of the Lord Jesus Christ According to the Authorized Version of King James I* (1931). Gill designed the text and illustrations to weave and intertwine, producing a modern homage to traditional illuminated manuscripts. The type was digitized by the International Typeface Corporation (ITC) in 1996.

Amika Press is proud to utilize these typefaces for the first time in this book.